THE CONFIDENCE-MAN

THE

Confidence-Man

His Masquerade

BY

HERMAN MELVILLE

EDITED WITH AN INTRODUCTION BY

HENNIG COHEN

Holt, Rinehart and Winston, Inc.

NEW YORK · CHICAGO · SAN FRANCISCO · TORONTO · LONDON

Second Printing, March, 1967

Introduction and Notes copyright © 1964 by
Holt, Rinehart and Winston, Inc.
All Rights Reserved
Library of Congress Catalog Card Number: 64–12514
2443000
Printed in the United States of America

CONTENTS

v

84410

Introduction

In the summer of 1856, Herman Melville became an object of serious concern to his family. His tenth book, *The Confidence-Man,* was almost finished, but the effort had exhausted him physically and spiritually. In ensuing correspondence his brother-in-law, Lemuel Shaw, Jr., reported that Melville was "preparing another book for the press," and voiced the family consensus when he added that he had "no confidence in his productions." Lemuel Shaw, Sr., Melville's father-in-law, noting "how very ill, Herman has been" because "he overworks himself and brings on severe nervous affections," suggested that "a voyage or a journey" might "be highly beneficial to him and probably restore him." He advanced the money, and on October 11, 1856, Melville sailed from New York for Europe and the Holy Land.

His boat landed in Glasgow on October 26. On November 10 he called his old friend, Nathaniel Hawthorne, then the American consul in Liverpool. In his journal Hawthorne wrote that Melville looked "much as he used to do (a little paler, and perhaps sadder), in a rough outside coat, and with his characteristic gravity of manner." He invited Melville to accompany him to Southport, a seashore resort where he had taken a house. The visit was a memorable one for both men, though the record that Melville made in his travel diary is abrupt and laconic: "Took a long walk by the sea. Sands and grass. Wild and desolate. A strong wind. Good talk." Hawthorne's journal is more revealing: ". . . we took a pretty long walk together, and sat down in a hollow among the sand hills. . . . Melville, as he always does, began to reason of

Providence and futurity, and of everything that lies beyond human ken, and informed me that he had 'pretty much made up his mind to be annihilated.' . . . He can neither believe, nor be comfortable in his unbelief; and he is too honest and courageous not to try to do one or the other." What Melville had done in a rare moment was to put aside his own masquerade, disclosing the ambiguities and complexities of his being which he had objectified in the novel so recently completed. For Melville, "annihilation" did not mean simply defeat or death, but the recognition of the limitations inherent in the human situation. As Hawthorne was aware, even more difficult and profound matters were involved—how to live in a world in which nothing is what it appears to be, in which the only thing knowable is that nothing can be known, and the only thing believable is that nothing can be believed. In this special sense "annihilation" is the theme of *The Confidence-Man* and the ultimate source of its structure and style.

The structure of *The Confidence-Man* is a symbolic counterpart of Melville's grim but basically compassionate agnosticism. With a cunning disregard for conventional form because it implied conventional values and attitudes, he designed a novel in which the unimportance of plot, movement, suspense and climax, and the lack of a sympathetic protagonist are positive qualities. Plot is replaced by a series of confrontations, at times so patterned that they suggest the performance of a ritual. But instead of moving toward a resolution or a climax, these recurring performances trail off into what at first seems an aimless direction. Upon closer scrutiny they appear to circle back upon themselves. The outcome of the confrontations is usually clear from the beginning, and suspense depends not on revelation but on process. Talk is substituted for action, and wit for emotion. Like a carrousel, the novel whirls in its circle while remaining in the same place, the tension between stasis and motion underscored through the flow of characters who slip in and out of their various guises, and the setting, a river steamer moving downstream on a voyage of more than a thousand miles.

The voyage begins at sunrise on April 1, All Fools' Day. As the riverboat *Fidèle* departs St. Louis for New Orleans, "a man in cream-colors" comes aboard. He is the first of a number of grotesque figures who momentarily become the center of attention as they demand a response from their fellow passengers. With their uncanny behavior, their curious costumes, their slippery language, and their strange comings and goings, they are quite distinct from one another. They also have much in common. In fact, it becomes apparent that they are identical, a single actor playing a number of different roles, a supernatural being of some kind in a variety of incarnations. Through a protagonist who shifts his shape as readily as he shifts his ground, Melville expresses his commitment to a belief in uncertainty. His sardonic reaction to the necessity for such a belief is to identify this protagonist with Satan in the form of the Confidence Man.

The Confidence Man appears in eight successive incarnations:

1. (Chapters 1-2)   His "advent" at dawn is in the role of "the man in cream-colors," a flaxen-haired "stranger" identified with Manco Capac, the Inca sun god. He arrives alone and without baggage, seemingly having traveled a great distance; writes his message of faith, hope, and charity on a slate which he holds aloft; falls asleep in "lamblike" innocence at the foot of a ladder; and departs unnoticed. He is pallid, weak, and ineffectual, and provokes little response from the passengers except when they observe him as he sleeps. Then their conflicting opinions regarding his origins and nature intensify the mystery of his significance, in general suggesting an unworldliness not entirely wholesome.

2. (Chapter 3)   In his second embodiment he assumes the shape of a Negro beggar, Black Guinea. Grotesquely stunted, he shuffles about like a performing dog, snuffling piteously, catching pennies in his mouth, seeking charity and trust. When he is accused of fraudulently playing upon the sympathies of the public, he offers the names of "honest ge'mmen" aboard the riverboat who will vouch for him. None of them can be found, but they later appear as incarnations of the Confidence Man. He is last seen as he "forlornly stumped out of sight" toward an uncertain destination.

3. (Chapters 4-5)   John Ringman, whom Black Guinea has

called "dat good man wid de weed," is the Confidence Man in his
third form. He wears a weed or crape to signify that he is in mourning. His pathetic appeal for money is effective with Henry Roberts,
a kindly, elderly merchant, but his effort to insinuate himself into
the confidence of a college student is less successful. Before being
left "to wander away," he tells the merchant and the college student about a quick profit to be made through stock speculation,
setting them up as marks for a future Confidence Man.

4. (Chapters 6-8) The Confidence Man is next seen as an
agent for "a Widow and Orphan Asylum recently founded among
the Seminoles." He obtains donations from a young Episcopal clergyman, "a charitable lady," and a good-hearted "gentleman with
gold sleeve-buttons" who is notable for his immaculate clothing and
his spotless hands, and who listens attentively, though with reser-
vations, to the Seminole agent's plans for a grandiose "World's
Charity" operated on a businesslike basis.

5. (Chapters 9-15) John Truman, president and transfer agent
of the Black Rapids Coal Company, is the fifth shape of the Confidence Man. A "brisk, ruddy-cheeked man . . . carrying under
his arm a ledger-like volume," he sells stock to the receptive college student and offers him the opportunity to invest in a real estate
development called New Jerusalem. He also sells stock to Roberts,
the kindly merchant. His chief coup is bilking a senile miser whose
greed overwhelms his reason.

6. (Chapters 16-21) The sixth appearance of the Confidence
Man is as a jovial quack dressed in a "snuff-colored surtout." An
herb doctor and bonesetter, he wanders about extolling the virtues
of Nature, especially natural medical remedies, and hawking his
cure-alls, "the Omni-Balsamic Reinvigorator" and "the Samaritan
Pain Dissuader." Making capital of misery and wan hopes, he places
his nostrums in the hands of an incurably "sick man," a crippled
"soldier of fortune" who is himself something of a charlatan, and
the senile miser; but not Pitch, a Missouri backwoodsman whose
associations with Nature have given him cause to doubt natural
remedies. As the riverboat approaches Cape Girardeau, he blandly
wishes Pitch well and takes his leave.

7. (Chapter 22) A few minutes after the boat is again under way, Pitch is addressed by a fawning little man wearing a brass plate around his neck engraved with the letters "P.I.O." He is the Confidence Man in his seventh manifestation. The initials are those of the Philosophical Intelligence Office, an employment agency conducted on philosophical, scientific principles, of which he is the representative. The cantankerous Pitch, on his way to buy a labor-saving machine to replace the rascally boys he had previously employed, cannot resist his arguments, based upon scientific rationalism, for trusting human nature. Essentially hopeful beneath his crusty skepticism, Pitch is persuaded to try one more boy, a decision he regrets as the employment agent disappears in the noxious fog that swirls about the wharf at Cairo.

8. (Chapters 23-45) The brooding reveries of Pitch are interrupted by Frank Goodman, a self-proclaimed cosmopolitan, a promoter of universal brotherhood, and the incarnation of the Confidence Man in his final form. He wears a multihued costume that includes "Highland plaid, Emir's robe, and French blouse," smokes a German pipe, and sprinkles his conversation with foreign phrases. In a chapter with the deliberately misleading title, "A Philanthropist Undertakes to Convert a Misanthrope," Pitch identifies the Cosmopolitan for what he is—a man-hater posing as a man-lover—and sends him on his way. Thereafter the Cosmopolitan encounters Charles Noble, a Mississippi sharper whose attempt to dupe the Cosmopolitan ends in his own befuddlement; Mark Winsome, a mystical philosopher shielded by his remoteness from human considerations; Egbert, his practical, logical disciple; William Cream, a barber who in the pursuit of his calling has learned something of how far a man can be trusted; and, as midnight approaches, "a clean, comely, old man" reading his Bible, "untainted by the world, because ignorant of it." Tired and confused, the old man turns to the Cosmopolitan for assistance. The Confidence Man puts out the reading lamp and leads him off into the darkness.

The design of the novel is established by the Confidence Man, but its meaning is determined by the response of the secondary characters, foils, and dupes to his machinations. In the simpler

situations these characters are gulled as a result of their own short-
comings—their weaknesses, follies, selfishness, and knavery. The
Episcopal clergyman, the charitable lady, and the old man represent
the vulnerability of the innocent. The college student, the sick man,
and the senile miser are the victims of self-interest. But things are
usually more complex. The senile miser, for example, is not merely
selfish. A knave as well as a fool, he pays for his box of restorative
in clipped and sweated coins. The herb doctor sees the fraud but
does not object. Charles Noble, the Mississippi operator, is even
more obviously playing the confidence game. For shady purposes
he seeks out the Cosmopolitan, tells him the story of the Indian-
hater, and plies him with wine and pledges of friendship, the
doubtful qualities of which the Cosmopolitan is aware. Thomas
Fry, the crippled beggar in tattered regimentals, thrives by pretending to be a veteran of the Mexican War. His confession, which reveals him as a confidence man in his own right yet more sinned
against than sinning, does not save him from being victimized. The
Confidence Man knows his own and consumes them with particular
relish. "That good dish, man, still delights me," the Cosmopolitan
tells Pitch, though whether he prefers fools of vice to fools of virtue is difficult to determine.

The vicious and the virtuous are not his only victims. In a more
subtle way, by forcing them to reveal their moral imbalance, the
Confidence Man sets his mark upon the well-disposed and the high-
principled. The man with gold sleeve-buttons is so "winsome" that
the mere sight of him diverts the agent for the Seminole Asylum
from lesser prey. He is mature, handsome, elegantly attired, and
beneficent. He listens attentively to the Seminole agent and gives
him three "virgin" banknotes to which he adds another "with a look
half humor, half pity" at the conclusion of their conversation. His
impeccable behavior and his immaculate clothing are possible, however, through his avoidance of situations in which he might be sul-
lied. His gloves and his hands are spotless because a "negro servant's hands did most of his master's handling for him." The winsome
man, like Pontius Pilate, "the Hebrew governor, knew how to keep
his hands clean . . . ," a distinction shared with another Melville

character, the Reverend Mr. Falsgrave in *Pierre,* "an image of white-browed and white-handed, and napkined immaculateness."

The mystical Mark Winsome, an Emersonian philosopher whose insights are as clear and transparent as ice, and as cold, is also aloof from commitment. He intuitively knows the nature of the Confidence Man and, like the winsome man of the clean hands, transcends the problem by dealing with it through a surrogate, his practical disciple Egbert. The applied transcendentalism of Egbert is adequate to the occasion. The doctrine of self-reliance protects him from the risk of making a loan to a friend, and the Cosmopolitan wryly gives him a shilling for fuel to "warm the frozen natures of you and your philosopher by."

Imbalance also characterizes the "gimlet-eyed, sour-faced" man with the wooden leg who is so suspicious of Black Guinea. He has learned that "looks are one thing, and facts another." A cynic and a railer, he tells an ugly story about a cuckold who refuses to face the evidence of his wife's duplicity. Though he can see where others are blind, his vision has blighted his spirit, and the militant Methodist preacher who attacks him for his want of charity is correct when he comments: "There he shambles off on his one lone leg, emblematic of his one-sided view of humanity." But the Methodist preacher reveals his own one-sidedness when he tries to teach the wooden-legged man charity by "shaking him till his timber-toe clattered on the deck like a nine-pin."

Rage of an even darker hue distinguishes the somber "invalid Titan in homespun," a swarthy, taciturn backwoodsman. Accompanied by a "little Cassandra" of a child, "perhaps Creole, or even Camanche," he boards the riverboat from a wilderness landing. He is suffering from an obscure hurt that seems as much spiritual as physical, but he ignores the herb doctor's playful overtures through the child, his sympathetic inquiries about imperfectly healed wounds and internal pains, and his offer of a "certain cure for any pain in the world," except to retort angrily that "some pains cannot be eased but by producing insensibility, and cannot be cured but by producing death." His fury increases to "hypochondriac mania" as he listens to the extravagant claims of the medicine man, and becomes so overpowering that he strikes him a vicious blow.

The imbalance evidenced by the hot anger of the wilderness Titan reaches its greatest degree in the cold, obsessive dedication of the Indian-hater, Colonel John Moredock. Born on the frontier, Moredock learned the "histories of Indian lying, Indian theft, Indian double-dealing, Indian blood-thirstiness, Indian diabolism." When his family fell victim to the treachery of the Indian chief, Mocmohoc, a kind of redskinned confidence man, he becomes the scourge of the race, "a Leather-stocking Nemesis." His strength, woodcraft, and implacable hatred transform him from a human to something very close to that which he would destroy. The defense of the Indian is maintained by the Cosmopolitan, who cites the names of celebrated chieftains (including several best known as leaders of bloody massacres) and denounces Moredock as a misanthrope "focused on one race of men," while Noble senses Moredock's original idealism and humanity, now twisted by his obsession. The implication is that Moredock exchanges imbalance in one direction for imbalance in another.

As Melville indicates, the source of the account of the Indian-hater is James Hall's *Sketches of History, Life, and Manners, in the West* (1835). He follows Judge Hall closely, but he departs from his source in one important particular. Hall carefully explains, and to some extent justifies, the behavior of the Indian on the basis of his mistreatment by white pioneers. Melville, who elsewhere makes clear his sympathies for the Indian on these very grounds, takes pains to have his narrator portray him as a diabolical monster who, like the Confidence Man, is an arch dissembler.

With the exception of the wooden-legged man, who is a kind of universal malcontent, the pattern of moral imbalance which culminates in the Indian-hater has specific geographical identifications. The immaculate gentleman represents the South and the moral dilemma of slavery. Mark Winsome is that type of New England transcendentalism so rarified as to be above ordinary human concerns. Egbert is the laissez-faire commercialism of the North sanctioned by the doctrines of individualism and self-reliance. The "invalid Titan," the Indian-hater, and Pitch are men of the wilderness of the West.

For Melville, the American wilderness had romantic and even Turnerian undertones, but more important here, it was associated with the biblical wilderness as a place of trial and temptation. In the wilderness the children of Israel wandered, prophets saw visions, and Christ confronted Satan. The wilderness experience shapes the response of Moredock to the diabolical Indians, and the Titan and Pitch to the Confidence Man. Moredock and the Titan are blasted by the evil they encounter there, and thenceforth respond instinctively, on the level of animals. Pitch is toughened and his vision enhanced. He learns that the Devil is abroad and he must be alert, but his humanity and his essential trust have not been shattered. His wilderness experience arms him against the herb doctor's notions of natural goodness, but his faith in human reason and his sympathy for his fellow man cause him to drop his guard with the Philosophical Intelligence Officer. He recovers immediately, recognizing the Cosmopolitan as "Diogenes in disguise," a true cynic and misanthrope. For his part, the Cosmopolitan calls Pitch "an Ishmael." Ishmael was a character toward whom Melville felt deep affinities, and Ishmael-Pitch, the American Westerner—thin-skinned but tough, skeptical but trusting, a solitary but a lover of mankind—is Melville's answer to impending "annihilation." The Confidence Man traps his victims by forcing them to commitments and extremes in a context in which, because the only certainty is uncertainty, such positions are suicidal. China Aster, whose story is an inversion of Colonel Moredock's, destroys himself by being persuaded "into the free indulgence of confidence and an ardently bright view of life, to the exclusion of that counsel which comes by heeding the opposite view." Though he totters close to the brink of destruction, Pitch survives because he accepts the counsel of moderation.

The repeated confrontations of the Confidence Man and his foils give the novel its fundamental design, but Melville achieves further coherence through a number of other devices. For example, the book divides into two parts of almost equal length. The first seven incarnations of the Confidence Man occur in the first part (Chapters 1-22); the eighth, and final, incarnation, the Confidence Man in the guise of the Cosmopolitan, dominates the second part (Chapters 24-45). The first part takes place in daylight, the second part at night. Pitch is the bridge between. In the short chapter at the precise center of the book (Chapter 23), Pitch, at twilight, after musing glumly on his having been taken in by the Philosophical Intelligence Officer, is gently accosted by the Cosmopolitan. The two parts are held together firmly by a number of framing devices and by compression of time and space: from daybreak until midnight on the "1st day of April, 18—," aboard a riverboat as it sails from St. Louis to some point beyond Cairo. The ship microcosm appears in Melville's novels as early as *Omoo* and is crucial to *White-Jacket* and *Moby-Dick*. The variety of the passengers, "an Anacharsis Cloots congress of all kinds of that multiform pilgrim species, man," suggests that they are to be taken as representative of the whole human race. That Melville has the man with the wooden leg call them "fools . . . in this ship of fools" is important to his theme, but it also serves as a subtle reminder that the *Fidèle* is in the tradition of Sebastian Brant's widely known medieval satire, *The Ship of Fools*.

Recurring episodes, such as the three in which the Confidence Man and a companion sit together over a bottle of wine, serve the double function of tightening the structure of the novel and elaborating its meaning. After John Truman and the kindly merchant, Henry Roberts, complete their stock transaction, they drink champagne. Touched to "his natural heart" by the wine, the kindly merchant blurts out: "Ah, wine is good, and confidence is good; but can wine or confidence percolate down through all the stony strata of hard considerations, and drop warmingly and ruddily into the cold cave of truth? Truth will *not* be comforted." Truman guilefully quotes the proverb "*In vino veritas*" and then argues that the truth which Roberts has seen as a result of his tippling is not true at all. The drinking bout of Charles Noble and the Cosmopolitan is an even more detailed inversion. (We are warned that it will be:

they drink immediately following the story of Moredock and the devilish Indians from a bottle served up in "a little bark basket, braided with porcupine quills, gayly tinted in the Indian fashion.") Ordinarily a source of geniality and good-fellowship, wine creates distrust when Noble encourages the Cosmopolitan to excess and the Cosmopolitan impugns its quality by his extravagant defense of winemakers and barkeeps and his sly talk of poisoners. When Noble retires, the Cosmopolitan invites Mark Winsome to help him finish the bottle, but Winsome prefers to keep wine "in the lasting condition of an abstraction" and takes a goblet of ice water instead. Pitch is also abstemious, but for a better reason. His water, though cold, is not iced. He replies to the Cosmopolitan's anecdote on the virtues of wine: "If I take your parable right . . . the meaning is, that one cannot enjoy life with gusto unless he renounce the too-sober view of life. But since the too-sober view is, doubtless, nearer truth than the too-drunken; I, who rate truth, though cold water, above untruth, though Tokay, will stick to my earthen jug." That Melville himself cherished wine, and in his later years worked on a series of sketches about an imaginary "Burgundy Club" whose winebibbing members he idealized, makes the function of wine in this novel even more poignant.

The recurrence of animal imagery contributes to the structural unity of the novel in addition to its primary purpose of characterization. The deaf mute is "lamblike" in his innocence and weakness. Black Guinea and the Philosophical Intelligence Officer are canine as they crouch, whine, and faun, and the etymology of the word is used to hint at their underlying cynicism. Pitch calls the herb doctor a fox and identifies the Cosmopolitan with a performing ape and "monkery." The peg-legged man is a porcupine and, according to the militant Methodist preacher, a "foiled wolf." The senile miser has a "ferret eye," a hand that is "a sort of wasted penguin-flipper," and a "buzzard nose." The vicious Goneril is a toad, and the sham Mexican War veteran a hyena. The Indian-hater sleeps on a pile of wolf skins and is compared to Hairy Orson, the wild man of medieval romance who was nurtured by a bear, and to a Shetland seal beneath whose "bristles lurks the fur." The valuable fur apparently represents such Emersonian traits as "self-reliance," "untutored sagacity," and "dwelling exclusively among the world of God," which Melville hastens to add are common to the lowly oppossum. Pitch, "eccentrically clothed in the skins of wild beasts," is the center of numerous bearish allusions and much ursine word-play, but for all his growling he is a rather tame "Bruin." His efforts to simulate a wildcat are "more or less dubious," and he is called, not unpleasantly, "Coonskins" and referred to as an "entertaining old 'coon." Pitch's garb of animal skins and his bearish behavior are a superficial masquerade.

Snake imagery associates the Confidence Man with Satan, especially in his role of the dissembler and tempter of Eden, and only the Titan from the wilderness, Pitch, and Mark Winsome are capable of seeing the serpent behind his disguise. The man with the weed, the herb doctor, the Philosophical Intelligence Officer, and the Cosmopolitan are all depicted in ophidian terms and sometimes in language close to the Bible and *Paradise Lost,* and they make use of their serpentine powers to "charm" and "fascinate" their prey (cf. Chapter 43, "Very Charming").

Several other means of enriching the texture of *The Confidence-Man* while at the same time enhancing its structure should be noted. Black Guinea's roll call of "honest ge'mmen" is justified by the immediate situation and fixes the episodic structure of the novel, but as the "honest ge'mmen" come forward one by one they also find appropriate reasons to mention those who have preceded them or will follow, thus linking the loose episodes more closely together. For example, Black Guinea wanders off ostensibly in search of the man with the weed; the agent for the Seminole Asylum claims to have helped him ashore and the herb doctor to having treated him. Shakespearian allusions operate in a similar way. They are drawn mainly from the darker plays like *Timon of Athens* and *Hamlet,* or those like *The Tempest, A Midsummer-Night's Dream,* and *As You Like It,* which are much concerned with transformations and disguises, and stress rogues like Autolycus, railers like Thersites, and hypocrites like Malvolio. Pertinent to particular passages in the novel and cumulatively to its total meaning, they also serve a structural purpose as they take their place in the configuration of references to the theater, costumes, dramatic performances, actors, role-playing, exchange of roles, and transformations, whether natural, such as the Philosophical Intelligence Officer's analogy of bad boys to caterpillars which metamorphose into butterflies, or artificial, such as the barber with his "hair dyes, cosmetics, false moustaches, wigs and toupees," or magical, such as the Cosmopolitan and his sorcery with the gold coins.

Among its picaresque elements, *The Confidence-Man* has a number of digressions tending, formally at least, to give the novel a slack, disjointed quality. They are of three kinds: authorial intrusions into the flow of the narrative (Chapters 14, 33, and 44); extravagant descriptive passages (e.g., Chapter 2, p. 7, and Chapter 16, p. 80); and tales (Chapters 25-27, 34, and 40), biographical accounts of characters in the novel (Chapters 12 and 19), and short anecdotes (e.g., Chapter 6, p. 31, Chapter 13, p. 66, and Chapter 24, p. 145). Unlike the picaresque novel in which they may occur for their own sake, the digressions in *The Confidence-Man* are closely integrated into the total structure. This is obvious enough in the instance of the various stories and anecdotes but less so with the other two categories. Somewhat like Fielding's asides in *Tom Jones* (a comparison of the chapter titles of the two novels is suggestive), Melville discourses on his theories of fiction, in themselves of interest, but not gratuitously, for he provides applications as well as expositions, and the theories in their contradictions and reversals are consistent with philosophical assumptions and literary techniques which he employs in the novel. Nor are the passages of rhapsodic description, though departing from the prevailing tone, disruptive. Their effect is to heighten the satire in which they are embedded.

Important elements in the last chapters of *The Confidence-Man* are foreshadowed in the first chapter. The barber and his "No Trust" sign reappear, and his description of the Cosmopolitan as "quite an original," a creature resembling East Indian snake charmers, brings to mind the placard warning against "a mysterious imposter . . . from the East; quite an original genius." Sunrise has declined into darkness, and the sun is now a "solar lamp" or argand light. On its ground glass shade are a figure of a man with a halo, emblematic of Christ and the New Testament, and the altar of the Old Testament, the horns of which signified sanctuary. Reading his Bible by the light of the solar lamp is the white-haired old man with "a countenance like . . . good Simeon." It was the aged Simeon who awaited the coming of the Messiah and whose blessing, the Nunc Dimittis, last of the canonical hours, hails Christ as "A light to the Gentiles." Identification of the old man with Simeon recalls the "advent" of the whitish deaf mute associated with the Inca sun deity. The old man's simple piety and patient expectancy is rewarded by the coming of the Cosmopolitan, an incarnation of Lucifer, who seems "to dispense a sort of morning through the night." The appeal for faith quoted from Corinthians in the first chapter is succeeded by skeptical verses from Ecclesiastes. Bewildered but still credulous, the old man asks for help in finding his stateroom. After making him the object of a coarse April Fool joke involving a life preserver, the Cosmopolitan extinguishes the solar lamp and leads the old man away.

More often than not, Melville ended his novels without concluding them. Taken in chronological order, *Typee* stops only to begin again in *Omoo*, the final phrase of which is "before us was the wide Pacific," and the last sentence of *Mardi*, which starts out where *Omoo* leaves off, is "And thus, pursuers and pursued flew on, over an endless sea." The subtitle of *Redburn* is *His First Voyage*, implying a certain incompleteness, and *White-Jacket* ends with the ship homeward bound but "still with the land out of sight—still with the brooding darkness on the face of the deep" because, in the words of the narrator, "I love an indefinite, infinite background—a vast, heaving, rolling, mysterious rear!" The last novel, *The Confidence-Man*, is more than mysteriously inconclusive and open-ended. The "something further" which "may follow of this Masquerade" is a circling back to the beginning, not in the way of the old natural cycles but like the conception of the universe of steady-state physics. The ship world of the *Fidèle* moves and yet remains the same in time and space. The framing devices are also links in a circular chain.

The Confidence-Man, for all its fantasy, is firmly set in a realistic structure. In 1840 Melville visited an uncle in Galena, Illinois, probably making part of the return trip by riverboat on the Mississippi and Ohio. He seems to have drawn upon Timothy Flint's well known *Recollections of the Last Ten Years in the Mississippi Valley* (1826), and *The History and Geography of the Mississippi Valley* (1828), and he may have seen John Banvard's famous "Moving Panorama of the Mississippi," which he mentions at the beginning of the novel and elsewhere. In any event, his descriptions of the landscape and the river steamer of the period are accurate. He is likewise true to the facts (and to American folklore) in his presentation of such types as the Negro slave, the skeptical barber, the medicine man, the promoter of fabulous schemes, the Mississippi operator, the bogus war veteran, the Indian-hater, and the rugged backwoodsman. He is careful to give his novel American roots, following his own admonition that "in nearly all original characters . . . there is discernible something prevailingly local, or of the age," but he does so in order to transcend them, to move beyond "severe fidelity to real life." Through the fanciful, the symbolic, he achieves "far more reality, than real life itself can show." This higher reality has its universal applications but is also a commentary on the American national character.

So much attention to structure can be misleading. Melville is not Henry James erecting a complex and delicately balanced edifice, all parts of which fit in neatly with all other parts. Nor is he John Bunyan sustaining a detailed, tightly knit allegory. His talents lay in the direction of extension, elaboration, involution, diversity, and digression. He used form effectively but he did not let it get in his way. He faced a related problem in the matter of style and tone, and this time accepted discipline, for the theme of *The Confidence-Man* is so mordant that unless there were rigid controls the novel could move beyond tragedy to rage and despair. Melville's solution was to adopt the masque of comedy. Puns, tricks, choplogic, high wit, and low humor prevail. But the best joke of all is that Melville, striking back through the structure and style of his novel, manages to beat the Confidence Man at his own game.

Swarthmore, Pa.   HENNIG COHEN
February, 1964

Chronology

1819   Herman Melville, third of eight children of Allan and Maria Gansevoort Melville, born on August 1 in New York City.

1829   With the election of Andrew Jackson, Herman's grandfather, Major Thomas Melville, is removed as Naval Officer for the Port of Boston. At the end of the term at New-York Male High School, Herman visits his grandparents in Boston.

1830   Family moves to Albany, N.Y., where Allan Melville enters the fur trade. Herman attends Albany Academy.

1832   Allan Melville dies, leaving the family in financial difficulties. Herman employed as a bank clerk.

1833   Herman spends summer at his Uncle Thomas Melville's farm near Pittsfield, Mass.

1835   Herman clerks in his brother Allan's store and attends Albany Classical School.

1835   His brother's business fails and Herman teaches school near Pittsfield.

1838   Family moves to Lansingburgh, N.Y. Herman studies engineering at Lansingburgh Academy.

1839   In June Herman sails as a member of the crew of the *St. Lawrence,* a trading packet, for Liverpool. Returns to New York in October and teaches at Greenbush, N.Y.

1840   At the end of the school term visits his Uncle Thomas Melville in Galena, Ill. In December ships on the *Acushnet,* a whaler.

1841   The *Acushnet* visits Rio de Janeiro, rounds Cape Horn, and sails among the Galapagos Islands.

1842   *Acushnet* lands at Nukahiva in the Marquesas Islands. In July, with Richard Greene, Melville deserts and hides in the interior. In August he signs on the *Lucy Ann,* an Australian whaler. At Tahiti, with other members of the crew, he refuses duty and is detained by the British consul. He escapes to nearby Eimo in October and joins the crew of a Nantucket whaler, the *Charles and Henry.*

1843   Melville discharged in May at Honolulu. Works at odd jobs until August when he enlists as an ordinary seaman on the frigate *United States.* The *United States* visits the Marquesas, Tahiti, and Peruvian ports.

1844   In the summer the *United States* sails for Boston where Melville is discharged in October and visits his family in Lansingburgh.

1845   Melville completes an account of his Marquesan adventures. It is rejected by a New York publisher but his brother, Gansevoort, Secretary of the American Legation at London, obtains a contract for publication in England.

1846   *Typee* published in London and New York. It is well received.

1847   *Omoo,* a sequel, published in London and New York. Melville marries Elizabeth Shaw in Boston and they establish a home in New York.

1849   *Mardi,* an allegorical novel, published in London and New York. *Redburn,* based on the voyage to Liverpool, published in London and New York. Melville sails for England to arrange for the publication of his fifth book. He visits Paris, Brussels, and Cologne. A son, Malcolm, is born.

1850   *White-Jacket,* on life aboard an American frigate, published in London and New York. Melville moves to Pittsfield. He meets Hawthorne.

1851   *Moby-Dick* published in New York and, as *The Whale,* in England. Hawthorne, living in nearby Lenox, Mass., and Melville exchange letters and visits. Stanwix, second son, born.

1852   *Pierre,* a melodramatic novel, published in London and New York.

1853   Melville contributes stories and sketches to *Putnam's* and *Harper's* magazines, including "Bartleby the Scrivener," "Benito Cereno," and "The Encantadas." First daughter, Elizabeth, born.

1854   *Israel Potter,* a narrative of a Revolutionary War veteran, published serially in *Putnam's.*

1855   Second daughter, Frances, born. *Israel Potter* published in New York and London in book form.

1856   *Piazza Tales,* a collection of magazine pieces, published in New York and London. Melville sails for Europe and the Holy Land.

1857   *The Confidence-Man* published in New York and London.

1858   Melville lectures, mainly in the Middle West.

1859   Melville lectures.

1860   Lectures. Prepares a volume of poetry which fails to obtain publication. Sails for San Francisco on a ship commanded by his brother, Thomas.

1861   Unsuccessfully seeks a naval appointment.

1863   Moves to New York.

1864   Visits the battlefront in Virginia.

1866   *Battle-Pieces,* a collection of Civil War poems, published in New York. Becomes an inspector of Customs at the Port of New York.

1867   Malcolm dies of a self-inflicted pistol wound.

1869   Stanwix goes to sea.

1876   *Clarel: A Poem and Pilgrimage in the Holy Land* published in New York with funds provided by Melville's uncle, Peter Gansevoort.

1885   Melville resigns as Customs inspector.

1886   Stanwix dies in San Francisco.

1888   Melville publishes privately a small book of verse, *John Marr and Other Sailors*. He works on *Billy Budd*.

1891   *Billy Budd* finished in April. *Timoleon,* another small collection of verse, privately printed. Melville dies on September 28 and is buried in Woodlawn Cemetery in The Bronx, N.Y.

A Note on the Text

The first American edition of *The Confidence-Man* was published, appropriately enough, on April 1, 1857, by Dix, Edwards and Company of New York. Melville did not see it or the London edition issued a few days later through the press. The novel was not well received in the United States, though the English reception was somewhat warmer and more perceptive. It was not reprinted until its inclusion in the London Standard Edition of Melville's works issued in 1922-1924. Elizabeth S. Foster supplied an excellent introduction and notes to an edition published in New York in 1954.

The present text is based on the original American edition which is closely followed except for the correction of typographical errors and emendation of spelling and punctuation for the sake of consistency.

Selected Bibliography

BIBLIOGRAPHY

"American Literature: Nineteenth Century, 1800-1870." Published in the annual bibliography of *PMLA*.

"Articles in American Literature Appearing in Current Periodicals." Published quarterly in *American Literature*.

Beebe, Maurice, Harrison Hayford, and Gordon Roper, "Criticism of Herman Melville: A Checklist," *Modern Fiction Studies*, VIII (1962), pp. 312-346.

Gerstenberger, Donna, and George Hendrick, *The American Novel 1789-1959: A Checklist of Twentieth-Century Criticism* (Denver, 1961), pp. 181-182.

Spiller, Robert E., Willard Thorp, Thomas H. Johnson, and Henry Seidel Canby, eds., *Literary History of the United States* (1948), III, pp. 647-654; *Supplement* (1959) ed. Richard M. Ludwig, pp. 164-169.

BIOGRAPHY

Howard, Leon, *Herman Melville* (Berkeley, 1951).

Leyda, Jay, *The Melville Log: A Documentary Life of Herman Melville, 1819-1891* (New York, 1951). 2 vols.

Mason, Ronald, *The Spirit Above the Dust: A Study of Herman Melville* (London, 1951).

Stone, Geoffrey, *Melville* (New York, 1949).

CRITICISM

Anderson, David D., "Melville and Mark Twain in Rebellion," *Mark Twain Journal,* XI (1961), pp. 8-9.

Beverly, Gordon, "Herman Melville's Confidence," London *Times Literary Supplement,* Nov. 11, 1949, p. 733.

Cawelti, John G., "Some Notes on the Structure of *The Confidence-Man,*" *American Literature,* XXIX (1957), pp. 278-288.

Chase, Richard, "Melville's *Confidence Man,*" *Kenyon Review,* XI (1949), pp. 122-140.

Dubler, Walter, "Theme and Structure in Melville's *The Confidence Man,*" *American Literature,* XXXIII (1961), pp. 307-319.

Gross, John J., "Melville's *The Confidence-Man:* The Problem of Source and Meaning," *Neuphilologische Mitteilungen,* LX (1959), pp. 299-310.

Hayford, Harrison, "Poe in *The Confidence-Man,*" *Nineteenth-Century Fiction,* XIV (1959), pp. 207-218.

Hayman, Allen, "The Real and the Original: Herman Melville's Theory of Prose Fiction," *Modern Fiction Studies,* VIII (1962), pp. 211-232.

Hoffman, Dan G., "Melville's 'Story of China Aster,'" *American Literature,* XXII (1950), pp. 137-149.

Horsford, Howard C., "Evidence of Melville's Plans for a Sequel to *The Confidence-Man,*" *American Literature,* XXIV (1952), pp. 85-89.

Miller, James E., Jr., *"The Confidence-Man:* His Guises," *PMLA,* LXXIV (1959), pp. 102-111.

Nichol, John W., "Melville and the Midwest," *PMLA,* LXVI (1951), pp. 613-625.

Oliver, Egbert S., "Melville's Goneril and Fanny Kemble," *New England Quarterly,* XVIII (1945), pp. 489-500.

————, "Melville's Picture of Emerson and Thoreau in 'The Confidence-Man,'" *College English,* VIII (1946), pp. 61-72.

Pearce, Roy Harvey, "Melville's Indian Hater: A Note on the Meaning of *The Confidence-Man,*" *PMLA,* LXVII (1952), pp. 942-948.

Reeves, Paschal, "The 'Deaf Mute' Confidence Man: Melville's Imposter in Action," *Modern Language Notes*, LXXV (1960), pp. 18-20.

Rosenberry, Edward H., "Melville's Ship of Fools," *PMLA*, LXXV (1960), pp. 604-608.

Seelye, John D., "Timothy Flint's 'Wicked River' and *The Confidence-Man*," *PMLA*, LXXVIII (1963), pp. 75-79.

Shroeder, John W., "Sources and Symbols for Melville's *Confidence-Man*," *PMLA*, LXVI (1951), pp. 363-380.

Smith, Paul, "*The Confidence-Man* and the Literary World of New York," *Nineteenth-Century Fiction*, XVI (1962), pp. 329-337.

Tanselle, G. Thomas, "Herman Melville's Visit to Galena in 1840," *Journal of the Illinois State Historical Society*, LIII (1960), pp. 376-388.

Weissbuch, Ted N., "A Note on the Confidence-Man's Counterfeit Detector," *Emerson Society Quarterly*, No. 19 (1960), pp. 16-18.

Wright, Nathalia, "The Confidence Men of Melville and Cooper: an American Indictment," *American Quarterly*, IV (1952), pp. 266-268.

THE CONFIDENCE-MAN

THE

CONFIDENCE-MAN:

HIS MASQUERADE.

BY

HERMAN MELVILLE,

AUTHOR OF "PIAZZA TALES," "OMOO," "TYPEE," ETC., ETC.

———

NEW YORK:

DIX, EDWARDS & CO., 321 BROADWAY.

1857.

Chapter 1 A MUTE GOES ABOARD A BOAT *on the Mississippi* ॐ

At sunrise on a first of April, there appeared, suddenly as Manco Capac at the lake Titicaca, a man in cream-colors, at the water-side in the city of St. Louis.

His cheek was fair, his chin downy, his hair flaxen, his hat a white fur one, with a long fleecy nap. He had neither trunk, valise, carpet-bag, nor parcel. No porter followed him. He was unaccompanied by friends. From the shrugged shoulders, titters, whispers, wonderings of the crowd, it was plain that he was, in the extremest sense of the word, a stranger.

In the same moment with his advent, he stepped aboard the favorite steamer Fidèle, on the point of starting for New Orleans. Stared at, but unsaluted, with the air of one neither courting nor shunning regard, but evenly pursuing the path of duty, lead it through solitudes or cities, he held on his way along the lower deck until he chanced to come to a placard nigh the captain's office, offering a reward for the capture of a mysterious impostor, supposed to have recently arrived from the East; quite an original genius in his vocation, as would appear, though wherein his originality consisted was not clearly given; but what purported to be a careful description of his person followed.

As if it had been a theatre-bill, crowds were gathered about the announcement, and among them certain chevaliers, whose eyes, it was plain, were on the capitals, or, at least, earnestly seeking sight of them from behind intervening coats; but as for their fingers, they were enveloped in some myth; though, during a chance interval, one of these chevaliers somewhat showed his hand in purchasing from another chevalier, ex-officio a peddler of money-belts, one of his popular safe-guards, while another peddler, who was still another versatile chevalier, hawked, in the thick of the throng, the lives of Measan, the bandit of Ohio, Murrel, the pirate of the Mississippi, and the brothers Harpe, the Thugs of the Green River country, in Kentucky—creatures, with others of the sort, one and all exterminated at the time, and for the most part, like the hunted generations of wolves in the same regions, leaving comparatively few successors; which would seem cause for unalloyed gratulation, and is such to all except those who think that in new countries, where the wolves are killed off, the foxes increase.

Pausing at this spot, the stranger so far succeeded in threading his way, as at last to plant himself just beside the placard, when, producing a small slate and tracing some words upon it, he held it up before him on a level with the placard, so that they who read the one might read the other. The words were these:—

Charity thinketh no evil.

As, in gaining his place, some little perseverance, not to say persistence, of a milaiy ffensive sort, had been unavoidable, it was not with the best relish that the crowd regarded his apparent intrusion; and upon a more attentive survey, perceiving no badge of authority about him, but rather something quite the contrary—he being of an aspect so singularly innocent; an aspect, too, which they took to be somehow inappropriate to the time and place, and inclining to the notion that his writing was of much the same sort: in short, taking him for some strange kind of simpleton, harmless enough, would he keep to himself, but not wholly unobnoxious as an intruder—they made no scruple to jostle him aside; while one, less kind than the rest, or more of a wag, by an unobserved stroke, dexterously flattened down his fleecy hat upon his head. Without readjusting it, the stranger quietly turned, and writing anew upon the slate, again held it up:—

Charity suffereth long, and is kind.

Illy pleased with his pertinacity, as they thought it, the crowd a second time thrust him aside, and not without epithets and some buffets, all of which were unresented. But, as if at last despairing of so difficult an adventure, wherein one, apparently a non-resistant, sought to impose his presence upon fighting characters, the stranger now moved slowly away, yet not before altering his writing to this:—

Charity endureth all things.

Shield-like bearing his slate before him, amid stares and jeers he moved slowly up and down, at his turning points again changing his inscription to—

Charity believeth all things.

and then—

Charity never faileth.

The word charity, as originally traced, remained throughout uneffaced, not unlike the left-hand numeral of a printed date, otherwise left for convenience in blank.

To some observers, the singularity, if not lunacy, of the stranger was heightened by his muteness, and, perhaps also, by the contrast to his proceedings afforded in the actions—quite in the wonted and sensible order of things—of the barber of the boat, whose quarters, under a smoking-saloon, and over against a bar-room, was next door but two to the captain's office. As if the long, wide, covered deck, hereabouts built up on both sides with shop-like windowed spaces, were some Constantinople arcade or bazaar, where more than one trade is plied, this river barber, aproned and slippered, but rather crusty-looking for the moment, it may be from being newly out of bed, was throwing open his premises for the day, and suitably arranging the exterior. With business-like dispatch, having rattled down his shutters, and at a palm-tree angle set out in the iron fixture his little ornamental pole, and this without overmuch tenderness for the elbows and toes of the crowd, he concluded his operations by bidding people stand still more aside, when, jumping on a stool, he hung over his door, on the customary nail, a gaudy sort of illuminated pasteboard sign, skillfully executed by himself, gilt with the likeness of a razor elbowed in readiness to shave, and also, for the public benefit, with two words not unfrequently seen ashore gracing other shops besides barbers':—

No TRUST.

An inscription which, though in a sense not less intrusive than the contrasted ones of the stranger, did not, as it seemed, provoke any corresponding derision or surprise, much less indignation; and still less, to all appearances, did it gain for the inscriber the repute of being a simpleton.

Meanwhile, he with the slate continued moving slowly up and down, not without causing some stares to change into jeers, and some jeers into pushes, and some pushes into punches; when suddenly, in one of his turns, he was hailed from behind by two porters carrying a large trunk; but as the summons, though loud, was without effect, they accidentally or otherwise swung their burden against him, nearly overthrowing him; when, by a quick start, a peculiar inarticulate moan, and a pathetic telegraphing of his fingers, he involuntarily betrayed that he was not alone dumb, but also deaf.

Presently, as if not wholly unaffected by his reception thus far, he went forward, seating himself in a retired spot on the forecastle, nigh the foot of a ladder there leading to a deck above, up and down which ladder some of the boatmen, in discharge of their duties, were occasionally going.

From his betaking himself to this humble quarter, it was evident that, as a deck-passenger, the stranger, simple though he seemed, was not entirely ignorant of his place, though his taking a deck-passage might have been partly for convenience; as, from his having no luggage, it was probable that his destination was one of the small wayside landings within a few hours' sail. But, though he might not have a long way to go, yet he seemed already to have come from a very long distance.

Though neither soiled nor slovenly, his cream-colored suit had a tossed look, almost linty, as if, traveling night and day from some far country beyond the prairies, he had long been without the solace of a bed. His aspect was at once gentle and jaded, and, from the moment of seating himself, increasing in tired abstraction and dreaminess. Gradually overtaken by slumber, his flaxen head drooped, his whole lamb-like figure relaxed, and, half reclining against the ladder's foot, lay motionless, as some sugar-snow in March, which, softly stealing down over night, with its white placidity startles the brown farmer peering out from his threshold at daybreak.

Chapter 2 *Showing That* MANY MEN HAVE MANY MINDS ॐ

"Odd fish!"
  "Poor fellow!"
  "Who can he be?"
  "Casper Hauser."
  "Bless my soul!"
  "Uncommon countenance."
  "Green prophet from Utah."
  "Humbug!"
  "Singular innocence."
  "Means something."
  "Spirit-rapper."
  "Moon-calf."
  "Piteous."
  "Trying to enlist interest."
  "Beware of him."
  "Fast asleep here, and, doubtless, pick-pockets on board."
  "Kind of daylight Endymion."
  "Escaped convict, worn out with dodging."
  "Jacob dreaming at Luz."

Such the epitaphic comments, conflictingly spoken or thought, of a miscellaneous company, who, assembled on the overlooking, crosswise balcony at the forward end of the upper deck near by, had not witnessed preceding occurrences.

Meantime, like some enchanted man in his grave, happily oblivious of all gossip, whether chiseled or chatted, the deaf and dumb stranger still tranquilly slept, while now the boat started on her voyage.

The great ship-canal of Ving-King-Ching in the Flowery Kingdom, seems the Mississippi in parts, where, amply flowing between low, vine-tangled banks, flat as tow-paths, it bears the huge toppling steamers, bedizened and lacquered within like imperial junks.

Pierced along its great white bulk with two tiers of small embrasure-like windows, well above the water-line, the Fidèle, though, might at distance have been taken by strangers for some white-washed fort on a floating isle.

Merchants on 'change seem the passengers that buzz on her decks, while, from quarters unseen, comes a murmur as of bees in the comb. Fine promenades, domed saloons, long galleries, sunny balconies, confidential passages, bridal chambers, state-rooms plenty as pigeon-holes, and out-of-the-way retreats like secret drawers in an escritoire, present like facilities for publicity or privacy. Auctioneer or coiner, with equal ease, might somewhere here drive his trade.

Though her voyage of twelve hundred miles extends from apple to orange, from clime to clime, yet, like any small ferry-boat, to right and left, at every landing, the huge Fidèle still receives additional passengers in exchange for those that disembark; so that, though always full of strangers, she continually, in some degree, adds to, or replaces them with strangers still more strange; like Rio Janeiro fountain, fed from the Cocovarde mountains, which is ever over-flowing with strange waters, but never with the same strange parti-cles in every part.

Though hitherto, as has been seen, the man in cream-colors had by no means passed unobserved, yet by stealing into retirement, and there going asleep and continuing so, he seemed to have courted oblivion, a boon not often withheld from so humble an applicant as he. Those staring crowds on the shore were now left far behind, seen dimly clustering like swallows on eaves; while the passengers' attention was soon drawn away to the rapidly shooting high bluffs and shot-towers on the Missouri shore, or the bluff-looking Missourians and towering Kentuckians among the throngs on the decks.

By and by—two or three random stoppages having been made, and the last transient memory of the slumberer vanished, and he himself, not unlikely, waked up and landed ere now—the crowd, as is usual, began in all parts to break up from a concourse into various clusters or squads, which in some cases disintegrated again into quartettes, trios, and couples, or even solitaires; involuntarily sub-mitting to that natural law which ordains dissolution equally to the mass, as in time to the member.

As among Chaucer's Canterbury pilgrims, or those oriental ones crossing the Red Sea towards Mecca in the festival month, there was no lack of variety. Natives of all sorts, and foreigners; men of business and men of pleasure; parlor men and backwoodsmen; farm-hunters and fame-hunters; heiress-hunters, gold-hunters, buffalo-hunters, bee-hunters, happiness-hunters, truth-hunters, and still keener hunters after all these hunters. Fine ladies in slippers, and moccasined squaws; Northern speculators and Eastern philosophers; English, Irish, German, Scotch, Danes; Santa Fé traders in striped blankets, and Broadway bucks in cravats of cloth of gold; fine-looking Mississippi cotton-planters; Quakers in full drab, and United States soldiers in full regimentals; slaves, black, mulatto, quadroon; modish young Spanish Creoles, and old-fashioned French Jews; Mormons and Papists; Dives and Lazarus; jesters and mourners, teetotalers and convivialists, deacons and blacklegs; hard-shell Baptists and clay-eaters; grinning negroes, and Sioux chiefs solemn as high-priests. In short, a piebald parliament, an Anacharsis Cloots congress of all kinds of that multiform pilgrim species, man.

As pine, beech, birch, ash, hackmatack, hemlock, spruce, basswood, maple, interweave their foliage in the natural wood, so these varieties of mortals blended their varieties of visage and garb. A Tartar-like picturesqueness; a sort of pagan abandonment and assurance. Here reigned the dashing and all-fusing spirit of the West, whose type is the Mississippi itself, which, uniting the streams of the most distant and opposite zones, pours them along, helter-skelter, in one cosmopolitan and confident tide.

Chapter 3 *In Which* A VARIETY OF CHARACTERS APPEAR ⌘

In the forward part of the boat, not the least attractive object, for a time, was a grotesque negro cripple, in tow-cloth attire and an old coal-sifter of a tambourine in his hand, who, owing to something wrong about his legs, was, in effect, cut down to the stature of a Newfoundland dog; his knotted black fleece and good-natured, honest black face rubbing against the upper part of people's thighs as he made shift to shuffle about, making music, such as it was, and raising a smile even from the gravest. It was curious to see him, out of his very deformity, indigence, and houselessness, so cheerily endured, raising mirth in some of that crowd, whose own purses, hearths, hearts, all their possessions, sound limbs included, could not make gay.

"What is your name, old boy?" said a purple-faced drover, putting his large purple hand on the cripple's bushy wool, as if it were the curled forehead of a black steer.

"Der Black Guinea dey calls me, sar."

"And who is your master, Guinea?"

"Oh sar, I am der dog widout massa."

"A free dog, eh? Well, on your account, I'm sorry for that, Guinea. Dogs without masters fare hard."

"So dey do, sar; so dey do. But you see, sar, dese here legs? What ge'mman want to own dese here legs?"

"But where do you live?"

"All 'long shore, sar; dough now I'se going to see brodder at der landing; but chiefly I libs in der city."

"St. Louis, ah? Where do you sleep there of nights?"

"On der floor of der good baker's oven, sar."

"In an oven? whose, pray? What baker, I should like to know, bakes such black bread in his oven, alongside of his nice white rolls, too. Who is that too charitable baker, pray?"

"Dar he be," with a broad grin lifting his tambourine high over his head.

8

"The sun is the baker, eh?"

"Yes sar, in der city dat good baker warms der stones for dis ole darkie when he sleeps out on der pabements o' nights."

"But that must be in the summer only, old boy. How about winter, when the cold Cossacks come clattering and jingling? How about winter, old boy?"

"Den dis poor old darkie shakes werry bad, I tell you, sar. Oh sar, oh! don't speak ob der winter," he added, with a reminiscent shiver, shuffling off into the thickest of the crowd, like a half-frozen black sheep nudging itself a cozy berth in the heart of the white flock.

Thus far not very many pennies had been given him, and, used at last to his strange looks, the less polite passengers of those in that part of the boat began to get their fill of him as a curious object; when suddenly the negro more than revived their first interest by an expedient which, whether by chance or design, was a singular temptation at once to *diversion* and charity, though, even more than his crippled limbs, it put him on a canine footing. In short, as in appearance he seemed a dog, so now, in a merry way, like a dog he began to be treated. Still shuffling among the crowd, now and then he would pause, throwing back his head and opening his mouth like an elephant for tossed apples at a menagerie; when, making a space before him, people would have a bout at a strange sort of pitch-penny game, the cripple's mouth being at once target and purse, and he hailing each expertly-caught copper with a cracked bravura from his tambourine. To be the subject of alms-giving is trying, and to feel in duty bound to appear cheerfully grateful under the trial, must be still more so; but whatever his secret emotions, he swallowed them, while still retaining each copper this side the œsophagus. And nearly always he grinned, and only once or twice did he wince, which was when certain coins, tossed by more playf almoners, came inconveniently nigh to his teeth, an acciden hose unwelcomeness was not unedged by the circumstance that the pennies thus thrown proved buttons.

While this game of charity was yet at its height, a limping, gimlet-eyed, sour-faced person—it may be some discharged customhouse officer, who, suddenly stripped of convenient means of support, had concluded to be avenged on government and humanity by making himself miserable for life, either by hating or suspecting everything and everybody—this shallow unfortunate, after sundry sorry observations of the negro, began to croak out something about his deformity being a sham, got up for financial purposes, which immediately threw a damp upon the frolic benignities of the pitch-penny players.

But that these suspicions came from one who himself on a wooden leg went halt, this did not appear to strike anybody present. That cripples, above all men should be companionable, or, at least, refrain from picking a fellow-limper to pieces, in short, should have a little sympathy in common misfortune, seemed not to occur to the company.

Meantime, the negro's countenance, before marked with even more than patient good-nature, drooped into a heavy-hearted expression, full of the most painful distress. So far abased beneath its proper physical level, that Newfoundland-dog face turned in passively hopeless appeal, as if instinct told it that the right or the wrong might not have overmuch to do with whatever wayward mood superior intelligences might yield to.

But instinct, though knowing, is yet a teacher set below reason, which itself says, in the grave words of Lysander in the comedy, after Puck has made a sage of him with his spell:—

The will of man is by his reason swayed.

So that, suddenly change as people may, in their dispositions, it is not always waywardness, but improved judgment, which, as in Lysander's case, or the present, operates with them.

Yes, they began to scrutinize the negro curiously enough; when, emboldened by this evidence of the efficacy of his words, the wooden-legged man hobbled up to the negro, and, with the air of a beadle, would, to prove his alleged imposture on the spot, have stripped him and then driven him away, but was prevented by the crowd's clamor, now taking part with the poor fellow, against one who had just before turned nearly all minds the other way. So he with the wooden leg was forced to retire; when the rest, finding themselves left sole judges in the case, could not resist the opportunity of acting the part: not because it is a human weakness to take pleasure in sitting in judgment upon one in a box, as surely this unfortunate negro now was, but that it strangely sharpens human perceptions, when, instead of standing by and having their fellow-feelings touched by the sight of an alleged culprit severely handled by some one justiciary, a crowd suddenly come to be all justiciaries in the same case themselves; as in Arkansas once, a man proved guilty, by law, of murder, but whose condemnation was deemed unjust by the people, so that they rescued him to try him themselves; whereupon, they, as it turned out, found him even guiltier than the court had done, and forthwith proceeded to execution; so that the gallows presented the truly warning spectacle of a man hanged by his friends.

But not to such extremities, or anything like them, did the present crowd come; they, for the time, being content with putting the negro fairly and discreetly to the question; among other things, asking him, had he any documentary proof, any plain paper about him, attesting that his case was not a spurious one.

"No, no, dis poor ole darkie hain't none o' dem waloable papers," he wailed.

"But is there not some one who can speak a good word for you?" here said a person newly arrived from another part of the boat, a young Episcopal clergyman, in a long, straight-bodied black coat; small in stature, but manly; with a clear face and blue eye; innocence, tenderness, and good sense triumvirate in his air.

"Oh yes, oh yes, ge'mmen," he eagerly answered, as if his memory, before suddenly frozen up by cold charity, as suddenly thawed back into fluidity at the first kindly word. "Oh yes, oh yes, dar is aboard here a werry nice, good ge'mman wid a weed, and a ge'mman in a gray coat and white tie, what knows all about me; and a ge'mman wid a big book, too; and a yarb-doctor; and a ge'mman in a yaller west; and a ge'mman wid a brass plate; and a ge'mman in a wiolet robe; and a ge'mman as is a sodjer; and ever so many good, kind, honest ge'mmen more aboard what knows me and will speak for me, God bress 'em; yes, and what knows me as well as dis poor ole darkie knows hisself, God bress him! Oh, find 'em, find 'em," he earnestly added, "and let 'em come quick, and show you all, ge'm-men, dat dis poor ole darkie is werry well wordy of all you kind ge'mmen's kind confidence."

"But how are we to find all these people in this great crowd?" was the question of a bystander, umbrella in hand; a middle-aged person, a country merchant apparently, whose natural good-feeling had been made at least cautious by the unnatural ill-feeling of the discharged custom-house officer.

"Where are we to find them?" half-rebukefully echoed the young Episcopal clergyman. "I will go find one to begin with," he quickly added, and, with kind haste suiting the action to the word, away he went.

"Wild goose chase!" croaked he with the wooden leg, now again drawing nigh. "Don't believe there's a soul of them aboard. Did ever beggar have such heaps of fine friends? He can walk fast enough when he tries, a good deal faster than I; but he can lie yet faster. He's some white operator, betwisted and painted up for a decoy. He and his friends are all humbugs."

"Have you no charity, friend?" here in self-subdued tones, singularly contrasted with his unsubdued person, said a Methodist minister, advancing; a tall, muscular, martial-looking man, a Tennessean by birth, who in the Mexican war had been volunteer chaplain to a volunteer rifle-regiment.

"Charity is one thing, and truth is another," rejoined he with the wooden leg: "he's a rascal, I say."

"But why not, friend, put as charitable a construction as one can upon the poor fellow?" said the soldier-like Methodist, with increased difficulty maintaining a pacific demeanor towards one whose own asperity seemed so little to entitle him to it: "he looks honest, don't he?"

"Looks are one thing, and facts are another," snapped out the other perversely; "and as to your constructions, what construction can you put upon a rascal, but that a rascal he is?"

"Be not such a Canada thistle," urged the Methodist, with something less of patience than before. "Charity, man, charity."

"To where it belongs with your charity! to heaven with it!" again snapped out the other, diabolically; "here on earth, true charity dotes, and false charity plots. Who betrays a fool with a kiss, the charitable fool has the charity to believe is in love with him, and the charitable knave on the stand gives charitable testimony for his comrade in the box."

"Surely, friend," returned the noble Methodist, with much ado restraining his still waxing indignation—"surely, to say the least, you forget yourself. Apply it home," he continued, with exterior calmness tremulous with inkept emotion. "Suppose, now, I should exercise no charity in judging your own character by the words which have fallen from you; what sort of vile, pitiless man do you think I would take you for?"

"No doubt"—with a grin—"some such pitiless man as has lost his piety in much the same way that the jockey loses his honesty."

"And how is that, friend?" still conscientiously holding back the old Adam in him, as if it were a mastiff he had by the neck.

"Never you mind how it is"—with a sneer; "but all horses ain't virtuous, no more than all men kind; and come close to, and much dealt with, some things are catching. When you find me a virtuous jockey, I will find you a benevolent wise man."

"Some insinuation there."

"More fool you that are puzzled by it."

"Reprobate!" cried the other, his indignation now at last almost boiling over; "godless reprobate! if charity did not restrain me, I could call you by names you deserve."

"Could you, indeed?" with an insolent sneer.

"Yea, and teach you charity on the spot," cried the goaded Methodist, suddenly catching this exasperating opponent by his shabby coat-collar, and shaking him till his timber-toe clattered on the deck like a nine-pin. "You took me for a non-combatant did you? —thought, seedy coward that you are, that you could abuse a Christian with impunity. You find your mistake"—with another hearty shake.

"Well said and better done, church militant!" cried a voice.

"The white cravat against the world!" cried another.

"Bravo, bravo!" chorused many voices, with like enthusiasm taking sides with the resolute champion.

"You fools!" cried he with the wooden leg, writhing himself loose and inflamedly turning upon the throng; "you flock of fools, under this captain of fools, in this ship of fools!"

With which exclamations, followed by idle threats against his admonisher, this condign victim to justice hobbled away, as disdaining to hold further argument with such a rabble. But his scorn was more than repaid by the hisses that chased him, in which the brave Methodist, satisfied with the rebuke already administered, was, to omit still better reasons, too magnanimous to join. All he said was, pointing towards the departing recusant, "There he shambles off on his one lone leg, emblematic of his one-sided view of humanity."

"But trust your painted decoy," retorted the other from a distance, pointing back to the black cripple, "and I have my revenge."

"But we ain't agoing to trust him!" shouted back a voice.

"So much the better," he jeered back. "Look you," he added, coming to a dead halt where he was; "look you, I have been called a Canada thistle. Very good. And a seedy one: still better. And the seedy Canada thistle has been pretty well shaken among ye: best of all. Dare say some seed has been shaken out; and won't it spring though? And when it does spring, do you cut down the young thistles, and won't they spring the more? It's encouraging and coaxing 'em. Now, when with my thistles your farms shall be well stocked, why then—you may abandon 'em!"

"What does all that mean, now?" asked the country merchant, staring.

"Nothing; the foiled wolf's parting howl," said the Methodist. "Spleen, much spleen, which is the rickety child of his evil heart of unbelief: it has made him mad. I suspect him for one naturally reprobate. Oh, friends," raising his arms as in the pulpit, "oh beloved, how are we admonished by the melancholy spectacle of this raver. Let us profit by the lesson; and is it not this: that if, next to mistrusting Providence, there be aught that man should pray against, it is against mistrusting his fellow-man. I have been in mad-houses full of tragic mopers, and seen there the end of suspicion: the cynic, in

the moody madness muttering in the corner; for years a barren fixture there; head lopped over, gnawing his own lip, vulture of himself; while, by fits and starts, from the corner opposite came the
grimace of the idiot at him."

"What an example," whispered one.

"Might deter Timon," was the response.

"Oh, oh, good ge'mmen, have you no confidence in dis poor ole
darkie?" now wailed the returning negro, who, during the late scene,
had stumped apart in alarm.

"Confidence in you?" echoed he who had whispered, with
abruptly changed air turning short round; "that remains to be seen."

"I tell you what it is, Ebony," in similarly changed tones said he
who had responded to the whisperer, "yonder churl," pointing toward the wooden leg in the distance, "is, no doubt, a churlish fellow
enough, and I would not wish to be like him; but that is no reason
why you may not be some sort of black Jeremy Diddler."

"No confidence in dis poor ole darkie, den?"

"Before giving you our confidence," said a third, "we will wait
the report of the kind gentleman who went in search of one of your
friends who was to speak for you."

"Very likely, in that case," said a fourth, "we shall wait here till
Christmas. Shouldn't wonder, did we not see that kind gentleman
again. After seeking awhile in vain, he will conclude he has been
made a fool of, and so not return to us for pure shame. Fact is, I begin to feel a little qualmish about the darkie myself. Something
queer about this darkie, depend upon it."

Once more the negro wailed, and turning in despair from the last
speaker, imploringly caught the Methodist by the skirt of his coat.
But a change had come over that before impassioned intercessor.
With an irresolute and troubled air, he mutely eyed the suppli-
against whom, somehow, by what seemed instinctive influ-
distrusts first set on foot were now generally reviving, and, if anything, with added severity.

"No confidence in dis poor ole darkie," yet again wailed the negro, letting go the coat-skirts and turning appealingly all round him.

"Yes, my poor fellow, *I* have confidence in you," now exclaimed the country merchant before named, whom the negro's appeal, coming so piteously on the heel of pitilessness, seemed at last humanely to have decided in his favor. "And here, here is some proof of my trust," with which, tucking his umbrella under his arm, and diving down his hand into his pocket, he fished forth a purse, and, accidentally, along with it, his business card, which, unobserved, dropped to the deck. "Here, here, my poor fellow," he continued, extending a half dollar.

Not more grateful for the coin than the kindness, the cripple's face glowed like a polished copper saucepan, and shuffling a pace nigher, with one upstretched hand he received the alms, while, as unconsciously, his one advanced leather stump covered the card.

Done in despite of the general sentiment, the good deed of the merchant was not, perhaps, without its unwelcome return from the crowd, since that good deed seemed somehow to convey to them a sort of reproach. Still again, and more pertinaciously than ever, the cry arose against the negro, and still again he wailed forth his lament and appeal; among other things, repeating that the friends, of whom already he had partially run off the list, would freely speak for 'im, would anybody go find them.

"Why don't you go find 'em yourself?" demanded a gruff boatman.

"How can I go find 'em myself? Dis poor ole game-legged darkie's friends must come to him. Oh, whar, whar is dat good friend of dis darkie's, dat good man wid de weed?"

At this point, a steward ringing a bell came along, summoning all persons who had not got their tickets to step to the captain's office; an announcement which speedily thinned the throng about the black cripple, who himself soon forlornly stumped out of sight, probably on much the same errand as the rest.

Chapter 4 RENEWAL OF OLD ACQUAINTANCE ❧

"How do you do, Mr. Roberts?"

"Eh?"

"Don't you know me?"

"No, certainly."

The crowd about the captain's office, having in good time melted away, the above encounter took place in one of the side balconies astern, between a man in mourning clean and respectable, but none of the glossiest, a long weed on his hat, and the country-merchant before-mentioned, whom, with the familiarity of an old acquaintance, the former had accosted.

"Is it possible, my dear sir," resumed he with the weed, "that you do not recall my countenance? Why yours I recall distinctly as if but half an hour, instead of half an age, had passed since I saw you. Don't you recall me, now? Look harder."

"In my conscience—truly—I protest," honestly bewildered, "bless my soul, sir, I don't know you—really, really. But stay, stay," he hurriedly added, not without gratification, glancing up at the crape on the stranger's hat, "stay—yes—seems to me, though I have not the pleasure of personally knowing you, yet I am pretty sure I have at least *heard* of you, and recently too, quite recently. A poor negro aboard here referred to you, among others, for a character, I think."

"Oh, the cripple. Poor fellow, I know him well. They found me. I have said all I could for him. I think I abated their distrust. Would I could have been of more substantial service. And apropos, sir," he added, "now that it strikes me, allow me to ask, whether the circumstance of one man, however humble, referring for a character to another man, however afflicted, does not argue more or less of moral worth in the latter?"

The good merchant looked puzzled.

"Still you don't recall my countenance?"

"Still does truth compel me to say that I cannot, despite my best efforts," was the reluctantly-candid reply.

"Can I be so changed? Look at me. Or is it I who am mistaken?— Are you not, sir, Henry Roberts, forwarding merchant, of Wheeling,

17

Pennsylvania? Pray, now, if you use the advertisement of business cards, and happen to have one with you, just look at it, and see whether you are not the man I take you for."

"Why," a bit chafed, perhaps, "I hope I know myself."

"And yet self-knowledge is thought by some not so easy. Who knows, my dear sir, but for a time you may have taken yourself for somebody else? Stranger things have happened."

The good merchant stared.

"To come to particulars, my dear sir, I met you, now some six years back, at Brade Brothers & Co.'s office, I think. I was traveling for a Philadelphia house. The senior Brade introduced us, you remember; some business-chat followed, then you forced me home with you to a family tea, and a family time we had. Have you forgotten about the urn, and what I said about Werther's Charlotte, and the bread and butter, and that capital story you told of the large loaf. A hundred times since, I have laughed over it. At least you must recall my name—Ringman, John Ringman."

"Large loaf? Invited you to tea? Ringman? Ringman? Ring? Ring?"

"Ah sir," sadly smiling, "don't ring the changes that way. I see you have a faithless memory, Mr. Roberts. But trust in the faithfulness of mine."

"Well, to tell the truth, in some things my memory ain't of the very best," was the honest rejoinder. "But still," he perplexedly added, "still I—"

"Oh sir, suffice it that it is as I say. Doubt not that we are all well acquainted."

"But—but I don't like this going dead against my own memory; I—"

"But didn't you admit, my dear sir, that in some things this memory of yours is a little faithless? Now, those who have faithless memories, should they not have some little confidence in the less faithless memories of others?"

"But, of this friendly chat and tea, I have not the slightest—"

"I see, I see; quite erased from the tablet. Pray, sir," with a sudden illumination, "about six years back, did it happen to you to volving calamities against which no integrity, no forethought, no energy, no genius, no piety, could guard.

At every disclosure, the hearer's commiseration increased. No sentimental pity. As the story went on, he drew from his wallet a bank note, but after a while, at some still more unhappy revelation, changed it for another, probably of a somewhat larger amount; which, when the story was concluded, with an air studiously disclamatory of alms-giving, he put into the stranger's hands; who, on his side, with an air studiously disclamatory of alms-taking, put it into his pocket.

Assistance being received, the stranger's manner assumed a kind and degree of decorum which, under the circumstances, seemed almost coldness. After some words, not over ardent, and yet not exactly inappropriate, he took leave, making a bow which had one knows not what of a certain chastened independence about it; as if misery, however burdensome, could not break down self-respect, nor gratitude, however deep, humiliate a gentleman.

He was hardly yet out of sight, when he paused as if thinking; then with hastened steps returning to the merchant, "I am just reminded that the president, who is also transfer-agent, of the Black Rapids Coal Company, happens to be on board here, and, having been subpœnaed as witness in a stock case on the docket in Kentucky, has his transfer-book with him. A month since, in a panic contrived by artful alarmists, some credulous stock-holders sold out; but, to frustrate the aim of the alarmists, the Company, previously advised of their scheme, so managed it as to get into its own hands those sacrificed shares, resolved that, since a spurious panic must be, the panic-makers should be no gainers by it. The Company, I hear, is now ready, but not anxious, to redispose of those shares; and having obtained them at their depressed value, will now sell them at par, though, prior to the panic, they were held at a handsome figure above. That the readiness of the Company to do this is not generally known, is shown by the fact that the stock still stands on the transfer-book in the Company's name, offering to one in funds a rare chance for investment. For, the panic subsiding more and more every day, it will daily be seen how it originated; confidence will be more than restored; there will be a reaction; from the stock's descent its rise will be higher than from no fall, the holders trusting themselves to fear no second fate."

Having listened at first with curiosity, at last with interest, the merchant replied to the effect, that some time since, through friends concerned with it, he had heard of the company, and heard well of it, but was ignorant that there had latterly been fluctuations. He added that he was no speculator; that hitherto he had avoided having to do with stocks of any sort, but in the present case he really felt something like being tempted. "Pray," in conclusion, "do you think that upon a pinch anything could be transacted on board here with the transfer-agent? Are you acquainted with him?"

"Not personally. I but happened to hear that he was a passenger. For the rest, though it might be somewhat informal, the gentleman might not object to doing a little business on board. Along the Mississippi, you know, business is not so ceremonious as at the East."

"True," returned the merchant, and looked down a moment in thought, then, raising his head quickly, said, in a tone not so benign as his wonted one, "This would seem a rare chance, indeed; why, upon first hearing it, did you not snatch at it? I mean for yourself!"

"I?—would it had been possible!"

Not without some emotion was this said, and not without some embarrassment was the reply. "Ah, yes, I had forgotten."

Upon this, the stranger regarded him with mild gravity, not a little disconcerting; the more so, as there was in it what seemed the aspect not alone of the superior, but, as it were, the rebuker; which sort of bearing, in a beneficiary towards his benefactor, looked strangely enough; none the less, that, somehow, it sat not altogether unbecomingly upon the beneficiary, being free from anything like the appearance of assumption, and mixed with a kind of painful conscientiousness, as though nothing but a proper sense of what he owed to himself swayed him. At length he spoke:

"To reproach a penniless man with remissness in not availing himself of an opportunity for pecuniary investment—but, no, no; it was forgetfulness; and this, charity will impute to some lingering effect of that unfortunate brain-fever, which, as to occurrences dating yet further back, disturbed Mr. Roberts's memory still more seriously."

"As to that," said the merchant, rallying, "I am not—"

"Pardon me, but you must admit, that just now, an unpleasant distrust, however vague, was yours. Ah, shallow as it is, yet, how subtle a thing is suspicion, which at times can invade the humanest of hearts and wisest of heads. But, enough. My object, sir, in calling your attention to this stock, is by way of acknowledgment of your goodness. I but seek to be grateful; if my information leads to nothing, you must remember the motive."

He bowed, and finally retired, leaving Mr. Roberts not wholly without self-reproach, for having momentarily indulged injurious thoughts against one who, it was evident, was possessed of a self-respect which forbade his indulging them himself.

"Well, there is sorrow in the world, but goodness too; and goodness that is not greenness, either, no more than sorrow is. Dear good man. Poor beating heart!"

It was the man with the weed, not very long after quitting the merchant, murmuring to himself with his hand to his side like one with the heart-disease.

Meditation over kindness received seemed to have softened him somewhat, too, it may be, beyond what might, perhaps, have been looked for from one whose unwonted self-respect in the hour of need, and in the act of being aided, might have appeared to some not wholly unlike pride out of place; and pride, in any place, is seldom very feeling. But the truth, perhaps, is, that those who are least touched with that vice, besides being not unsusceptible to goodness, are sometimes the ones whom a ruling sense of propriety makes appear cold, if not thankless, under a favor. For, at such a time, to be full of warm, earnest words, and heart-felt protestations, is to create a scene; and well-bred people dislike few things more than that; which would seem to look as if the world did not relish earnestness; but, not so; because the world, being earnest itself, likes an earnest scene, and an earnest man, very well, but only in their place—the stage. See what sad work they make of it, who, ignorant of this, flame out in Irish enthusiasm and with Irish sincerity, to a benefactor, who, if a man of sense and respectability, as well as kindliness, can but be more or less annoyed by it; and, if of a nervously fastidious nature, as some are, may be led to think almost as much less favorably of the beneficiary paining him by his gratitude, as if he had been guilty of its contrary, instead only of an indiscretion. But, beneficiaries who know better, though they may feel as much, if not more, neither inflict such pain, nor are inclined to run any risk of so doing. And these, being wise, are the majority. By which one sees how inconsiderate those persons are, who, from the absence of its

24

officious manifestations in the world, complain that there is not much gratitude extant; when the truth is, that there is as much of it as there is of modesty; but, both being for the most part votarists of the shade, for the most part keep out of sight.

What started this was, to account, if necessary, for the changed air of the man with the weed, who, throwing off in private the cold garb of decorum, and so giving warmly loose to his genuine heart, seemed almost transformed into another being. This subdued air of softness, too, was toned with melancholy, melancholy unreserved; a thing which, however at variance with propriety, still the more attested his earnestness; for one knows not how it is, but it sometimes happens that, where earnestness is, there, also, is melancholy.

At the time, he was leaning over the rail at the boat's side, in pensiveness, unmindful of another pensive figure near—a gentleman with a swan-neck, wearing a lady-like open shirt la thrown back, and tied with a black ribbon. From a square ableted broach, curiously engraved with Greek characters, he s d a collegian—not improbably, a sophomore—on his travel ossibly, his first. A small book bound in Roman vellum was in hi d.

Overhearing his murmuring neighbor, the yo regarded him with some surprise, not to say interest. But, sing ly for a collegian, being apparently of a retiring nature, he di speak; when the other still more increased his diffidence by changing from soliloquy to colloquy, in a manner strangely mixed of familiarity and pathos.

"Ah, who is this? You did not hear me, my young friend, did you? Why, you, too, look sad. My melancholy is not catching!"

"Sir, sir," stammered the other.

"Pray, now," with a sort of sociable sorrowfulness, slowly sliding along the rail, "Pray, now, my young friend, what volume have you there? Give me leave," gently drawing it from him. "Tacitus!" Then opening it at random, read: "In general a black and shameful period lies before me." "Dear young sir," touching his arm alarmedly, "don't read this book. It is poison, moral poison. Even were there truth in Tacitus, such truth would have the operation of falsity, and so still be poison, moral poison. Too well I know this Tacitus. In my college days he came near souring me into cynicism. Yes, I began to turn down my collar, and go about with a disdainfully joyless expression."

"Sir, sir, I—I—"

"Trust me. Now, young friend, perhaps you think that Tacitus, like me, is only melancholy; but he's more—he's ugly. A vast difference, young sir, between the melancholy view and the ugly. The one may show the world still beautiful, not so the other. The one may be compatible with benevolence, the other not. The one may deepen insight, the other shallows it. Drop Tacitus. Phrenologically, my young friend, you would seem to have a well-developed head, and large; but cribbed within the ugly view, the Tacitus view, your large brain, like your large ox in the contracted field, will but starve the more. And don't dream, as some of you students may, that, by taking this same ugly view, the deeper meanings of the deeper books will so alone become revealed to you. Drop Tacitus. His subtlety is falsity. To him, in his double-refined anatomy of human nature, is well applied the Scripture saying—'There is a subtle man, and the same is deceived.' Drop Tacitus. Come, now, let me throw the book overboard."

"Sir, I—I—"

"Not a word; I know just what is in your mind, and that is just what I am speaking to. Yes, learn from me that, though the sorrows of the world are great, its wickedness—that is, its ugliness—is small. Much cause to pity man, little to distrust him. I myself have known adversity, and know it still. But for that, do I turn cynic? No, no: it is small beer that sours. To my fellow-creatures I owe alleviations. So, whatever I may have undergone, it but deepens my confidence in my kind. Now, then" (winningly), "this book—will you let me drown it for you?"

"Really, sir—I—"

"I see, I see. But of course you read Tacitus in order to aid you in understanding human nature—as if truth was ever got at by libel. My young friend, if to know human nature is your object, drop Tacitus and go north to the cemeteries of Auburn and Greenwood."

"Upon my word, I—I—"

"Nay, I foresee all that. But you carry Tacitus, that shallow Tacitus. What do *I* carry? See"—producing a pocket-volume—"Aken-side—his 'Pleasures of Imagination.' One of these days you will know it. Whatever our lot, we should read serene and cheery books, fitted to inspire love and trust. But Tacitus! I have long been of opinion that these classics are the bane of colleges; for—not to hint of the immorality of Ovid, Horace, Anacreon, and the rest, and the dangerous theology of Æschylus and others—where will one find views so injurious to human nature as in Thycidides, Juvenal, Lucian, but more particularly Tacitus? When I consider that, ever since the revival of learning, these classics have been the favorites of successive generations of students and studious men, I tremble to think of that mass of unsuspected heresy on every vital topic which for centuries must have simmered unsurmised in the heart of Christendom. But Tacitus—he is the most extraordinary example of a heretic; not one iota of confidence in his kind. What a mockery that such an one should be reputed wise, and Thucydides be esteemed the statesman's manual! But Tacitus—I hate Tacitus; not, though, I trust, with the hate that sins, but a righteous hate. Without confidence himself, Tacitus destroys it in all his readers. Destroys confidence, paternal confidence, of which God knows that there is in this world none to spare. For, comparatively inexperienced as you are, my dear young friend, did you never observe how little, very little, confidence, there is? I mean between man and man—more particularly between stranger and stranger. In a sad world it is the saddest fact. Confidence! I have sometimes almost thought that confidence is fled; that confidence is the New Astrea—emigrated—vanished—gone." Then softly sliding nearer, with the softest air, quivering down and looking up, "could you now, my dear young sir, under such circumstances, by way of experiment, simply have confidence in *me?*"

From the outset, the sophomore, as has been seen, had struggled with an ever-increasing embarrassment, arising, perhaps, from such strange remarks coming from a stranger—such persistent and prolonged remarks, too. In vain had he more than once sought to break the spell by venturing a deprecatory or leave-taking word. In vain.

Somehow, the stranger fascinated him. Little wonder, then, that, when the appeal came, he could hardly speak, but, as before intimated, being apparently of a retiring nature, abruptly retired from the spot, leaving the chagrined stranger to wander away in the opposite direction.

"You—pish! Why will the captain suffer these begging fellows on board?"

These pettish words were breathed by a well-to-do gentleman in a ruby-colored velvet vest, and with a ruby-colored cheek, a ruby-headed cane in his hand, to a man in a gray coat and white tie, who, shortly after the interview last described, had accosted him for contributions to a Widow and Orphan Asylum recently founded among the Seminoles. Upon a cursory view, this last person might have seemed, like the man with the weed, one of the less unrefined children of misfortune; but, on a closer observation, his countenance revealed little of sorrow, though much of sanctity.

With added words of touchy disgust, the well-to-do gentleman hurried away. But, though repulsed, and rudely, the man in gray did not reproach, for a time patiently remaining in the chilly loneliness to which he had been left, his countenance, however, not without token of latent though chastened reliance.

At length an old gentleman, somewhat bulky, drew nigh, and from him also a contribution was sought.

"Look, you," coming to a dead halt, and scowling upon him. "Look, you," swelling his bulk out before him like a swaying balloon, "look, you, you on others' behalf ask for money; you, a fellow with a face as long as my arm. Hark ye, now: there is such a thing as gravity, and in condemned felons it may be genuine; but of long faces there are three sorts; that of grief's drudge, that of the lantern-jawed man, and that of the impostor. You know best which yours is."

"Heaven give you more charity, sir."

"And you less hypocrisy, sir."

With which words, the hard-hearted old gentleman marched off.

While the other still stood forlorn, the young clergyman, before introduced, passing that way, catching a chance sight of him, seemed suddenly struck by some recollection; and, after a moment's pause, hurried up with: "Your pardon, but shortly since I was all over looking for you."

"For me?" as marveling that one of so little account should be sought for.

"Yes, for you; do you know anything about the negro, apparently a cripple, aboard here? Is he, or is he not, what he seems to be?"

"Ah, poor Guinea! have you, too, been distrusted? you, upon whom nature has placarded the evidence of your claims?"

"Then you do really know him, and he is quite worthy? It relieves me to hear it—much relieves me. Come, let us go find him, and see what can be done."

"Another instance that confidence may come too late. I am sorry to say that at the last landing I myself—just happening to catch sight of him on the gangway-plank—assisted the cripple ashore. No time to talk, only to help. He may not have told you, but he has a brother in that vicinity."

"Really, I regret his going without my seeing him again; regret it, more, perhaps, than you can readily think. You see, shortly after leaving St. Louis, he was on the forecastle, and there, with many others, I saw him, and put trust in him; so much so, that, to convince those who did not, I, at his entreaty, went in search of you, you being one of several individuals he mentioned, and whose personal appearance he more or less described, individuals who he said would willingly speak for him. But, after diligent search, not finding you, and catching no glimpse of any of the others he had enumerated, doubts were at last suggested; but doubts indirectly originating, as I can but think, from prior distrust unfeelingly proclaimed by another. Still, certain it is, I began to suspect."

"Ha, ha, ha!"

A sort of laugh more like a groan than a laugh; and yet, somehow, it seemed intended for a laugh.

Both turned, and the young clergyman started at seeing the wooden-legged man close behind him, morosely grave as a criminal judge with a mustard-plaster on his back. In the present case the mustard-plaster might have been the memory of certain recent biting rebuffs and mortifications.

"Wouldn't think it was I who laughed, would you?"

"But who was it you laughed at? or rather, tried to laugh at?" demanded the young clergyman, flushing, "me?"

"Neither you nor any one within a thousand miles of you. But perhaps you don't believe it."

"If he were of a suspicious temper, he might not," interposed the man in gray calmly, "it is one of the imbecilities of the suspicious person to fancy that every stranger, however absent-minded, he sees so much as smiling or gesturing to himself in any odd sort of way, is secretly making him his butt. In some moods, the movements of an entire street, as the suspicious man walks down it, will seem an express pantomimic jeer at him. In short, the suspicious man kicks himself with his own foot."

"Whoever can do that, ten to one he saves other folks' sole-leather," said the wooden-legged man with a crusty attempt at humor. But with augmented grin and squirm, turning directly upon the young clergyman, "you still think it was *you* I was laughing at, just now. To prove your mistake, I will tell you what I *was* laughing at; a story I happened to call to mind just then."

Whereupon, in his porcupine way, and with sarcastic details, unpleasant to repeat, he related a story, which might, perhaps, in a good-natured version, be rendered as follows:

A certain Frenchman of New Orleans, an old man, less slender in purse than limb, happening to attend the theatre one evening, was so charmed with the character of a faithful wife, as there represented to the life, that nothing would do but he must marry upon it. So, marry he did, a beautiful girl from Tennessee, who had first attracted his attention by her liberal mould, and was subsequently recommended to him through her kin, for her equally liberal education and disposition. Though large, the praise proved not too much. For, ere long, rumor more than corroborated it, by whispering that the lady was liberal to a fault. But though various circumstances, which by most Benedicts would have been deemed all but conclusive, were duly recited to the old Frenchman by his friends, yet such was his confidence that not a syllable would he credit, till, chancing one night to return unexpectedly from a journey, upon entering his apartment, a stranger burst from the alcove: "Begar!" cried he, "now I *begin* to suspec."

His story told, the wooden-legged man threw back his head, and gave vent to a long, gasping, rasping sort of taunting cry, intolerable as that of a high-pressure engine jeering off steam; and that done, with apparent satisfaction hobbled away.

"Who is that scoffer," said the man in gray, not without warmth. "Who is he, who even were truth on his tongue, his way of speaking it would make truth almost offensive as falsehood. Who is he?"

"He who I mentioned to you as having boasted his suspicion of the negro," replied the young clergyman, recovering from disturbance, "in short, the person to whom I ascribe the origin of my own distrust; he maintained that Guinea was some white scoundrel, betwisted and painted up for a decoy. Yes, these were his very words, I think."

"Impossible! he could not be so wrong-headed. Pray, will you call him back, and let me ask him if he were really in earnest?"

The other complied; and, at length, after no few surly objections, prevailed upon the one-legged individual to return for a moment. Upon which, the man in gray thus addressed him: "This reverend gentleman tells me, sir, that a certain cripple, a poor negro, is by you considered an ingenious impostor. Now, I am not unaware that there are some persons in this world, who, unable to give better proof of being wise, take a strange delight in showing what they think they have sagaciously read in mankind by uncharitable suspicions of them. I hope you are not one of these. In short, would you tell me now, whether you were not merely joking in the notion you threw out about the negro. Would you be so kind?"

"No, I won't be so kind, I'll be so cruel."

"As you please about that."

"Well, he's just what I said he was."

"A white masquerading as a black?"

"Exactly."

The man in gray glanced at the young clergyman a moment, then quietly whispered to him, "I thought you represented your friend here as a very distrustful sort of person, but he appears endued with a singular credulity.—Tell me, sir, do you really think that a white could look the negro so? For one, I should call it pretty good acting."

"Not much better than any other man acts."

"How? Does all the world act? Am *I*, for instance, an actor? Is my reverend friend here, too, a performer?"

"Yes, don't you both perform acts? To do, is to act; so all doers are actors."

"You trifle.—I ask again, if a white, how could he look the negro so?"

"Never saw the negro-minstrels, I suppose?"

"Yes, but they are apt to overdo the ebony; exemplifying the old saying, not more just than charitable, that 'the devil is never so black as he is painted.' But his limbs, if not a cripple, how could he twist his limbs so?"

"How do other hypocritical beggars twist theirs? Easy enough to see how they are hoisted up."

"The sham is evident, then?"

"To the discerning eye," with a horrible screw of his gimlet one.

"Well, where is Guinea?" said the man in gray; "where is he? Let us at once find him, and refute beyond cavil this injurious hypothesis."

"Do so," cried the one-eyed man, "I'm just in the humor now for having him found, and leaving the streaks of these fingers on his paint, as the lion leaves the streaks of his nails on a Caffre. They wouldn't let me touch him before. Yes, find him, I'll make wool fly, and him after."

"You forget," here said the young clergyman to the man in gray, "that yourself helped poor Guinea ashore."

"So I did, so I did; how unfortunate. But look now," to the other, "I think that without personal proof I can convince you of your mistake. For I put it to you, is it reasonable to suppose that a man with brains, sufficient to act such a part as you say, would take all that trouble, and run all that hazard, for the mere sake of those few paltry coppers, which, I hear, was all he got for his pains, if pains they were?"

"That puts the case irrefutably," said the young clergyman, with a challenging glance towards the one-legged man.

"You two green-horns! Money, you think, is the sole motive to pains and hazard, deception and deviltry, in this world. How much money did the devil make by gulling Eve?"

Whereupon he hobbled off again with a repetition of his intolerable jeer.

The man in gray stood silently eying his retreat a while, and then, turning to his companion, said: "A bad man, a dangerous man; a man to be put down in any Christian community.—And this was he who was the means of begetting your distrust? Ah, we should shut our ears to distrust, and keep them open only for its opposite."

"You advance a principle, which, if I had acted upon it this morning, I should have spared myself what I now feel.—That but one man, and he with one leg, should have such ill power given him; his one sour word leavening into congenial sourness (as, to my knowledge, it did) the dispositions, before sweet enough, of a numerous company. But, as I hinted, with me at the time his ill words went for nothing; the same as now; only afterwards they had effect: and I confess, this puzzles me."

"It should not. With humane minds, the spirit of distrust works something as certain potions do; it is a spirit which may enter such minds, and yet, for a time, longer or shorter, lie in them quiescent; but only the more deplorable its ultimate activity."

"An uncomfortable solution; for, since that baneful man did but just now anew drop on me his bane, how shall I be sure that my present exemption from its effects will be lasting?"

"You cannot be sure, but you can strive against it."

"How?"

"By strangling the least symptom of distrust, of any sort, which hereafter, upon whatever provocation, may arise in you."

"I will do so." Then added as in soliloquy, "Indeed, indeed, I was to blame in standing passive under such influences as that one-legged man's. My conscience upbraids me.—The poor negro: you see him occasionally, perhaps?"

"No, not often; though in a few days, as it happens, my engagements will call me to the neighborhood of his present retreat; and, no doubt, honest Guinea, who is a grateful soul, will come to see me there."

"Then you have been his benefactor?"

"His benefactor? I did not say that. I have known him."

"Take this mite. Hand it to Guinea when you see him; say it comes from one who has full belief in his honesty, and is sincerely sorry for having indulged, however transiently, in a contrary thought."

"I accept the trust. And, by-the-way, since you are of this truly charitable nature, you will not turn away an appeal in behalf of the Seminole Widow and Orphan Asylum?"

"I have not heard of that charity."

"But recently founded."

After a pause, the clergyman was irresolutely putting his hand in his pocket, when, caught by something in his companion's expression, he eyed him inquisitively, almost uneasily.

"Ah, well," smiled the other wanly, "if that subtle bane, we were speaking of but just now, is so soon beginning to work, in vain my appeal to you. Good-bye."

"Nay," not untouched, "you do me injustice; instead of indulging present suspicions, I had rather make amends for previous ones. Here is something for your asylum. Not much; but every drop helps. Of course you have papers?"

"Of course," producing a memorandum book and pencil. "Let me take down name and amount. We publish these names. And now let me give you a little history of our asylum, and the providential way in which it was started."

At an interesting point of the narration, and at the moment when, with much curiosity, indeed, urgency. the narrator was being particularly questioned upon that point, he was, as it happened, altogether diverted both from it and his story, by just then catching sight of a gentleman who had been standing in sight from the beginning, but, until now, as it seemed, without being observed by him.

"Pardon me," said he, rising, "but yonder is one who I know will contribute, and largely. Don't take it amiss if I quit you."

"Go: duty before all things," was the conscientious reply.

The stranger was a man of more than winsome aspect. There he stood apart and in repose, and yet, by his mere look, lured the man in gray from his story, much as, by its graciousness of bearing, some full-leaved elm, alone in a meadow, lures the noon sickleman to throw down his sheaves, and come and apply for the alms of its shade.

But, considering that goodness is no such rare thing among men —the world familiarly know the noun; a common one in every language—it was curious that what so signalized the stranger, and made him look like a kind of foreigner, among the crowd (as to some it may make him appear more or less unreal in this portraiture), was but the expression of so prevalent a quality. Such goodness seemed his, allied with such fortune, that, so far as his own personal experience could have gone, scarcely could he have known ill, physical or moral; and as for knowing or suspecting the latter in any serious degree (supposing such degree of it to be), by observation or philosophy; for that, probably, his nature, by its opposition, imperfectly qualified, or from it wholly exempted. For the rest, he might have been five and fifty, perhaps sixty, but tall, rosy, between plump and portly, with a primy, palmy air, and for the time and place, not to hint of his years, dressed with a strangely festive finish and elegance. The inner-side of his coat-skirts was of white satin, which might have looked especially inappropriate, had it not seemed less a bit of mere tailoring than something of an emblem, as it were; an involuntary emblem, let us say, that what seemed so good about him was not all outside; no, the fine covering had a still finer lining. Upon one hand he wore a white kid glove, but the other hand, which was ungloved, looked hardly less white. Now, as the Fidèle, like most steamboats, was upon deck a little soot-streaked here and there, especially about the railings, it was a marvel how, under such circumstances, these hands retained their spotlessness. But, if you watched them a while, you noticed that they avoided touching anything; you noticed, in short, that a certain negro body-servant, whose hands nature had dyed black, perhaps with the same purpose that millers wear white, this negro servant's hands did most of his master's handling for him; having to do with dirt on his account, but not to his prejudice. But if, with the same undefiledness of consequences to himself, a gentleman could also sin by deputy, how shocking would that be! But it is not permitted to be; and even if it were, no judicious moralist would make proclamation of it.

This gentleman, therefore, there is reason to affirm, was one who, like the Hebrew governor, knew how to keep his hands clean, and who never in his life happened to be run suddenly against by hurrying house-painter, or sweep; in a word, one whose very good luck it was to be a very good man.

Not that he looked as if he were a kind of Wilberforce at all; that superior merit, probably, was not his; nothing in his manner bespoke him righteous, but only good, and though to be good is much below being righteous, and though there is a difference between the two, yet not, it is to be hoped, so incompatible as that a righteous man can not be a good man; though, conversely, in the pulpit it has been with much cogency urged, that a merely good man, that is, one good merely by his nature, is so far from thereby being righteous, that nothing short of a total change and conversion can make him so; which is something which no honest mind, well read in the history of righteousness, will care to deny; nevertheless, since St. Paul himself, agreeing in a sense with the pulpit distinction, though not altogether in the pulpit deduction, and also pretty plainly intimating which of the two qualities in question enjoys his apostolic preference; I say, since St. Paul has so meaningly said, that, "scarcely for a righteous man will one die, yet peradventure for a good man some would even dare to die;" therefore, when we repeat of this gentleman, that he was only a good man, whatever else by severe censors may be objected to him, it is still to be hoped that his goodness will not at least be considered criminal in him. At all events, no man, not even a righteous man, would think it quite right to commit this gentleman to prison for the crime, extraordinary as he might deem it; more especially, as, until everything could be known, there would be some chance that the gentleman might after all be quite as innocent of it as he himself.

It was pleasant to mark the good man's reception of the salute of the righteous man, that is, the man in gray; his inferior, apparently, not more in the social scale than in stature. Like the benign elm again, the good man seemed to wave the canopy of his goodness over that suitor, not in conceited condescension, but with that even amenity of true majesty, which can be kind to any one without stooping to it.

To the plea in behalf of the Seminole widows and orphans, the gentleman, after a question or two duly answered, responded by producing an ample pocket-book in the good old capacious style, of fine green French morocco and workmanship, bound with silk of the same color, not to omit bills crisp with newness, fresh from the bank, no muckworms' grime upon them. Lucre those bills might be, but as yet having been kept unspotted from the world, not of the filthy sort. Placing now three of those virgin bills in the applicant's hands, he hoped that the smallness of the contribution would be pardoned; to tell the truth, and this at last accounted for his toilet, he was bound but a short run down the river, to attend, in a festive grove, the afternoon wedding of his niece: so did not carry much money with him.

The other was about expressing his thanks when the gentleman in his pleasant way checked him: the gratitude was on the other side. To him, he said, charity was in one sense not an effort, but a luxury; against too great indulgence in which his steward, a humorist, had sometimes admonished him.

In some general talk which followed, relative to organized modes of doing good, the gentleman expressed his regrets that so many benevolent societies as there were, here and there isolated in the land, should not act in concert by coming together, in the way that already in each society the individuals composing it had done, which would result, he thought, in like advantages upon a larger scale. Indeed, such a confederation might, perhaps, be attended with as happy results as politically attended that of the states.

Upon his hitherto moderate enough companion, this suggestion had an effect illustrative in a sort of that notion of Socrates, that the soul is a harmony; for as the sound of a flute, in any particular key, will, it is said, audibly affect the corresponding chord of any harp in good tune, within hearing, just so now did some string in him respond, and with animation.

Which animation, by the way, might seem more or less out of character in the man in gray, considering his unsprightly manner when first introduced, had he not already, in certain after colloquies, given proof, in some degree, of the fact, that, with certain natures, a soberly continent air at times, so far from arguing emptiness of stuff, is good proof it is there, and plenty of it, because unwasted, and may be used the more effectively, too, when opportunity offers. What now follows on the part of the man in gray will still further exemplify, perhaps somewhat strikingly, the truth, or what appears to be such, of this remark.

"Sir," said he eagerly, "I am before you. A project, not dissimilar to yours, was by me thrown out at the World's Fair in London."

"World's Fair? You there? Pray how was that?"

"First, let me——"

"Nay, but first tell me what took you to the Fair?"

"I went to exhibit an invalid's easy-chair I had invented."

"Then you have not always been in the charity business?"

"Is it not charity to ease human suffering? I am, and always have been, as I always will be, I trust, in the charity business, as you call it; but charity is not like a pin, one to make the head, and the other the point; charity is a work to which a good workman may be competent in all its branches. I invented my Protean easy-chair in odd intervals stolen from meals and sleep."

"You call it the Protean easy-chair; pray describe it."

"My Protean easy-chair is a chair so all over bejointed, behinged, and bepadded, everyway so elastic, springy, and docile to the airiest touch, that in some one of its endlessly-changeable accommodations of back, seat, footboard, and arms, the most restless body, the body most racked, nay, I had almost added the most tormented conscience must, somehow and somewhere, find rest. Believing that I owed it to suffering humanity to make known such a chair to the utmost, I scraped together my little means and off to the World's Fair with it."

"You did right. But your scheme; how did you come to hit upon that?"

"I was going to tell you. After seeing my invention duly catalogued and placed, I gave myself up to pondering the scene about me. As I dwelt upon that shining pageant of arts, and moving concourse of nations, and reflected that here was the pride of the world glorying in a glass house, a sense of the fragility of worldly grandeur profoundly impressed me. And I said to myself, I will see if this occasion of vanity cannot supply a hint toward a better profit than was designed. Let some world-wide good to the world-wide cause be now done. In short, inspired by the scene, on the fourth day I issued at the World's Fair my prospectus of the World's Charity."

"Quite a thought. But, pray explain it."

"The World's Charity is to be a society whose members shall comprise deputies from every charity and mission extant; the one object of the society to be the methodization of the world's benevolence; to which end, the present system of voluntary and promiscuous contribution to be done away, and the Society to be empowered by the various governments to levy, annually, one grand benevolence tax upon all mankind; as in Augustus Cæsar's time, the whole world to come up to be taxed; a tax which, for the scheme of it, should be something like the income-tax in England, a tax, also, as before hinted, to be a consolidation-tax of all possible benevolence taxes; as in America here, the state-tax, and the county-tax, and the town-tax, and the poll-tax, are by the assessors rolled into one. This tax, according to my tables, calculated with care, would result in the yearly raising of a fund little short of eight hundred millions; this fund to be annually applied to such objects, and in such modes, as the various charities and missions, in general congress represented, might decree; whereby, in fourteen years, as I estimate, there would have been devoted to good works the sum of eleven thousand two hundred millions; which would warrant the dissolution of the society, as that fund judiciously expended, not a pauper or heathen could remain the round world over."

"Eleven thousand two hundred millions! And all by passing round a *hat,* as it were."

"Yes, I am no Fourier, the projector of an impossible scheme, but a philanthropist and a financier setting forth a philanthropy and a finance which are practicable."

"Practicable?"

"Yes. Eleven thousand two hundred millions; it will frighten none but a retail philanthropist. What is it but eight hundred millions for each of fourteen years? Now eight hundred millions— what is that, to average it, but one little dollar a head for the population of the planet? And who will refuse, what Turk or Dyak even, his own little dollar for sweet charity's sake? Eight hundred millions! More than that sum is yearly expended by mankind, not only in vanities, but miseries. Consider that bloody spendthrift, War. And are mankind so stupid, so wicked, that, upon the demonstration of these things they will not, amending their ways, devote their superfluities to blessing the world instead of cursing it? Eight hundred millions! They have not to make it, it is theirs already; they have but to direct it from ill to good. And to this, scarce a self-denial is demanded. Actually, they would not in the mass be one farthing the poorer for it; as certainly would they be all the better and happier. Don't you see? But admit, as you must, that mankind is not mad, and my project is practicable. For, what creature but a madman would not rather do good than ill, when it is plain that, good or ill, it must return upon himself?"

"Your sort of reasoning," said the good gentleman, adjusting his gold sleeve-buttons, "seems all reasonable enough, but with mankind it won't do."

"Then mankind are not reasoning beings, if reason won't do with them."

"That is not to the purpose. By-the-way, from the manner in which you alluded to the world's census, it would appear that, according to your world-wide scheme, the pauper not less than the nabob is to contribute to the relief of pauperism, and the heathen not less than the Christian to the conversion of heathenism. How is that?"

"Why, that—pardon me—is quibbling. Now, no philanthropist likes to be opposed with quibbling."

"Well, I won't quibble any more. But, after all, if I understand your project, there is little specially new in it, further than the magnifying of means now in operation."

"Magnifying and energizing. For one thing, missions I would thoroughly reform. Missions I would quicken with the Wall street spirit."

"The Wall street spirit?"

"Yes; for if, confessedly, certain spiritual ends are to be gained but through the auxiliary agency of worldly means, then, to the surer gaining of such spiritual ends, the example of worldly policy in worldly projects should not by spiritual projectors be slighted. In brief, the conversion of the heathen, so far, at least, as depending on human effort, would, by the world's charity, be let out on contract. So much by bid for converting India, so much for Borneo, so much for Africa. Competition allowed, stimulus would be given. There would be no lethargy of monopoly. We should have no mission-house or tract-house of which slanderers could, with any plausibility, say that it had degenerated in its clerkships into a sort of custom-house. But the main point is the Archimedean money-power that would be brought to bear."

"You mean the eight hundred million power?"

"Yes. You see, this doing good to the world by driblets amounts to just nothing. I am for doing good to the world with a will. I am for doing good to the world once for all and having done with it.

Do but think, my dear sir, of the eddies and maëlstroms of pagans in China. People here have no conception of it. Of a frosty morning in Hong Kong, pauper pagans are found dead in the streets like so many nipped peas in a bin of peas. To be an immortal being in China is no more distinction than to be a snow-flake in a snow-squall. What are a score or two of missionaries to such a people? A pinch of snuff to the kraken. I am for sending ten thousand missionaries in a body and converting the Chinese *en masse* within six months of the debarkation. The thing is then done, and turn to something else."

"I fear you are too enthusiastic."

"A philanthropist is necessarily an enthusiast; for without enthusiasm what was ever achieved but commonplace? But again: consider the poor in London. To that mob of misery, what is a joint here and a loaf there? I am for voting to them twenty thousand bullocks and one hundred thousand barrels of flour to begin with. They are then comforted, and no more hunger for one while among the poor of London. And so all round."

"Sharing the character of your general project, these things, I take it, are rather examples of wonders that were to be wished, than wonders that will happen."

"And is the age of wonders passed? Is the world too old? Is it barren? Think of Sarah."

"Then I am Abraham reviling the angel (with a smile). But still, as to your design at large, there seems a certain audacity."

"But if to the audacity of the design there be brought a commensurate circumspectness of execution, how then?"

"Why, do you really believe that your world's charity will ever go into operation?"

"I have confidence that it will."

"But may you not be over-confident?"

"For a Christian to talk so!"

"But think of the obstacles!"

"Obstacles? I have confidence to remove obstacles, though mountains. Yes, confidence in the world's charity to that degree, that, as no better person offers to supply the place, I have nominated myself provisional treasurer, and will be happy to receive subscriptions, for the present to be devoted to striking off a million more of my prospectuses."

The talk went on; the man in gray revealed a spirit of benevolence which, mindful of the millennial promise, had gone abroad over all the countries of the globe, much as the diligent spirit of the husbandman, stirred by forethought of the coming seed-time, leads him, in March reveries at his fireside, over every field of his farm. The master chord of the man in gray had been touched, and it seemed as if it would never cease vibrating. A not unsilvery tongue, too, was his, with gestures that were a Pentecost of added ones, and persuasiveness before which granite hearts might crumble into gravel.

Strange, therefore, how his auditor, so singularly good-hearted as he seemed, remained proof to such eloquence; though not, as it turned out, to such pleadings. For, after listening a while longer with pleasant incredulity, presently, as the boat touched his place of destination, the gentleman, with a look half humor, half pity, put another bank-note into his hands; charitable to the last, if only to the dreams of enthusiasm.

If a drunkard in a sober fit is the dullest of mortals, an enthusiast in a reason-fit is not the most lively. And this, without prejudice to his greatly improved understanding; for, if his elation was the height of his madness, his despondency is but the extreme of his sanity. Something thus now, to all appearance, with the man in gray. Society his stimulus, loneliness was his lethargy. Loneliness, like the sea-breeze, blowing off from a thousand leagues of blankness, he did not find, as veteran solitaires do, if anything, too bracing. In short, left to himself, with none to charm forth his latent lymphatic, he insensibly resumes his original air, a quiescent one, blended of sad humility and demureness.

Ere long he goes laggingly into the ladies' saloon, as in spiritless quest of somebody; but, after some disappointed glances about him, seats himself upon a sofa with an air of melancholy exhaustion and depression.

At the sofa's further end sits a plump and pleasant person, whose aspect seems to hint that, if she have any weak point, it must be anything rather than her excellent heart. From her twilight dress, neither dawn nor dark, apparently she is a widow just breaking the chrysalis of her mourning. A small gilt testament is in her hand, which she has just been reading. Half-relinquished, she holds the book in reverie, her finger inserted at the xiii. of 1st Corinthians, to which chapter possibly her attention might have recently been turned, by witnessing the scene of the monitory mute and his slate.

The sacred page no longer meets her eye; but, as at evening, when for a time the western hills shine on though the sun be set, her thoughtful face retains its tenderness though the teacher is forgotten.

Meantime, the expression of the stranger is such as ere long to attract her glance. But no responsive one. Presently, in her somewhat inquisitive survey, her volume drops. It is restored. No encroaching politeness in the act, but kindness, unadorned. The eyes of the lady sparkle. Evidently, she is not now unprepossessed. Soon, bending over, in a low, sad tone, full of deference, the stran-

45

ger breathes, "Madam, pardon my freedom, but there is something in that face which strangely draws me. May I ask, are you a sister of the Church?"

"Why—really—you—"

In concern for her embarrassment, he hastens to relieve it, but, without seeming so to do. "It is very solitary for a brother here," eying the showy ladies brocaded in the background, "I find none to mingle souls with. It may be wrong—I *know* it is—but I cannot force myself to be easy with the people of the world. I prefer the company, however silent, of a brother or sister in good standing. By the way, madam, may I ask if you have confidence?"

"Really, sir—why, sir—really—I—"

"Could you put confidence in *me* for instance?"

"Really, sir—as much—I mean, as one may wisely put in a—a—stranger, an entire stranger, I had almost said," rejoined the lady, hardly yet at ease in her affability, drawing aside a little in body, while at the same time her heart might have been drawn as far the other way. A natural struggle between charity and prudence.

"Entire stranger!" with a sigh. "Ah, who would be a stranger? In vain, I wander; no one will have confidence in me."

"You interest me," said the good lady, in mild surprise. "Can I any way befriend you?"

"No one can befriend me, who has not confidence."

"But I—I have—at least to that degree—I mean that—"

"Nay, nay, you have none—none at all. Pardon, I see it. No confidence. Fool, fond fool that I am to seek it!"

"You are unjust, sir," rejoins the good lady with heightened interest; "but it may be that something untoward in your experiences has unduly biased you. Not that I would cast reflections. Believe me, I—yes, yes—I may say—that—that—"

"That you have confidence? Prove it. Let me have twenty dollars."

"Twenty dollars!"

"There, I told you, madam, you had no confidence."

The lady was, in an extraordinary way, touched. She sat in a sort of restless torment, knowing not which way to turn. She began twenty different sentences, and left off at the first syllable of each. At last, in desperation, she hurried out, "Tell me, sir, for what you want the twenty dollars?"

"And did I not—" then glancing at her half-mourning, "for the widow and the fatherless. I am traveling agent of the Widow and Orphan Asylum, recently founded among the Seminoles."

"And why did you not tell me your object before?" As not a little relieved. "Poor souls—Indians, too—those cruelly-used Indians. Here, here; how could I hesitate. I am so sorry it is no more."

"Grieve not for that, madam," rising and folding up the bank-notes. "This is an inconsiderable sum, I admit, but," taking out his pencil and book, "though I here but register the amount, there is another register, where is set down the motive. Good-bye; you have confidence. Yea, you can say to me as the apostle said to the Corinthians, 'I rejoice that I have confidence in you in all things.'"

Chapter 9 TWO BUSINESS MEN *Transact a Little Business* ᔐ

"Pray, sir, have you seen a gentleman with a weed hereabouts, rather a saddish gentleman? Strange where he can have gone to. I was talking with him not twenty minutes since."

By a brisk, ruddy-cheeked man in a tasseled traveling-cap, carrying under his arm a ledger-like volume, the above words were addressed to the collegian before introduced, suddenly accosted by the rail to which not long after his retreat, as in a previous chapter recounted, he had returned, and there remained.

"Have you seen him, sir?"

Rallied from his apparent diffidence by the genial jauntiness of the stranger, the youth answered with unwonted promptitude: "Yes, a person with a weed was here not very long ago."

"Saddish?"

"Yes, and a little cracked, too, I should say."

"It was he. Misfortune, I fear, has disturbed his brain. Now quick, which way did he go?"

"Why just in the direction from which you came, the gangway yonder."

"Did he? Then the man in the gray coat, whom I just met, said right: he must have gone ashore. How unlucky!"

He stood vexedly twitching at his cap-tassel, which fell over by his whisker, and continued: "Well, I am very sorry. In fact, I had something for him here."—Then drawing nearer, "You see, he applied to me for relief, no, I do him injustice, not that, but he began to intimate, you understand. Well, being very busy just then, I declined; quite rudely, too, in a cold, morose, unfeeling way, I fear. At all events, not three minutes afterwards I felt self-reproach, with a kind of prompting, very peremptory, to deliver over into that unfortunate man's hands a ten-dollar bill. You smile. Yes, it may be superstition, but I can't help it; I have my weak side, thank God. Then again," he rapidly went on, "we have been so very prosperous lately in our affairs—by we, I mean the Black Rapids Coal Company—that, really, out of my abundance, associative and individual,

48

it is but fair that a charitable investment or two should be made, don't you think so?"

"Sir," said the collegian without the least embarrassment, "do I understand that you are officially connected with the Black Rapids Coal Company?"

"Yes, I happen to be president and transfer-agent."

"You are?"

"Yes, but what is it to you? You don't want to invest?"

"Why, do you sell the stock?"

"Some might be bought, perhaps; but why do you ask? you don't want to invest?"

"But supposing I did," with cool self-collectedness, "could you do up the thing for me, and here?"

"Bless my soul," gazing at him in amaze, "really, you are quite a business man. Positively, I feel afraid of you."

"Oh, no need of that.—You could sell me some of that stock, then?"

"I don't know, I don't know. To be sure, there are a few shares under peculiar circumstances bought in by the Company; but it would hardly be the thing to convert this boat into the Company's office. I think you had better defer investing. So," with an indifferent air, "you have seen the unfortunate man I spoke of?"

"Let the unfortunate man go his ways.—What is that large book you have with you?"

"My transfer-book. I am subpœnaed with it to court."

"Black Rapids Coal Company," obliquely reading the gilt inscription on the back; "I have heard much of it. Pray do you happen to have with you any statement of the condition of your company?"

"A statement has lately been printed."

"Pardon me, but I am naturally inquisitive. Have you a copy with you?"

"I tell you again, I do not think that it would be suitable to convert this boat into the Company's office.—That unfortunate man, did you relieve him at all?"

"Let the unfortunate man relieve himself.—Hand me the statement."

"Well, you are such a business-man, I can hardly deny you. Here," handing a small, printed pamphlet.

The youth turned it over sagely.

"I hate a suspicious man," said the other, observing him; "but I must say I like to see a cautious one."

"I can gratify you there," languidly returning the pamphlet; "for, as I said before, I am naturally inquisitive; I am also circumspect. No appearances can deceive me. Your statement," he added "tells a very fine story; but pray, was not your stock a little heavy a while ago? downward tendency? Sort of low spirits among holders on the subject of that stock?"

"Yes, there was a depression. But how came it? who devised it? the 'bears,' sir. The depression of our stock was solely owing to the growling, the hypocritical growling, of the bears."

"How, hypocritical?"

"Why, the most monstrous of all hypocrites are these bears: hypocrites by inversion; hypocrites in the simulation of things dark instead of bright; souls that thrive, less upon depression, than the fiction of depression; professors of the wicked art of manufacturing depressions; spurious Jeremiahs; sham Heraclituses, who, the lugubrious day done, return, like sham Lazaruses among the beggars, to make merry over the gains got by their pretended sore heads—scoundrelly bears!"

"You are warm against these bears?"

"If I am, it is less from the remembrance of their stratagems as to our stock, than from the persuasion that these same destroyers of confidence, and gloomy philosophers of the stock-market, though false in themselves, are yet true types of most destroyers of confidence and gloomy philosophers, the world over. Fellows who, whether in stocks, politics, bread-stuffs, morals, metaphysics, religion—be it what it may—trump up their black panics in the naturally-quiet brightness, solely with a view to some sort of covert advantage. That corpse of calamity which the gloomy philosopher parades, is but his Good-Enough-Morgan."

"I rather like that," knowingly drawled the youth. "I fancy these gloomy souls as little as the next one. Sitting on my sofa after a champagne dinner, smoking my plantation cigar, if a gloomy fellow come to me—what a bore!"

"You tell him it's all stuff, don't you?"

"I tell him it ain't natural. I say to him, you are happy enough, and you know it; and everybody else is as happy as you, and you know that, too; and we shall all be happy after we are no more, and you know that, too; but no, still you must have your sulk."

"And do you know whence this sort of fellow gets his sulk? not from life; for he's often too much of a recluse, or else too young to have seen anything of it. No, he gets it from some of those old plays he sees on the stage, or some of those old books he finds up in garrets. Ten to one, he has lugged home from auction a musty old Seneca, and sets about stuffing himself with that stale old hay; and, thereupon, thinks it looks wise and antique to be a croaker, thinks it's taking a stand way above his kind."

"Just so," assented the youth. "I've lived some, and seen a good many such ravens at second hand. By the way, strange how that man with the weed, you were inquiring for, seemed to take me for some soft sentimentalist, only because I kept quiet, and thought, because I had a copy of Tacitus with me, that I was reading him for his gloom, instead of his gossip. But I let him talk. And, indeed, by my manner humored him."

"You shouldn't have done that, now. Unfortunate man, you must have made quite a fool of him."

"His own fault if I did! But I like prosperous fellows, comfortable fellows; fellows that talk comfortably and prosperously, like you. Such fellows are generally honest. And, I say now, I happen to have a superfluity in my pocket, and I'll just—"

"—Act the part of a brother to that unfortunate man?"

"Let the unfortunate man be his own brother. What are you dragging him in for all the time? One would think you didn't care to register any transfers, or dispose of any stock—mind running on something else. I say I will invest."

"Stay, stay, here come some uproarious fellows—this way, this way."

And with off-handed politeness the man with the book escorted his companion into a private little haven removed from the brawling swells without.

Business transacted, the two came forth, and walked the deck.

"Now tell me, sir," said he with the book, "how comes it that a young gentleman like you, a sedate student at the first appearance, should dabble in stocks and that sort of thing?"

"There are certain sophomorean errors in the world," drawled the sophomore, deliberately adjusting his shirt-collar, "not the least of which is the popular notion touching the nature of the modern scholar, and the nature of the modern scholastic sedateness."

"So it seems, so it seems. Really, this is quite a new leaf in my experience."

"Experience, sir," originally observed the sophomore, "is the only teacher."

"Hence am I your pupil; for it's only when experience speaks, that I can endure to listen to speculation."

"My speculations, sir," dryly drawing himself up, "have been chiefly governed by the maxim of Lord Bacon; I speculate in those philosophies which come home to my business and bosom—pray, do you know of any other good stocks?"

"You wouldn't like to be concerned in the New Jerusalem, would you?"

"New Jerusalem?"

"Yes, the new and thriving city, so called, in northern Minnesota. It was originally founded by certain fugitive Mormons. Hence the name. It stands on the Mississippi. Here, here is the map," producing a roll. "There—there, you see are the public buildings—here the landing—there the park—yonder the botanic gardens—and this, this little dot here, is a perpetual fountain, you understand. You observe there are twenty asterisks. Those are for the lyceums. They have lignum-vitæ rostrums."

"And are all these buildings now standing?"

"All standing—*bona fide.*"

"These marginal squares here, are they the water-lots?"

"Water-lots in the city of New Jerusalem? All terra firma—you don't seem to care about investing, though?"

"Hardly think I should read my title clear, as the law students say," yawned the collegian.

"Prudent—you are prudent. Don't know that you are wholly out, either. At any rate, I would rather have one of your shares of coal stock than two of this other. Still, considering that the first settlement was by two fugitives, who had swum over naked from the opposite shore—it's a surprising place. It is, *bona fide*.—But dear me, I must go. Oh, if by possibility you should come across that unfortunate man—"

"—In that case," with drawling impatience, "I will send for the steward, and have him and his misfortunes consigned overboard."

"Ha ha!—now were some gloomy philosopher here, some theological bear, forever taking occasion to growl down the stock of human nature (with ulterior views, d'ye see, to a fat benefice in the gift of the worshippers of Arimanius), he would pronounce that the sign of a hardening heart and a softening brain. Yes, that would be his sinister construction. But it's nothing more than the oddity of a genial humor—genial but dry. Confess it. Good-bye."

Stools, settees, sofas, divans, ottomans; occupying them are clusters of men, old and young, wise and simple; in their hands are cards spotted with diamonds, spades, clubs, hearts; the favorite games are whist, cribbage, and brag. Lounging in arm-chairs or sauntering among the marble-topped tables, amused with the scene, are the comparatively few, who, instead of having hands in the games, for the most part keep their hands in their pockets. These may be the *philosophes*. But here and there, with a curious expression, one is reading a small sort of handbill of anonymous poetry, rather wordily entitled:

ODE

ON THE INTIMATIONS

OF

DISTRUST IN MAN,

UNWILLINGLY INFERRED FROM REPEATED REPULSES,

IN DISINTERESTED ENDEAVORS

TO PROCURE HIS

CONFIDENCE.

On the floor are many copies, looking as if fluttered down from a balloon. The way they came there was this: A somewhat elderly person, in the quaker dress, had quietly passed through the cabin, and, much in the manner of those railway book-peddlers who precede their proffers of sale by a distribution of puffs, direct or indirect, of the volumes to follow, had, without speaking, handed about the odes, which, for the most part, after a cursory glance, had been disrespectfully tossed aside, as no doubt, the moonstruck production of some wandering rhapsodist.

In due time, book under arm, in trips the ruddy man with the traveling-cap, who, lightly moving to and fro, looks animatedly about him, with a yearning sort of gratulatory affinity and longing, expressive of the very soul of sociality; as much as to say, "Oh, boys, would that I were personally acquainted with each mother's son of you, since what a sweet world, to make sweet acquaintance in, is ours, my brothers; yea, and what dear, happy dogs are we all!"

And just as if he had really warbled it forth, he makes fraternally up to one lounging stranger or another, exchanging with him some pleasant remark.

"Pray, what have you there?" he asked of one newly accosted, a little, dried-up man, who looked as if he never dined.

"A little ode, rather queer, too," was the reply, "of the same sort you see strewn on the floor here."

"I did not observe them. Let me see;" picking one up and looking it over. "Well now, this is pretty; plaintive, especially the opening:—

> *Alas for man, he hath small sense*
> *Of genial trust and confidence.*

—If it be so, alas for him, indeed. Runs off very smoothly, sir. Beautiful pathos. But do you think the sentiment just?"

"As to that," said the little dried-up man, "I think it a kind of queer thing altogether, and yet I am almost ashamed to add, it really has set me to thinking; yes and to feeling. Just now, somehow, I feel as it were trustful and genial. I don't know that ever I felt so much so before. I am naturally numb in my sensibilities; but this ode, in its way, works on my numbness not unlike a sermon, which, by lamenting over my lying dead in trespasses and sins, thereby stirs me up to be all alive in well-doing."

"Glad to hear it, and hope you will do well, as the doctors say. But who snowed the odes about here?"

"I cannot say; I have not been here long."

"Wasn't an angel, was it? Come, you say you feel genial, let us do as the rest, and have cards."

"Thank you, I never play cards."

"A bottle of wine?"

"Thank you, I never drink wine."

"Cigars?"

"Thank you, I never smoke cigars."

"Tell stories?"

"To speak truly, I hardly think I know one worth telling."

"Seems to me, then, this geniality you say you feel waked in you, is as water-power in a land without mills. Come, you had better take a genial hand at the cards. To begin, we will play for as small a sum as you please; just enough to make it interesting."

"Indeed, you must excuse me. Somehow I distrust cards."

"What, distrust cards? Genial cards? Then for once I join with our sad Philomel here:—

> Alas for man, he hath small sense
> Of genial trust and confidence.

Good-bye!"

Sauntering and chatting here and there, again, he with the book at length seems fatigued, looks round for a seat, and spying a partly-vacant settee drawn up against the side, drops down there; soon, like his chance neighbor, who happens to be the good merchant, becoming not a little interested in the scene more immediately before him; a party at whist; two cream-faced, giddy, unpolished youths, the one in a red cravat, the other in a green, opposed to two bland, grave, handsome, self-possessed men of middle age, decorously dressed in a sort of professional black, and apparently doctors of some eminence in the civil law.

By-and-by, after a preliminary scanning of the new comer next him the good merchant, sideways leaning over, whispers behind a crumpled copy of the Ode which he holds: "Sir, I don't like the looks of those two, do you?"

"Hardly," was the whispered reply; "those colored cravats are not in the best taste, at least not to mine; but my taste is no rule for all."

"You mistake; I mean the other two, and I don't refer to dress, but countenance. I confess I am not familiar with such gentry any further than reading about them in the papers—but those two are —are sharpers, ain't they?"

"Far be from us the captious and fault-finding spirit, my dear sir."

"Indeed, sir, I would not find fault; I am little given that way;

but certainly, to say the least, these two youths can hardly be adepts, while the opposed couple may be even more."

"You would not hint that the colored cravats would be so bungling as to lose, and the dark cravats so dextrous as to cheat?—Sour imaginations, my dear sir. Dismiss them. To little purpose have you read the Ode you have there. Years and experience, I trust, have not sophisticated you. A fresh and liberal construction would teach us to regard those four players—indeed, this whole cabin-full of players—as playing at games in which every player plays fair, and not a player but shall win."

"Now, you hardly mean that; because games in which all may win, such games remain as yet in this world uninvented, I think."

"Come, come," luxuriously laying himself back, and casting a free glance upon the players, "fares all paid; digestion sound; care, toil, penury, grief, unknown; lounging on this sofa, with waistband relaxed, why not be cheerfully resigned to one's fate, nor peevishly pick holes in the blessed fate of the world?"

Upon this, the good merchant, after staring long and hard, and then rubbing his forehead, fell into meditation, at first uneasy, but at last composed, and in the end, once more addressed his companion: "Well, I see it's good to out with one's private thoughts now and then. Somehow, I don't know why, a certain misty suspiciousness seems inseparable from most of one's private notions about some men and some things; but once out with these misty notions, and their mere contact with other men's soon dissipates, or, at least, modifies them."

"You think I have done you good, then? may be, I have. But don't thank me, don't thank me. If by words, casually delivered in the social hour, I do any good to right or left, it is but involuntary influence—locust-tree sweetening the herbage under it; no merit at all; mere wholesome accident, of a wholesome nature.—Don't you see?"

Another stare from the good merchant, and both were silent again.

Finding his book, hitherto resting on his lap, rather irksome there, the owner now places it edgewise on the settee, between himself and neighbor; in so doing, chancing to expose the lettering on the back—*"Black Rapids Coal Company"*—which the good merchant, scrupulously honorable, had much ado to avoid reading, so directly would it have fallen under his eye, had he not conscientiously averted it. On a sudden, as if just reminded of something, the stranger starts up, and moves away, in his haste leaving his book; which the merchant observing, without delay takes it up, and, hurrying after, civilly returns it; in which act he could not avoid catching sight by an involuntary glance of part of the lettering.

"Thank you, thank you, my good sir," said the other, receiving the volume, and was resuming his retreat, when the merchant spoke: "Excuse me, but are you not in some way connected with the—the Coal Company I have heard of?"

"There is more than one Coal Company that may be heard of, my good sir," smiled the other, pausing with an expression of painful impatience, disinterestedly mastered.

"But you are connected with one in particular.—The 'Black Rapids,' are you not?"

"How did you find that out?"

"Well, sir, I have heard rather tempting information of your Company."

"Who is your informant, pray," somewhat coldly.

"A—a person by the name of Ringman."

"Don't know him. But, doubtless, there are plenty who know our Company, whom our Company does not know; in the same way that one may know an individual, yet be unknown to him.—Known this Ringman long? Old friend, I suppose.—But pardon, I must leave you."

"Stay, sir, that—that stock."

"Stock?"

"Yes, it's a little irregular, perhaps, but—"

"Dear me, you don't think of doing any business with me, do you? In my official capacity I have not been authenticated to you. This transfer-book, now," holding it up so as to bring the lettering in sight, "how do you know that it may not be a bogus one? And I, being personally a stranger to you, how can you have confidence in me?"

"Because," knowingly smiled the good merchant, "if you were other than I have confidence that you are, hardly would you challenge distrust that way."

"But you have not examined my book."

"What need to, if already I believe that it is what it is lettered to be?"

"But you had better. It might suggest doubts."

"Doubts, may be, it might suggest, but not knowledge; for how, by examining the book, should I think I knew any more than I now think I do; since, if it be the true book, I think it so already; and since if it be otherwise, then I have never seen the true one, and don't know what that ought to look like."

"Your logic I will not criticize, but your confidence I admire, and earnestly, too, jocose as was the method I took to draw it out. Enough, we will go to yonder table, and if there be any business which, either in my private or official capacity, I can help you do, pray command me."

The transaction concluded, the two still remained seated, falling into familiar conversation, by degrees verging into that confidential sort of sympathetic silence, the last refinement and luxury of unaffected good feeling. A kind of social superstition, to suppose that to be truly friendly one must be saying friendly words all the time, any more than be doing friendly deeds continually. True friendliness, like true religion, being in a sort independent of works.

At length, the good merchant, whose eyes were pensively resting upon the gay tables in the distance, broke the spell by saying that, from the spectacle before them, one would little divine what other quarters of the boat might reveal. He cited the case, accidentally encountered but an hour or two previous, of a shrunken old miser, clad in shrunken old moleskin, stretched out, an invalid, on a bare plank in the emigrants' quarters, eagerly clinging to life and lucre, though the one was gasping for outlet, and about the other he was in torment lest death, or some other unprincipled cutpurse, should be the means of his losing it; by like feeble tenure holding lungs and pouch, and yet knowing and desiring nothing beyond them; for his mind, never raised above mould, was now all but mouldered away. To such a degree, indeed, that he had no trust in anything, not even in his parchment bonds, which, the better to preserve from the tooth of time, he had packed down and scaled up, like brandy peaches, in a tin case of spirits.

The worthy man proceeded at some length with these dispiriting particulars. Nor would his cheery companion wholly deny that there might be a point of view from which such a case of extreme want of confidence might, to the humane mind, present features not altogether welcome as wine and olives after dinner. Still, he was not without compensatory considerations, and, upon the whole, took his companion to task for evincing what, in a good-natured, round-about way, he hinted to be a somewhat jaundiced sentimentality. Nature, he added, in Shakespeare's words, had meal and bran; and, rightly regarded, the bran in its way was not to be condemned.

The other was not disposed to question the justice of Shakespeare's thought, but would hardly admit the propriety of the application in this instance, much less of the comment. So, after some further temperate discussion of the pitiable miser, finding that they could not entirely harmonize, the merchant cited another case, that of the negro cripple. But his companion suggested whether the alleged hardships of that alleged unfortunate might not exist more in the pity of the observer than the experience of the observed. He knew nothing about the cripple, nor had seen him, but ventured to surmise that, could one but get at the real state of his heart, he would be found about as happy as most men, if not, in fact, full as happy as the speaker himself. He added that negroes were by nature a singularly cheerful race; no one ever heard of a native-born African Zimmermann or Torquemada; that even from religion they dismissed all gloom; in their hilarious rituals they danced, so to speak, and, as it were, cut pigeon-wings. It was improbable, therefore, that a negro, however reduced to his stumps by fortune, could be ever thrown off the legs of a laughing philosophy.

Foiled again, the good merchant would not desist, but ventured still a third case, that of the man with the weed, whose story, as narrated by himself, and confirmed and filled out by the testimony of a certain man in a gray coat, whom the merchant had afterwards met, he now proceeded to give; and that, without holding back those particulars disclosed by the second informant, but which delicacy had prevented the unfortunate man himself from touching upon.

But as the good merchant could, perhaps, do better justice to the man than the story, we shall venture to tell it in other words than his, though not to any other effect.

Chapter 12 STORY OF THE UNFORTUNATE MAN,
*From Which May Be Gathered Whether or No He Has Been
Justly So Entitled* ই

It appeared that the unfortunate man had had for a wife one of
those natures, anomalously vicious, which would almost tempt a
metaphysical lover of our species to doubt whether the human
form be, in all cases, conclusive evidence of humanity, whether,
sometimes, it may not be a kind of unpledged and indifferent taber-
nacle, and whether, once for all to crush the saying of Thrasea, (an
unaccountable one, considering that he himself was so good a man)
that "he who hates vice, hates humanity," it should not, in self-
defense, be held for a reasonable maxim, that none but the good
are human.

Goneril was young, in person lithe and straight, too straight, indeed, for a woman, a complexion naturally rosy, and which would
have been charmingly so, but for a certain hardness and bakedness,
like that of the glazed colors on stone-ware. Her hair was of a deep,
rich chestnut, but worn in close, short curls all round her head.
Her Indian figure was not without its impairing effect on her bust,
while her mouth would have been pretty but for a trace of moustache. Upon the whole, aided by the resources of the toilet, her
appearance at distance was such, that some might have thought
her, if anything, rather beautiful, though of a style of beauty rather
peculiar and cactus-like.

It was happy for Goneril that her more striking peculiarities were
less of the person than of temper and taste. One hardly knows how
to reveal, that, while having a natural antipathy to such things as
the breast of chicken, or custard, or peach, or grape, Goneril could
yet in private make a satisfactory lunch on hard crackers and brawn
of ham. She liked lemons, and the only kind of candy she loved
were little dried sticks of blue clay, secretly carried in her pocket.
Withal she had hard, steady health like a squaw's, with as firm a
spirit and resolution. Some other points about her were likewise
such as pertain to the women of savage life. Lithe though she was,

she loved supineness, but upon occasion could endure like a stoic. She was taciturn, too. From early morning till about three o'clock in the afternoon she would seldom speak—it taking that time to thaw her, by all accounts, into but talking terms with humanity. During the interval she did little but look, and keep looking out of her large, metallic eyes, which her enemies called cold as a cuttle-fish's, but which by her were esteemed gazelle-like; for Goneril was not without vanity. Those who thought they best knew her, often wondered what happiness such a being could take in life, not considering the happiness which is to be had by some natures in the very easy way of simply causing pain to those around them. Those who suffered from Goneril's strange nature, might, with one of those hyberboles to which the resentful incline, have pronounced her some kind of toad; but her worst slanderers could never, with any show of justice, have accused her of being a toady. In a large sense she possessed the virtue of independence of mind. Goneril held it flattery to hint praise even of the absent, and even if merited; but honesty, to fling people's imputed faults into their faces. This was thought malice, but it certainly was not passion. Passion is human. Like an icicle-dagger, Goneril at once stabbed and froze; so at least they said; and when she saw frankness and innocence tyrannized into sad nervousness under her spell, according to the same authority, inly she chewed her blue clay, and you could mark that she chuckled. These peculiarities were strange and unpleasing; but another was alleged, one really incomprehensible. In company she had a strange way of touching, as by accident, the arm or hand of comely young men, and seemed to reap a secret delight from it, but whether from the humane satisfaction of having given the evil-touch, as it is called, or whether it was something else in her, not equally wonderful, but quite as deplorable, remained an enigma.

Needless to say what distress was the unfortunate man's, when, engaged in conversation with company, he would suddenly perceive his Goneril bestowing her mysterious touches, especially in such cases where the strangeness of the thing seemed to strike upon the touched person, notwithstanding good-breeding forbade his proposing the mystery, on the spot, as a subject of discussion for the company. In these cases, too, the unfortunate man could never endure so much as to look upon the touched young gentleman afterwards, fearful of the mortification of meeting in his countenance some kind of more or less quizzingly-knowing expression. He would shudderingly shun the young gentleman. So that here, to the husband, Goneril's touch had the dread operation of the heathen taboo. Now Goneril brooked no chiding. So, at favorable times, he, in a wary manner, and not indelicately, would venture in private interviews gently to make distant allusions to this questionable propensity. She divined him. But, in her cold loveless way, said it was witless to be telling one's dreams, especially foolish ones; but if the unfortunate man liked connubially to rejoice his soul with such chimeras, much connubial joy might they give him. All this was sad —a touching case—but all might, perhaps, have been borne by the unfortunate man—conscientiously mindful of his vow—for better or for worse—to love and cherish his dear Goneril so long as kind heaven might spare her to him—but when, after all that had happened, the devil of jealousy entered her, a calm, clayey, cakey devil, for none other could possess her, and the object of that deranged jealousy, her own child, a little girl of seven, her father's consolation and pet; when he saw Goneril artfully torment the little innocent, and then play the maternal hypocrite with it, the unfortunate man's patient long-suffering gave way. Knowing that she would neither confess nor amend, and might, possibly, become even worse than she was, he thought it but duty as a father, to withdraw the child from her; but, loving it as he did, he could not do so without accompanying it into domestic exile himself. Which, hard though it was, he did. Whereupon the whole female neighborhood, who till now had little enough admired dame Goneril, broke out in indignation against a husband, who, without assigning a cause, could deliberately abandon the wife of his bosom, and sharpen the sting to her, too, by depriving her of the solace of retaining her offspring. To all this, self-respect, with Christian charity towards Goneril, long kept the unfortunate man dumb. And well had it been had he continued so; for when, driven to desperation, he hinted something of the truth of the case, not a soul would credit it; while for Goneril, she pronounced all he said to be a malicious invention. Ere long, at the suggestion of some woman's-rights women, the injured wife began a suit, and, thanks to able counsel and accommodating testimony, succeeded in such a way, as not only to recover custody of the child, but to get such a settlement awarded upon a separation, as to make penniless the unfortunate man (so he averred), besides, through the legal sympathy she enlisted, effecting a judicial blasting of his private reputation. What made it yet more lamentable was, that the unfortunate man, thinking that, before the court, his wisest plan, as well as the most Christian besides, being, as he deemed, not at variance with the truth of the matter, would be to put forth the plea of the mental derangement of Goneril, which done, he could, with less of mortification to himself, and odium to her, reveal in self-defense those eccentricities which had led to his retirement from the joys of wedlock, had much ado in the end to prevent this charge of derangement from fatally recoiling upon himself—especially, when, among other things, he alleged her mysterious touchings. In vain did his counsel, striving to make out the derangement to be where, in fact, if anywhere, it was, urge that, to hold otherwise, to hold that such a being as Goneril was sane, this was constructively a libel upon womankind. Libel be it. And all ended by the unfortunate man's subsequently getting wind of Goneril's intention to procure him to be permanently committed for a lunatic. Upon which he fled, and was now an innocent outcast, wandering forlorn in the great valley of the Mississippi, with a weed on his hat for the loss of his Goneril; for he had lately seen by the papers that she was dead, and thought it but proper to comply with the prescribed form of mourning in such cases. For some days past he had been trying to get money enough to return to his child, and was but now started with inadequate funds.

Now all of this, from the beginning, the good merchant could not but consider rather hard for the unfortunate man.

*Evinces Much Humanity, and in a Way Which Would Seem
To Show Him To Be One of the Most Logical of Optimists* ⧼

Years ago, a grave American savant, being in London, observed at
an evening party there, a certain coxcombical fellow, as he thought,
an absurd riband in his lapel, and full of smart persiflage, whisking
about to the admiration of as many as were disposed to admire.
Great was the savant's disdain; but, chancing ere long to find himself in a corner with the jackanapes, got into conversation with him,
when he was somewhat ill-prepared for the good sense of the jackanapes, but was altogether thrown aback, upon subsequently being
whispered by a friend that the jackanapes was almost as great a
savant as himself, being no less a personage than Sir Humphry Davy.

The above anecdote is given just here by way of an anticipative
reminder to such readers as, from the kind of jaunty levity, or what
may have passed for such, hitherto for the most part appearing in
the man with the traveling-cap, may have been tempted into a more
or less hasty estimate of him; that such readers, when they find the
same person, as they presently will, capable of philosophic and
humanitarian discourse—no mere casual sentence or two as hereto-
fore at times, but solidly sustained throughout an almost entire
sitting; that they may not, like the American savant, be thereupon
betrayed into any surprise incompatible with their own good opinion of their previous penetration.

The merchant's narration being ended, the other would not deny
but that it did in some degree affect him. He hoped he was not
without proper feeling for the unfortunate man. But he begged to
know in what spirit he bore his alleged calamities. Did he despond
or have confidence?

The merchant did not, perhaps, take the exact import of the last
member of the question; but answered, that, if whether the unfortunate man was becomingly resigned under his affliction or no,
was the point, he could say for him that resigned he was, and to
an exemplary degree: for not only, so far as known, did he refrain
from any one-sided reflections upon human goodness and human

justice, but there was observable in him an air of chastened reliance, and at times tempered cheerfulness.

Upon which the other observed, that since the unfortunate man's alleged experience could not be deemed very conciliatory towards a view of human nature better than human nature was, it largely redounded to his fair-mindedness, as well as piety, that under the alleged dissuasives, apparently so, from philanthropy, he had not, in a moment of excitement, been warped over to the ranks of the misanthropes. He doubted not, also, that with such a man his experience would, in the end, act by a complete and beneficent inversion, and so far from shaking his confidence in his kind, confirm it, and rivet it. Which would the more surely be the case, did he (the unfortunate man) at last become satisfied (as sooner or later he probably would be) that in the distraction of his mind his Goneril had not in all respects had fair play. At all events, the description of the lady, charity could not but regard as more or less exaggerated, and so far unjust. The truth probably was that she was a wife with some blemishes mixed with some beauties. But when the blemishes were displayed, her husband, no adept in the female nature, had tried to use reason with her, instead of something far more persuasive. Hence his failure to convince and convert. The act of withdrawing from her, seemed, under the circumstances, abrupt. In brief, there were probably small faults on both sides, more than balanced by large virtues; and one should not be hasty in judging.

When the merchant, strange to say, opposed views so calm and impartial, and again, with some warmth, deplored the case of the unfortunate man, his companion, not without seriousness, checked him, saying, that this would never do; that, though but in the most exceptional case, to admit the existence of unmerited misery, more particularly if alleged to have been brought about by unhindered arts of the wicked, such an admission was, to say the least, not prudent; since, with some, it might unfavorably bias their most important persuasions. Not that those persuasions were legitimately servile to such influences. Because, since the common occurrences of life could never, in the nature of things, steadily look one way and tell one story, as flags in the trade-wind; hence, if the conviction of a Providence, for instance, were in any way made dependent upon such variabilities as everyday events, the degree of that conviction would, in thinking minds, be subject to fluctuations akin to those of the stock-exchange during a long and uncertain war. Here he glanced aside at his transfer-book, and after a moment's pause continued. It was of the essence of a right conviction of the divine nature, as with a right conviction of the human, that, based less on experience than intuition, it rose above the zones of weather.

When now the merchant, with all his heart, coincided with this (as being a sensible, as well as religious person, he could not but do), his companion expressed satisfaction, that, in an age of some distrust on such subjects, he could yet meet with one who shared with him, almost to the full, so sound and sublime a confidence.

Still, he was far from the illiberality of denying that philosphy duly bounded was not permissible. Only he deemed it at least desirable that, when such a case as that alleged of the unfortunate man was made the subject of philosophic discussion, it should be so philosophized upon, as not to afford handles to those unblessed with the true light. For, but to grant that there was so much as a mystery about such a case, might by those persons be held for a tacit surrender of the question. And as for the apparent license temporarily permitted sometimes, to the bad over the good (as was by implication alleged with regard to Goneril and the unfortunate man), it might be injudicious there to lay too much polemic stress upon the doctrine of future retribution as the vindication of present impunity. For though, indeed, to the right-minded that doctrine was true, and of sufficient solace, yet with the perverse the polemic mention of it might but provoke the shallow, though mischievous conceit, that such a doctrine was but tantamount to the one which should affirm that Providence was not now, but was going to be. In short, with all sorts of cavilers, it was best, both for them and everybody, that whoever had the true light should stick behind the secure Malakoff of confidence, nor be tempted forth to hazardous skirmishes on the open ground of reason. Therefore, he deemed it unadvisable in the good man, even in the privacy of his own mind, or

in communion with a congenial one, to indulge in too much latitude
of philosophizing, or, indeed, of compassionating, since this might
beget an indiscreet habit of thinking and feeling which might unexpectedly betray him upon unsuitable occasions. Indeed, whether
in private or public, there was nothing which a good man was more
bound to guard himself against than, on some topics, the emotional
unreserve of his natural heart; for, that the natural heart, in certain
points, was not what it might be, men had been authoritatively admonished.

But he thought he might be getting dry.

The merchant, in his good-nature, thought otherwise, and said
that he would be glad to refresh himself with such fruit all day. It
was sitting under a ripe pulpit, and better such a seat than under a
ripe peach-tree.

The other was pleased to find that he had not, as he feared, been
prosing; but would rather not be considered in the formal light of a
preacher; he preferred being still received in that of the equal and
genial companion. To which end, throwing still more of sociability
into his manner, he again reverted to the unfortunate man. Take
the very worst view of that case; admit that his Goneril was, indeed,
a Goneril; how fortunate to be at last rid of this Goneril, both by
nature and by law? If he were acquainted with the unfortunate
man, instead of condoling with him, he would congratulate him.
Great good fortune had this unfortunate man. Lucky dog, he dared
say, after all.

To which the merchant replied, that he earnestly hoped it might
be so, and at any rate he tried his best to comfort himself with the
persuasion that, if the unfortunate man was not happy in this world,
he would, at least, be so in another.

His companion made no question of the unfortunate man's happiness in both worlds; and, presently calling for some champagne,
invited the merchant to partake, upon the playful plea that, whatever notions other than felicitous ones he might associate with the
unfortunate man, a little champagne would readily bubble away.

At intervals they slowly quaffed several glasses in silence and thoughtfulness. At last the merchant's expressive face flushed, his eye moistly beamed, his lips trembled with an imaginative and feminine sensibility. Without sending a single fume to his head, the wine seemed to shoot to his heart, and begin soothsaying there. "Ah," he cried, pushing his glass from him, "Ah, wine is good, and confidence is good; but can wine or confidence percolate down through all the stony strata of hard considerations, and drop warmly and ruddily into the cold cave of truth? Truth will *not* be comforted. Led by dear charity, lured by sweet hope, fond fancy essays this feat; but in vain; mere dreams and ideals, they explode in your hand, leaving naught but the scorching behind!"

"Why, why, why!" in amaze, at the burst; "bless me, if *In vino veritas* be a true saying, then, for all the fine confidence you professed with me, just now, distrust, deep distrust, underlies it; and ten thousand strong, like the Irish Rebellion, breaks out in you now. That wine, good wine, should do it! Upon my soul," half seriously, half humorously, securing the bottle, "you shall drink no more of it. Wine was meant to gladden the heart, not grieve it; to heighten confidence, not depress it."

Sobered, shamed, all but confounded, by this raillery, the most telling rebuke under such circumstances, the merchant stared about him, and then, with altered mien, stammeringly confessed, that he was almost as much surprised as his companion, at what had escaped him. He did not understand it; was quite at a loss to account for such a rhapsody popping out of him unbidden. It could hardly be the champagne; he felt his brain unaffected; in fact, if anything, the wine had acted upon it something like white of egg in coffee, clarifying and brightening.

"Brightening? brightening it may be, but less like the white of egg in coffee, than like stove-lustre on a stove—black, brightening seriously. I repent calling for the champagne. To a temperament like yours, champagne is not to be recommended. Pray, my dear sir, do you feel quite yourself again? Confidence restored?"

"I hope so; I think I may say it is so. But we have had a long talk, and I think I must retire now."

So saying, the merchant rose, and making his adieus, left the table with the air of one, mortified at having been tempted by his own honest goodness, accidentally stimulated into making mad disclosures—to himself as to another—of the queer, unaccountable caprices of his natural heart.

Chapter 14 WORTH THE CONSIDERATION *of Those to Whom It May Prove Worth Considering* 🦢

As the last chapter was begun with a reminder looking forwards, so the present must consist of one glancing backwards.

To some, it may raise a degree of surprise that one so full of confidence, as the merchant has throughout shown himself, up to the moment of his late sudden impulsiveness, should, in that instance, have betrayed such a depth of discontent. He may be thought inconsistent, and even so he is. But for this, is the author to be blamed? True, it may be urged that there is nothing a writer of fiction should more carefully see to, as there is nothing a sensible reader will more carefully look for, than that, in the depiction of any character, its consistency should be preserved. But this, though at first blush, seeming reasonable enough, may, upon a closer view, prove not so much so. For how does it couple with another requirement—equally insisted upon, perhaps—that, while to all fiction is allowed some play of invention, yet, fiction based on fact should never be contradictory to it; and is it not a fact, that, in real life, a consistent character is a *rara avis*? Which being so, the distaste of readers to the contrary sort in books, can hardly arise from any sense of their untrueness. It may rather be from perplexity as to understanding them. But if the acutest sage be often at his wits' ends to understand living character, shall those who are not sages expect to run and read character in those mere phantoms which flit along a page, like shadows along a wall? That fiction, where every character can, by reason of its consistency, be comprehended at a glance, either exhibits but sections of character, making them appear for wholes, or else is very untrue to reality; while, on the other hand, that author who draws a character, even though to common view incongruous in its parts, as the flying-squirrel, and, at different periods, as much at variance with itself as the caterpillar is with the butterfly into which it changes, may yet, in so doing, be not false but faithful to facts.

If reason be judge, no writer has produced such inconsistent characters as nature herself has. It must call for no small sagacity in a reader unerringly to discriminate in a novel between the inconsistencies of conception and those of life as elsewhere. Experience is the only guide here; but as no one man can be coextensive with *what is,* it may be unwise in every case to rest upon it. When the duck-billed beaver of Australia was first brought stuffed to England, the naturalists, appealing to their classifications, maintained that there was, in reality, no such creature; the bill in the specimen must needs be, in some way, artificially stuck on.

But let nature, to the perplexity of the naturalists, produce her duck-billed beavers as she may, lesser authors, some may hold, have no business to be perplexing readers with duck-billed characters. Always, they should represent human nature not in obscurity, but transparency, which, indeed, is the practice with most novelists, and is, perhaps, in certain cases, someway felt to be a kind of honor rendered by them to their kind. But whether it involve honor or otherwise might be mooted, considering that, if these waters of human nature can be so readily seen through, it may be either that they are very pure or very shallow. Upon the whole, it might rather be thought, that he, who, in view of its inconsistencies, says of human nature the same that, in view of its contrasts, is said of the divine nature, that it is past finding out, thereby evinces a better appreciation of it than he who, by always representing it in a clear light, leaves it to be inferred that he clearly knows all about it.

But though there is a prejudice against inconsistent characters in books, yet the prejudice bears the other way, when what seemed at first their inconsistency, afterwards, by the skill of the writer, turns out to be their good keeping. The great masters excel in nothing so much as in this very particular. They challenge astonishment at the tangled web of some character, and then raise admiration still greater at their satisfactory unraveling of it; in this way throwing open, sometimes to the understanding even of school misses, the last complications of that spirit which is affirmed by its Creator to be fearfully and wonderfully made.

At least, something like this is claimed for certain psychological novelists; nor will the claim be here disputed. Yet, as touching this point, it may prove suggestive, that all those sallies of ingenuity, having for their end the revelation of human nature on fixed principles, have, by the best judges, been excluded with contempt from the ranks of the sciences—palmistry, physiognomy, phrenology, psychology. Likewise, the fact, that in all ages such conflicting views have, by the most eminent minds, been taken of mankind, would, as with other topics, seem some presumption of a pretty general and pretty thorough ignorance of it. Which may appear the less improbable if it be considered that, after poring over the best novels professing to portray human nature, the studious youth will still run risk of being too often at fault upon actually entering the world; whereas, had he been furnished with a true delineation, it ought to fare with him something as with a stranger entering, map in hand, Boston town; the streets may be very crooked, he may often pause; but, thanks to his true map, he does not hopelessly lose his way. Nor, to this comparison, can it be an adequate objection, that the twistings of the town are always the same, and those of human nature subject to variation. The grand points of human nature are the same to-day they were a thousand years ago. The only variability in them is in expression, not in feature.

But as, in spite of seeming discouragement, some mathematicians are yet in hopes of hitting upon an exact method of determining the longitude, the more earnest psychologists may, in the face of previous failures, still cherish expectations with regard to some mode of infallibly discovering the heart of man.

But enough has been said by way of apology for whatever may have seemed amiss or obscure in the character of the merchant; so nothing remains but to turn to our comedy, or, rather, to pass from the comedy of thought to that of action.

The merchant having withdrawn, the other remained seated alone
for a time, with the air of one who, after having conversed with
some excellent man, carefully ponders what fell from him, however
intellectually inferior it may be, that none of the profit may be lost;
happy if from any honest word he has heard he can derive some
hint, which, besides confirming him in the theory of virtue, may,
likewise, serve for a finger-post to virtuous action.

Ere long his eye brightened, as if some such hint was now caught.
He rises, book in hand, quits the cabin, and enters upon a sort of
corridor, narrow and dim, a by-way to a retreat less ornate and
cheery than the former; in short, the emigrants' quarters; but which,
owing to the present trip being a down-river one, will doubtless be
found comparatively tenantless. Owing to obstructions against the
side windows, the whole place is dim and dusky; very much so, for
the most part; yet, by starts, haggardly lit here and there by narrow, capricious sky-lights in the cornices. But there would seem
no special need for light, the place being designed more to pass the
night in, than the day; in brief, a pine barrens dormitory, of
knotty pine bunks, without bedding. As with the nests in the geo-
metrical towns of the associate penguin and pelican, these bunks
were disposed with Philadelphian regularity, but, like the cradle
of the oriole, they were pendulous, and, moreover, were, so to
speak, three-story cradles; the description of one of which will suffice for all.

Four ropes, secured to the ceiling, passed downwards through
auger-holes bored in the corners of three rough planks, which at
equal distances rested on knots vertically tied in the ropes, the
lowermost plank but an inch or two from the floor, the whole affair
resembling, on a large scale, rope book-shelves; only, instead of
hanging firmly against a wall, they swayed to and fro at the least
suggestion of motion, but were more especially lively upon the
provocation of a green emigrant sprawling into one, and trying to
lay himself out there, when the cradling would be such as almost to

toss him back whence he came. In consequence, one less inexperienced, essaying repose on the uppermost shelf, was liable to serious disturbance, should a raw beginner select a shelf beneath. Sometimes a throng of poor emigrants, coming at night in a sudden rain to occupy these oriole nests, would—through ignorance of their peculiarity—bring about such a rocking uproar of carpentry, joining to it such an uproar of exclamations, that it seemed as if some luckless ship, with all its crew, was being dashed to pieces among the rocks. They were beds devised by some sardonic foe of poor travelers, to deprive them of that tranquillity which should precede, as well as accompany, slumber.—Procrustean beds, on whose hard grain humble worth and honesty writhed, still invoking repose, while but torment responded. Ah, did anyone make such a bunk for himself, instead of having it made for him, it might be just, but how cruel, to say, You must lie on it!

But, purgatory as the place would appear, the stranger advances into it; and, like Orpheus in his gay descent to Tartarus, lightly hums to himself an opera snatch.

Suddenly there is a rustling, then a creaking, one of the cradles swings out from a murky nook, a sort of wasted penguin-flipper is supplicatingly put forth, while a wail like that of Dives is heard:—"Water, water!"

It was the miser of whom the merchant had spoken.

Swift as a sister-of-charity, the stranger hovers over him:—

"My poor, poor sir, what can I do for you?"

"Ugh, ugh—water!"

Darting out, he procures a glass, returns, and, holding it to the sufferer's lips, supports his head while he drinks: "And did they let you lie here, my poor sir, racked with this parching thirst?"

The miser, a lean old man, whose flesh seemed salted cod-fish, dry as combustibles; head, like one whittled by an idiot out of a knot; flat, bony mouth, nipped between buzzard nose and chin; expression, flitting between hunks and imbecile—now one, now the other—he made no response. His eyes were closed, his cheek lay upon an old white moleskin coat, rolled under his head like a wizened apple upon a grimy snow-bank.

Revived at last, he inclined towards his ministrant, and, in a voice disastrous with a cough, said:—"I am old and miserable, a poor beggar, not worth a shoe-string—how can I repay you?"

"By giving me your confidence."

"Confidence!" he squeaked, with changed manner, while the pallet swung, "little left at my age, but take the stale remains, and welcome."

"Such as it is, though, you give it. Very good. Now give me a hundred dollars."

Upon this the miser was all panic. His hands groped towards his waist, then suddenly flew upward beneath his moleskin pillow, and there lay clutching something out of sight. Meantime, to himself he incoherently mumbled:—"Confidence? Cant, gammon! Confidence? hum, bubble!—Confidence? fetch, gouge!—Hundred dollars?—hundred devils!"

Half spent, he lay mute awhile, then feebly raising himself, in a voice for the moment made strong by the sarcasm, said, "A hundred dollars? rather high price to put upon confidence. But don't you see I am a poor, old rat here, dying in the wainscot? You have served me; but, wretch that I am, I can but cough you my thanks,—ugh, ugh, ugh!"

This time his cough was so violent that its convulsions were imparted to the plank, which swung him about like a stone in a sling preparatory to its being hurled.

"Ugh, ugh, ugh!"

"What a shocking cough. I wish, my friend, the herb-doctor was here now; a box of his Omni-Balsamic Reinvigorator would do you good."

"Ugh, ugh, ugh!"

"I've a good mind to go find him. He's aboard somewhere. I saw his long, snuff-colored surtout. Trust me, his medicines are the best in the world."

"Ugh, ugh, ugh!"

"Oh, how sorry I am."

"No doubt of it," squeaked the other again, "but go, get your charity out on deck. There parade the pursy peacocks; they don't cough down here in desertion and darkness, like poor old me. Look how scaly a pauper I am, clove with this churchyard cough. Ugh, ugh, ugh!"

"Again, how sorry I feel, not only for your cough, but your poverty. Such a rare chance made unavailable. Did you have but the sun named, how I could invest it for you. Treble profits. But confidence—I fear that, even had you the precious cash, you would not have the more precious confidence I speak of."

"Ugh, ugh, ugh!" flightily raising himself. "What's that? How, how? Then you don't want the money for yourself?"

"My dear, *dear* sir, how could you impute to me such preposterous self-seeking? To solicit out of hand, for my private behoof, an hundred dollars from a perfect stranger? I am not mad, my dear sir."

"How, how?" still more bewildered, "do you, then, go about the world, gratis, seeking to invest people's money for them?"

"My humble profession, sir. I live not for myself; but the world will not have confidence in me, and yet confidence in me were great gain."

"But, but," in a kind of vertigo, "what do—do you do—do with people's money? Ugh, ugh! How is the gain made?"

"To tell that would ruin me. That known, every one would be going into the business, and it would be overdone. A secret, a mystery—all I have to do with you is to receive your confidence, and all you have to do with me is, in due time, to receive it back, thrice paid in trebling profits."

"What, what?" imbecility in the ascendant once more; "but the vouchers, the vouchers," suddenly hunkish again.

"Honesty's best voucher is honesty's face."

"Can't see yours, though," peering through the obscurity.

From this last alternating flicker of rationality, the miser fell back, sputtering, into his previous gibberish, but it took now an arithmetical turn. Eyes closed, he lay muttering to himself—

"One hundred, one hundred—two hundred, two hundred—three hundred, three hundred."

He opened his eyes, feebly stared, and still more feebly said—

"It's a little dim here, ain't it? Ugh, ugh! But, as well as my poor old eyes can see, you look honest."

"I am glad to hear that."

"If—if, now, I should put"—trying to raise himself, but vainly, excitement having all but exhausted him—"if, if now, I should put, put—"

"No ifs. Downright confidence, or none. So help me heaven, I will have no half-confidences."

He said it with an indifferent and superior air, and seemed moving to go.

"Don't, don't leave me, friend; bear with me; age can't help some distrust; it can't, friend, it can't. Ugh, ugh, ugh! Oh, I am so old and miserable. I ought to have a guard*ee*an. Tell me, if—"

"If? No more!"

"Stay! how soon—ugh, ugh!—would my money be trebled? How soon, friend?"

"You won't confide. Good-bye!"

"Stay, stay," falling back now like an infant, "I confide, I confide; help, friend, my distrust!"

From an old buckskin pouch, tremulously dragged forth, ten hoarded eagles, tarnished into the appearance of ten old horn-buttons, were taken, and half-eagerly, half-reluctantly, offered.

"I know not whether I should accept this slack confidence," said the other coldly, receiving the gold, "but an eleventh-hour confidence, a sick-bed confidence, a distempered, death-bed confidence, after all. Give me the healthy confidence of healthy men, with their healthy wits about them. But let that pass. All right. Good-bye!"

"Nay, back, back—receipt, my receipt! Ugh, ugh, ugh! Who are you? What have I done? Where go you? My gold, my gold! Ugh, ugh, ugh!"

But, unluckily for this final flicker of reason, the stranger was now beyond ear-shot, nor was any one else within hearing of so feeble a call.

Chapter 16 A SICK MAN, *after Some Impatience, Is Induced to Become a Patient* ⧫

The sky slides into blue, the bluffs into bloom; the rapid Mississippi expands; runs sparkling and gurgling, all over in eddies; one magnified wake of a seventy-four. The sun comes out, a golden hussar, from his tent, flashing his helm on the world. All things, warmed in the landscape, leap. Speeds the dædal boat as a dream.

But, withdrawn in a corner, wrapped about in a shawl, sits an unparticipating man, visited, but not warmed, by the sun—a plant whose hour seems over, while buds are blowing and seeds are astir. On a stool at his left sits a stranger in a snuff-colored surtout, the collar thrown back; his hand waving in persuasive gesture, his eye beaming with hope. But not easily may hope be awakened in one long tranced into hopelessness by a chronic complaint.

To some remark the sick man, by word or look, seemed to have just made an impatiently querulous answer, when, with a deprecatory air, the other resumed:

"Nay, think not I seek to cry up my treatment by crying down that of others. And yet, when one is confident he has truth on his side, and that it is not on the other, it is no very easy thing to be charitable; not that temper is the bar, but conscience; for charity would beget toleration, you know, which is a kind of implied permitting, and in effect a kind of countenancing; and that which is countenanced is so far furthered. But should untruth be furthered? Still, while for the world's good I refuse to further the cause of these mineral doctors, I would fain regard them, not as willful wrong-doers, but good Samaritans erring. And is this—I put it to you, sir —is this the view of an arrogant rival and pretender?"

His physical power all dribbled and gone, the sick man replied not by voice or by gesture; but, with feeble dumb-show of his face, seemed to be saying, "Pray leave me; who was ever cured by talk?"

But the other, as if not unused to make allowances for such despondency, proceeded; and kindly, yet firmly:

"You tell me, that by advice of an eminent physiologist in Louisville, you took tincture of iron. For what? To restore your lost energy. And how? Why, in healthy subjects iron is naturally found in the blood, and iron in the bar is strong; ergo, iron is the source of animal invigoration. But you being deficient in vigor, it follows that the cause is deficiency of iron. Iron, then, must be put into you; and so your tincture. Now as to the theory here, I am mute. But in modesty assuming its truth, and then, as a plain man viewing that theory in practice, I would respectfully question your eminent physiologist: 'Sir,' I would say, 'though by natural processes, lifeless natures taken as nutriment become vitalized, yet is a lifeless nature, under any circumstances, capable of a living transmission, with all its qualities as a lifeless nature unchanged? If, sir, nothing can be incorporated with the living body but by assimilation, and if that implies the conversion of one thing to a different thing (as, in a lamp, oil is assimilated into flame), is it, in this view, likely, that by banqueting on fat, Calvin Edson will fatten? That is, will what is fat on the board prove fat on the bones? If it will, then, sir, what is iron in the vial will prove iron in the vein.' Seems that conclusion too confident?"

But the sick man again turned his dumb-show look, as much as to say, "Pray leave me. Why, with painful words, hint the vanity of that which the pains of this body have too painfully proved?"

But the other, as if unobservant of that querulous look, went on: "But this notion, that science can play farmer to the flesh, making there what living soil it pleases, seems not so strange as that other conceit—that science is now-a-days so expert that, in consumptive cases, as yours, it can, by prescription of the inhalation of certain vapors, achieve the sublimest act of omnipotence, breathing ⁀ ₒ all but lifeless dust the breath of life. For did you not tell me, my poor sir, that by order of the great chemist in Baltimore, for three weeks you were never driven out without a respirator, and for a given time of every day sat bolstered up in a sort of gasometer, inspiring vapors generated by the burning of drugs? as if this concocted atmosphere of man were an antidote to the poison of God's natural air. Oh, who can wonder at that old reproach against science, that it is atheistical? And here is my prime reason for opposing these chemical practitioners, who have sought out so many inventions. For what do their inventions indicate, unless it be that kind and degree of pride in human skill, which seems scarce compatible with reverential dependence upon the power above? Try to rid my mind of it as I may, yet still these chemical practitioners with their tinctures, and fumes, and braziers, and occult incantations, seem to me like Pharaoh's vain sorcerers, trying to beat down the will of heaven. Day and night, in all charity, I intercede for them, that heaven may not, in its own language, be provoked to anger with their inventions; may not take vengeance of their inventions. A thousand pities that you should ever have been in the hands of these Egyptians."

But again came nothing but the dumb-show look, as much as to say, "Pray leave me; quacks, and indignation against quacks, both are vain."

But, once more, the other went on: "How different we herb-doctors! who claim nothing, invent nothing; but staff in hand, in glades, and upon hillsides, go about in nature, humbly seeking her cures. True Indian doctors, though not learned in names, we are not unfamiliar with essences—successors of Solomon the Wise, who knew all vegetables, from the cedar of Lebanon, to the hyssop on the wall. Yes, Solomon was the first of herb-doctors. Nor were the virtues of herbs unhonored by yet older ages. Is it not writ, that on a moonlight night,

> *Medea gathered the enchanted herbs*
> *That did renew old Æson?*

Ah, would you but have confidence, you should be the new Æson, and I your Medea. A few vials of my Omni-Balsamic Reinvigorator would, I am certain, give you some strength."

Upon this, indignation and abhorrence seemed to work by their excess the effect promised of the balsam. Roused from that long apathy of impotence, the cadaverous man started, and, in a voice that was as the sound of obstructed air gurgling through a maze of broken honey-combs, cried: "Begone! You are all alike. The name of doctor, the dream of helper, condemns you. For years I have been but a gallipot for you experimentizers to rinse your experiments into, and now, in this livid skin, partake of the nature of my contents. Begone! I hate ye."

"I were inhuman, could I take affront at a want of confidence, born of too bitter an experience of betrayers. Yet, permit one who is not without feeling—"

"Begone! Just in that voice talked to me, not six months ago, the German doctor at the water cure, from which I now return, six months and sixty pangs nigher my grave."

"The water-cure? Oh, fatal delusion of the well-meaning Preissnitz!—Sir, trust me—"

"Begone!"

"Nay, an invalid should not always have his own way. Ah, sir, reflect how untimely this distrust in one like you. How weak you are; and weakness, is it not the time for confidence? Yes, when through weakness everything bids despair, then is the time to get strength by confidence."

Relenting in his air, the sick man cast upon him a long glance of beseeching, as if saying, "With confidence must come hope; and how can hope be?"

The herb-doctor took a sealed paper box from his surtout pocket, and holding it towards him, said solemnly, "Turn not away. This may be the last time of health's asking. Work upon yourself; invoke confidence, though from ashes; rouse it; for your life, rouse it, and invoke it, I say."

The other trembled, was silent; and then, a little commanding himself, asked the ingredients of the medicine.

"Herbs."

"What herbs? And the nature of them? And the reason for giving them?"

"It cannot be made known."

"Then I will none of you."

Sedately observant of the juiceless, joyless form before him, the herb-doctor was mute a moment, then said:—"I give up."

"How?"

"You are sick, and a philosopher."

"No, no;—not the last."

"But, to demand the ingredient, with the reason for giving, is the mark of a philosopher; just as the consequence is the penalty of a fool. A sick philosopher is incurable."

"Why?"

"Because he has no confidence."

"How does that make him incurable?"

"Because either he spurns his powder, or, if he take it, it proves a blank cartridge, though the same given to a rustic in like extremity, would act like a charm. I am no materialist; but the mind so acts upon the body, that if the one have no confidence, neither has the other."

Again, the sick man appeared not unmoved. He seemed to be thinking what in candid truth could be said to all this. At length, "You talk of confidence. How comes it that when brought low himself, the herb-doctor, who was most confident to prescribe in other cases, proves least confident to prescribe in his own; having small confidence in himself for himself?"

"But he has confidence in the brother he calls in. And that he does so, is no reproach to him, since he knows that when the body is prostrated, the mind is not erect. Yes, in this hour the herb-doctor does distrust himself, but not his art."

The sick man's knowledge did not warrant him to gainsay this. But he seemed not grieved at it; glad to be confuted in a way tending towards his wish.

"Then you give me hope?" his sunken eye turned up.

"Hope is proportioned to confidence. How much confidence you give me, so much hope do I give you. For this," lifting the box, "if all depended upon this, I should rest. It is nature's own."

"Nature!"

"Why do you start?"

"I know not," with a sort of shudder, "but I have heard of a book entitled 'Nature in Disease.'"

"A title I cannot approve; it is suspiciously scientific. 'Nature in Disease?' As if nature, divine nature, were aught but health; as if through nature disease is decreed! But did I not before hint of the tendency of science, that forbidden tree? Sir, if despondency is yours from recalling that title, dismiss it. Trust me, nature is health; for health is good, and nature cannot work ill. As little can she work error. Get nature, and you get well. Now, I repeat, this medicine is nature's own."

Again the sick man could not, according to his light, conscientiously disprove what was said. Neither, as before, did he seem overanxious to do so; the less, as in his sensitiveness it seemed to him, that hardly could he offer so to do without something like the appearance of a kind of implied irreligion; nor in his heart was he ungrateful, that since a spirit opposite to that pervaded all the herbdoctor's hopeful words, therefore, for hopefulness, he (the sick man) had not alone medical warrant, but also doctrinal.

"Then you do really think," hectically, "that if I take this medicine," mechanically reaching out for it, "I shall regain my health?"

"I will not encourage false hopes," relinquishing to him the box, "I will be frank with you. Though frankness is not always the weakness of the mineral practitioner, yet the herb doctor must be frank, or nothing. Now then, sir, in your case, a radical cure—such a cure, understand, as should make you robust—such a cure, sir, I do not and cannot promise."

"Oh, you need not! only restore me the power of being something else to others than a burdensome care, and to myself a droning grief. Only cure me of this misery of weakness; only make me so that I can walk about in the sun and not draw the flies to me, as lured by the coming of decay. Only do that—but that."

"You ask not much; you are wise; not in vain have you suffered. That little you ask, I think, can be granted. But remember, not in a day, nor a week, nor perhaps a month, but sooner or later; I say not exactly when, for I am neither prophet nor charlatan. Still, if, according to the directions in your box there, you take my medicine steadily, without assigning an especial day, near or remote, to discontinue it, then may you calmly look for some eventual result of good. But again I say, you must have confidence."

Feverishly he replied that he now trusted he had, and hourly should pray for its increase. When suddenly relapsing into one of those strange caprices peculiar to some invalids, he added: "But to one like me, it is so hard, so hard. The most confident hopes so often have failed me, and as often have I vowed never, no, never, to trust them again. Oh," feebly wringing his hands, "you do not know, you do not know."

"I know this, that never did a right confidence come to naught. But time is short; you hold your cure, to retain or reject."

"I retain," with a clinch, "and now how much?"

"As much as you can evoke from your heart and heaven."

"How?—the price of this medicine?"

"I thought it was confidence you meant; how much confidence you should have. The medicine,—that is half a dollar a vial. Your box holds six."

The money was paid.

"Now, sir," said the herb-doctor, "my business calls me away, and it may so be that I shall never see you again; if then—"

He paused, for the sick man's countenance fell blank.

"Forgive me," cried the other, "forgive that imprudent phrase 'never see you again.' Though I solely intended it with reference to myself, yet I had forgotten what your sensitiveness might be. I repeat, then, that it may be that we shall not soon have a second interview, so that hereafter, should another of my boxes be needed, you may not be able to replace it except by purchase at the shops; and, in so doing, you may run more or less risk of taking some not salutary mixture. For such is the popularity of the Omni-Balsamic Reinvigorator—thriving not by the credulity of the simple, but the trust of the wise—that certain contrivers have not been idle, though I would not, indeed, hastily affirm of them that they are aware of the sad consequences to the public. Homicides and murderers, some call those contrivers; but I do not; for murder (if such a crime be possible) comes from the heart, and these men's motives come from the purse. Were they not in poverty, I think they would hardly do what they do. Still, the public interests forbid that I should let their needy device for a living succeed. In short, I have adopted precautions. Take the wrapper from any of my vials and hold it to the light, you will see water-marked in capitals the word 'confidence,' which is the countersign of the medicine, as I wish it was of the world. The wrapper bears that mark or else the medicine is counterfeit. But if still any lurking doubt should remain, pray enclose the wrapper to this address," handing a card, "and by return mail I will answer."

At first the sick man listened, with the air of vivid interest, but gradually, while the other was still talking, another strange caprice came over him, and he presented the aspect of the most calamitous dejection.

"How now?" said the herb-doctor.

"You told me to have confidence, said that confidence was indispensable, and here you preach to me distrust. Ah, truth will out!"

"I told you, you must have confidence, unquestioning confidence, I meant confidence in the genuine medicine, and the genuine *me*."

"But in your absence, buying vials purporting to be yours, it seems I cannot have unquestioning confidence."

"Prove all the vials; trust those which are true."

"But to doubt, to suspect, to prove—to have all this wearing work to be doing continually—how opposed to confidence. It is evil!"

"From evil comes good. Distrust is a stage to confidence. How has it proved in our interview? But your voice is husky; I have let you talk too much. You hold your cure; I leave you. But stay—when I hear that health is yours, I will not, like some I know, vainly make boasts; but, giving glory where all glory is due, say, with the devout herb-doctor, Japus in Virgil, when, in the unseen but efficacious presence of Venus, he with simples healed the wound of Æneas:—

> *This is no mortal work, no cure of mine,*
> *Nor art's effect, but done by power divine.*"

Chapter 17 Towards the End of Which THE HERB-DOCTOR Proves Himself a Forgiver of Injuries ࿔

In a kind of ante-cabin, a number of respectable looking people, male and female, way-passengers, recently come on board, are listlessly sitting in a mutually shy sort of silence.

Holding up a small, square bottle, ovally labeled with the engraving of a countenance full of soft pity as that of the Romish-painted Madonna, the herb-doctor passes slowly among them, benignly urbane, turning this way and that, saying:—

"Ladies and gentlemen, I hold in my hand here the Samaritan Pain Dissuader, thrice-blessed discovery of that disinterested friend of humanity whose portrait you see. Pure vegetable extract. Warranted to remove the acutest pain within less than ten minutes. Five hundred dollars to be forfeited on failure. Especially efficacious in heart disease and tic-douloureux. Observe the expression of this pledged friend of humanity.—Price only fifty cents."

In vain. After the first idle stare, his auditors—in pretty good health, it seemed—instead of encouraging his politeness, appeared, if anything, impatient of it; and, perhaps, only diffidence, or some small regard for his feelings, prevented them from telling him so. But, insensible to their coldness, or charitably overlooking it, he more wooingly than ever resumed: "May I venture upon a small supposition? Have I your kind leave, ladies and gentlemen?"

To which modest appeal, no one had the kindness to answer a syllable.

"Well," said he, resignedly, "silence is at least not denial, and may be consent. My supposition is this: possibly some lady, here present, has a dear friend at home, a bed-ridden sufferer from spinal complaint. If so, what gift more appropriate to that sufferer than this tasteful little bottle of Pain Dissuader?"

Again he glanced about him, but met much the same reception as before. Those faces, alien alike to sympathy or surprise, seemed patiently to say, "We are travelers; and, as such, must expect to meet, and quietly put up with, many antic fools, and more antic quacks."

88

"Ladies and gentlemen," (deferentially fixing his eyes upon their now self-complacent faces), "ladies and gentlemen, might I, by your kind leave, venture upon one other small supposition? It is this: that there is scarce a sufferer, this noonday, writhing on his bed, but in his hour he sat satisfactorily healthy and happy; that the Samaritan Pain Dissuader is the one only balm for that to which each living creature—who knows?—may be a draughted victim, present or prospective. In short:—Oh, Happiness on my right hand, and oh, Security on my left, can ye wisely adore a Providence, and not think it wisdom to provide?—Provide!" (Uplifting the bottle.)

What immediate effect, if any, this appeal might have had, is uncertain. For just then the boat touched at a houseless landing, scooped, as by a land-slide, out of sombre forests; back through which led a road, the sole one, which, from its narrowness, and its being walled up with story on story of dusk, matted foliage, presented the vista of some cavernous old gorge in a city, like haunted Cock Lane in London. Issuing from that road, and crossing that landing, there stooped his shaggy form in the door-way, and entered the ante-cabin, with a step so burdensome that shot seemed in his pockets, a kind of invalid Titan in homespun; his beard blackly pendant, like the Carolina-moss, and dank with cypress dew; his countenance tawny and shadowy as an iron-ore country in a clouded day. In one hand he carried a heavy walking-stick of swamp-oak; with the other, led a puny girl, walking in moccasins, not improbably his child, but evidently of alien maternity, perhaps Creole, or even Camanche. Her eye would have been large for a woman, and was inky as the pools of falls among mountain-pines. An Indian blanket, orange-hued, and fringed with lead tassel-work, appeared that morning to have shielded the child from heavy showers. Her limbs were tremulous; she seemed a little Cassandra, in nervousness.

No sooner was the pair spied by the herb-doctor, than with a cheerful air, both arms extended like a host's, he advanced, and taking the child's reluctant hand, said, trippingly: "On your travels, ah, my little May Queen? Glad to see you. What pretty moccasins. Nice to dance in." Then with a half caper sang—

> "Hey diddle, diddle, the cat and the fiddle;
> The cow jumped over the moon. '

Come, chirrup, chirrup, my little robin!"

Which playful welcome drew no responsive playfulness from the child, nor appeared to gladden or conciliate the father; but rather, if anything, to dash the dead weight of his heavy-hearted expression with a smile hypochondriacally scornful.

Sobering down now, the herb-doctor addressed the stranger in a manly, business-like way—a transition which, though it might seem a little abrupt, did not appear constrained, and, indeed, served to show that his recent levity was less the habit of a frivolous nature, than the frolic condescension of a kindly heart.

"Excuse me," said he. "but, if I am not, I was speaking to you the other day;—on a Kentucky boat, wasn't it?"

"Never to me," was the reply; the voice deep and lonesome enough to have come from the bottom of an abandoned coal-shaft.

"Ah!—But am I again mistaken, (his eye falling on the swamp-oak stick), or don't you go a little lame, sir?"

"Never was lame in my life."

"Indeed? I fancied I had perceived not a limp, but a hitch, a slight hitch;—some experience in these things—divined some hidden cause of the hitch—buried bullet, may be—some dragoons in the Mexican war discharged with such, you know.—Hard fate!" he sighed, "little pity for it, for who sees   have you dropped anything?"

Why, there is no telling, but the stranger was bowed over, and might have seemed bowing for the purpose of picking up something, were it not that, as arrested in the imperfect posture, he for the moment so remained; slanting his tall stature like a mainmast yielding to the gale, or Adam to the thunder.

The little child pulled him. With a kind of a surge he righted himself, for an instant looked toward the herb-doctor; but, either from emotion or aversion, or both together, withdrew his eyes, saying nothing. Presently, still stooping, he seated himself, drawing his child between his knees, his massy hands tremulous, and still averting his face, while up into the compassionate one of the herb-doctor the child turned a fixed, melancholy glance of repugnance.

The herb-doctor stood observant a moment, then said:

"Surely you have pain, strong pain, somewhere; in strong frames pain is strongest. Try, now, my specific," (holding it up). "Do but look at the expression of this friend of humanity. Trust me, certain cure for any pain in the world. Won't you look?"

"No," choked the other.

"Very good. Merry time to you, little May Queen."

And so, as if he would intrude his cure upon no one, moved pleasantly off, again crying his wares, nor now at last without result. A new-comer, not from the shore, but another part of the boat, a sickly young man, after some questions, purchased a bottle. Upon this, others of the company began a little to wake up as it were; the scales of indifference or prejudice fell from their eyes; now, at last, they seemed to have an inkling that here was something not undesirable which might be had for the buying.

But while, ten times more briskly bland than ever, the herb-doctor was driving his benevolent trade, accompanying each sale with added praises of the thing traded, all at once the dusk giant, seated at some distance, unexpectedly raised his voice with—

"What was that you last said?"

The question was put distinctly, yet resonantly, as when a great cock-bell—stunning admonisher—strikes one; and the stroke, though single, comes bedded in the belfry clamor.

All proceedings were suspended. Hands held forth for the specific were withdrawn, while every eye turned towards the direction whence the question came. But, no way abashed, the herb-doctor, elevating his voice with even more than wonted self-possession, replied—

"I was saying what, since you wish it, I cheerfully repeat, that the Samaritan Pain Dissuader, which I here hold in my hand, will either cure or ease any pain you please, within ten minutes after its application."

"Does it produce insensibility?"

"By no means. Not the least of its merits is, that it is not an opiate. It kills pain without killing feeling."

"You lie! Some pains cannot be eased but by producing insensibility, and cannot be cured but by producing death."

Beyond this the dusk giant said nothing; neither, for impairing the other's market, did there appear much need to. After eying the rude speaker a moment with an expression of mingled admiration and consternation, the company silently exchanged glances of mutual sympathy under unwelcome conviction. Those who had purchased looked sheepish or ashamed; and a cynical-looking little man, with a thin flaggy beard, and a countenance ever wearing the rudiments of a grin, seated alone in a corner commanding a good view of the scene, held a rusty hat before his face.

But, again, the herb-doctor, without noticing the retort, over-bearing though it was, began his panegyrics anew, and in a tone more assured than before, going so far now as to say that his specific was sometimes almost as effective in cases of mental suffering as in cases of physical; or rather, to be more precise, in cases when, through sympathy, the two sorts of pain coöperated into a climax of both—in such cases, he said, the specific had done very well. He cited an example: Only three bottles, faithfully taken, cured a Louisiana widow (for three weeks sleepless in a darkened chamber) of neuralgic sorrow for the loss of husband and child, swept off in one night by the last epidemic. For the truth of this, a printed voucher was produced, duly signed.

While he was reading it aloud, a sudden side-blow all but felled him.

It was the giant, who, with a countenance lividly epileptic with hypochondriac mania, exclaimed—

"Profane fiddler on heart-strings! Snake!"

More he would have added, but, convulsed, could not; so, without another word, taking up the child, who had followed him, went with a rocking pace out of the cabin.

"Regardless of decency, and lost to humanity!" exclaimed the herb-doctor, with much ado recovering himself. Then, after a pause, during which he examined his bruise, not omitting to apply externally a little of his specific, and with some success, as it would seem, plained to himself:

"No, no, I won't seek redress; innocence is my redress. But," turning upon them all, "if that man's wrathful blow provokes me to no wrath, should his evil distrust arouse you to distrust? I do devoutly hope," proudly raising voice and arm, "for the honor of humanity—hope that, despite this coward assault, the Samaritan Pain Dissuader stands unshaken in the confidence of all who hear me!"

But, injured as he was, and patient under it, too, somehow his case excited as little compassion as his oratory now did enthusiasm. Still, pathetic to the last, he continued his appeals, notwithstanding the frigid regard of the company, till, suddenly interrupting himself, as if in reply to a quick summons from without, he said hurriedly, "I come, I come," and so with every token of precipitate dispatch, out of the cabin the herb-doctor went.

"Sha'n't see that fellow again in a hurry," remarked an auburn-haired gentleman, to his neighbor with a hook-nose. "Never knew an operator so completely unmasked."

"But do you think it the fair thing to unmask an operator that way?"

"Fair? It is right."

"Supposing that at high 'change on the Paris Bourse, Asmodeus should lounge in, distributing hand-bills, revealing the true thoughts and designs of all the operators present—would that be the fair thing in Asmodeus? Or, as Hamlet says, were it 'to consider the thing too curiously?' "

"We won't go into that. But since you admit the fellow to be a knave—"

"I don't admit it. Or, if I did, I take it back. Shouldn't wonder if, after all, he is no knave at all, or, but little of one. What can you prove against him?"

"I can prove that he makes dupes."

"Many held in honor do the same; and many, not wholly knaves, do it too."

"How about that last?"

"He is not wholly at heart a knave, I fancy, among whose dupes is himself. Did you not see our quack friend apply to himself his own quackery? A fanatic quack; essentially a fool, though effectively a knave."

Bending over, and looking down between his knees on the floor, the auburn-haired gentleman meditatively scribbled there awhile with his cane, then, glancing up, said:

"I can't conceive how you, in any way, can hold him a fool. How he talked—so glib, so pat, so well."

"A smart fool always talks well; takes a smart fool to be tonguey."

In much the same strain the discussion continued—the hook-nosed gentleman talking at large and excellently, with a view of demonstrating that a smart fool always talks just so. Ere long he talked to such purpose as almost to convince.

Presently, back came the person of whom the auburn-haired gentleman had predicted that he would not return. Conspicuous in the door-way he stood, saying, in a clear voice, "Is the agent of the Seminole Widow and Orphan Asylum within here?"

No one replied.

"Is there within here any agent or any member of any charitable institution whatever?"

No one seemed competent to answer, or, no one thought it worth while to.

"If there be within here any such person, I have in my hand two dollars for him."

Some interest was manifested.

"I was called away so hurriedly, I forgot this part of my duty. With the proprietor of the Samaritan Pain Dissuader it is a rule, to devote, on the spot, to some benevolent purpose, the half of the proceeds of sales. Eight bottles were disposed of among this company. Hence, four half-dollars remain to charity. Who, as steward, takes the money?"

One or two pair of feet moved upon the floor, as with a sort of itching; but nobody rose.

"Does diffidence prevail over duty? If, I say, there be any gentleman, or any lady, either, here present, who is in any connection with any charitable institution whatever, let him or her come forward. He or she happening to have at hand no certificate of such connection, makes no difference. Not of a suspicious temper, thank God, I shall have confidence in whoever offers to take the money."

A demure-looking woman, in a dress rather tawdry and rumpled, here drew her veil well down and rose; but, marking every eye upon her, thought it advisable, upon the whole, to sit down again.

"Is it to be believed that, in this Christian company, there is no one charitable person? I mean, no one connected with any charity? Well, then, is there no object of charity here?"

Upon this, an unhappy-looking woman, in a sort of mourning,

neat, but sadly worn, hid her face behind a meagre bundle, and was heard to sob. Meantime, as not seeing or hearing her, the herb-doctor again spoke, and this time not unpathetically:

"Are there none here who feel in need of help, and who, in accepting such help, would feel that they, in their time, have given or done more than may ever be given or done to them? Man or woman, is there none such here?"

The sobs of the woman were more audible, though she strove to repress them. While nearly every one's attention was bent upon her, a man of the appearance of a day-laborer, with a white bandage across his face, concealing the side of the nose, and who, for coolness' sake, had been sitting in his red-flannel shirt-sleeves, his coat thrown across one shoulder, the darned cuffs drooping behind—this man shufflingly rose, and, with a pace that seemed the lingering memento of the lock-step of convicts, went up for a duly-qualified claim.

"Poor wounded hussar!" sighed the herb-doctor, and dropping the money into the man's clam-shell of a hand turned and departed.

The recipient of the alms was about moving after, when the auburn-haired gentleman staid him: "Don't be frightened, you; but I want to see those coins. Yes, yes; good silver, good silver. There, take them again, and while you are about it, go bandage the rest of yourself behind something. D'ye hear? Consider yourself, wholly, the scar of a nose, and be off with yourself."

Being of a forgiving nature, or else from emotion not daring to trust his voice, the man silently, but not without some precipitancy, withdrew.

"Strange," said the auburn-haired gentleman, returning to his friend, "the money was good money."

"Aye, and where your fine knavery now? Knavery to devote the half of one's receipts to charity? He's a fool I say again."

"Others might call him an original genius."

"Yes, being original in his folly. Genius? His genius is a cracked pate, and, as this age goes, not much originality about that."

"May he not be knave, fool, and genius altogether?"

"I beg pardon," here said a third person with a gossiping expres-

You look up now. Give me your story. Ere I undertake a cure, I require a full account of the case."

"You can't help me," returned the cripple gruffly. "Go away."

"You seem sadly destitute of—"

"No I ain't destitute; to-day, at least, I can pay my way."

"The Natural Bone-setter is happy, indeed, to hear that. But you were premature. I was deploring your destitution, not of cash, but of confidence. You think the Natural Bone-setter can't help you. Well, suppose he can't, have you any objection to telling him your story? You, my friend, have, in a signal way, experienced adversity. Tell me, then, for my private good, how, without aid from the noble cripple, Epictetus, you have arrived at his heroic *sang-froid* in misfortune."

At these words the cripple fixed upon the speaker the hard ironic eye of one toughened and defiant in misery, and, in the end, grinned upon him with his unshaven face like an ogre.

"Come, come, be sociable—be human, my friend. Don't make that face; it distresses me."

"I suppose," with a sneer, "you are the man I've long heard of— The Happy Man."

"Happy? my friend. Yes, at least I ought to be. My conscience is peaceful. I have confidence in everybody. I have confidence that, in my humble profession, I do some little good to the world. Yes, I think that, without presumption, I may venture to assent to the proposition that I am the Happy Man—the Happy Bone-setter."

"Then you shall hear my story. Many a month I have longed to get hold of the Happy Man, drill him, drop the powder, and leave him to explode at his leisure."

"What a demoniac unfortunate," exclaimed the herb-doctor retreating. "Regular infernal machine!"

"Look ye," cried the other, stumping after him, and with his horny hand catching him by a horn button, "my name is Thomas Fry. Until my—"

—"Any relation of Mrs. Fry?" interrupted the other. "I still correspond with that excellent lady on the subject of prisons. Tell me, are you anyway connected with *my* Mrs. Fry?"

"Blister Mrs. Fry! What do them sentimental souls know of prisons or any other black fact? I'll tell ye a story of prisons. Ha, ha!"

The herb-doctor shrank, and with reason, the laugh being strangely startling.

"Positively, my friend," said he, "you must stop that; I can't stand that; no more of that. I hope I have the milk of kindness, but your thunder will soon turn it."

"Hold, I haven't come to the milk-turning part yet. My name is Thomas Fry. Until my twenty-third year I went by the nickname of Happy Tom—happy—ha, ha! They called me Happy Tom, d'ye see? because I was so good-natured and laughing all the time, just as I am now—ha, ha!"

Upon this the herb-doctor would, perhaps, have run, but once more the hyæna clawed him. Presently, sobering down, he continued:

"Well, I was born in New York, and there I lived a steady, hard-working man, a cooper by trade. One evening I went to a political meeting in the Park—for you must know, I was in those days a great patriot. As bad luck would have it, there was trouble near, between a gentleman who had been drinking wine, and a pavior who was sober. The pavior chewed tobacco, and the gentleman said it was beastly in him, and pushed him, wanting to have his place. The pavior chewed on and pushed back. Well, the gentleman carried a sword-cane, and presently the pavior was down—skewered."

"How was that?"

"Why you see the pavior undertook something above his strength."

"The other must have been a Samson then. 'Strong as a pavior,' is a proverb."

"So it is, and the gentleman was in body a rather weakly man, but, for all that, I say again, the pavior undertook something above his strength."

"What are you talking about? He tried to maintain his rights, didn't he?"

"Yes; but, for all that, I say again, he undertook something above his strength."

"I don't understand you. But go on."

"Along with the gentleman, I, with other witnesses, was taken to the Tombs. There was an examination, and, to appear at the trial, the gentleman and witnesses all gave bail—I mean all but me."

"And why didn't you?"

"Couldn't get it."

"Steady, hard-working cooper like you; what was the reason you couldn't get bail?"

"Steady, hard-working cooper hadn't no friends. Well, souse I went into a wet cell, like a canal-boat splashing into the lock; locked up in pickle, d'ye see? against the time of the trial."

"But what had you done?"

"Why, I hadn't got any friends, I tell ye. A worse crime than murder, as ye'll see afore long."

"Murder? Did the wounded man die?"

"Died the third night."

"Then the gentleman's bail didn't help him. Imprisoned now, wasn't he?"

"Had too many friends. No, it was *I* that was imprisoned.—But I was going on: They let me walk about the corridor by day; but at night I must into lock. There the wet and the damp struck into my bones. They doctored me, but no use. When the trial came, I was boosted up and said my say."

"And what was that?"

"My say was that I saw the steel go in, and saw it sticking in."

"And that hung the gentleman."

"Hung him with a gold chain! His friends called a meeting in the Park, and presented him with a gold watch and chain upon his acquittal."

"Acquittal?"

"Didn't I say he had friends?"

There was a pause, broken at last by the herb-doctor's saying: "Well, there is a bright side to everything. If this speak prosaically for justice, it speaks romantically for friendship! But go on, my fine fellow."

"My say being said, they told me I might go. I said I could not without help. So the constables helped me, asking *where* would I go? I told them back to the 'Tombs.' I knew no other place. 'But where are your friends?' said they. 'I have none.' So they put me into a hand-barrow with an awning to it, and wheeled me down to the dock and on board a boat, and away to Blackwell's Island to the Corporation Hospital. There I got worse—got pretty much as you see me now. Couldn't cure me. After three years, I grew sick of lying in a grated iron bed alongside of groaning thieves and moul-dering burglars. They gave me five silver dollars, and these crutches, and I hobbled off. I had an only brother who went to Indiana, years ago. I begged about, to make up a sum to go to him; got to Indiana at last, and they directed me to his grave. It was on a great plain, in a log-church yard with a stump fence, the old gray roots sticking all ways like moose-antlers. The bier, set over the grave, it being the last dug, was of green hickory; bark on, and green twigs sprouting from it. Some one had planted a bunch of violets on the mound, but it was a poor soil (always choose the poorest soils for grave-yards), and they were all dried to tinder. I was going to sit and rest myself on the bier and think about my brother in heaven, but the bier broke down, the legs being only tacked. So, after driving some hogs out of the yard that were root-ing there, I came away, and, not to make too long a story of it, here I am, drifting down stream like any other bit of wreck."

The herb-doctor was silent for a time, buried in thought. At last, raising his head, he said: "I have considered your whole story, my friend, and strove to consider it in the light of a commentary on what I believe to be the system of things; but it so jars with all, is so incompatible with all, that you must pardon me, if I honestly tell you, I cannot believe it."

"That don't surprise me."

"How?"

"Hardly anybody believes my story, and so to most I tell a dif-ferent one."

"How, again?"

"Wait here a bit and I'll show ye."

With that, taking off his rag of a cap, and arranging his tattered regimentals the best he could, off he went stumping among the passengers in an adjoining part of the deck, saying with a jovial kind of air: "Sir, a shilling for Happy Tom, who fought at Buena Vista. Lady, something for General Scott's soldier, crippled in both pins at glorious Contreras."

Now, it so chanced that, unbeknown to the cripple, a prim-looking stranger had overheard part of his story. Beholding him, then, on his present begging adventure, this person, turning to the herb-doctor, indignantly said: "Is it not too bad, sir, that yonder rascal should lie so?"

"Charity never faileth, my good sir," was the reply. "The vice of this unfortunate is pardonable. Consider, he lies not out of wantonness."

"Not out of wantonness. I never heard more wanton lies. In one breath to tell you what would appear to be his true story, and, in the next, away and falsify it."

"For all that, I repeat he lies not out of wantonness. A ripe philosopher, turned out of the great Sorbonne of hard times, he thinks that woes, when told to strangers for money, are best sugared. Though the inglorious lock-jaw of his knee-pans in a wet dungeon is a far more pitiable ill than to have been crippled at glorious Contreras, yet he is of opinion that this lighter and false ill shall attract, while the heavier and real one might repel."

"Nonsense; he belongs to the Devil's regiment; and I have a great mind to expose him."

"Shame upon you. Dare to expose that poor unfortunate, and by heaven—don't you do it, sir."

Noting something in his manner, the other thought it more prudent to retire than retort. By-and-by, the cripple came back, and with glee, having reaped a pretty good harvest.

"There," he laughed, "you know now what sort of soldier I am."

"Aye, one that fights not the stupid Mexican, but a foe worthy your tactics—Fortune!"

"Hi, hi!" clamored the cripple, like a fellow in the pit of a six-penny theatre, then said, "don't know much what you meant, but it went off well."

This over, his countenance capriciously put on a morose ogreness. To kindly questions he gave no kindly answers. Unhandsome notions were thrown out about "free Ameriky," as he sarcastically called his country. These seemed to disturb and pain the herb-doctor, who, after an interval of thoughtfulness, gravely addressed him in these words:

"You, my worthy friend, to my concern, have reflected upon the government under which you live and suffer. Where is your patriotism? Where is your gratitude? True, the charitable may find something in your case, as you put it, partly to account for such reflections as coming from you. Still, be the facts how they may, your reflections are none the less unwarrantable. Grant, for the moment, that your experiences are as you give them; in which case I would admit that government might be thought to have more or less to do with what seems undesirable in them. But it is never to be forgotten that human government, being subordinate to the divine, must needs, therefore, in its degree, partake of the characteristics of the divine. That is, while in general efficacious to happiness, the world's law may yet, in some cases, have, to the eye of reason, an unequal operation, just as, in the same imperfect view, some inequalities may appear in the operations of heaven's law; nevertheless, to one who has a right confidence, final benignity is, in every instance, as sure with the one law as the other. I expound the point at some length, because these are the considerations, my poor fellow, which, weighed as they merit, will enable you to sustain with unimpaired trust the apparent calamities which are yours."

"What do you talk your hog-latin to me for?" cried the cripple, who, throughout the address, betrayed the most illiterate obduracy; and, with an incensed look, anew he swung himself.

Glancing another way till the spasm passed, the other continued:

"Charity marvels not that you should be somewhat hard of conviction, my friend, since you, doubtless, believe yourself hardly dealt by; but forget not that those who are loved are chastened."

"Mustn't chasten them too much, though, and too long, because their skin and heart get hard, and feel neither pain nor tickle."

"To mere reason, your case looks something piteous, I grant. But never despond; many things—the choicest—yet remain. You breathe this bounteous air, are warmed by this gracious sun, and, though poor and friendless, indeed, nor so agile as in your youth, yet, how sweet to roam, day by day, through the groves, plucking the bright mosses and flowers, till forlornness itself becomes a hilarity, and, in your innocent independence, you skip for joy."

"Fine skipping with these 'ere horse-posts—ha, ha!"

"Pardon; I forgot the crutches. My mind, figuring you after receiving the benefit of my art, overlooked you as you stand before me."

"Your art? You call yourself a bone-setter—a natural bone-setter, do ye? Go, bone-set the crooked world, and then come bone-set crooked me."

"Truly, my honest friend, I thank you for again recalling me to my original object. Let me examine you," bending down; "ah, I see, I see; much such a case as the negro's. Did you see him? Oh no, you came aboard since. Well, his case was a little something like yours. I prescribed for him, and I shouldn't wonder at all if, in a very short time, he were able to walk almost as well as myself. Now, have you no confidence in my art?"

"Ha, ha!"

The herb-doctor averted himself; but, the wild laugh dying away, resumed:

"I will not force confidence on you. Still, I would fain do the friendly thing by you. Here, take this box; just rub that liniment on the joints night and morning. Take it. Nothing to pay. God bless you. Good-bye."

"Stay," pausing in his swing, not untouched by so unexpected an act; "stay—thank'ee—but will this really do me good? Honor bright, now; will it? Don't deceive a poor fellow," with changed mien and glistening eye.

"Try it. Good-bye."

"Stay stay! *Sure* it will do me good?"

"Possibly, possibly; no harm in trying. Good-bye."

"Stay, stay; give me three more boxes, and here's the money."

"My friend," returning towards him with a sadly pleased sort of air, "I rejoice in the birth of your confidence and hopefulness. Believe me that, like your crutches, confidence and hopefulness will long support a man when his own legs will not. Stick to confidence and hopefulness, then, since how mad for the cripple to throw his crutches away. You ask for three more boxes of my liniment. Luckily, I have just that number remaining. Here they are. I sell them at half-a-dollar apiece. But I shall take nothing from you. There; God bless you again; good-bye."

"Stay," in a convulsed voice, and rocking himself, "stay, stay! You have made a better man of me. You have borne with me like a good Christian, and talked to me like one, and all that is enough without making me a present of these boxes. Here is the money. I won't take nay. There, there; and may Almighty goodness go with you."

As the herb-doctor withdrew, the cripple gradually subsided from his hard rocking into a gentle oscillation. It expressed, perhaps, the soothed mood of his reverie.

Chapter 20 REAPPEARANCE *of One Who May Be Remembered* ૐ

The herb-doctor had not moved far away, when, in advance of him, this spectacle met his eye. A dried-up old man, with the stature of a boy of twelve, was tottering about like one out of his mind, in rumpled clothes of old moleskin, showing recent contact with bedding, his ferret eyes, blinking in the sunlight of the snowy boat, as imbecilely eager, and, at intervals, coughing, he peered hither and thither as if in alarmed search for his nurse. He presented the aspect of one who, bed-rid, has, through overruling excitement, like that of a fire, been stimulated to his feet.

"You seek some one," said the herb-doctor, accosting him. "Can I assist you?"

"Do, do; I am so old and miserable," coughed the old man. "Where is he? This long time I've been trying to get up and find him. But I haven't any friends, and couldn't get up till now. Where is he?"

"Who do you mean?" drawing closer, to stay the further wanderings of one so weakly.

"Why, why, why," now marking the other's dress, "why you, yes, you—you, you—ugh, ugh, ugh!"

"I?"

"Ugh, ugh, ugh!—you are the man he spoke of. Who is he?"

"Faith, that is just what I want to know."

"Mercy, mercy!" coughed the old man, bewildered, "ever since seeing him, my head spins round so. I ought to have a guardeean. Is this a snuff-colored surtout of yours, or ain't it? Somehow, can't trust my senses any more, since trusting him—ugh, ugh, ugh!"

"Oh, you have trusted somebody? Glad to hear it. Glad to hear of any instance of that sort. Reflects well upon all men. But you inquire whether this is a snuff-colored surtout. I answer it is; and will add that a herb-doctor wears it."

Upon this the old man, in his broken way, replied that then he (the herb-doctor) was the person he sought—the person spoken of by the other person as yet unknown. He then, with flighty

107

eagerness, wanted to know who this last person was, and where he was, and whether he could be trusted with money to treble it.

"Aye, now, I begin to understand; ten to one you mean my worthy friend, who, in pure goodness of heart, makes people's fortunes for them—their everlasting fortunes, as the phrase goes —only charging his one small commission of confidence. Aye, aye; before intrusting funds with my friend, you want to know about him. Very proper—and, I am glad to assure you, you need have no hesitation; none, none, just none in the world; *bona fide,* none. Turned me in a trice a hundred dollars the other day into as many eagles."

"Did he? did he? But where is he? Take me to him."

"Pray, take my arm! The boat is large! We may have something of a hunt! Come on! Ah, is that he?"

"Where? where?"

"Oh, no; I took yonder coat-skirts for his. But no, my honest friend would never turn tail that way. Ah!—"

"Where? where?"

"Another mistake. Surprising resemblance. I took yonder clergyman for him. Come on!"

Having searched that part of the boat without success, they went to another part, and, while exploring that, the boat sided up to a landing, when, as the two were passing by the open guard, the herbdoctor suddenly rushed towards the disembarking throng, crying out: "Mr. Truman, Mr. Truman! There he goes—that's he. Mr. Truman, Mr. Truman!—Confound that steam-pipe. Mr. Truman! for God's sake, Mr. Truman!—No, no.—There, the plank's in—too late—we're off."

With that, the huge boat, with a mighty, walrus wallow, rolled away from the shore, resuming her course.

"How vexatious!" exclaimed the herb-doctor, returning. "Had we been but one single moment sooner.—There he goes, now, towards yon hotel, his portmanteau following. You see him, don't you?"

"Where? where?"

"Can't see him any more. Wheel-house shot between. I am very sorry. I should have so liked you to have let him have a hundred or so of your money. You would have been pleased with the investment, believe me."

"Oh, I *have* let him have some of my money," groaned the old man.

"You have? My dear sir," seizing both the miser's hands in both his own and heartily shaking them. "My dear sir, how I congratulate you. You don't know."

"Ugh, ugh! I fear I don't," with another groan. "His name is Truman, is it?"

"John Truman."

"Where does he live?"

"In St. Louis."

"Where's his office?"

"Let me see. Jones street, number one hundred and—no, no—anyway, it's somewhere or other up-stairs in Jones street."

"Can't you remember the number? Try, now."

"One hundred—two hundred—three hundred—"

"Oh, my hundred dollars! I wonder whether it will be one hundred, two hundred, three hundred, with them! Ugh, ugh! Can't remember the number?"

"Positively, though I once knew, I have forgotten, quite forgotten it. Strange. But never mind. You will easily learn in St. Louis. He is well known there."

"But I have no receipt—ugh, ugh! Nothing to show—don't know where I stand—ought to have a guardeean—ugh, ugh! Don't know anything. Ugh, ugh!"

"Why, you know that you gave him your confidence, don't you?"

"Oh, yes."

"Well, then?"

"But what, what—how, how—ugh, ugh!"

"Why, didn't he tell you?"

"No."

"What! Didn't he tell you that it was a secret, a mystery?"

"Oh—yes."

"Well, then?"

"But I have no bond."

"Don't need any with Mr. Truman. Mr. Truman's word is his bond."

"But how am I to get my profits—ugh, ugh!—and my money back? Don't know anything. Ugh, ugh!"

"Oh, you must have confidence."

"Don't say that word again. Makes my head spin so. Oh, I'm so old and miserable, nobody caring for me, everybody fleecing me, and my head spins so—ugh, ugh!—and this cough racks me so. I say again, I ought to have a guard*ee*an."

"So you ought; and Mr. Truman is your guardian to the extent you invested with him. Sorry we missed him just now. But you'll hear from him. All right. It's imprudent, though, to expose yourself this way. Let me take you to your berth."

Forlornly enough the old miser moved slowly away with him. But, while descending a stairway, he was seized with such coughing that he was fain to pause.

"That is a very bad cough."

"Church-yard—ugh, ugh!—church-yard cough.—Ugh!"

"Have you tried anything for it?"

"Tired of trying. Nothing does me any good—ugh! ugh! Not even the Mammoth Cave. Ugh! ugh! Denned there six months, but coughed so bad the rest of the coughers—ugh! ugh!—black-balled me out. Ugh, ugh! Nothing does me good."

"But have you tried the Omni-Balsamic Reinvigorator, sir?"

"That's what that Truman—ugh, ugh!—said I ought to take. Yarb-medicine; you are that yarb-doctor, too?"

"The same. Suppose you try one of my boxes now. Trust me, from what I know of Mr. Truman, he is not the gentleman to recommend, even in behalf of a friend, anything of whose excellence he is not conscientiously satisfied."

"Ugh!—how much?"

"Only two dollars a box."

"Two dollars? Why don't you say two millions? ugh, ugh! Two dollars, that's two hundred cents; that's eight hundred farthings; that's two thousand mills; and all for one little box of yarb-medicine. My head, my head!—oh, I ought to have a guardeean for my head. Ugh, ugh, ugh, ugh!"

"Well, if two dollars a box seems too much, take a dozen boxes at twenty dollars; and that will be getting four boxes for nothing, and you need use none but those four, the rest you can retail out at a premium, and so cure your cough, and make money by it. Come, you had better do it. Cash down. Can fill an order in a day or two. Here now," producing a box; "pure herbs."

At that moment, seized with another spasm, the miser snatched each interval to fix his half distrustful, half hopeful eye upon the medicine, held alluringly up. "Sure—ugh! Sure it's all nat'ral? Nothing but yarbs? If I only thought it was a purely nat'ral medicine now—all yarbs—ugh, ugh!—oh this cough, this cough—ugh, ugh! —shatters my whole body. Ugh, ugh, ugh!"

"For heaven's sake try my medicine, if but a single box. That it is pure nature you may be confident. Refer you to Mr. Truman."

"Don't know his number—ugh, ugh, ugh, ugh! Oh this cough. He did speak well of this medicine though; said solemnly it would cure me—ugh, ugh, ugh, ugh!—take off a dollar and I'll have a box."

"Can't sir, can't."

"Say a dollar-and-half. Ugh!"

"Can't. Am pledged to the one-price system, only honorable one."

"Take off a shilling—ugh, ugh!"

"Can't."

"Ugh, ugh, ugh—I'll take it. There."

Grudgingly he handed eight silver coins, but while still in his hand, his cough took him, and they were shaken upon the deck.

One by one, the herb-doctor picked them up, and, examining them, said: "These are not quarters, these are pistareens; and clipped, and sweated, at that."

"Oh don't be so miserly—ugh, ugh!—better a beast than a miser —ugh, ugh!"

"Well, let it go. Anything rather than the idea of your not being cured of such a cough. And I hope, for the credit of humanity, you have not made it appear worse than it is, merely with a view to working upon the weak point of my pity, and so getting my medicine the cheaper. Now, mind, don't take it till night. Just before retiring is the time. There, you can get along now, can't you? I would attend you further, but I land presently, and must go hunt up my luggage."

Chapter 21 A HARD CASE ❧

"Yarbs, yarbs; natur, natur; you foolish old file you! He diddled you with that hocus-pocus, did he? Yarbs and natur will cure your incurable cough, you think."

It was a rather eccentric-looking person who spoke; somewhat ursine in aspect; sporting a shaggy spencer of the cloth called bear's-skin; a high-peaked cap of raccoon-skin, the long bushy tail switching over behind; raw-hide leggings; grim stubble chin; and to end, a double-barreled gun in hand—a Missouri bachelor, a Hoosier gentleman, of Spartan leisure and fortune, and equally Spartan manners and sentiments; and, as the sequel may show, not less acquainted, in a Spartan way of his own, with philosophy and books, than with woodcraft and rifles.

He must have overheard some of the talk between the miser and the herb-doctor; for, just after the withdrawal of the one, he made up to the other—now at the foot of the stairs leaning against the baluster there—with the greeting above.

"Think it will cure me?" coughed the miser in echo; "why shouldn't it? The medicine is nat'ral yarbs, pure yarbs; yarbs must cure me."

"Because a thing is nat'ral, as you call it, you think it must be good. But who gave you that cough? Was it, or was it not, nature?"

"Sure, you don't think that natur, Dame Natur, will hurt a body, do you?"

"Natur is good Queen Bess; but who's responsible for the cholera?"

"But yarbs, yarbs; yarbs are good?"

"What's deadly-nightshade? Yarb, ain't it"

"Oh, that a Christian man should speak agin natur and yarbs— ugh, ugh, ugh!—ain't sick men sent out into the country; sent out to natur and grass?"

"Aye, and poets send out the sick spirit to green pastures, like lame horses turned out unshod to the turf to renew their hoofs. A sort of yarb-doctors in their way, poets have it that for sore hearts, as for sore lungs, nature is the grand cure. But who froze to death my teamster on the prairie? And who made an idiot of Peter the Wild Boy?"

"Then you don't believe in these 'ere yarb-doctors?"

"Yarb-doctors? I remember the lank yarb-doctor I saw once on a hospital-cot in Mobile. One of the faculty passing round and seeing who lay there, said with professional triumph, "Ah, Dr. Green, your yarbs don't help ye now, Dr. Green. Have to come to us and the mercury now, Dr. Green.—Natur! Y-a-r-b-s!"

"Did I hear something about herbs and herb-doctors?" here said a flute-like voice, advancing.

It was the herb-doctor in person. Carpet-bag in hand, he happened to be strolling back that way.

"Pardon me," addressing the Missourian, "but if I caught your words aright, you would seem to have little confidence in nature; which, really, in my way of thinking, looks like carrying the spirit of distrust pretty far."

"And who of my sublime species may you be?" turning short round upon him, clicking his rifle-lock, with an air which would have seemed half cynic, half wild-cat, were it not for the grotesque excess of the expression, which made its sincerity appear more or less dubious.

"One who has confidence in nature, and confidence in man, with some little modest confidence in himself."

"That's your Confession of Faith, is it? Confidence in man, eh? Pray, which do you think are most, knaves or fools?"

"Having met with few or none of either, I hardly think I am competent to answer."

"I will answer for you. Fools are most."

"Why do you think so?"

"For the same reason that I think oats are numerically more than horses. Don't knaves munch up fools just as horses do oats?"

"A droll, sir; you are a droll. I can appreciate drollery—ha, ha, ha!"

"But I'm in earnest."

"That's the drollery, to deliver droll extravagance with an earnest air—knaves munching up fools as horses oats.—Faith, very droll, indeed, ha, ha, ha! Yes, I think I understand you now, sir. How silly I was to have taken you seriously, in your droll conceits, too, about having no confidence in nature. In reality you have just as much as I have."

"*I* have confidence in nature? *I?* I say again there is nothing I am more suspicious of. I once lost ten thousand dollars by nature. Nature embezzled that amount from me; absconded with ten thousand dollars' worth of my property; a plantation on this stream, swept clean away by one of those sudden shiftings of the banks in a freshet; ten thousand dollars' worth of alluvion thrown broad off upon the waters."

"But have you no confidence that by a reverse shifting that soil will come back after many days?—ah, here is my venerable friend," observing the old miser, "not in your berth yet? Pray, if you *will* keep afoot, don't lean against that baluster; take my arm."

It was taken; and the two stood together; the old miser leaning against the herb-doctor with something of that air of trustful fraternity with which, when standing, the less strong of the Siamese twins habitually leans against the other.

The Missourian eyed them in silence, which was broken by the herb-doctor.

"You look surprised, sir. Is it because I publicly take under my protection a figure like this? But I am never ashamed of honesty, whatever his coat."

"Look you," said the Missourian, after a scrutinizing pause, "you are a queer sort of chap. Don't know exactly what to make of you. Upon the whole though, you somewhat remind me of the last boy I had on my place."

"Good, trustworthy boy, I hope?"

"Oh, very! I am now started to get me made some kind of machine to do the sort of work which boys are supposed to be fitted for."

"Then you have passed a veto upon boys?"

"And men, too."

"But, my dear sir, does not that again imply more or less lack of confidence?—(Stand up a little, just a very little, my venerable friend; you lean rather hard.)—No confidence in boys, no confidence in men, no confidence in nature. Pray, sir, who or what may you have confidence in?"

"I have confidence in distrust; more particularly as applied to you and your herbs."

"Well," with a forbearing smile, "that is frank. But pray, don't forget that when you suspect my herbs you suspect nature."

"Didn't I say that before?"

"Very good. For the argument's sake I will suppose you are in earnest. Now, can you, who suspect nature, deny, that this same nature not only kindly brought you into being, but has faithfully nursed you to your present vigorous and independent condition? Is it not to nature that you are indebted for that robustness of mind which you so unhandsomely use to her scandal? Pray, is it not to nature that you owe the very eyes by which you criticise her?"

"No! for the privilege of vision I am indebted to an oculist, who in my tenth year operated upon me in Philadelphia. Nature made me blind and would have kept me so. My oculist counterplotted her."

"And yet, sir, by your complexion, I judge you live an out-of-door life; without knowing it, you are partial to nature; you fly to nature, the universal mother."

"Very motherly! Sir, in the passion-fits of nature, I've known birds fly from nature to me, rough as I look; yes, sir, in a tempest, refuge here," smiting the folds of his bearskin. "Fact, sir, fact. Come, come, Mr. Palaverer, for all your palavering, did you yourself never shut out nature of a cold, wet night? Bar her out? Bolt her out? Lint her out?"

"As to that," said the herb-doctor calmly, "much may be said."

"Say it, then," ruffling all his hairs. "You can't, sir, can't." Then, as in apostrophe: "Look you, nature! I don't deny but your clover is sweet, and your dandelions don't roar; but whose hailstones smashed my windows?"

"Sir," with unimpaired affability, producing one of his boxes, "I am pained to meet with one who holds nature a dangerous character. Though your manner is refined your voice is rough; in short, you seem to have a sore throat. In the calumniated name of nature, I present you with this box; my venerable friend here has a similar one; but to you, a free gift, sir. Through her regularly-authorized agents, of whom I happen to be one, Nature delights in benefiting those who most abuse her. Pray, take it."

"Away with it! Don't hold it so near. Ten to one there is a torpedo in it. Such things have been. Editors been killed that way. Take it further off, I say."

"Good heavens! my dear sir—"

"I tell you I want none of your boxes," snapping his rifle.

"Oh, take it—ugh, ugh! do take it," chimed in the old miser; "I wish he would give me one for nothing."

"You find it lonely, eh," turning short round; "gulled yourself, you would have a companion."

"How can he find it lonely," returned the herb-doctor, "or how desire a companion, when here I stand by him; I, even I, in whom he has trust. For the gulling, tell me, is it humane to talk so to this poor old man? Granting that his dependence on my medicine is vain, is it kind to deprive him of what, in mere imagination, if nothing more, may help eke out, with hope, his disease? For you, if you have no confidence, and, thanks to your native health, can get along without it, so far, at least, as trusting in my medicine goes; yet, how cruel an argument to use, with this afflicted one here. Is it not for all the world as if some brawny pugilist, aglow in December, should rush in and put out a hospital-fire, because, forsooth, he feeling no need of artificial heat, the shivering patients shall have none? Put it to your conscience, sir, and you will admit, that, whatever be the nature of this afflicted one's trust, you, in opposing it, evince either an erring head or a heart amiss. Come, own, are you not pitiless?"

"Yes, poor soul," said the Missourian, gravely eying the old man —"yes, it *is* pitiless in one like me to speak too honestly to one like you. You are a late sitter-up in this life; past man's usual bed-time;

and truth, though with some it makes a wholesome breakfast, proves to all a supper too hearty. Hearty food, taken late, gives bad dreams."

"What, in wonder's name—ugh, ugh!—is he talking about?" asked the old miser, looking up to the herb-doctor.

"Heaven be praised for that!" cried the Missourian.

"Out of his mind, ain't he?" again appealed the old miser.

"Pray, sir," said the herb-doctor to the Missourian, "for what were you giving thanks just now?"

"For this: that, with some minds, truth is, in effect, not so cruel a thing after all, seeing that, like a loaded pistol found by poor devils of savages, it raises more wonder than terror—its peculiar virtue being unguessed, unless, indeed, by indiscreet handling, it should happen to go off of itself."

"I pretend not to divine your meaning there," said the herb-doctor, after a pause, during which he eyed the Missourian with a kind of pinched expression, mixed of pain and curiosity, as if he grieved at his state of mind, and, at the same time, wondered what had brought him to it, "but this much I know," he added, "that the general cast of your thoughts is, to say the least, unfortunate. There is strength in them, but a strength, whose source, being physical, must wither. You will yet recant."

"Recant?"

"Yes, when, as with this old man, your evil days of decay come on, when a hoary captive in your chamber, then will you, something like the dungeoned Italian we read of, gladly seek the breast of that confidence begot in the tender time of your youth, blessed beyond telling if it return to you in age."

"Go back to nurse again, eh? Second childhood, indeed. You are soft."

"Mercy, mercy!" cried the old miser, "what is all this!—ugh, ugh! Do talk sense, my good friends. Ain't you," to the Missourian, "going to buy some of that medicine?"

"Pray, my venerable friend," said the herb-doctor, now trying to straighten himself, "don't lean *quite* so hard; my arm grows numb; abate a little, just a very little."

"Go," said the Missourian, "go lay down in your grave, old man, if you can't stand of yourself. It's a hard world for a leaner."

"As to his grave," said the herb-doctor, "that is far enough off, so he but faithfully take my medicine."

"Ugh, ugh, ugh!—He says true. No, I ain't—ugh! a going to die yet—ugh, ugh, ugh! Many years to live yet, ugh, ugh, ugh!"

"I approve your confidence," said the herb-doctor; "but your coughing distresses me, besides being injurious to you. Pray, let me conduct you to your berth. You are best there. Our friend here will wait till my return, I know."

With which he led the old miser away, and then, coming back, the talk with the Missourian was resumed.

"Sir," said the herb-doctor, with some dignity and more feeling, "now that our infirm friend is withdrawn, allow me, to the full, to express my concern at the words you allowed to escape you in his hearing. Some of those words, if I err not, besides being calculated to beget deplorable distrust in the patient, seemed fitted to convey unpleasant imputations against me, his physician."

"Suppose they did?" with a menacing air.

"Why, then—then, indeed," respectfully retreating, "I fall back upon my previous theory of your general facetiousness. I have the fortune to be in company with a humorist—a wag."

"Fall back you had better, and wag it is," cried the Missourian, following him up, and wagging his raccoon tail almost into the herb-doctor's face, "look you!"

"At what?"

"At this coon. Can you, the fox, catch him?"

"If you mean," returned the other, not unselfpossessed, "whether I flatter myself that I can in any way dupe you, or impose upon you, or pass myself off upon you for what I am not, I, as an honest man, answer that I have neither the inclination nor the power to do aught of the kind."

"Honest man? Seems to me you talk more like a craven."

"You in vain seek to pick a quarrel with me, or put any affront upon me. The innocence in me heals me."

"A healing like your own nostrums. But you are a queer man—

a very queer and dubious man; upon the whole, about the most so I ever met."

The scrutiny accompanying this seemed unwelcome to the diffidence of the herb-doctor. As if at once to attest the absence of resentment, as well as to change the subject, he threw a kind of familiar cordiality into his air, and said: "So you are going to get some machine made to do your work? Philanthropic scruples, doubtless, forbid your going as far as New Orleans for slaves?"

"Slaves?" morose again in a twinkling, "won't have 'em! Bad enough to see whites ducking and grinning round for a favor, without having those poor devils of niggers congeeing round for their corn. Though, to me, the niggers are the freer of the two. You are an abolitionist, ain't you?" he added, squaring himself with both hands on his rifle, used for a staff, and gazing in the herb-doctor's face with no more reverence than if it were a target. "You are an abolitionist, ain't you?"

"As to that, I cannot so readily answer. If by abolitionist you mean a zealot, I am none; but if you mean a man, who, being a man, feels for all men, slaves included, and by any lawful act, opposed to nobody's interest, and therefore, rousing nobody's enmity, would willingly abolish suffering (supposing it, in its degree, to exist) from among mankind, irrespective of color, then am I what you say."

"Picked and prudent sentiments. You are the moderate man, the invaluable understrapper of the wicked man. You, the moderate man, may be used for wrong, but are useless for right."

"From all this," said the herb-doctor, still forgivingly, "I infer, that you, a Missourian, though living in a slave-state, are without slave sentiments."

"Aye, but are you? Is not that air of yours, so spiritlessly enduring and yielding, the very air of a slave? Who is your master, pray; or are you owned by a company?"

"*My* master?"

"Aye, for come from Maine or Georgia, you come from a slave-state, and a slave-pen, where the best breeds are to be bought up at any price from a livelihood to the Presidency. Abolitionism, ye gods, but expresses the fellow-feeling of slave for slave."

"The back-woods would seem to have given you rather eccentric notions," now with polite superiority smiled the herb-doctor, still with manly intrepidity forbearing each unmanly thrust, "but to return; since, for your purpose, you will have neither man nor boy, bond nor free, truly, then some sort of machine for you is all there is left. My desires for your success attend you, sir.—Ah!" glancing shoreward, "here is Cape Giradeau; I must leave you."

" 'PHILOSOPHICAL INTELLIGENCE OFFICE'—novel idea! But how did you come to dream that I wanted anything in your absurd line, eh?"

About twenty minutes after leaving Cape Giradeau, the above was growled out over his shoulder by the Missourian to a chance stranger who had just accosted him; a round-backed, baker-kneed man, in a mean five-dollar suit, wearing, collar-wise by a chain, a small brass plate, inscribed P. I. O., and who, with a sort of canine deprecation, slunk obliquely behind.

"How did you come to dream that I wanted anything in your line, eh?"

"Oh, respected sir," whined the other, crouching a pace nearer, and, in his obsequiousness, seeming to wag his very coat-tails behind him, shabby though they were, "oh, sir, from long experience, one glance tells me the gentleman who is in need of our humble services."

"But suppose I did want a boy—what they jocosely call a good boy—how could your absurd office help me?—Philosophical Intelligence Office?"

"Yes, respected sir, an office founded on strictly philosophical and physio—"

"Look you—come up here—how, by philosophy or physiology either, make good boys to order? Come up here. Don't give me a crick in the neck. Come up here, come, sir, come," calling as if to his pointer. "Tell me, how put the requisite assortment of good qualities into a boy, as the assorted mince into the pie?"

"Respected sir, our office—"

"You talk much of that office. Where is it? On board this boat?"

"Oh no, sir, I just came aboard. Our office—"

"Came aboard at that last landing, eh? Pray, do you know a herb-doctor there? Smooth scamp in a snuff-colored surtout?"

"Oh, sir, I was but a sojourner at Cape Giradeau. Though, now that you mention a snuff-colored surtout, I think I met such a man as you speak of stepping ashore as I stepped aboard, and 'pears to me I have seen him somewhere before. Looks like a very mild Christian sort of person, I should say. Do you know him, respected sir?"

"Not much, but better than you seem to. Proceed with your business."

With a low, shabby bow, as grateful for the permission, the other began: "Our office—"

"Look you," broke in the bachelor with ire, "have you the spinal complaint? What are you ducking and groveling about? Keep still. Where's your office?"

"The branch one which I represent, is at Alton, sir, in the free state we now pass," (pointing somewhat proudly ashore).

"Free, eh? You a freeman, you flatter yourself? With those coat-tails and that spinal complaint of servility? Free? Just cast up in your private mind who is your master, will you?"

"Oh, oh, oh! I don't understand—indeed—indeed. But, respected sir, as before said, our office, founded on principles wholly new—"

"To the devil with your principles! Bad sign when a man begins to talk of his principles. Hold, come back, sir; back here, back, sir, back! I tell you no more boys for me. Nay, I'm a Mede and Persian. In my old home in the woods I'm pestered enough with squirrels, weasels, chipmunks, skunks. I want no more wild vermin to spoil my temper and waste my substance. Don't talk of boys; enough of your boys; a plague of your boys; chilblains on your boys! As for Intelligence Offices, I've lived in the East, and know 'em. Swindling concerns kept by low-born cynics, under a fawning exterior wreaking their cynic malice upon mankind. You are a fair specimen of 'em."

"Oh dear, dear, dear!"

"Dear? Yes, a thrice dear purchase one of your boys would be to me. A rot on your boys!"

"But, respected sir, if you will have not have boys, might we not, in our small way, accommodate you with a man?"

"Accommodate? Pray, no doubt you could accommodate me with a bosom-friend too, couldn't you? Accommodate! Obliging word accommodate: there's accommodation notes now, where one accommodates another with a loan, and if he don't pay it pretty quickly, accommodates him with a chain to his foot. Accommodate! God forbid that I should ever be accommodated. No, no. Look you, as I told that cousin-german of yours, the herb-doctor, I'm now on the road to get me made some sort of machine to do my work. Machines for me. My cider-mill—does that ever steal my cider? My mowing-machine—does that ever lay a-bed mornings? My corn-husker—does that ever give me insolence? No: cider-mill, mowing-machine, corn-husker—all faithfully attend to their business. Disinterested, too; no board, no wages; yet doing good all their lives long; shining examples that virtue is its own reward—the only practical Christians I know."

"Oh dear, dear, dear, dear!"

"Yes, sir:—boys? Start my soul-bolts, what a difference, in a moral point of view, between a corn-husker and a boy! Sir, a corn-husker, for its patient continuance in well-doing, might not unfitly go to heaven. Do you suppose a boy will?"

"A corn-husker in heaven! (turning up the whites of his eyes). Respected sir, this way of talking as if heaven were a kind of Washington patent-office museum—oh, oh, oh!—as if mere machine-work and puppet-work went to heaven—oh, oh, oh! Things incapable of free agency, to receive the eternal reward of well-doing —oh, oh, oh!"

"You Praise-God-Barebones you, what are you groaning about? Did I say anything of that sort? Seems to me, though you talk so good, you are mighty quick at a hint the other way, or else you want to pick a polemic quarrel with me."

"It may be so or not, respected sir," was now the demure reply; "but if it be, it is only because as a soldier out of honor is quick in taking affront, so a Christian out of religion is quick, sometimes perhaps a little too much so, in spying heresy."

"Well," after an astonished pause, "for an unaccountable pair, you and the herb-doctor ought to yoke together."

So saying, the bachelor was eying him rather sharply, when he with the brass plate recalled him to the discussion by a hint, not unflattering, that he (the man with the brass plate) was all anxiety to hear him further on the subject of servants.

"About that matter," exclaimed the impulsive bachelor, going off at the hint like a rocket, "all thinking minds are, now-a-days, coming to the conclusion—one derived from an immense hereditary experience—see what Horace and others of the ancients say of servants—coming to the conclusion, I say, that boy or man, the human animal is, for most work-purposes, a losing animal. Can't be trusted; less trustworthy than oxen; for conscientiousness a turn-spit dog excels him. Hence these thousand new inventions—carding machines, horseshoe machines, tunnel-boring machines, reaping machines, apple-paring machines, boot-blacking machines, sewing machines, shaving machines, run-of-errand machines, dumb-waiter machines, and the Lord-only-knows-what machines; all of which announce the era when that refractory animal, the working or serving man, shall be a buried by-gone, a superseded fossil. Shortly prior to which glorious time, I doubt not that a price will be put upon their peltries as upon the knavish 'possums, especially the boys. Yes, sir (ringing his rifle down on the deck), I rejoice to think that the day is at hand, when, prompted to it by law, I shall shoulder this gun and go out a boy-shooting."

"Oh, now! Lord, Lord, Lord!—But *our* office, respected sir, conducted as I ventured to observe—"

"No, sir," bristlingly settling his stubble chin in his coon-skins. "Don't try to oil me; the herb-doctor tried that. My experience, carried now through a course—worse than salivation—a course of five and thirty boys, proves to me that boyhood is a natural state of rascality."

"Save us, save us!"

"Yes, sir, yes. My name is Pitch; I stick to what I say. I speak from fifteen years' experience; five and thirty boys; American, Irish, English, German, African, Mulatto; not to speak of that China boy sent me by one who well knew my perplexities, from California; and that Lascar boy from Bombay. Thug! I found him sucking the embryo life from my spring eggs. All rascals, sir, every soul of them; Caucasian or Mongol. Amazing the endless variety of rascality in human nature of the juvenile sort. I remember that, having discharged, one after another, twenty-nine boys—each, too, for some wholly unforeseen species of viciousness peculiar to that one peculiar boy—I remember saying to myself: Now, then, surely, I have got to the end of the list, wholly exhausted it; I have only now to get me a boy, any boy different from those twenty-nine preceding boys, and he infallibly shall be that virtuous boy I have so long been seeking. But, bless me! this thirtieth boy—by the way, having at the time long forsworn your intelligence offices, I had him sent to me from the Commissioners of Emigration, all the way from New York, culled out carefully, in fine, at my particular request, from a standing army of eight hundred boys, the flowers of all nations, so they wrote me, temporarily in barracks on an East River island —I say, this thirtieth boy was in person not ungraceful; his deceased mother a lady's maid, or something of that sort; and in manner, why, in a plebeian way, a perfect Chesterfield; very intelligent, too—quick as a flash. But, such suavity! 'Please sir! please sir!' always bowing and saying, 'Please sir.' In the strangest way, too, combining a filial affection with a menial respect. Took such warm, singular interest in my affairs. Wanted to be considered one of the family—sort of adopted son of mine, I suppose. Of a morning, when I would go out to my stable, with what childlike good nature he would trot out my nag, 'Please sir, I think he's getting fatter and fatter.' 'But, he don't look very clean, does he?' unwilling to be downright harsh with so affectionate a lad; 'and he seems a little hollow inside the haunch there, don't he? or no, perhaps I don't see plain this morning.' 'Oh, please sir, it's just there I think he's gaining so, please.' Polite scamp! I soon found he never gave that wretched nag his oats of nights; didn't bed him either. Was above that sort of chambermaid work. No end to his willful neglects. But the more he abused my service, the more polite he grew."

"Oh, sir, some way you mistook him."

"Not a bit of it. Besides, sir, he was a boy who under a Chesterfieldian exterior hid strong destructive propensities. He cut up my horse-blanket for the bits of leather, for hinges to his chest. Denied it point-blank. After he was gone, found the shreds under his mattress. Would slyly break his hoe-handle, too, on purpose to get rid of hoeing. Then be so gracefully penitent for his fatal excess of industrious strength. Offer to mend all by taking a nice stroll to the nighest settlement—cherry-trees in full bearing all the way—to get the broken thing cobbled. Very politely stole my pears, odd pennies, shillings, dollars, and nuts; regular squirrel at it. But I could prove nothing. Expressed to him my suspicions. Said I, moderately enough, 'A little less politeness, and a little more honesty would suit me better.' He fired up; threatened to sue for libel. I won't say anything about his afterwards, in Ohio, being found in the act of gracefully putting a bar across a rail-road track, for the reason that a stoker called him the rogue that he was. But enough: polite boys or saucy boys, white boys or black boys, smart boys or lazy boys, Caucasian boys or Mongol boys—all are rascals."

"Shocking, shocking!" nervously tucking his frayed cravat-end out of sight. "Surely, respected sir, you labor under a deplorable hallucination. Why, pardon again, you seem to have not the slightest confidence in boys. I admit, indeed, that boys, some of them at least, are but too prone to one little foolish foible or other. But, what then, respected sir, when, by natural laws, they finally outgrow such things, and wholly?"

Having until now vented himself mostly in plaintive dissent of canine whines and groans, the man with the brass plate seemed beginning to summon courage to a less timid encounter. But, upon his maiden essay, was not very encouragingly handled, since the dialogue immediately continued as follows:

"Boys outgrow what is amiss in them? From bad boys spring good men? Sir, 'the child is father of the man'; hence, as all boys are rascals, so are all men. But, God bless me, you must know these things better than I; keeping an intelligence office as you do; a business which must furnish peculiar facilities for studying mankind. Come, come up here, sir; confess you know these things pretty well, after all. Do you not know that all men are rascals, and all boys, too?"

"Sir," replied the other, spite of his shocked feelings seeming to pluck up some spirit, but not to an indiscreet degree, "Sir, heaven be praised, I am far, very far from knowing what you say. True," he thoughtfully continued, "with my associates, I keep an intelligence office, and for ten years, come October, have, one way or other, been concerned in that line; for no small period in the great city of Cincinnati, too; and though, as you hint, within that long interval, I must have had more or less favorable opportunity for studying mankind—in a business way, scanning not only the faces, but ransacking the lives of several thousands of human beings, male and female, of various nations, both employers and employed, genteel and ungenteel, educated and uneducated; yet—of course, I candidly admit, with some random exceptions, I have, so far as my small observation goes, found that mankind thus domestically viewed, confidentially viewed, I may say; they, upon the whole—making some reasonable allowances for human imperfection—present as pure a moral spectacle as the purest angel could wish. I say it, respected sir, with confidence."

"Gammon! You don't mean what you say. Else you are like a landsman at sea: don't know the ropes, the very things everlastingly pulled before your eyes. Serpent-like, they glide about, traveling blocks too subtle for you. In short, the entire ship is a riddle. Why, you green ones wouldn't know if she were unseaworthy; but still, with thumbs stuck back into your arm-holes, pace the rotten planks, singing, like a fool, words put into your green mouth by the cunning owner, the man who, heavily insuring it, sends his ship to be wrecked—

> A wet sheet and a flowing sea!—

and, sir, now that it occurs to me, your talk, the whole of it, is but a wet sheet and a flowing sea, and an idle wind that follows fast, offering a striking contrast to my own discourse."

"Sir," exclaimed the man with the brass plate, his patience now more or less tasked, "permit me with deference to hint that some of your remarks are injudiciously worded. And thus we say to our patrons, when they enter our office full of abuse of us because of some worthy boy we may have sent them—some boy wholly misjudged for the time. Yes, sir, permit me to remark that you do not sufficiently consider that, though a small man, I may have my small share of feelings."

"Well, well, I didn't mean to wound your feelings at all. And that they are small, very small, I take your word for it. Sorry, sorry. But truth is like a thrashing-machine; tender sensibilities must keep out of the way. Hope you understand me. Don't want to hurt you. All I say is, what I said in the first place, only now I swear it, that all boys are rascals."

"Sir," lowly replied the other, still forbearing like an old lawyer badgered in court, or else like a good-hearted simpleton, the butt of mischievous wags, "Sir, since you come back to the point, will you allow me, in my small, quiet way, to submit to you certain small, quiet views of the subject in hand?"

"Oh, yes!" with insulting indifference, rubbing his chin and looking the other way. "Oh, yes; go on."

"Well, then, respected sir," continued the other, now assuming as genteel an attitude as the irritating set of his pinched five-dollar suit would permit; "well, then, sir, the peculiar principles, the strictly philosophical principles, I may say," guardedly rising in dignity, as he guardedly rose on his toes, "upon which our office is founded, has led me and my associates, in our small, quiet way, to a careful analytical study of man, conducted, too, on a quiet theory, and with an unobtrusive aim wholly our own. That theory I will not now at large set forth. But some of the discoveries resulting from it, I will, by your permission, very briefly mention; such of them, I mean, as refer to the state of boyhood scientifically viewed."

"Then you have studied the thing? expressly studied boys, eh? Why didn't you out with that before?"

"Sir, in my small business way, I have not conversed with so many masters, gentlemen masters, for nothing. I have been taught that in this world there is a precedence of opinions as well as of persons. You have kindly given me your views, I am now, with modesty, about to give you mine."

"Stop flunkying—go on."

"In the first place, sir, our theory teaches us to proceed by analogy from the physical to the moral. Are we right there, sir? Now, sir, take a young boy, a young male infant rather, a man-child in short—what sir, I respectfully ask, do you in the first place remark?"

"A rascal, sir! present and prospective, a rascal!"

"Sir, if passion is to invade, surely science must evacuate. May I proceed? Well, then, what, in the first place, in a general view, do you remark, respected sir, in that male baby or man-child?"

The bachelor privily growled, but this time, upon the whole, better governed himself than before, though not, indeed, to the degree of thinking it prudent to risk an articulate response.

"What do you remark? I respectfully repeat." But, as no answer came, only the low, half-suppressed growl, as of Bruin in a hollow trunk, the questioner continued: "Well, sir, if you will permit me, in my small way, to speak for you, you remark, respected sir, an incipient creation; loose sort of sketchy thing; a little preliminary rag-paper study, or careless cartoon, so to speak, of a man. The idea, you see, respected sir, is there; but, as yet, wants filling out. In a word, respected sir, the man-child is at present but little, every way; I don't pretend to deny it; but, then, he *promises* well, does he not? Yes, promises very well indeed, I may say. (So, too, we say to our patrons in reference to some noble little youngster objected to for being a *dwarf*.) But, to advance one step further," extending his thread bare leg, as he drew a pace nearer, "we must now drop the figure of the rag-paper cartoon, and borrow one—to use presently, when wanted—from the horticultural kingdom. Some bud, lily-bud, if you please. Now, such points as the new-born man-child has—as yet not all that could be desired, I am free to confess —still, such as they are, there they are, and palpable as those of an adult. But we stop not here," taking another step. "The man-child not only possesses these present points, small though they are, but, likewise—now our horticultural image comes into play—like the bud of the lily, he contains concealed rudiments of others; that is, points at present invisible, with beauties at present dormant."

"Come, come, this talk is getting too horticultural and beautiful altogether. Cut it short, cut it short!"

"Respected sir," with a rustily martial sort of gesture, like a decayed corporal's, "when deploying into the field of discourse the vanguard of an important argument, much more in evolving the grand central forces of a new philosophy of boys, as I may say, surely you will kindly allow scope adequate to the movement in hand, small and humble in its way as that movement may be. Is it worth my while to go on, respected sir?"

"Yes, stop flunkying and go on."

Thus encouraged, again the philosopher with the brass plate proceeded:

"Supposing, sir, that worthy gentleman (in such terms, to an applicant for service, we allude to some patron we chance to have in our eye), supposing, respected sir, that worthy gentleman, Adam, to have been dropped overnight in Eden, as a calf in the pasture; supposing that, sir—then how could even the learned serpent himself have foreknown that such a downy-chinned little innocent would eventually rival the goat in a beard? Sir, wise as the serpent was, that eventuality would have been entirely hidden from his wisdom."

"I don't know about that. The devil is very sagacious. To judge by the event, he appears to have understood man better even than the Being who made him."

"For God's sake, don't say that, sir! To the point. Can it now with fairness be denied that, in his beard, the man-child prospectively possesses an appendix, not less imposing than patriarchal; and for this goodly beard, should we not by generous anticipation give the man-child, even in his cradle, credit? Should we not now, sir? respectfully I put it."

"Yes, if like pig-weed he mows it down soon as it shoots," porcinely rubbing his stubble-chin against his coon-skins.

"I have hinted at the analogy," continued the other, calmly disregardful of the digression; "now to apply it. Suppose a boy evince no noble quality. Then generously give him credit for his prospective one. Don't you see? So we say to our patrons when they would fain return a boy upon us as unworthy: 'Madam, or sir, (as the case may be) has this boy a beard?' 'No.' 'Has he, we respectfully ask, as yet, evinced any noble quality?' 'No, indeed.' 'Then, madam, or sir, take him back, we humbly beseech; and keep him till that same noble quality sprouts; for, have confidence, it, like the beard, is in him.' "

"Very fine theory," scornfully exclaimed the bachelor, yet in secret, perhaps, not entirely undisturbed by these strange new views of the matter; "but what trust is to be placed in it?"

"The trust of perfect confidence, sir. To proceed. Once more, if you please, regard the man-child."

"Hold!" paw-like thrusting out his bearskin arm, "don't intrude that man-child upon me too often. He who loves not bread, dotes not on dough. As little of your man-child as your logical arrangements will admit."

"Anew regard the man-child," with inspired intrepidity repeated he with the brass plate, "in the perspective of his developments, I mean. At first the man-child has no teeth, but about the sixth month—am I right, sir?"

"Don't know anything about it."

"To proceed then: though at first deficient in teeth, about the sixth month the man-child begins to put forth in that particular. And sweet those tender little puttings-forth are."

"Very, but blown out of his mouth directly, worthless enough."

"Admitted. And, therefore, we say to our patrons returning with a boy alleged not only to be deficient in goodness, but redundant in ill: 'The lad, madam or sir, evinces very corrupt qualities, does he?' 'No end to them.' 'But, have confidence, there will be; for pray, madam, in this lad's early childhood, were not those frail first teeth, then his, followed by his present sound, even, beautiful and permanent set? And the more objectionable those first teeth became, was not that, madam, we respectfully submit, so much the more reason to look for their speedy substitution by the present sound, even, beautiful and permanent ones?' 'True, true, can't deny that.' 'Then, madam, take him back, we respectfully beg, and wait till, in the now swift course of nature, dropping those transient moral blemishes you complain of, he replacingly buds forth in the sound, even, beautiful and permanent virtues.' "

"Very philosophical again," was the contemptuous reply—the outward contempt, perhaps, proportioned to the inward misgiving. "Vastly philosophical, indeed, but tell me—to continue your analogy—since the second teeth followed—in fact, came from—the first, is there no chance the blemish may be transmitted?"

"Not at all." Abating in humility as he gained in the argument. "The second teeth follow, but do not come from, the first; successors, not sons. The first teeth are not like the germ blossom of the apple, at once the father of, and incorporated into, the growth it foreruns; but they are thrust from their place by the independent undergrowth of the succeeding set—an illustration, by the way, which shows more for me than I meant, though not more than I wish."

"What does it show?" Surly-looking as a thundercloud with the inkept unrest of unacknowledged conviction.

"It shows this, respected sir, that in the case of any boy, especially an ill one, to apply unconditionally the saying, that the 'child is father of the man,' is, besides implying an uncharitable aspersion of the race, affirming a thing very wide of—"

"—Your analogy," like a snapping turtle.

"Yes, respected sir."

"But is analogy argument? You are a punster."

"Punster, respected sir?" with a look of being aggrieved.

"Yes, you pun with ideas as aother man may with words."

"Oh well, sir, whoever talks in that strain, whoever has no confidence in human reason, whoever despises human reason, in vain to reason with him. Still, respected sir," altering his air, "permit me to hint that, had not the force of analogy moved you somewhat, you would hardly have offered to contemn it."

"Talk away," disdainfully; "but pray tell me what has that last analogy of yours to do with your intelligence office business?"

"Everything to do with it, respected sir. From that analogy we derive the reply made to such a patron as, shortly after being supplied by us with an adult servant, proposes to return him upon our hands; not that, while with the patron, said adult has given any cause of dissatisfaction, but the patron has just chanced to hear something unfavorable concerning him from some gentleman who employed said adult long before, while a boy. To which too fastidious patron, we, taking said adult by the hand, and graciously reintroducing him to the patron, say: 'Far be it from you, madam, or sir, to proceed in your censure against this adult, in anything of the spirit of an ex-post-facto law. Madam, or sir, would you visit upon the butterfly the sins of the caterpillar? In the natural advance of all creatures, do they not bury themselves over and over again in the endless resurrection of better and better? Madam, or sir, take back this adult; he may have been a caterpillar, but is now a butterfly."

"Pun away; but even accepting your analogical pun, what does it amount to? Was the caterpillar one creature, and is the butterfly another? The butterfly is the caterpillar in a gaudy cloak; stripped of which, there lies the impostor's long spindle of a body, pretty much worm-shaped as before."

"You reject the analogy. To the facts then. You deny that a youth of one character can be transformed into a man of an opposite character. Now then—yes, I have it. There's the founder of La Trappe, and Ignatius Loyola; in boyhood, and some way into manhood, both devil-may-care bloods, and yet, in the end, the wonders of the world for anchoritish self-command. These two examples, by-the-way, we cite to such patrons as would hastily return rakish young waiters upon us. 'Madam, or sir—patience; patience,' we say; 'good madam, or sir, would you discharge forth your cask of good wine, because, while working, it riles more or less? Then discharge not forth this young waiter; the good in him is working.' 'But he is a sad rake.' 'Therein is his promise; the rake being crude material for the saint.' "

"Ah, you are a talking man—what I call a wordy man. You talk, talk."

"And with submission, sir, what is the greatest judge, bishop or prophet, but a talking man? He talks, talks. It is the peculiar vocation of a teacher to talk. What's wisdom itself but table-talk? The best wisdom in this world, and the last spoken by its teacher, did it not literally and truly come in the form of table-talk?"

"You, you, you!" rattling down his rifle.

"To shift the subject, since we cannot agree. Pray, what is your opinion, respected sir, of St. Augustine?"

"St. Augustine? What should I, or you either, know of him? Seems to me, for one in such a business, to say nothing of such a coat, that though you don't know a great deal, indeed, yet you know a good deal more than you ought to know, or than you have a right to know, or than it is safe or expedient for you to know, or than, in the fair course of life, you could have honestly come to know. I am of opinion you should be served like a Jew in the middle ages with his gold; this knowledge of yours, which you haven't enough knowledge to know how to make a right use of, it should be taken from you. And so I have been thinking all along."

"You are merry, sir. But you have a little looked into St. Augustine, I suppose."

"St. Augustine on Original Sin is my text book. But you, I ask again, where do you find time or inclination for these out-of-the-way speculations? In fact, your whole talk, the more I think of it, is altogether unexampled and extraordinary."

"Respected sir, have I not already informed you that the quite new method, the strictly philosophical one, on which our office is founded, has led me and my associates to an enlarged study of mankind. It was my fault, if I did not, likewise, hint, that these studies directed always to the scientific procuring of good servants of all sorts, boys included, for the kind gentlemen, our patrons—that these studies, I say, have been conducted equally among all books of all libraries, as among all men of all nations. Then, you rather like St. Augustine, sir?"

"Excellent genius!"

"In some points he was; yet, how comes it that under his own hand, St. Augustine confesses that, until his thirtieth year, he was a very sad dog?"

"A saint a sad dog?"

"Not the saint, but the saint's irresponsible little forerunner—the boy."

"All boys are rascals, and so are all men," again flying off at his tangent; "my name is Pitch; I stick to what I say."

"Ah, sir, permit me—when I behold you on this mild summer's eve, thus eccentrically clothed in the skins of wild beasts, I cannot but conclude that the equally grim and unsuitable habit of your mind is likewise but an eccentric assumption, having no basis in your genuine soul, no more than in nature herself."

"Well, really, now—really," fidgeted the bachelor, not un-affected in his conscience by these benign personalities, "really, really, now, I don't know but that I may have been a little bit too hard upon those five and thirty boys of mine."

"Glad to find you a little softening, sir. Who knows now, but that flexile gracefulness, however questionable at the time of that thir-tieth boy of yours, might have been the silky husk of the most solid qualities of maturity. It might have been with him as with the ear of the Indian corn."

"Yes, yes, yes," excitedly cried the bachelor, as the light of this new illustration broke in, "yes, yes; and now that I think of it, how often I've sadly watched my Indian corn in May, wondering whether such sickly, half-eaten sprouts, could ever thrive up into the stiff, stately spear of August."

"A most admirable reflection, sir, and you have only, according to the analogical theory first started by our office, to apply it to that thirtieth boy in question, and see the result. Had you but kept that thirtieth boy—been patient with his sickly virtues, cultivated them, hoed round them, why what a glorious guerdon would have been yours, when at last you should have had a St. Augustine for an ostler."

"Really, really—well, I am glad I didn't send him to jail, as at first I intended."

"Oh that would have been too bad. Grant he was vicious. The petty vices of boys are like the innocent kicks of colts, as yet im-perfectly broken. Some boys know not virtue only for the same rea-son they know not French; it was never taught them. Established upon the basis of parental charity, juvenile asylums exist by law for the benefit of lads convicted of acts which, in adults, would have received other requital. Why? Because, do what they will, society, like our office, at bottom has a Christian confidence in boys. And all this we say to our patrons."

"Your patrons, sir, seem your marines to whom you may say anything," said the other, relapsing. "Why do knowing employers shun youths from asylums, though offered them at the smallest wages? I'll none of your reformado boys."

"Such a boy, respected sir, I would not get for you, but a boy that never needed reform. Do not smile, for as whooping-cough and measles are juvenile diseases, and yet some juveniles never have them, so are there boys equally free from juvenile vices. True, for the best of boys, measles may be contagious, and evil communications corrupt good manners; but a boy with a sound mind in a sound body—such is the boy I would get you. If hitherto, sir, you have struck upon a peculiarly bad vein of boys, so much the more hope now of your hitting a good one."

"That sounds a kind of reasonable, as it were—a little so, really. In fact, though you have said a great many foolish things, very foolish and absurd things, yet, upon the whole, your conversation has been such as might almost lead one less distrustful than I to repose a certain conditional confidence in you, I had almost added in your office, also. Now, for the humor of it, supposing that even I, I myself, really had this sort of conditional confidence, though but a grain, what sort of a boy, in sober fact, could you send me? And what would be your fee?"

"Conducted," replied the other somewhat loftily, rising now in eloquence as his proselyte, for all his pretenses, sunk in conviction, "conducted upon principles involving care, learning, and labor, exceeding what is usual in kindred institutions, the Philosophical Intelligence Office is forced to charges somewhat higher than customary. Briefly, our fee is three dollars in advance. As for the boy, by a lucky chance, I have a very promising little fellow now in my eye —a very likely little fellow, indeed."

"Honest?"

"As the day is long. Might trust him with untold millions. Such, at least, were the marginal observations on the phrenological chart of his head, submitted to me by the mother."

"How old?"

"Just fifteen."

"Tall? Stout?"

"Uncommonly so, for his age, his mother remarked."

"Industrious?"

"The busy bee."

The bachelor fell into a troubled reverie. At last, with much hesitancy, he spoke:

"Do you think now, candidly, that—I say candidly—candidly— could I have some small, limited—some faint, conditional degree of confidence in that boy? Candidly, now?"

"Candidly, you could."

"A sound boy? A good boy?"

"Never knew one more so."

The bachelor fell into another irresolute reverie; then said: "Well, now, you have suggested some rather new views of boys, and men, too. Upon those views in the concrete I at present decline to determine. Nevertheless, for the sake purely of a scientific experiment, I will try that boy. I don't think him an angel, mind. No, no. But I'll try him. There are my three dollars, and here is my address. Send him along this day two weeks. Hold, you will be wanting the money for his passage. There," handing it somewhat reluctantly.

"Ah, thank you. I had forgotten his passage"; then, altering in manner, and gravely holding the bills, continued: "Respected sir, never willingly do I handle money not with perfect willingness, nay, with a certain alacrity, paid. Either tell me that you have a perfect and unquestioning confidence in me (never mind the boy now) or permit me respectfully to return these bills."

"Put 'em up, put 'em up!"

"Thank you. Confidence is the indispensable basis of all sorts of business transactions. Without it, commerce between man and man, as between country and country, would, like a watch, run down and stop. And now, supposing that against present expectation the lad should, after all, evince some little undesirable trait, do not, respected sir, rashly dismiss him. Have but patience, have but confidence. Those transient vices will, ere long, fall out, and be replaced by the sound, firm, even and permanent virtues. Ah," glancing shoreward, towards a grotesquely-shaped bluff, "there's the Devil's Joke, as they call it; the bell for landing will shortly ring. I must go look up the cook I brought for the innkeeper at Cairo."

Chapter 23 *In Which the Powerful Effect of Natural Scenery Is Evinced in the Case of the Missourian, Who, in View of the Region Round-about Cairo, Has* A RETURN OF HIS CHILLY FIT 🙠

At Cairo, the old established firm of Fever & Ague is still settling up its unfinished business; that Creole grave-digger, Yellow Jack— his hand at the mattock and spade has not lost its cunning; while Don Saturninus Typhus taking his constitutional with Death, Calvin Edson and three undertakers, in the morass, snuffs up the mephitic breeze with zest.

In the dank twilight, fanned with mosquitoes, and sparkling with fire-flies, the boat now lies before Cairo. She has landed certain passengers, and tarries for the coming of expected ones. Leaning over the rail on the inshore side, the Missourian eyes through the dubious medium that swampy and squalid domain; and over it audibly mumbles his cynical mind to himself, as Apemantus' dog may have mumbled his bone. He bethinks him that the man with the brass plate was to land on this villainous bank, and for that cause, if no other, begins to suspect him. Like one beginning to rouse himself from a dose of chloroform treacherously given, he half divines, too, that he, the philosopher, had unwittingly been betrayed into being an unphilosophical dupe. To what vicissitudes of light and shade is man subject! He ponders the mystery of human subjectivity in general. He thinks he perceives with Crossbones, his favorite author, that, as one may wake up well in the morning, very well, indeed, and brisk as a buck, I thank you, but ere bed-time get under the weather, there is no telling how—so one may wake up wise, and slow of assent, very wise and very slow, I assure you, and for all that, before night, by like trick in the atmosphere, be left in the lurch a ninny. Health and wisdom equally precious, and equally little as unfluctuating possessions to be relied on.

But where was slipped in the entering wedge? Philosophy, knowledge, experience—were those trusty knights of the castle recreant? No, but unbeknown to them, the enemy stole on the castle's south side, its genial one, where Suspicion, the warder, parleyed. In fine, his too indulgent, too artless and companionable nature betrayed him. Admonished by which, he thinks he must be a little splenetic in his intercourse henceforth.

He revolves the crafty process of sociable chat, by which, as he fancies, the man with the brass plate wormed into him, and made such a fool of him as insensibly to persuade him to waive, in his exceptional case, that general law of distrust systematically applied to the race. He revolves, but cannot comprehend, the operation, still less the operator. Was the man a trickster, it must be more for the love than the lucre. Two or three dirty dollars the motive to so many nice wiles? And yet how full of mean needs his seeming. Before his mental vision the person of that threadbare Talleyrand, that impoverished Machiavelli, that seedy Rosicrucian—for something of all these he vaguely deems him—passes now in puzzled review. Fain, in his disfavor, would he make out a logical case. The doctrine of analogies recurs. Fallacious enough doctrine when wielded against one's prejudices, but in corroboration of cherished suspicions not without likelihood. Analogically, he couples the slanting cut of the equivocator's coat-tails with the sinister cast in his eye; he weighs slyboot's sleek speech in the light imparted by the oblique import of the smooth slope of his worn boot-heels; the insinuator's undulating flunkyisms dovetail into those of the flunky beast that windeth his way on his belly.

From these uncordial reveries he is roused by a cordial slap on the shoulder, accompanied by a spicy volume of tobacco-smoke, out of which came a voice, sweet as a seraph's:

"A penny for your thoughts, my fine fellow."

"Hands off!" cried the bachelor, involuntarily covering dejection with moroseness.

"Hands off? That sort of label won't do in our Fair. Whoever in our Fair has fine feelings loves to feel the nap of fine cloth, especially when a fine fellow wears it."

"And who of my fine-fellow species may you be? From the Brazils, ain't you? Toucan fowl. Fine feathers on foul meat."

This ungentle mention of the toucan was not improbably suggested by the parti-hued, and rather plumagy aspect of the stranger, no bigot it would seem, but a liberalist, in dress, and whose wardrobe, almost anywhere than on the liberal Mississippi, used to all sorts of fantastic informalities, might, even to observers less critical than the bachelor, have looked, if anything, a little out of the common; but not more so perhaps, than, considering the bear and raccoon costume, the bachelor's own appearance. In short, the stranger sported a vesture barred with barious hues, that of the cochineal predominating, in style participating of a Highland plaid, Emir's robe, and French blouse; from its plaited sort of front peeped glimpses of a flowered regatta-shirt, while, for the rest, white trowsers of ample duck flowed over maroon-colored slippers, and a jaunty smoking-cap of regal purple crowned him off at top; king of traveled good-fellows, evidently. Grotesque as all was, nothing looked stiff or unused; all showed signs of easy service, the least wonted thing setting like a wonted glove. That genial hand, which had just been laid on the ungenial shoulder, was now carelessly thrust down before him, sailor-fashion, into a sort of Indian belt, confining the redundant vesture; the other held, by its long bright cherry-stem, a Nuremberg pipe in blast, its great porcelain bowl painted in miniature with linked crests and arms of interlinked nations—a florid show. As by subtle saturations of its mellowing essence the tobacco had ripened the bowl, so it looked as if something similar of the interior spirit came rosily out on the cheek. But rosy pipe-bowl, or rosy countenance, all was lost on that unrosy man, the bachelor, who, waiting a moment till the commotion, caused by the boat's renewed progress, had a little abated, thus continued:

"Hark ye," jeeringly eying the cap and belt, "did you ever see Signor Marzetti in the African pantomime?"

"No;—good performer?"

"Excellent; plays the intelligent ape till he seems it. With such naturalness can a being endowed with an immortal spirit enter into that of a monkey. But where's your tail? In the pantomime, Marzetti, no hypocrite in his monkery, prides himself on that."

The stranger, now at rest, sideways and genially, on one hip, his right leg cavalierly crossed before the other, the toe of his vertical slipper pointed easily down on the deck, whiffed out a long, leisurely sort of indifferent and charitable puff, betokening him more or less of the mature man of the world, a character which, like its opposite, the sincere Christian's, is not always swift to take offense; and then, drawing near, still smoking, again laid his hand, this time with mild impressiveness, on the ursine shoulder, and not unamiably said: "That in your address there is a sufficiency of the *fortiter in re* few unbiased observers will question; but that this is duly attempered with the *suaviter in modo* may admit, I think, of an honest doubt. My dear fellow," beaming his eyes full upon him, "what injury have I done you, that you should receive my greeting with a curtailed civility?"

"Off hands"; once more shaking the friendly member from him. "Who in the name of the great chimpanzee, in whose likeness, you, Marzetti, and the other chatterers are made, who in thunder are you?"

"A cosmopolitan, a catholic man; who, being such, ties himself to no narrow tailor or teacher, but federates, in heart as in costume, something of the various gallantries of men under various suns. Oh, one roams not over the gallant globe in vain. Bred by it, is a fraternal and fusing feeling. No man is a stranger. You accost anybody. Warm and confiding, you wait not for measured advances. And though, indeed, mine, in this instance, have met with no very hilarious encouragement, yet the principle of a true citizen of the world is still to return good for ill.—My dear fellow, tell me how I can serve you."

"By dispatching yourself, Mr. Popinjay-of-the-world, into the heart of the Lunar Mountains. You are another of them. Out of my sight!"

"Is the sight of humanity so very disagreeable to you then? Ah, I may be foolish, but for my part, in all its aspects, I love it. Served up à la Pole, or à la Moor, à la Ladrone, or à la Yankee, that good dish, man, still delights me; or rather is man a wine I never weary of comparing and sipping; wherefore am I a pledged cosmopolitan, a sort of London-Dock-Vault connoisseur, going about from Teheran to Natchitoches, a taster of races; in all his vintages, smacking my lips over this racy creature, man, continually. But as there are tee-total palates which have a distaste even for Amontillado, so I suppose there may be teetotal souls which relish not even the very best brands of humanity. Excuse me, but it just occurs to me that you, my dear fellow, possibly lead a solitary life."

"Solitary?" starting as at a touch of divination.

"Yes: in a solitary life one insensibly contracts oddities,—talking to one's self now."

"Been eaves-dropping, eh?"

"Why, a soliloquist in a crowd can hardly but be overheard, and without much reproach to the hearer."

"You are an eaves-dropper."

"Well. Be it so."

"Confess yourself an eaves-dropper?"

"I confess that when you were muttering here I, passing by, caught a word or two, and, by like chance, something previous of your chat with the Intelligence-office man;—a rather sensible fellow, by the way; much of my style of thinking; would, for his own sake, he were of my style of dress. Grief to good minds, to see a man of superior sense forced to hide his light under the bushel of an inferior coat.—Well, from what little I heard, I said to myself, 'Here now is one with the unprofitable philosophy of disesteem for man.' Which disease, in the main, I have observed—excuse me—

to spring from a certain lowness, if not sourness, of spirits inseparable from sequestration. Trust me, one had better mix in, and do
like others. Sad business, this holding out against having a good
time. Life is a pic-nic *en costume;* one must take a part, assume a
character, stand ready in a sensible way to play the fool. To come
in plain clothes, with a long face, as a wiseacre, only makes one a
discomfort to himself, and a blot upon the scene. Like your jug of
cold water among the wine-flasks, it leaves you unelated among
the elated ones. No, no. This austerity won't do. Let me tell you
too—*en confiance*—that while revelry may not always merge into
ebriety, soberness, in too deep potations, may become a sort of sottishness. Which sober sottishness, in my way of thinking, is only
to be cured by beginning at the other end of the horn, to tipple a
little."

"Pray, what society of vintners and old topers are you hired to
lecture for?"

"I fear I did not give my meaning clearly. A little story may help.
The story of the worthy old woman of Goshen, a very moral old
woman, who wouldn't let her shoats eat fattening apples in fall, for
fear the fruit might ferment upon their brains, and so make them
swinish. Now, during a green Christmas, inauspicious to the old,
this worthy old woman fell into a moping decline, took to her bed,
no appetite, and refused to see her best friends. In much concern
her good man sent for the doctor, who, after seeing the patient and
putting a question or two, beckoned the husband out, and said:
'Deacon, do you want her cured?' 'Indeed I do.' 'Go directly, then,
and buy a jug of Santa Cruz.' 'Santa Cruz? my wife drink Santa
Cruz?' 'Either that or die.' 'But how much?' 'As much as she can
get down.' 'But she'll get drunk!' 'That's the cure.' Wise men, like
doctors, must be obeyed. Much against the grain, the sober deacon got the unsober medicine, and, equally against her conscience,
the poor old woman took it; but, by so doing, ere long recovered
health and spirits, famous appetite, and glad again to see her
friends; and having by this experience broken the ice of arid absti-
nence, never afterwards kept herself a cup too low."

This story had the effect of surprising the bachelor into interest, though hardly into approval.

"If I take your parable right," said he, sinking no little of his former churlishness, "the meaning is, that one cannot enjoy life with gusto unless he renounce the too-sober view of life. But since the too-sober view is, doubtless, nearer true than the too-drunken; I, who rate truth, though cold water, above untruth, though Tokay, will stick to my earthen jug."

"I see," slowly spirting upward a spiral staircase of lazy smoke, "I see; you go in for the lofty."

"How?"

"Oh, nothing! but if I wasn't afraid of prosing, I might tell another story about an old boot in a pieman's loft, contracting there between sun and oven an unseemly, dry-seasoned curl and warp. You've seen such leathery old garretteers, haven't you? Very high, sober, solitary, philosophic, grand, old boots, indeed; but I, for my part, would rather be the pieman's trodden slipper on the ground. Talking of piemen, humble-pie before proud-cake for me. This notion of being lone and lofty is a sad mistake. Men I hold in this respect to be like roosters; the one that betakes himself to a lone and lofty perch is the hen-pecked one, or the one that has the pip."

"You are abusive!" cried the bachelor, evidently touched.

"Who is abused? You, or the race? You won't stand by and see the human race abused? Oh, then, you have some respect for the human race."

"I have some respect for *myself*," with a lip not so firm as before.

"And what race may *you* belong to? now don't you see, my dear fellow, in what inconsistencies one involves himself by affecting disesteem for men? To a charm, my little stratagem succeeded. Come, come, think better of it, and, as a first step to a new mind, give up solitude. I fear, by the way, you have at some time been reading Zimmermann, that old Mr. Megrims of a Zimmermann, whose book on Solitude is as vain as Hume's on Suicide, as Bacon's on Knowledge; and, like these, will betray him who seeks to steer soul and body by it, like a false religion. All they, be they what boasted ones you please, who, to the yearning of our kind after a founded rule of content, offer aught not in the spirit of fellowly gladness based on due confidence in what is above, away with them for poor dupes, or still poorer impostors."

His manner here was so earnest that scarcely any auditor, perhaps, but would have been more or less impressed by it, while, possibly, nervous opponents might have a little quailed under it. Thinking within himself a moment, the bachelor replied: "Had you experience, you would know that your tippling theory, take it in what sense you will, is poor as any other. And Rabelais's pro-wine Koran no more trustworthy than Mahomet's anti-wine one."

"Enough," for a finality knocking the ashes from his pipe, "we talk and keep talking, and still stand where we did. What do you say for a walk? My arm, and let's a turn. They are to have dancing on the hurricane-deck to-night. I shall fling them off a Scotch jig, while, to save the pieces, you hold my loose change; and following that, I propose that you, my dear fellow, stack your gun, and throw your bearskins in a sailor's hornpipe—I holding your watch. What do you say?"

At this proposition the other was himself again, all raccoon.

"Look you," thumping down his rifle, "are you Jeremy Diddler No. 3?"

"Jeremy Diddler? I have heard of Jeremy the prophet, and Jeremy Taylor the divine, but your other Jeremy is a gentleman I am unacquainted with."

"You are his confidential clerk, ain't you?"

"*Whose*, pray? Not that I think myself unworthy of being confided in, but I don't understand."

"You are another of them. Somehow I meet with the most extraordinary metaphysical scamps to-day. Sort of visitation of them. And yet that herb-doctor Diddler somehow takes off the raw edge of the Diddlers that come after him."

"Herb-doctor? who is he?"

"Like you—another of them."

"*Who?*" Then drawing near, as if for a good long explanatory chat, his left hand spread, and his pipe-stem coming crosswise down upon it like a ferule, "You think amiss of me. Now to undeceive you, I will just enter into a little argument and—"

"No you don't. No more little arguments for me. Had too many little arguments to-day."

"But put a case. Can you deny—I dare you to deny—that the man leading a solitary life is peculiarly exposed to the sorriest misconceptions touching strangers?"

"Yes, I *do* deny it," again, in his impulsiveness, snapping at the controversial bait, "and I will confute you there in a trice. Look, you—"

"Now, now, now, my dear fellow," thrusting out both vertical palms for double shields, "you crowd me too hard. You don't give one a chance. Say what you will, to shun a social proposition like mine, to shun society in any way, evinces a churlish nature— cold, loveless; as, to embrace it, shows one warm and friendly, in fact, sunshiny."

Here the other, all agog again, in his perverse way, launched forth into the unkindest references to deaf old worldlings keeping in the deafening world; and gouty gluttons limping to their gouty gormandizings; and corseted coquettes clasping their corseted cavaliers in the waltz, all for disinterested society's sake; and thousands, bankrupt through lavishness, ruining themselves out of pure love of the sweet company of man—no envies, rivalries, or other unhandsome motive to it.

"Ah, now," deprecating with his pipe, "irony is so unjust; never could abide irony; something Satanic about irony. God defend me from Irony, and Satire, his bosom friend."

"A right knave's prayer, and a right fool's, too," snapping his riflelock.

"Now be frank. Own that was a little gratuitous. But, no, no, you didn't mean it; anyway, I can make allowances. Ah, did you but know it, how much pleasanter to puff at this philanthropic pipe, than still to keep fumbling at that misanthropic rifle. As for your worldling, glutton, and coquette, though, doubtless, being such, they may have their little foibles—as who has not?—yet not one of the three can be reproached with that awful sin of shunning society; awful I call it, for not seldom it presupposes a still darker thing than itself—remorse."

"Remorse drives man away from man? How came your fellow-creature, Cain, after the first murder, to go and build the first city? And why is it that the modern Cain dreads nothing so much as solitary confinement?"

"My dear fellow, you get excited. Say what you will, I for one must have my fellow-creatures round me. Thick, too—I must have them thick."

"The pick-pocket, too, loves to have his fellow-creatures round him. Tut, man! no one goes into the crowd but for his end; and the end of too many is the same as the pick-pocket's—a purse."

"Now, my dear fellow, how can you have the conscience to say that, when it is as much according to natural law that men are social as sheep gregarious. But grant that, in being social, each man has his end, do you, upon the strength of that, do you yourself, I say, mix with man, now, immediately, and be your end a more genial philosophy. Come, let's take a turn."

Again he offered his fraternal arm; but the bachelor once more flung it off, and, raising his rifle in energetic invocation, cried: "Now the high-constable catch and confound all knaves in towns and rats in grain-bins, and if in this boat, which is a human grain-bin for the time, any sly, smooth, philandering rat be dodging now, pin him, thou high rat-catcher, against this rail."

"A noble burst! shows you at heart a trump. And when a card's that, little matters it whether it be spade or diamond. You are good wine that, to be still better, only needs a shaking up. Come, let's agree that we'll to New Orleans, and there embark for London —I staying with my friends nigh Primrose-hill, and you putting up at the Piazza, Covent Garden—Piazza, Covent Garden; for tell me—since you will not be a disciple to the full—tell me, was not that humor, of Diogenes, which led him to live, a merry-andrew, in the flower-market, better than that of the less wise Athenian, which made him a skulking scare-crow in pine-barrens? An injudicious gentleman, Lord Timon."

"Your hand!" seizing it.

"Bless me, how cordial a squeeze. It is agreed we shall be brothers, then?"

"As much so as a brace of misanthropes can be," with another and terrific squeeze. "I had thought that the moderns had degenerated beneath the capacity of misanthropy. Rejoiced, though but in one instance, and that disguised, to be undeceived."

The other stared in blank amaze.

"Won't do. You are Diogenes, Diogenes in disguise. I say—Diogenes masquerading as a cosmopolitan."

With ruefully altered mien, the stranger still stood mute awhile. At length, in a pained tone, spoke: "How hard the lot of that pleader who, in his zeal conceding too much, is taken to belong to a side which he but labors, however ineffectually, to convert!" Then with another change of air: "To you, an Ishmael, disguising in sportiveness my intent, I came ambassador from the human race, charged with the assurance that for your mislike they bore no answering grudge, but sought to conciliate accord between you and them. Yet you take me not for the honest envoy, but I know not what sort of unheard-of spy. Sir," he less lowly added, "this mistaking of your man should teach you how you may mistake all men. For God's sake," laying both hands upon him, "get you confidence. See how distrust has duped you. I, Diogenes? I, he who, going a step beyond misanthropy, was less a man-hater than a man-hooter? Better were I stark and stiff!"

With which the philanthropist moved away less lightsome than he had come, leaving the discomfited misanthrope to the solitude he held so sapient.

Chapter 25 *The Cosmopolitan Makes* AN ACQUAINT-ANCE ❦

In the act of retiring, the cosmopolitan was met by a passenger, who, with the bluff *abord* of the West, thus addressed him, though a stranger.

"Queer 'coon, your friend. Had a little skrimmage with him myself. Rather entertaining old 'coon, if he wasn't so deuced analytical. Reminded me somehow of what I've heard about Colonel John Moredock, of Illinois, only your friend ain't quite so good a fellow at bottom, I should think."

It was in the semicircular porch of a cabin, opening a recess from the deck, lit by a zoned lamp swung overhead, and sending its light vertically down, like the sun at noon. Beneath the lamp stood the speaker, affording to any one disposed to it no unfavorable chance for scrutiny; but the glance now resting on him betrayed no such rudeness.

A man neither tall nor stout, neither short nor gaunt; but with a body fitted, as by measure, to the service of his mind. For the rest, one less favored perhaps in his features than his clothes; and of these the beauty may have been less in the fit than the cut; to say nothing of the fineness of the nap, seeming out of keeping with something the reverse of fine in the skin; and the unsuitableness of a violet vest, sending up sunset hues to a countenance betokening a kind of bilious habit.

But, upon the whole, it could not be fairly said that his appearance was unprepossessing; indeed, to the congenial, it would have been doubtless not uncongenial; while to others, it could not fail to be at least curiously interesting, from the warm air of florid cordiality, contrasting itself with one knows not what kind of aguish sallowness of saving discretion lurking behind it. Ungracious critics might have thought that the manner flushed the man, something in the same fictitious way that the vest flushed the cheek. And though his teeth were singularly good, those same ungracious ones might have hinted that they were too good to be true; or rather, were not so good as they might be; since the best false teeth are those made with at least two or three blemishes, the more to look like life. But fortunately for better constructions, no such critics had the stranger now in eye; only the cosmopolitan, who, after, in the first place, acknowledging his advances with a mute salute—in which acknowledgment, if there seemed less of spirit than in his way of accosting the Missourian, it was probably because of the saddening sequel of that late interview—thus now replied: "Colonel John Moredock," repeating the words abstractedly; "that surname recalls reminiscences. Pray," with enlivened air, "was he anyway connected with the Moredocks of Moredock Hall, Northamptonshire, England?"

"I know no more of the Moredocks of Moredock Hall than of the Burdocks of Burdock Hut," returned the other, with the air somehow of one whose fortunes had been of his own making; "all I know is, that the late Colonel John Moredock was a famous one in his time; eye like Lochiel's; finger like a trigger; nerve like a catamount's; and with but two little oddities—seldom stirred without his rifle, and hated Indians like snakes."

"Your Moredock, then, would seem a Moredock of Misanthrope Hall—the Woods. No very sleek creature, the colonel, I fancy."

"Sleek or not, he was no uncombed one, but silky bearded and curly headed, and to all but Indians juicy as a peach. But Indians— how the late Colonel John Moredock, Indian-hater of Illinois, did hate Indians, to be sure!"

"Never heard of such a thing. Hate Indians? Why should he or anybody else hate Indians? *I* admire Indians. Indians I have always heard to be one of the finest of the primitive races, possessed of many heroic virtues. Some noble women, too. When I think of Pocahontas, I am ready to love Indians. Then there's Massasoit, and Philip of Mount Hope, and Tecumseh, and Red-Jacket, and Logan— all heroes; and there's the Five Nations, and Araucanians—federations and communities of heroes. God bless me; hate Indians? Surely the late Colonel John Moredock must have wandered in his mind."

"Wandered in the woods considerably, but never wandered elsewhere, that I ever heard."

"Are you in earnest? Was there ever one who so made it his particular mission to hate Indians that, to designate him, a special word has been coined—Indian-hater?"

"Even so."

"Dear me, you take it very calmly.—But really, I would like to know something about this Indian-hating. I can hardly believe such a thing to be. Could you favor me with a little history of the extraordinary man you mentioned?"

"With all my heart," and immediately stepping from the porch, gestured the cosmopolitan to a settee near by, on deck. "There, sir, sit you there, and I will sit here beside you—you desire to hear of Colonel John Moredock. Well, a day in my boyhood is marked with a white stone—the day I saw the colonel's rifle, powder-horn attached, hanging in a cabin on the West bank of the Wabash river. I was going westward a long journey through the wilderness with my father. It was high noon, and we had stopped at the cabin to unsaddle and bait. The man at the cabin pointed out the rifle, and told whose it was, adding that the colonel was that moment sleeping on wolf-skins in the corn-loft above, so we must not talk very loud, for the colonel had been out all night hunting (Indians, mind), and it would be cruel to disturb his sleep. Curious to see one so famous, we waited two hours over, in hopes he would come forth; but he did not. So, it being necessary to get to the next cabin before nightfall, we had at last to ride off without the wished-for satisfaction. Though, to tell the truth, I, for one, did not go away entirely ungratified, for, while my father was watering the horses, I slipped back into the cabin, and stepping a round or two up the ladder, pushed my head through the trap, and peered about. Not much light in the loft; but off, in the further corner, I saw what I took to be the wolf-skins, and on them a bundle of something, like a drift of leaves; and at one end, what seemed a moss-ball; and over it, deer-antlers branched; and close by, a small squirrel sprang out from a maple-bowl of nuts, brushed the moss-ball with his tail, through a hole, and vanished, squeaking. That bit of woodland scene was all I saw. No Colonel Moredock there, unless that moss-ball was his curly head, seen in the back view. I would have gone clear up, but the man below had warned me, that though, from his camping habits, the Colonel could sleep through thunder, he was for the same cause amazing quick to waken at the sound of footsteps, however soft, and especially if human."

"Excuse me," said the other, softly laying his hand on the narrator's wrist, "but I fear the colonel was of a distrustful nature—little or no confidence. He *was* a little suspicious-minded, wasn't he?"

"Not a bit. Knew too much. Suspected nobody, but was not ignorant of Indians. Well: though, as you may gather, I never fully saw the man, yet, have I, one way and another, heard about as much of him as any other; in particular, have I heard his history again and again from my father's friend, James Hall, the judge, you know. In every company being called upon to give this history, which none could better do, the judge at last fell into a style so methodic, you would have thought he spoke less to mere auditors than to an invisible amanuensis; seemed talking for the press; very impressive way with him indeed. And I, having an equally impressible memory, think that, upon a pinch, I can render you the judge upon the colonel almost word for word."

"Do so, by all means," said the cosmopolitan, well pleased.

"Shall I give you the judge's philosophy, and all?"

"As to that," rejoined the other gravely, pausing over the pipe-bowl he was filling, "the desirableness, to a man of a certain mind, of having another man's philosophy given, depends considerably upon what school of philosophy that other man belongs to. Of what school or system was the judge, pray?"

"Why, though he knew how to read and write, the judge never had much schooling. But, I should say he belonged, if anything, to the free-school system. Yes, a true patriot, the judge went in strong for free-schools."

"In philosophy? The man of a certain mind, then, while respecting the judge's patriotism, and not blind to the judge's capacity for narrative, such as he may prove to have, might, perhaps, with prudence, waive an opinion of the judge's probable philosophy.

But I am no rigorist; proceed, I beg; his philosophy or not, as you please."

"Well, I would mostly skip that part, only, to begin, some reconnoitering of the ground in a philosophical way the judge always deemed indispensable with strangers. For you must know that Indian-hating was no monopoly of Colonel Moredock's; but a passion, in one form or other, and to a degree, greater or less, largely shared among the class to which he belonged. And Indian-hating still exists; and, no doubt, will continue to exist, so long as Indians do. Indian-hating, then, shall be my first theme, and Colonel Moredock, the Indian-hater, my next and last."

With which the stranger, settling himself in his seat, commenced —the hearer paying marked regard, slowly smoking, his glance, meanwhile, steadfastly abstracted towards the deck, but his right ear so disposed towards the speaker that each word came through as little atmospheric intervention as possible. To intensify the sense of hearing, he seemed to sink the sense of sight. No complaisance of mere speech could have been so flattering, or expressed such striking politeness as this mute eloquence of thoroughly digesting attention.

"The judge always began in these words: 'The backwoodsman's hatred of the Indian has been a topic for some remark. In the earlier times of the frontier the passion was thought to be readily accounted for. But Indian rapine having mostly ceased through regions where it once prevailed, the philanthropist is surprised that Indian-hating has not in like degree ceased with it. He wonders why the backwoodsman still regards the red man in much the same spirit that a jury does a murderer, or a trapper a wild cat—a creature, in whose behalf mercy were not wisdom; truce is vain; he must be executed.

"'A curious point,' the judge would continue, 'which perhaps not everybody, even upon explanation, may fully understand; while, in order for any one to approach to an understanding, it is necessary for him to learn, or if he already know, to bear in mind, what manner of man the backwoodsman is; as for what manner of man the Indian is, many know, either from history or experience.

"'The backwoodsman is a lonely man. He is a thoughtful man. He is a man strong and unsophisticated. Impulsive, he is what some might call unprincipled. At any rate, he is self-willed; being one who less hearkens to what others may say about things, than looks for himself, to see what are things themselves. If in straits, there are few to help; he must depend upon himself; he must continually look to himself. Hence self-reliance, to the degree of standing by his own judgment, though it stand alone. Not that he deems himself infallible; too many mistakes in following trails prove the contrary; but he thinks that nature destines such sagacity as she has given him, as she destines it to the 'possum. To these fellow-beings of the wilds their untutored sagacity is their best dependence. If with either it prove faulty, if the 'possum's betray it to the trap, or the backwoodsman's mislead him into ambuscade, there are consequences to be undergone, but no self-blame. As with the 'possum, instincts prevail with the backwoodsman over precepts.

Like the 'possum, the backwoodsman presents the spectacle of a creature dwelling exclusively among the works of God, yet these, truth must confess, breed little in him of a godly mind. Small bowing and scraping is his, further than when with bent knee he points his rifle, or picks its flint. With few companions, solitude by necessity his lengthened lot, he stands the trial—no slight one, since, next to dying, solitude, rightly borne, is perhaps of fortitude the most rigorous test. But not merely is the backwoodsman content to be alone, but in no few cases is anxious to be so. The sight of smoke ten miles off is provocation to one more remove from man, one step deeper into nature. Is it that he feels that whatever man may be, man is not the universe? that glory, beauty, kindness, are not all engrossed by him? that as the presence of man frights birds away, so, many bird-like thoughts? Be that how it will, the backwoodsman is not without some fineness to his nature. Hairy Orson as he looks, it may be with him as with the Shetland seal—beneath the bristles lurks the fur.

" 'Though held in a sort a barbarian, the backwoodsman would seem to America what Alexander was to Asia—captain in the vanguard of conquering civilization. Whatever the nation's growing opulence or power, does it not lackey his heels? Pathfinder, provider of security to those who come after him, for himself he asks nothing but hardship. Worthy to be compared with Moses in the Exodus, or the Emperor Julian in Gaul, who on foot, and barebrowed, at the head of covered or mounted legions, marched so through the elements, day after day. The tide of emigration, let it roll as it will, never overwhelms the backwoodsman into itself; he rides upon advance, as the Polynesian upon the comb of the surf.

" 'Thus, though he keep moving on through life, he maintains with respect to nature much the same unaltered relation throughout; with her creatures, too, including panthers and Indians. Hence, it is not unlikely that, accurate as the theory of the Peace Congress may be with respect to those two varieties of beings, among others, yet the backwoodsman might be qualified to throw out some practical suggestions.

" 'As the child born to a backwoodsman must in turn lead his father's life—a life which, as related to humanity, is related mainly to Indians—it is thought best not to mince matters, out of delicacy; but to tell the boy pretty plainly what an Indian is, and what he must expect from him. For however charitable it may be to view Indians as members of the Society of Friends, yet to affirm them such to one ignorant of Indians, whose lonely path lies a long way through their lands, this, in the event, might prove not only injudicious but cruel. At least something of this kind would seem the maxim upon which backswoods' education is based. Accordingly, if in youth the backwoodsman incline to knowledge, as is generally the case, he hears little from his schoolmasters, the old chroniclers of the forest, but histories of Indian lying, Indian theft, Indian double-dealing, Indian fraud and perfidy, Indian want of conscience, Indian blood-thirstiness, Indian diabolism—histories which, though of wild woods, are almost as full of things unangelic as the Newgate Calendar or the Annals of Europe. In these Indian narratives and traditions the lad is thoroughly grounded. "As the twig is bent the tree's inclined." The instinct of antipathy against an Indian grows in the backwoodsman with the sense of good and bad, right and wrong. In one breath he learns that a brother is to be loved, and an Indian to be hated.

" 'Such are the facts,' the judge would say, 'upon which, if one seek to moralize, he must do so with an eye to them. It is terrible that one creature should so regard another, should make it conscience to abhor an entire race. It is terrible; but is it surprising? Surprising, that one should hate a race which he believes to be red from a cause akin to that which makes some tribes of garden insects green? A race whose name is upon the frontier a *memento mori;* painted to him in every evil light; now a horse-thief like those in Moyamensing; now an assassin like a New York rowdy; now a treaty-breaker like an Austrian; now a Palmer with poisoned arrows; now a judicial murderer and Jeffries, after a fierce farce of trial condemning his victim to bloody death; or a Jew with hospitable speeches cozening some fainting stranger into ambuscade, there to burke him, and account it a deed grateful to Manitou, his god.

" 'Still, all this is less advanced as truths of the Indians than as examples of the backwoodsman's impression of them—in which the charitable may think he does them some injustice. Certain it is, the Indians themselves think so; quite unanimously, too. The Indians, indeed, protest against the backwoodsman's view of them; and some think that one cause of their returning his antipathy so sincerely as they do, is their moral indignation at being so libeled by him, as they really believe and say. But whether, on this or any point, the Indians should be permitted to testify for themselves, to the exclusion of other testimony, is a question that may be left to the Supreme Court. At any rate, it has been observed that when an Indian becomes a genuine proselyte to Christianity (such cases, however, not being very many; though, indeed, entire tribes are sometimes nominally brought to the true light), he will not in that case conceal his enlightened conviction, that his race's portion by nature is total depravity; and, in that way, as much as admits that the backwoodsman's worst idea of it is not very far from true; while, on the other hand, those red men who are the greatest sticklers for the theory of Indian virtue, and Indian loving-kindness, are sometimes the arrantest horse-thieves and tomahawkers among them. So, at least, avers the backwoodsman. And though, knowing the Indian nature, as he thinks he does, he fancies he is not ignorant that an Indian may in some points deceive himself almost as effectually as in bush-tactics he can another, yet his theory and his practice as above contrasted seem to involve an inconsistency so extreme, that the backwoodsman only accounts for it on the supposition that when a tomahawking red man advances the notion of the benignity of the red race, it is but part and parcel with that subtle strategy which he finds so useful in war, in hunting, and the general conduct of life.'

"In further explanation of that deep abhorrence with which the backwoodsman regards the savage, the judge used to think it might perhaps a little help, to consider what kind of stimulus to it is furnished in those forest histories and traditions before spoken of. In which behalf, he would tell the story of the little colony of Wrights and Weavers, originally seven cousins from Virginia, who, after successive removals with their families, at last established themselves near the southern frontier of the Bloody Ground, Kentucky: 'They were strong, brave men; but, unlike many of the pioneers in those days, theirs was no love of conflict for conflict's sake. Step by step they had been lured to their lonely resting-place by the ever-beckoning seductions of a fertile and virgin land, with a singular exemption, during the march, from Indian molestation. But clearings made and houses built, the bright shield was soon to turn its other side. After repeated persecutions and eventual hostilities, forced on them by a dwindled tribe in their neighborhood—persecutions resulting in loss of crops and cattle; hostilities in which they lost two of their number, illy to be spared, besides others getting painful wounds—the five remaining cousins made, with some serious concessions, a kind of treaty with Mocmohoc, the chief—being to this induced by the harryings of the enemy, leaving them no peace. But they were further prompted, indeed, first incited, by the suddenly changed ways of Mocmohoc, who, though hitherto deemed a savage almost perfidious as Cæsar Borgia, yet now put on a seeming the reverse of this, engaging to bury the hatchet, smoke the pipe, and be friends forever; not friends in the mere sense of renouncing enmity; but in the sense of kindliness, active and familiar.

" 'But what the chief now seemed, did not wholly blind them to what the chief had been; so that, though in no small degree influenced by his change of bearing, they still distrusted him enough to covenant with him, among other articles on their side, that though friendly visits should be exchanged between the wigwams and the cabins, yet the five cousins should never, on any account, be expected to enter the chief's lodge together. The intention was, though they reserved it, that if ever, under the guise of amity, the chief should mean them mischief, and effect it, it should be but partially; so that some of the five might survive, not only for their families' sake, but also for retribution's. Nevertheless, Mocmohoc did, upon a time, with such fine art and pleasing carriage win their confidence, that he brought them all together to a feast of bear's meat, and there, by stratagem, ended them. Years after, over their calcined bones and those of all their families, the chief, reproached for his treachery by a proud hunter whom he had made captive, jeered out, "Treachery? pale face! 'Twas they who broke their covenant first, in coming all together; they that broke it first, in trusting Mocmohoc." '

"At this point the judge would pause, and lifting his hand, and rolling his eyes, exclaim in a solemn enough voice, 'Circling wiles and bloody lusts. The acuteness and genius of the chief but make him the more atrocious.'

"After another pause, he would begin an imaginary kind of dialogue between a backwoodsman and a questioner:

" 'But are all Indians like Mocmohoc?—Not all have proved such; but in the least harmful may lie his germ. There is an Indian nature. "Indian blood is in me," is the half-breed's threat.—But are not some Indians kind?—Yes, but kind Indians are mostly lazy, and reputed simple—at all events, are seldom chiefs; chiefs among the red men being taken from the active, and those accounted wise. Hence, with small promotion, kind Indians have but proportionate influence. And kind Indians may be forced to do unkind biddings. So "beware the Indian, kind or unkind," said Daniel Boone, who lost his sons by them.—But, have all you backwoodsmen been some way victimized by Indians?—No.—Well, and in certain cases may not at least some few of you be favored by them? —Yes, but scarce one among us so self-important, or so selfish-minded, as to hold his personal exemption from Indian outrage such a set-off against the contrary experience of so many others, as that he must needs, in a general way, think well of Indians; or, if he do, an arrow in his flank might suggest a pertinent doubt.

" 'In short,' according to the judge, 'if we at all credit the backwoodsman, his feeling against Indians, to be taken aright, must be considered as being not so much on his own account as on others', or jointly on both accounts. True it is, scarce a family he knows but some member of it, or connection, has been by Indians maimed or scalped. What avails, then, that some one Indian, or some two or three, treat a backwoodsman friendly-like? He fears me, he thinks. Take my rifle from me, give him motive, and what will come? Or if not so, how know I what involuntary preparations may be going on in him for things as unbeknown in present time to him as me—a sort of chemical preparation in the soul for malice, as chemical preparation in the body for malady.'

"Not that the backwoodsman ever used those words, you see, but the judge found him expression for his meaning. And this point he would conclude with saying, that, 'what is called a "friendly Indian" is a very rare sort of creature; and well it was so, for no ruthlessness exceeds that of a "friendly Indian" turned enemy. A coward friend, he makes a valiant foe.

" 'But, thus far the passion in question has been viewed in a general way as that of a community. When to his due share of this the backwoodsman adds his private passion, we have then the stock out of which is formed, if formed at all, the Indian-hater *par excellence*.'

"The Indian-hater *par excellence* the judge defined to be one 'who, having with his mother's milk drank in small love for red men, in youth or early manhood, ere the sensibilities become osseous, receives at their hand some signal outrage, or, which in effect is much the same, some of his kin have, or some friend. Now, nature all around him by her solitudes wooing or bidding him muse upon this matter, he accordingly does so, till the thought develops such attraction, that much as straggling vapors troop from all sides to a storm-cloud, so straggling thoughts of other outrages troop to the nucleus thought, assimiliate with it, and swell it. At last, taking counsel with the elements, he comes to his resolution. An intenser Hannibal, he makes a vow, the hate of which is a vortex from whose suction scarce the remotest chip of the guilty race may reasonably feel secure. Next, he declares himself and settles his temporal affairs. With the solemnity of a Spaniard turned monk, he takes leave of his kin; or rather, these leave-takings have something of the still more impressive finality of death-bed adieus. Last, he commits himself to the forest primeval; there, so long as life shall be his, to act upon a calm, cloistered scheme of strategical, implacable, and lonesome vengeance. Ever on the noiseless trail; cool, collected, patient; less seen than felt; snuffing, smelling—a Leather-stocking Nemesis. In the settlements he will not be seen again; in eyes of old companions tears may start at some chance thing that speaks of him; but they never look for him, nor call; they know he will not come. Suns and seasons fleet; the tiger-lily blows and falls; babes are born and leap in their mothers' arms; but, the Indian-hater is good as gone to his long home, and "Terror" is his epitaph.'

"Here the judge, not unaffected, would pause again, but presently resume: 'How evident that in strict speech there can be no biography of an Indian-hater *par excellence,* any more than one of a sword-fish, or other deep-sea denizen; or, which is still less imaginable, one of a dead man. The career of the Indian-hater *par excellence* has the impenetrability of the fate of a lost steamer. Doubtless, events, terrible ones, have happened, must have happened; but the powers that be in nature have taken order that they shall never become news.

" 'But, luckily for the curious, there is a species of diluted Indian-hater, one whose heart proves not so steely as his brain. Soft enticements of domestic life too often draw him from the ascetic trail; a monk who apostatizes to the world at times. Like a mariner, too, though much abroad, he may have a wife and family in some green harbor which he does not forget. It is with him as with the Papist converts in Senegal; fasting and mortification prove hard to bear.'

"The judge, with his usual judgment, always thought that the intense solitude to which the Indian-hater consigns himself, has, by its overawing influence, no little to do with relaxing his vow. He would relate instances where, after some months' lonely scoutings, the Indian-hater is suddenly seized with a sort of calenture; hurries openly towards the first smoke, though he knows it is an Indian's, announces himself as a lost hunter, gives the savage his rifle, throws himself upon his charity, embraces him with much affection, imploring the privilege of living a while in his sweet companionship. What is too often the sequel of so distempered a procedure may be best known by those who best know the Indian. Upon the whole, the judge, by two and thirty good and sufficient reasons, would maintain that there was no known vocation whose consistent following calls for such self-containings as that of the Indian-hater *par excellence*. In the highest view, he considered such a soul one peeping out but once an age.

"For the diluted Indian-hater, although the vacations he permits himself impair the keeping of the character, yet, it should not be overlooked that this is the man who, by his very infirmity, enables us to form surmises, however inadequate, of what Indian-hating in its perfection is."

"One moment," gently interrupted the cosmopolitan here, "and let me refill my calumet."

Which being done, the other proceeded:—

Chapter **27** *Some Account of* A MAN OF QUESTIONABLE MORALITY, *but Who, Nevertheless, Would Seem Entitled to the Esteem of That Eminent English Moralist Who Said He Liked a Good Hater* 〰

"Coming to mention the man to whose story all thus far said was but the introduction, the judge, who, like you, was a great smoker, would insist upon all the company taking cigars, and then lighting a fresh one himself, rise in his place, and, with the solemnest voice, say—'Gentlemen, let us smoke to the memory of Colonel John Moredock'; when, after several whiffs taken standing in deep silence and deeper reverie, he would resume his seat and his discourse, something in these words:

" 'Though Colonel John Moredock was not an Indian-hater *par excellence*, he yet cherished a kind of sentiment towards the red man, and in that degree, and so acted out his sentiment as sufficiently to merit the tribute just rendered to his memory.

" 'John Moredock was the son of a woman married thrice, and thrice widowed by a tomahawk. The three successive husbands of this woman had been pioneers, and with them she had wandered from wilderness to wilderness, always on the frontier. With nine children, she at last found herself at a little clearing, afterwards Vincennes. There she joined a company about to remove to the new country of Illinois. On the eastern side of Illinois there were then no settlements; but on the west side, the shore of the Mississippi, there were, near the mouth of the Kaskaskia, some old hamlets of French. To the vicinity of those hamlets, very innocent and pleasant places, a new Arcadia, Mrs. Moredock's party was destined; for thereabouts, among the vines, they meant to settle. They embarked upon the Wabash in boats, proposing descending that stream into the Ohio, and the Ohio into the Mississippi, and so, northwards, towards the point to be reached. All went well till they made the rock of the Grand Tower on the Mississippi, where they had to land and drag their boats round a point swept by a strong current. Here a party of Indians, lying in wait, rushed out and mur-

dered nearly all of them. The widow was among the victims
with her children, John excepted, who, some fifty miles distant,
was following with a second party.

"'He was just entering upon manhood, when thus left in nature
sole survivor of his race. Other youngsters might have turned
mourners; he turned avenger. His nerves were electric wires—
sensitive, but steel. He was one who, from self-possession, could be
made neither to flush nor pale. It is said that when the tidings were
brought him, he was ashore sitting beneath a hemlock eating his
dinner of venison—and as the tidings were told him, after the first
start he kept on eating, but slowly and deliberately, chewing the
wild news with the wild meat, as if both together, turned to chyle,
together should sinew him to his intent. From that meal he rose an
Indian-hater. He rose; got his arms, prevailed upon some com-
rades to join him, and without delay started to discover who were
the actual transgressors. They proved to belong to a band of twenty
renegades from various tribes, outlaws even among Indians, and
who had formed themselves into a marauding crew. No opportunity for action being at the time presented, he dismissed his
friends; told them to go on, thanking them, and saying he would
ask their aid at some future day. For upwards of a year, alone in
the wilds, he watched the crew. Once, what he thought a favorable
chance having occurred—it being midwinter, and the savages en-
camped, apparently to remain so—he anew mustered his friends,
and marched against them; but, getting wind of his coming, the
enemy fled, and in such panic that everything was left behind but
their weapons. During the winter, much the same thing happened
upon two subsequent occasions. The next year he sought them at
the head of a party pledged to serve him for forty days. At last
the hour came. It was on the shore of the Mississippi. From their
covert, Moredock and his men dimly descried the gang of Cains
in the red dusk of evening, paddling over to a jungled island in
mid-stream, there the more securely to lodge; for Moredock's retributive spirit in the wilderness spoke ever to their trepidations
now, like the voice calling through the garden. Waiting until dead
of night, the whites swam the river, towing after them a raft laden

with their arms. On landing, Moredock cut the fastenings of the enemy's canoes, and turned them, with his own raft, adrift; resolved that there should be neither escape for the Indians, nor safety, except in victory, for the whites. Victorious the whites were; but three of the Indians saved themselves by taking to the stream. Moredock's band lost not a man.

"'Three of the murderers survived. He knew their names and persons. In the course of three years each successively fell by his own hand. All were now dead. But this did not suffice. He made no avowal, but to kill Indians had become his passion. As an athlete, he had few equals; as a shot, none; in single combat, not to be beaten. Master of that woodland-cunning enabling the adept to subsist where the tyro would perish, and expert in all those arts by which an enemy is pursued for weeks, perhaps months, without once suspecting it, he kept to the forest. The solitary Indian that met him, died. When a murder was descried, he would either secretly pursue their track for some chance to strike at least one blow; or if, while thus engaged, he himself was discovered, he would elude them by superior skill.

"'Many years he spent thus; and though after a time he was, in a degree, restored to the ordinary life of the region and period, yet it is believed that John Moredock never let pass an opportunity of quenching an Indian. Sins of commission in that kind may have been his, but none of omission.

"'It were to err to suppose,' the judge would say, 'that this gentleman was naturally ferocious, or peculiarly possessed of those qualities, which, unhelped by provocation of events, tend to withdraw man from social life. On the contrary, Moredock was an example of something apparently self-contradicting, certainly curious, but, at the same time, undeniable: namely, that nearly all Indian-haters have at bottom loving hearts; at any rate, hearts, if anything, more generous than the average. Certain it is, that, to the degree in which he mingled in the life of the settlements, Moredock showed himself not without humane feelings. No cold husband or colder father, he; and, though often and long away from his household, bore its needs in mind, and provided for them. He could be very convivial; told a good story (though never of his more private exploits), and sung a capital song. Hospitable, not backward to help a neighbor; by report, benevolent, as retributive, in secret; while, in a general manner, though sometimes grave—as is not unusual with men of his complexion, a sultry and tragical brown—yet with nobody, Indians excepted, otherwise than courteous in a manly fashion; a moccasined gentleman, admired and loved. In fact, no one more popular, as an incident to follow may prove.

" 'His bravery, whether in Indian fight or any other, was unquestionable. An officer in the ranging service during the war of 1812, he acquitted himself with more than credit. Of his soldierly character, this anecdote is told: Not long after Hull's dubious surrender at Detroit, Moredock with some of his rangers rode up at night to a log-house, there to rest till morning. The horses being attended to, supper over, and sleeping-places assigned the troop, the host showed the colonel his best bed, not on the ground like the rest, but a bed that stood on legs. But out of delicacy, the guest declined to monopolize it, or, indeed, to occupy it at all; when, to increase the inducement, as the host thought, he was told that a general officer had once slept in that bed. "Who, pray?" asked the colonel. "General Hull." "Then you must not take offense," said the colonel, buttoning up his coat, "but, really, no coward's bed, for me, however comfortable." Accordingly he took up with valor's bed—a cold one on the ground.

" 'At one time the colonel was a member of the territorial council of Illinois, and at the formation of the state government, was pressed to become candidate for governor, but begged to be excused. And, though he declined to give his reasons for declining, yet by those who best knew him the cause was not wholly unsurmised. In his official capacity he might be called upon to enter into friendly treaties with Indian tribes, a thing not to be thought of. And even did no such contingency arise, yet he felt there would be an impropriety in the Governor of Illinois stealing out now and then, during a recess of the legislative bodies, for a few days' shooting at human beings, within the limits of his paternal chief-magistracy. If the governorship offered large honors, from Moredock it demanded larger sacrifices. These were incompatibles. In short, he was not unaware that to be a consistent Indian-hater involves the renunciation of ambition, with its objects—the pomps and glories of the world; and since religion, pronouncing such things vanities, accounts it merit to renounce them, therefore, so far as this goes, Indian-hating, whatever may be thought of it in other respects, may be regarded as not wholly without the efficacy of a devout sentiment.' "

Here the narrator paused. Then, after his long and irksome sitting, started to his feet, and regulating his disordered shirt-frill, and at the same time adjustingly shaking his legs down in his rumpled pantaloons, concluded: "There, I have done; having given you, not my story, mind, or my thoughts, but another's. And now, for your friend Coonskins, I doubt not, that, if the judge were here, he would pronounce him a sort of comprehensive Colonel Moredock, who, too much spreading his passion, shallows it."

"Charity, charity!" exclaimed the cosmopolitan, "never a sound judgment without charity. When man judges man, charity is less a bounty from our mercy than just allowance for the insensible lee-way of human fallibility. God forbid that my eccentric friend should be what you hint. You do not know him, or but imperfectly. His outside deceived you; at first it came near deceiving even me. But I seized a chance, when, owing to indignation against some wrong, he laid himself a little open; I seized that lucky chance, I say, to inspect his heart, and found it an inviting oyster in a forbidding shell. His outside is but put on. Ashamed of his own goodness, he treats mankind as those strange old uncles in romances do their nephews—snapping at them all the time and yet loving them as the apple of their eye."

"Well, my words with him were few. Perhaps he is not what I took him for. Yes, for aught I know, you may be right."

"Glad to hear it. Charity, like poetry, should be cultivated, if only for its being graceful. And now, since you have renounced your notion, I should be happy would you, so to speak, renounce your story, too. That story strikes me with even more incredulity than wonder. To me some parts don't hang together. If the man of hate, how could John Moredock be also the man of love? Either his lone campaigns are fabulous as Hercules'; or else, those being true, what was thrown in about his geniality is but garnish. In short, if ever there was such a man as Moredock, he, in my way of thinking, was either misanthrope or nothing; and his misanthropy the more intense from being focused on one race of men. Though, like suicide, man-hatred would seem peculiarly a Roman and a Grecian passion—that is, Pagan; yet, the annals of neither Rome nor Greece can produce the equal in man-hatred of Colonel More-dock, as the judge and you have painted him. As for this Indian-hating in general, I can only say of it what Dr. Johnson said of the alleged Lisbon earthquake: 'Sir, I don't believe it.'"

"Didn't believe it? Why not? Clashed with any little prejudice of his?"

"Doctor Johnson had no prejudice; but, like a certain other person," with an ingenuous smile, "he had sensibilities, and those were pained."

"Dr. Johnson was a good Christian, wasn't he?"

"He was."

"Suppose he had been something else."

"Then small incredulity as to the alleged earthquake."

"Suppose he had been also a misanthrope?"

"Then small incredulity as to the robberies and murders alleged to have been perpetrated under the pall of smoke and ashes. The infidels of the time were quick to credit those reports and worse. So true is it that, while religion, contrary to the common notion, implies, in certain cases, a spirit of slow reserve as to assent, infidelity, which claims to despise credulity, is sometimes swift to it."

"You rather jumble together misanthropy and infidelity."

"I do not jumble them; they are coördinates. For misanthropy, springing from the same root with disbelief of religion, is twin with that. It springs from the same root, I say; for, set aside materialism, and what is an atheist, but one who does not, or will not, see in the universe a ruling principle of love; and what a misanthrope, but one who does not, or will not, see in man a ruling principle of kindness? Don't you see? In either case the vice consists in a want of confidence."

"What sort of a sensation is misanthropy?"

"Might as well ask me what sort of sensation is hydrophobia. Don't know; never had it. But I have often wondered what it can be like. Can a misanthrope feel warm, I ask myself; take ease? be companionable with himself? Can a misanthrope smoke a cigar and muse? How fares he in solitude? Has the misanthrope such a thing as an appetite? Shall a peach refresh him? The effervescence of champagne, with what eye does he behold it? Is summer good to him? Of long winters how much can he sleep? What are his dreams? How feels he, and what does he, when suddenly awakened, alone, at dead of night, by fusilades of thunder?"

"Like you," said the stranger, "I can't understand the misanthrope. So far as my experience goes, either mankind is worthy one's best love, or else I have been lucky. Never has it been my lot to have been wronged, though but in the smallest degree. Cheating, backbiting, superciliousness, disdain, hard-heartedness, and all that brood, I know but by report. Cold regards tossed over the sinister shoulder of a former friend, ingratitude in a beneficiary, treachery in a confidant—such things may be; but I must take somebody's word for it. Now the bridge that has carried me so well over, shall I not praise it?"

"Ingratitude to the worthy bridge not to do so. Man is a noble fellow, and in an age of satirists, I am not displeased to find one who has confidence in him, and bravely stands up for him."

"Yes, I always speak a good word for man; and what is more, am always ready to do a good deed for him."

"You are a man after my own heart," responded the cosmopolitan, with a candor which lost nothing by its calmness. "Indeed," he added, "our sentiments agree so, that were they written in a book, whose was whose, few but the nicest critics might determine."

"Since we are thus joined in mind," said the stranger, "why not be joined in hand?"

"My hand is always at the service of virtue," frankly extending it to him as to virtue personified.

"And now," said the stranger, cordially retaining his hand, "you know our fashion here at the West. It may be a little low, but it is kind. Briefly, we being newly-made friends must drink together. What say you?"

"Thank you; but indeed, you must excuse me."

"Why?"

"Because, to tell the truth, I have to-day met so many old friends, all free-hearted, convivial gentlemen, that really, really, though for the present I succeed in mastering it, I am at bottom almost in the condition of a sailor who, stepping ashore after a long voyage, ere night reels with loving welcomes, his head of less capacity than his heart."

At the allusion to old friends, the stranger's countenance a little fell, as a jealous lover's might at hearing from his sweetheart of former ones. But rallying, he said: "No doubt they treated you to something strong; but wine—surely, that gentle creature, wine; come, let us have a little gentle wine at one of these little tables here. Come, come." Then essaying to roll about like a full pipe in the sea, sang in a voice which had had more of good-fellowship, had there been less of a latent squeak to it:

> *"Let us drink of the wine of the vine benign,*
> *That sparkles warm in Zansovine."*

The cosmopolitan, with longing eye upon him, stood as sorely tempted and wavering a moment; then, abruptly stepping towards him, with a look of dissolved surrender, said: "When mermaid songs move figure-heads, then may glory, gold, and women try their blandishments on me. But a good fellow, singing a good song, he woos forth my every spike, so that my whole hull, like a ship's, sailing by a magnetic rock, caves in with acquiescence. Enough: when one has a heart of a certain sort, it is in vain trying to be resolute."

Chapter 29 THE BOON COMPANIONS ❧

The wine, port, being called for, and the two seated at the little table, a natural pause of convivial expectancy ensued; the stranger's eye turned towards the bar near by, watching the red-cheeked, white-aproned man there, blithely dusting the bottle, and invitingly arranging the salver and glasses; when, with a sudden impulse turning round his head towards his companion, he said, "Ours is friendship at first sight, ain't it?"

"It is," was the placidly pleased reply: "and the same may be said of friendship at first sight as of love at first sight: it is the only true one, the only noble one. It bespeaks confidence. Who would go sounding his way into love or friendship, like a strange ship by night, into an enemy's harbor?"

"Right. Boldly in before the wind. Agreeable, how we always agree. By-the-way, though but a formality, friends should know each other's names. What is yours, pray?"

"Francis Goodman. But those who love me, call me Frank. And yours?"

"Charles Arnold Noble. But do you call me Charlie."

"I will, Charlie; nothing like preserving in manhood the fraternal familiarities of youth. It proves the heart a rosy boy to the last."

"My sentiments again. Ah!"

It was a smiling waiter, with the smiling bottle, the cork drawn; a common quart bottle, but for the occasion fitted at bottom into a little bark basket, braided with porcupine quills, gayly tinted in the Indian fashion. This being set before the entertainer, he regarded it with affectionate interest, but seemed not to understand, or else to pretend not to, a handsome red label pasted on the bottle, bearing the capital letters, P. W.

"P. W.," said he at last, perplexedly eying the pleasing poser, "now what does P. W. mean?"

"Shouldn't wonder," said the cosmopolitan gravely, "if it stood for port wine. You called for port wine, didn't you?"

"Why so it is, so it is!"

"I find some little mysteries not very hard to clear up," said the other, quietly crossing his legs.

This commonplace seemed to escape the stranger's hearing, for, full of his bottle, he now rubbed his somewhat sallow hands over it, and with a strange kind of cackle, meant to be a chirrup, cried: "Good wine, good wine; is it not the peculiar bond of good feeling?" Then brimming both glasses, pushed one over, saying, with what seemed intended for an air of fine disdain: "I'll betide those gloomy skeptics who maintain that now-a-days pure wine is unpurchasable; that almost every variety on sale is less the vintage of vineyards than laboratories; that most bar-keepers are but a set of male Brinvillierses, with complaisant arts practicing against the lives of their best friends, their customers."

A shade passed over the cosmopolitan. After a few minutes' downcast musing, he lifted his eyes and said: "I have long thought, my dear Charlie, that the spirit in which wine is regarded by too many in these days is one of the most painful examples of want of confidence. Look at these glasses. He who could mistrust poison in this wine would mistrust consumption in Hebe's cheek. While, as for suspicions against the dealers in wine and sellers of it, those who cherish such suspicions can have but limited trust in the human heart. Each human heart they must think to be much like each bottle of port, not such port as this, but such port as they hold to. Strange traducers, who see good faith in nothing, however sacred. Not medicines, not the wine in sacraments, has escaped them. The doctor with his phial, and the priest with his chalice, they deem equally the unconscious dispensers of bogus cordials to the dying."

"Dreadful!"

"Dreadful indeed," said the cosmopolitan solemnly. "These distrusters stab at the very soul of confidence. If this wine," impressively holding up his full glass, "if this wine with its bright promise be not true, how shall man be, whose promise can be no brighter? But if wine be false, while men are true, whither shall fly convivial geniality? To think of sincerely-genial souls drinking each other's health at unawares in perfidious and murderous drugs!"

"Horrible!"

"Much too much so to be true, Charlie. Let us forget it. Come, you are my entertainer on this occasion, and yet you don't pledge me. I have been waiting for it."

"Pardon, pardon," half confusedly and half ostentatiously lifting his glass. "I pledge you, Frank, with my whole heart, believe me," taking a draught too decorous to be large, but which, small though it was, was followed by a slight involuntary wryness to the mouth.

"And I return you the pledge, Charlie, heart-warm as it came to me, and honest as this wine I drink it in," reciprocated the cosmopolitan with princely kindliness in his gesture, taking a generous swallow, concluding in a smack, which, though audible, was not so much so as to be unpleasing.

"Talking of alleged spuriousness of wines," said he, tranquilly setting down his glass, and then sloping back his head and with friendly fixedness eying the wine, "perhaps the strangest part of those allegings is, that there is, as claimed, a kind of man who, while convinced that on this continent most wines are shams, yet still drinks away at them; accounting wine so fine a thing, that even the sham article is better than none at all. And if the temperance people urge that, by this course, he will sooner or later be undermined in health, he answers, 'And do you think I don't know that? But health without cheer I hold a bore; and cheer, even of the spurious sort, has its price, which I am willing to pay.'"

"Such a man, Frank, must have a disposition ungovernably bacchanalian."

"Yes, if such a man there be, which I don't credit. It is a fable, but a fable from which I once heard a person of less genius than grotesqueness draw a moral even more extravagant than the fable itself. He said that it illustrated, as in a parable, how that a man of a disposition ungovernably good-natured might still familiarly associate with men, though, at the same time, he believed the greater part of men false-hearted—accounting society so sweet a thing that even the spurious sort was better than none at all. And if the Rochefoucaultites urge that, by this course, he will sooner or later be undermined in security, he answers, 'And do you think I don't know that? But security without society I hold a bore; and society, even of the spurious sort, has its price, which I am willing to pay.'"

"A most singular theory," said the stranger with a slight fidget, eying his companion with some inquisitiveness, "indeed, Frank, a most slanderous thought," he exclaimed in sudden heat and with an involuntary look almost of being personally aggrieved.

"In one sense it merits all you say, and more," rejoined the other with wonted mildness, "but, for a kind of drollery in it, charity might, perhaps, overlook something of the wickedness. Humor is, in fact, so blessed a thing, that even in the least virtuous product of the human mind, if there can be found but nine good jokes, some philosophers are clement enough to affirm that those nine good jokes should redeem all the wicked thoughts, though plenty as the populace of Sodom. At any rate, this same humor has something, there is no telling what, of beneficence in it, it is such a catholicon and charm—nearly all men agreeing in relishing it, though they may agree in little else—and in its way it undeniably does such a deal of familiar good in the world, that no wonder it is almost a proverb, that a man of humor, a man capable of a good loud laugh—seem how he may in other things—can hardly be a heartless scamp."

"Ha, ha, ha!" laughed the other, pointing to the figure of a pale pauper-boy on the deck below, whose pitiableness was touched, as it were, with ludicrousness by a pair of monstrous boots, apparently some mason's discarded ones, cracked with drouth, half eaten by lime, and curled up about the toe like a bassoon. "Look—ha, ha ha!"

"I see," said the other, with what seemed quiet appreciation, but of a kind expressing an eye to the grotesque, without blindness to what in this case accompanied it, "I see; and the way in which it moves you, Charlie, comes in very apropos to point the proverb I was speaking of. Indeed, had you intended this effect, it could not have been more so. For who that heard that laugh, but would as naturally argue from it a sound heart as sound lungs? True, it is said that a man may smile, and smile, and smile, and be a villain; but it is not said that a man may laugh, and laugh, and laugh, and be one, is it, Charlie?"

"Ha, ha, ha!—no no, no no."

"Why Charlie, your explosions illustrate my remarks almost as aptly as the chemist's imitation volcano did his lectures. But even if experience did not sanction the proverb, that a good laugher cannot be a bad man, I should yet feel bound in confidence to believe it, since it is a saying current among the people, and I doubt not originated among them, and hence *must* be true; for the voice of the people is the voice of truth. Don't you think so?"

"Of course I do. If Truth don't speak through the people, it never speaks at all; so I heard one say."

"A true saying. But we stray. The popular notion of humor, considered as index to the heart, would seem curiously confirmed by Aristotle—I think, in his "Politics," (a work, by-the-by, which, however it may be viewed upon the whole, yet, from the tenor of certain sections, should not, without precaution, be placed in the hands of youth)—who remarks that the least lovable men in history seem to have had for humor not only a disrelish, but a hatred; and this, in some cases, along with an extraordinary dry taste for practical punning. I remember it is related of Phalaris, the capricious tyrant of Sicily, that he once caused a poor fellow to be beheaded on a horse-block, for no other cause than having a horse-laugh."

"Funny Phalaris!"

"Cruel Phalaris!"

As after fire-crackers, there was a pause, both looking downward on the table as if mutually struck by the contrast of exclamations, and pondering upon its significance, if any. So, at least, it seemed; but on one side it might have been otherwise: for presently glancing up, the cosmopolitan said: "In the instance of the moral, drolly cynic, drawn from the queer bacchanalian fellow we were speaking of, who had his reasons for still drinking spurious wine, though knowing it to be such—there, I say, we have an example of what is certainly a wicked thought, but conceived in humor. I will now give you one of a wicked thought conceived in wickedness. You shall compare the two, and answer, whether in the one case the sting is not neutralized by the humor, and whether in the other the absence of humor does not leave the sting free play. I once heard a wit, a mere wit, mind, an irreligious Parisian wit, say, with regard to the temperance movement, that none, to their personal benefit, joined it sooner than niggards and knaves; because, as he affirmed, the one by it saved money and the other made money, as in ship-owners cutting off the spirit ration without giving its equivalent, and gamblers and all sorts of subtle tricksters sticking to cold water, the better to keep a cool head for business."

"A wicked thought, indeed!" cried the stranger, feelingly.

"Yes," leaning over the table on his elbow and genially gesturing at him with his forefinger: "yes, and, as I said, you don't remark the sting of it?"

"I do, indeed. Most calumnious thought, Frank!"

"No humor in it?"

"Not a bit!"

"Well now, Charlie," eying him with moist regard, "let us drink. It appears to me you don't drink freely."

"Oh, oh—indeed, indeed—I am not backward there. I pro-test, a freer drinker than friend Charlie you will find nowhere," with feverish zeal snatching his glass, but only in the sequel to dally with it. "By-the-way, Frank," said he, perhaps, or perhaps not, to draw attention from himself, "by-the-way, I saw a good thing the other day; capital thing; a panegyric on the press. It pleased me so, I got it by heart at two readings. It is a kind of poetry, but in a form which stands in something the same relation to blank verse which that does to rhyme. A sort of free-and-easy chant with re-frains to it. Shall I recite it?"

"Anything in praise of the press I shall be happy to hear," re-joined the cosmopolitan, "the more so," he gravely proceeded, "as of late I have observed in some quarters a disposition to disparage the press."

"Disparage the press?"

"Even so some gloomy souls affirming that it is proving with that great invention as with brandy or eau-de-vie, which, upon its first discovery, was believed by the doctors to be, as its French name implies, a panacea—a notion which experience, it may be thought, has not fully verified."

"You surprise me, Frank. Are there really those who so decry the press? Tell me more. Their reasons."

"Reasons they have none, but affirmations they have many; among other things affirming that, while under dynastic despotisms, the press is to the people little but an improvisatore, under popular ones it is too apt to be their Jack Cade. In fine, these sour sages regard the press in the light of a Colt's revolver, pledged to no cause but his in whose chance hands it may be; deeming the one invention an improvement upon the pen, much akin to what the other is upon the pistol; involving, along with the multiplication of the barrel, no consecration of the aim. The term 'freedom of the press' they consider on a par with *freedom of Colt's revolver*. Hence, for truth and the right, they hold, to indulge hopes from the one is little more sensible than for Kossuth and Mazzini to indulge hopes from the other. Heart-breaking views enough, you think; but their refutation is in every true reformer's contempt. Is it not so?"

"Without doubt. But go on, go on. I like to hear you," flatteringly brimming up his glass for him.

"For one," continued the cosmopolitan, grandly swelling his chest, "I hold the press to be neither the people's improvisatore, nor Jack Cade; neither their paid fool, nor conceited drudge. I think interest never prevails with it over duty. The press still speaks for truth though impaled, in the teeth of lies though intrenched. Disdaining for it the poor name of cheap diffuser of news, I claim for it the independent apostleship of Advancer of Knowledge:—the iron Paul! Paul, I say; for not only does the press advance knowledge, but righteousness. In the press, as in the sun, resides, my dear Charlie, a dedicated principle of beneficent force and light. For the Satanic press, by its coappearance with the apostolic, it is no more an aspersion to that, than to the true sun is the coappearance of the mock one. For all the baleful-looking parhelion, god Apollo dispenses the day. In a word, Charlie, what the sovereign of

England is titularly, I hold the press to be actually—Defender of the Faith!—defender of the faith in the final triumph of truth over error, metaphysics over superstition, theory over falsehood, machinery over nature, and the good man over the bad. Such are my views, which, if stated at some length, you, Charlie, must pardon, for it is a theme upon which I cannot speak with cold brevity. And now I am impatient for your panegyric, which, I doubt not, will put mine to the blush."

"It is rather in the blush-giving vein," smiled the other; "but such as it is, Frank, you shall have it."

"Tell me when you are about to begin," said the cosmopolitan, "for, when at public dinners the press is toasted, I always drink the toast standing, and shall stand while you pronounce the panegyric."

"Very good, Frank; you may stand up now."

He accordingly did so, when the stranger likewise rose, and uplifting the ruby wine-flask, began.

Chapter **30** *Opening with a* POETICAL EULOGY OF THE PRESS *and Continuing with Talk Inspired by the Same* ॐ

" 'Praise be unto the press, not Faust's, but Noah's; let us extol and magnify the press, the true press of Noah, from which breaketh the true morning. Praise be unto the press, not the black press but the red; let us extol and magnify the press, the red press of Noah, from which cometh inspiration. Ye pressmen of the Rhineland and the Rhine, join in with all ye who tread out the glad tidings on isle Madeira or Mitylene.—Who giveth redness of eyes by making men long to tarry at the fine print?—Praise be unto the press, the rosy press of Noah, which giveth rosiness of hearts, by making men long to tarry at the rosy wine.—Who hath babblings and contentions? Who, without cause, inflicteth wounds? Praise be unto the press, the kindly press of Noah, which knitteth friends, which fuseth foes. —Who may be bribed?—Who may be bound?—Praise be unto the press, the free press of Noah, which will not lie for tyrants, but make tyrants speak the truth.—Then praise be unto the press, the frank old press of Noah; then let us extol and magnify the press, the brave old press of Noah; then let us with roses garland and enwreathe the press, the grand old press of Noah, from which flow streams of knowledge which give man a bliss no more unreal than his pain.' "

"You deceived me," smiled the cosmopolitan, as both now resumed their seats; "you roguishly took advantage of my simplicity; you archly played upon my enthusiasm. But never mind; the offense, if any, was so charming, I almost wish you would offend again. As for certain poetic left-handers in your panegyric, those I cheerfully concede to the indefinite privileges of the poet. Upon the whole, it was quite in the lyric style—a style I always admire on account of that spirit of Sibyllic confidence and assurance which is, perhaps, its prime ingredient. But come," glancing at his companion's glass, "for a lyrist, you let the bottle stay with you too long."

"The lyre and the vine forever!" cried the other in his rapture, or what seemed such, heedless of the hint, "the vine, the vine! is it

182

not the most graceful and bounteous of all growths? And, by its being such, is not something meant—divinely meant? As I live, a vine, a Catawba vine, shall be planted on my grave!"

"A genial thought; but your glass there."

"Oh, oh," taking a moderate sip, "but you, why don't you drink?"

"You have forgotten, my dear Charlie, what I told you of my previous convivialities to-day."

"Oh," cried the other, now in manner quite abandoned to the lyric mood, not without contrast to the easy sociability of his companion. "Oh, one can't drink too much of good old wine—the genuine, mellow old port. Pooh, pooh! drink away."

"Then keep me company."

"Of course," with a flourish, taking another sip—"suppose we have cigars. Never mind your pipe there; a pipe is best when alone. I say, waiter, bring some cigars—your best."

They were brought in a pretty little bit of western pottery, representing some kind of Indian utensil, mummy-colored, set down in a mass of tobacco leaves, whose long, green fans, fancifully grouped, formed with peeps of red the sides of the receptacle.

Accompanying it were two accessories, also bits of pottery, but smaller, both globes; one in guise of an apple flushed with red and gold to the life, and, through a cleft at top, you saw it was hollow. This was for the ashes. The other, gray, with wrinkled surface, in the likeness of a wasp's nest, was the match-box.

"There," said the stranger, pushing over the cigar-stand, "help yourself, and I will touch you off," taking a match. "Nothing like tobacco," he added, when the fumes of the cigar began to wreathe, glancing from the smoker to the pottery, "I will have a Virginia tobacco-plant set over my grave beside the Catawba vine."

"Improvement upon your first idea, which by itself was good—but you don't smoke."

"Presently, presently—let me fill your glass again. You don't drink."

"Thank you; but no more just now. Fill *your* glass."

"Presently, presently; do you drink on. Never mind me. Now

that it strikes me, let me say, that he who, out of superfine gentility or fanatic morality, denies himself tobacco, suffers a more serious abatement in the cheap pleasures of life than the dandy in his iron boot, or the celibate on his iron cot. While for him who would fain revel in tobacco, but cannot, it is a thing at which philanthropists must weep, to see such an one, again and again, madly returning to the cigar, which, for his incompetent stomach, he cannot enjoy, while still, after each shameful repulse, the sweet dream of the impossible good goads him on to his fierce misery once more—poor eunuch!"

"I agree with you," said the cosmopolitan, still gravely social, "but you don't smoke."

"Presently, presently, do you smoke on. As I was saying about—"

"But *why* don't you smoke—come. You don't think that tobacco, when in league with wine, too much enhances the latter's vinous quality—in short, with certain constitutions tends to impair self-possession, do you?"

"To think that, were treason to good fellowship," was the warm disclaimer. "No, no. But the fact is, there is an unpropitious flavor in my mouth just now. Ate of a diabolical ragout at dinner, so I shan't smoke till I have washed away the lingering memento of it with wine. But smoke away, you, and pray, don't forget to drink. By-the-way, while we sit here so companionably, giving loose to any companionable nothing, your uncompanionable friend, Coonskins, is, by pure contrast, brought to recollection. If he were but here now, he would see how much of real heart-joy he denies himself by not hob-a-nobbing with his kind."

"Why," with loitering emphasis, slowly withdrawing his cigar, "I thought I had undeceived you there. I thought you had come to a better understanding of my eccentric friend."

"Well, I thought so, too; but first impressions will return, you know. In truth, now that I think of it, I am led to conjecture from chance things which dropped from Coonskins, during the little interview I had with him, that he is not a Missourian by birth, but years ago came West here, a young misanthrope from the other side of the Alleghanies, less to make his fortune, than to flee man.

Now, since they say trifles sometimes effect great results, I shouldn't wonder, if his history were probed, it would be found that what first indirectly gave his sad bias to Coonskins was his disgust at reading in boyhood the advice of Polonius to Laertes—advice which, in the selfishness it inculcates, is almost on a par with a sort of ballad upon the economies of money-making, to be occasionally seen pasted against the desk of small retail traders in New England."

"I do hope now, my dear fellow," said the cosmopolitan with an air of bland protest, "that, in my presence at least, you will throw out nothing to the prejudice of the sons of the Puritans."

"Hey-day and high times indeed," exclaimed the other, nettled, "sons of the Puritans forsooth! And who be Puritans, that I, an Alabamaian, must do them reverence? A set of sourly conceited old Malvolios, whom Shakespeare laughs his fill at in his comedies."

"Pray, what were you about to suggest with regard to Polonius," observed the cosmopolitan with quiet forbearance, expressive of the patience of a superior mind at the petulance of an inferior one; "how do you characterize his advice to Laertes?"

"As false, fatal, and calumnious," exclaimed the other, with a degree of ardor befitting one resenting a stigma upon the family escutcheon, "and for a father to give his son—monstrous. The case you see is this: The son is going abroad, and for the first time. What does the father? Invoke God's blessing upon him? Put the blessed Bible in his trunk? No. Crams him with maxims smacking of my Lord Chesterfield, with maxims of France, with maxims of Italy."

"No, no, be charitable, not that. Why, does he not among other things say:—

'*The friends thou hast, and their adoption tried,*
Grapple them to thy soul with hooks of steel'?

Is that compatible with maxims of Italy?"

"Yes, it is, Frank. Don't you see? Laertes is to take the best of care of his friends—his proved friends, on the same principle that a wine-corker takes the best of care of his proved bottles. When a bottle gets a sharp knock and don't break, he says, 'Ah, I'll keep that bottle.' Why? Because he loves it? No, he has particular use for it."

"Dear, dear!" appealingly turning in distress, "that—that kind of criticism is—is—in fact—it won't do."

"Won't truth do, Frank? You are so charitable with everybody, do but consider the tone of the speech. Now I put it to you, Frank; is there anything in it hortatory to high, heroic, disinterested effort? Anything like 'sell all thou hast and give to the poor?' And, in other points, what desire seems most in the father's mind, that his son should cherish nobleness for himself, or be on his guard against the contrary thing in others? An irreligious warner, Frank —no devout counselor, is Polonius. I hate him. Nor can I bear to hear your veterans of the world affirm, that he who steers through life by the advice of old Polonius will not steer among the break-ers."

"No, no—I hope nobody affirms that," rejoined the cosmopolitan, with tranquil abandonment; sideways reposing his arm at full length upon the table. "I hope nobody affirms that; because, if Polonius' advice be taken in your sense, then the recommendation of it by men of experience would appear to involve more or less of an un-handsome sort of reflection upon human nature. And yet," with a perplexed air, "your suggestions have put things in such a strange light to me as in fact a little to disturb my previous notions of Polonius and what he says. To be frank, by your ingenuity you have unsettled me there, to that degree that were it not for our coincidence of opinion in general, I should almost think I was now at length beginning to feel the ill effect of an immature mind, too much consorting with a mature one, except on the ground of first principles in common."

"Really and truly," cried the other with a kind of tickled modesty and pleased concern, "mine is an understanding too weak to throw out grapnels and hug another to it. I have indeed heard of some great scholars in these days, whose boast is less that they have made disciples than victims. But for me, had I the power to do such things, I have not the heart to desire."

"I believe you, my dear Charlie. And yet, I repeat, by your commentaries on Polonius you have, I know not how, unsettled me; so that now I don't exactly see how Shakespeare meant the words he puts in Polonius' mouth."

"Some say that he meant them to open people's eyes; but I don't think so."

"Open their eyes?" echoed the cosmopolitan, slowly expanding his; "what is there in this world for one to open his eyes to? I mean in the sort of invidious sense you cite?"

"Well, others say he meant to corrupt people's morals; and still others, that he had no express intention at all, but in effect opens their eyes and corrupts their morals in one operation. All of which I reject."

"Of course you reject so crude an hypothesis; and yet, to confess, in reading Shakespeare in my closet, struck by some passage, I have laid down the volume, and said: 'This Shakespeare is a queer man.' At times seeming irresponsible, he does not always seem reliable. There appears to be a certain—what shall I call it?—hidden sun, say, about him, at once enlightening and mystifying. Now, I should be afraid to say what I have sometimes thought that hidden sun might be."

"Do you think it was the true light?" with clandestine geniality again filling the other's glass.

"I would prefer to decline answering a categorical question there. Shakespeare has got to be a kind of deity. Prudent minds, having certain latent thoughts concerning him, will reserve them in a condition of lasting probation. Still, as touching avowable speculations, we are permitted a tether. Shakespeare himself is to be adored, not arraigned; but, so we do it with humility, we may a little canvass his characters. There's his Autolycus now, a fellow that always puzzled me. How is one to take Autolycus? A rogue so happy, so lucky, so triumphant, of so almost captivatingly vicious a career that a virtuous man reduced to the poor-house (were such a contingency conceivable), might almost long to change sides with him. And yet, see the words put into his mouth: 'Oh,' cries Autolycus, as he comes galloping, gay as a buck, upon the stage, 'oh,' he laughs, 'oh what a fool is Honesty, and Trust, his sworn brother, a very simple gentleman.' Think of that. Trust, that is, confidence—that is, the thing in this universe the sacredest—is rattlingly pronounced just the simplest. And the scenes in which the rogue figures seem purposely devised for verification of his principles. Mind, Charlie, I do not say it *is* so, far from it; but I *do* say it seems so. Yes, Autolycus would seem a needy varlet acting upon the persuasion that less is to be got by invoking pockets than picking them, more to be made by an expert knave than a bungling beggar; and for this reason, as he thinks, that the soft heads outnumber the soft hearts. The devil's drilled recruit, Autolycus is joyous as if he wore the livery of heaven. When disturbed by the character and career of one thus wicked and thus happy, my sole consolation is in the fact that no such creature ever existed, except in the powerful imagination which evoked him. And yet, a creature, a living creature, he is, though only a poet was his maker. It may be, that in that paper-and-ink investiture of his, Autolycus acts more effectively upon mankind than he would in a flesh-and-blood one. Can his influence be salutary? True, in Autolycus there is humor; but though, according to my principle, humor is in general to be held a saving quality, yet the case of Autolycus is an exception; because it is his humor which, so to speak, oils his mischievousness. The bravadoing mischievousness of Autolycus is slid into the world on humor, as a pirate schooner, with colors flying, is launched into the sea on greased ways."

"I approve of Autolycus as little as you," said the stranger, who, during his companion's commonplaces, had seemed less attentive to them than to maturing within his own mind the original conceptions destined to eclipse them. "But I cannot believe that Autolycus, mischievous as he must prove upon the stage, can be near so much so as such a character as Polonius."

"I don't know about that," bluntly, and yet not impolitely, returned the cosmopolitan; "to be sure, accepting your view of the old courtier, then if between him and Autolycus you raise the question of unprepossessingness, I grant you the latter comes off best.

For a moist rogue may tickle the midriff, while a dry worldling may but wrinkle the spleen."

"But Polonius is not dry," said the other excitedly; "he drules. One sees the fly-blown old fop drule and look wise. His vile wisdom is made the viler by his vile rheuminess. The bowing and cringing, time-serving old sinner—is such an one to give manly precepts to youth? The discreet, decorous, old dotard-of-state; senile prudence; fatuous soullessness! The ribanded old dog is paralytic all down one side, and that the side of nobleness. His soul is gone out. Only nature's automatonism keeps him on his legs. As with some old trees, the bark survives the pith, and will still stand stiffly up, though but to rim round punk, so the body of old Polonius has outlived his soul."

"Come, come," said the cosmopolitan with serious air, almost displeased; "though I yield to none in admiration of earnestness, yet, I think, even earnestness may have limits. To human minds, strong language is always more or less distressing. Besides, Polonius is an old man—as I remember him upon the stage—with snowy locks. Now charity requires that such a figure—think of it how you will —should at least be treated with civility. Moreover, old age is ripeness, and I once heard say, 'Better ripe than raw.'"

"But not better rotten than raw!" bringing down his hand with energy on the table.

"Why, bless me," in mild surprise contemplating his heated comrade, "how you fly out against this unfortunate Polonius—a being that never was, nor will be. And yet, viewed in a Christian light," he added pensively, "I don't know that anger against this man of straw is a whit less wise than anger against a man of flesh. Madness, to be mad with anything."

"That may be, or may not be," returned the other, a little testily, perhaps; "but I stick to what I said, that it is better to be raw than rotten. And what is to be feared on that head, may be known from this: that it is with the best of hearts as with the best of pears—a dangerous experiment to linger too long upon the scene. This did Polonius. Thank fortune, Frank, I am young, every tooth sound in my head, and if good wine can keep me where I am, long shall I remain so."

"True," with a smile. "But wine, to do good, must be drunk. You have talked much and well, Charlie; but drunk little and indifferently—fill up."

"Presently, presently," with a hasty and preoccupied air. "If I remember right, Polonius hints as much as that one should, under no circumstances, commit the indiscretion of aiding in a pecuniary way an unfortunate friend. He drules out some stale stuff about 'loan losing both itself and friend,' don't he? But our bottle; is it glued fast? Keep it moving, my dear Frank. Good wine, and upon my soul I begin to feel it, and through me old Polonius—yes, this wine, I fear, is what excites me so against that detestable old dog without a tooth."

Upon this, the cosmopolitan, cigar in mouth, slowly raised the bottle, and brought it slowly to the light, looking at it steadfastly, as one might at a thermometer in August, to see not how low it was, but how high. Then whiffing out a puff, set it down, and said: "Well, Charlie, if what wine you have drunk came out of this bottle, in that case I should say that if—supposing a case—that if one fellow had an object in getting another fellow fuddled, and this fellow to be fuddled was of your capacity, the operation would be comparatively inexpensive. What do you think, Charlie?"

"Why, I think I don't much admire the supposition," said Charlie, with a look of resentment; "it ain't safe, depend upon it, Frank, to venture upon too jocose suppositions with one's friends."

"Why, bless you, Frank, my supposition wasn't personal, but general. You mustn't be so touchy."

"If I am touchy it is the wine. Sometimes, when I freely drink, it has a touchy effect on me, I have observed."

"Freely drink? you haven't drunk the perfect measure of one glass, yet. While for me, this must be my fourth or fifth, thanks to your importunity; not to speak of all I drank this morning, for old acquaintance' sake. Drink, drink; you must drink."

"Oh, I drink while you are talking," laughed the other; "you have not noticed it, but I have drunk my share. Have a queer way

I learned from a sedate old uncle, who used to tip off his glass unperceived. Do you fill up, and my glass, too. There! Now away with that stump, and have a new cigar. Good fellowship forever!" again in the lyric mood. "Say, Frank, are we not men? I say are we not human? Tell me, were they not human who engendered us, as before heaven I believe they shall be whom we shall engender? Fill up, up, up, my friend. Let the ruby tide aspire, and all ruby aspirations with it! Up, fill up! Be we convivial. And conviviality, what is it? The word, I mean; what expresses it? A living together. But bats live together, and did you ever hear of convivial bats?"

"If I ever did," observed the cosmopolitan, "it has quite slipped my recollection."

"But *why* did you never hear of convivial bats, nor anybody else? Because bats, though they live together, live not together genially. Bats are not genial souls. But men are; and how delightful to think that the word which among men signifies the highest pitch of geniality, implies, as indispensable auxiliary, the cheery benediction of the bottle. Yes, Frank, to live together in the finest sense, we must drink together. And so, what wonder that he who loves not wine, that sober wretch has a lean heart—a heart like a wrung-out old bluing-bag, and loves not his kind? Out upon him, to the rag-house with him, hang him—the ungenial soul!"

"Oh, now, now, can't you be convivial without being censorious? I like easy, unexcited conviviality. For the sober man, really, though for my part I naturally love a cheerful glass, I will not prescribe my nature as the law to other natures. So don't abuse the sober man. Conviviality is one good thing, and sobriety is another good thing. So don't be one-sided."

"Well, if I am one-sided, it is the wine. Indeed, indeed, I have indulged too genially. My excitement upon slight provocation shows it. But yours is a stronger head; drink you. By the way, talking of geniality, it is much on the increase in these days, ain't it?"

"It is, and I hail the fact. Nothing better attests the advance of the humanitarian spirit. In former and less humanitarian ages—the ages of amphitheatres and gladiators—geniality was mostly confined to the fireside and table. But in our age—the age of joint-stock companies and free-and-easies—it is with this precious quality as with precious gold in old Peru, which Pizarro found making up the scullion's sauce-pot as the Inca's crown. Yes, we golden boys, the moderns, have geniality everywhere—a bounty broadcast like noonlight."

"True, true; my sentiments again. Geniality has invaded each department and profession. We have genial senators, genial authors, genial lecturers, genial doctors, genial clergymen, genial surgeons, and the next thing we shall have genial hangmen."

"As to the last-named sort of person," said the cosmopolitan, "I trust that the advancing spirit of geniality will at last enable us to dispense with him. No murderers—no hangmen. And surely, when the whole world shall have been genialized, it will be as out of place to talk of murderers, as in a Christianized world to talk of sinners."

"To pursue the thought," said the other, "every blessing is attended with some evil, and—"

"Stay," said the cosmopolitan, "that may be better let pass for a loose saying, than for hopeful doctrine."

"Well, assuming the saying's truth, it would apply to the future supremacy of the genial spirit, since then it will fare with the hangman as it did with the weaver when the spinning-jenny whizzed into the ascendant. Thrown out of employment, what could Jack Ketch turn his hand to? Butchering?"

"That he could turn his hand to it seems probable; but that, under the circumstances, it would be appropriate, might in some minds admit of a question. For one, I am inclined to think—and I trust it will not be held fastidiousness—that it would hardly be suitable to the dignity of our nature, that an individual, once employed in attending the last hours of human unfortunates, should, that office being extinct, transfer himself to the business of attending the last hours of unfortunate cattle. I would suggest that the individual turn valet—a vocation to which he would, perhaps, appear not wholly inadapted by his familiar dexterity about the person. In particular, for giving a finishing tie to a gentleman's cravat,

I know few who would, in all likelihood, be, from previous occupation, better fitted than the professional person in question."

"Are you in earnest?" regarding the serene speaker with unaffected curiosity; "are you really in earnest?"

"I trust I am never otherwise," was the mildly earnest reply; "but talking of the advance of geniality, I am not without hopes that it will eventually exert its influence even upon so difficult a subject as the misanthrope."

"A genial misanthrope! I thought I had stretched the rope pretty hard in talking of genial hangmen. A genial misanthrope is no more conceivable than a surly philanthropist."

"True," lightly depositing in an unbroken little cylinder the ashes of his cigar, "true, the two you name are well opposed."

"Why, you talk as if there *was* such a being as a surly philanthropist."

"I do. My eccentric friend, whom you call Coonskins, is an example. Does he not, as I explained to you, hide under a surly air a philanthropic heart? Now, the genial misanthrope, when, in the process of eras, he shall turn up, will be the converse of this; under an affable air, he will hide a misanthropical heart. In short, the genial misanthrope will be a new kind of monster, but still no small improvement upon the original one, since, instead of making faces and throwing stones at people, like that poor old crazy man, Timon, he will take steps, fiddle in hand, and set the tickled world a' dancing. In a word, as the progress of Christianization mellows those in manner whom it cannot mend in mind, much the same will it prove with the progress of genialization. And so, thanks to geniality, the misanthrope, reclaimed from his boorish address, will take on refinement and softness—to so genial a degree, indeed, that it may possibly fall out that the misanthrope of the coming century will be almost as popular as, I am sincerely sorry to say, some philanthropists of the present time would seem not to be, as witness my eccentric friend named before."

"Well," cried the other, a little weary, perhaps, of a speculation so abstract, "well, however it may be with the century to come, certainly in the century which is, whatever else one may be, he must be genial or he is nothing. So fill up, fill up, and be genial!"

"I am trying my best," said the cosmopolitan, still calmly companionable. "A moment since, we talked of Pizarro, gold, and Peru; no doubt, now, you remember that when the Spaniard first entered Atahualpa's treasure-chamber, and saw such profusion of plate stacked up, right and left, with the wantonness of old barrels in a brewer's yard, the needy fellow felt a twinge of misgiving, of want of confidence, as to the genuineness of an opulence so profuse. He went about rapping the shining vases with his knuckles. But it was all gold, pure gold, good gold, sterling gold, which how cheerfully would have been stamped such at Goldsmiths' Hall. And just so those needy minds, which, through their own insincerity, having no confidence in mankind, doubt lest the liberal geniality of this age be spurious. They are small Pizarros in their way—by the very princeliness of men's geniality stunned into distrust of it."

"Far be such distrust from you and me, my genial friend," cried the other fervently; "fill up, fill up!"

"Well, this all along seems a division of labor," smiled the cosmopolitan. "I do about all the drinking, and you do about all—the genial. But yours is a nature competent to do that to a large population. And now, my friend," with a peculiarly grave air, evidently foreshadowing something not unimportant, and very likely of close personal interest; "wine, you know, opens the heart, and—"

"Opens it!" with exultation, "it thaws it right out. Every heart is ice-bound till wine melt it, and reveal the tender grass and sweet herbage budding below, with every dear secret, hidden before like a dropped jewel in a snow-bank, lying there unsuspected through winter till spring."

"And just in that way, my dear Charlie, is one of my little secrets now to be shown forth."

"Ah!" eagerly moving round his chair, "what is it?"

"Be not so impetuous, my dear Charlie. Let me explain. You see, naturally, I am a man not overgifted with assurance; in general, I am, if anything, diffidently reserved; so, if I shall presently seem otherwise, the reason is, that you, by the geniality you have evinced in all your talk, and especially the noble way in which, while affirming your good opinion of men, you intimated that you never could prove false to any man, but most by your indignation at a particularly illiberal passage in Polonius' advice—in short, in short," with extreme embarrassment, "how shall I express what I mean, unless I add that by your whole character you impel me to throw myself upon your nobleness; in one word, put confidence in you, a generous confidence?"

"I see, I see," with heightened interest, "something of moment you wish to confide. Now, what is it, Frank? Love affair?"

"No, not that."

"What then, my *dear* Frank? Speak—depend upon me to the last. Out with it."

"Out it shall come, then," said the cosmopolitan, "I am in want, urgent want, of money."

Chapter 31 A METAMORPHOSIS MORE SURPRISING
Than Any in Ovid ᔰ

"In want of money!" pushing back his chair as from a suddenly-disclosed man-trap or crater.

"Yes," naïvely assented the cosmopolitan, "and you are going to loan me fifty dollars. I could almost wish I was in need of more, only for your sake. Yes, my dear Charlie, for your sake; that you might the better prove your noble kindliness, my dear Charlie."

"None of your dear Charlies," cried the other, springing to his feet, and buttoning up his coat, as if hastily to depart upon a long journey.

"Why, why, why?" painfully looking up.

"None of your why, why, whys!" tossing out a foot, "go to the devil, sir! Beggar, impostor!—never so deceived in a man in my life."

While speaking or rather hissing those words, the boon companion underwent much such a change as one reads of in fairy-books. Out of old materials sprang a new creature. Cadmus glided into the snake.

The cosmopolitan rose, the traces of previous feeling vanished; looked steadfastly at his transformed friend a moment, then, taking ten half-eagles from his pocket, stooped down, and laid them, one by one, in a circle round him; and, retiring a pace, waved his long tasseled pipe with the air of a necromancer, an air heightened by his costume, accompanying each wave with a solemn murmur of cabalistical words.

Meantime, he within the magic-ring stood suddenly rapt, exhibiting every symptom of a successful charm—a turned cheek, a fixed attitude, a frozen eye; spell-bound, not more by the waving wand than by the ten invincible talismans on the floor.

"Reappear, reappear, reappear, oh, my former friend! Replace this hideous apparition with thy blest shape, and be the token of thy return the words, 'My dear Frank.'"

"My dear Frank," now cried the restored friend, cordially stepping out of the ring, with regained self-possession regaining lost identity, "My dear Frank, what a funny man you are; full of fun as an egg of meat. How could you tell me that absurd story of your being in need? But I relish a good joke too well to spoil it by letting on. Of course, I humored the thing; and, on my side, put on all the cruel airs you would have me. Come, this little episode of fictitious estrangement will but enhance the delightful reality. Let us sit down again, and finish our bottle."

"With all my heart," said the cosmopolitan, dropping the necromancer with the same facility with which he had assumed it. "Yes," he added, soberly picking up the gold pieces, and returning them with a chink to his pocket, "yes, I am something of a funny man now and then; while for you, Charlie," eying him in tenderness, "what you say about your humoring the thing is true enough; never did man second a joke better than you did just now. You played your part better than I did mine; you played it, Charlie, to the life."

"You see, I once belonged to an amateur play company; that accounts for it. But come, fill up, and let's talk of something else."

"Well," acquiesced the cosmopolitan, seating himself, and quietly brimming his glass, "what shall we talk about?"

"Oh, anything you please," a sort of nervously accommodating.

"Well, suppose we talk about Charlemont?"

"Charlemont? What's Charlemont? Who's Charlemont?"

"You shall hear, my dear Charlie," answered the cosmopolitan. "I will tell you the story of Charlemont, the gentleman-madman."

But ere be given the rather grave story of Charlemont, a reply must in civility be made to a certain voice which methinks I hear, that, in view of past chapters, and more particularly the last, where certain antics appear, exclaims: How unreal all this is! Who did ever dress or act like your cosmopolitan? And who, it might be returned, did ever dress or act like harlequin?

Strange, that in a work of amusement, this severe fidelity to real life should be exacted by any one, who, by taking up such a work, sufficiently shows that he is not unwilling to drop real life, and turn, for a time, to something different. Yes, it is, indeed, strange that any one should clamor for the thing he is weary of; that any one, who, for any cause, finds real life dull, should yet demand of him who is to divert his attention from it, that he should be true to that dullness.

There is another class, and with this class we side, who sit down to a work of amusement tolerantly as they sit at a play, and with much the same expectations and feelings. They look that fancy shall evoke scenes different from those of the same old crowd round the custom-house counter, and same old dishes on the boarding-house table, with characters unlike those of the same old acquaint-ances they meet in the same old way every day in the same old street. And as, in real life, the proprieties will not allow people to act out themselves with that unreserve permitted to the stage; so, in books of fiction, they look not only for more entertainment, but, at bottom, even for more reality, than real life itself can show. Thus, though they want novelty, they want nature, too; but nature un-fettered, exhilarated, in effect transformed. In this way of think-ing, the people in a fiction, like the people in a play, must dress as nobody exactly dresses, talk as nobody exactly talks, act as nobody exactly acts. It is with fiction as with religion: it should present an-other world, and yet one to which we feel the tie.

If, then, something is to be pardoned to well-meant endeavor, surely a little is to be allowed to that writer who, in all his scenes, does but seek to minister to what, as he understands it, is the implied wish of the more indulgent lovers of entertainment, before whom harlequin can never appear in a coat too parti-colored, or cut capers too fantastic.

One word more. Though every one knows how bootless it is to be in all cases vindicating one's self, never mind how convinced one may be that he is never in the wrong; yet, so precious to man is the approbation of his kind, that to rest, though but under an imaginary censure applied to but a work of imagination, is no easy thing. The mention of this weakness will explain why all such readers as may think they perceive something inharmonious between the boisterous hilarity of the cosmopolitan with the bristling cynic, and his restrained good-nature with the boon-companion, are now referred to that chapter where some similar apparent inconsistency in another character is, on general principles, modestly endeavored to be apologized for.

"Charlemont was a young merchant of French descent, living in St. Louis—a man not deficient in mind, and possessed of that sterling and captivating kindliness, seldom in perfection seen but in youthful bachelors, united at times to a remarkable sort of gracefully devil-may-care and witty good-humor. Of course, he was admired by everybody, and loved, as only mankind can love, by not a few. But in his twenty-ninth year a change came over him. Like one whose hair turns gray in a night, so in a day Charlemont turned from affable to morose. His acquaintances were passed without greeting; while, as for his confidential friends, them he pointedly, unscrupulously, and with a kind of fierceness, cut dead.

"One, provoked by such conduct, would fain have resented it with words as disdainful; while another, shocked by the change, and, in concern for a friend, magnanimously overlooking affronts, implored to know what sudden, secret grief had distempered him. But from resentment and from tenderness Charlemont alike turned away.

"Ere long, to the general surprise, the merchant Charlemont was gazetted, and the same day it was reported that he had withdrawn from town, but not before placing his entire property in the hands of responsible assignees for the benefit of creditors.

"Whither he had vanished, none could guess. At length, nothing being heard, it was surmised that he must have made away with himself—a surmise, doubtless, originating in the remembrance of the change some months previous to his bankruptcy—a change of a sort only to be ascribed to a mind suddenly thrown from its balance.

"Years passed. It was spring-time, and lo, one bright morning, Charlemont lounged into the St. Louis coffee-houses—gay, polite, humane, companionable, and dressed in the height of costly elegance. Not only was he alive, but he was himself again. Upon meeting with old acquaintances, he made the first advances, and in such a manner that it was impossible not to meet him half-way.

Upon other old friends, whom he did not chance casually to meet, he either personally called, or left his card and compliments for them; and to several, sent presents of game or hampers of wine.

"They say the world is sometimes harshly unforgiving, but it was not so to Charlemont. The world feels a return of love for one who returns to it as he did. Expressive of its renewed interest was a whisper, an inquiring whisper, how now, exactly, so long after his bankruptcy, it fared with Charlemont's purse. Rumor, seldom at a loss for answers, replied that he had spent nine years in Marseilles in France, and there acquiring a second fortune, had returned with it, a man devoted henceforth to genial friendships.

"Added years went by, and the restored wanderer still the same; or rather, by his noble qualities, grew up like golden maize in the encouraging sun of good opinions. But still the latent wonder was, what had caused that change in him at a period when, pretty much as now, he was, to all appearance, in the possession of the same fortune, the same friends, the same popularity. But nobody thought it would be the thing to question him here.

"At last, at a dinner at his house, when all the guests but one had successively departed; this remaining guest, an old acquaintance, being just enough under the influence of wine to set aside the fear of touching upon a delicate point, ventured, in a way which perhaps spoke more favorably for his heart than his tact, to beg of his host to explain the one enigma of his life. Deep melancholy overspread the before cheery face of Charlemont; he sat for some moments tremulously silent; then pushing a full decanter towards the guest, in a choked voice, said: 'No, no! when by art, and care, and time, flowers are made to bloom over a grave, who would seek to dig all up again only to know the mystery?—The wine.' When both glasses were filled, Charlemont took his, and lifting it, added lowly: 'If ever, in days to come, you shall see ruin at hand, and, thinking you understand mankind, shall tremble for your friendships, and tremble for your pride; and, partly through love for the one and fear for the other, shall resolve to be beforehand with the world, and save it from a sin by prospectively taking that sin to yourself, then will you do as one I now dream of once did, and like him will you suffer; but how fortunate and how grateful should you be, if like him, after all that had happened, you could be a little happy again.'

"When the guest went away, it was with the persuasion, that though outwardly restored in mind as in fortune, yet, some taint of Charlemont's old malady survived, and that it was not well for friends to touch one dangerous string."

"Well, what do you think of the story of Charlemont?" mildly asked he who had told it.

"A very strange one," answered the auditor, who had been such not with perfect ease, "but is it true?"

"Of course not; it is a story which I told with the purpose of every story-teller—to amuse. Hence, if it seem strange to you, that strangeness is the romance; it is what contrasts it with real life; it is the invention, in brief, the fiction as opposed to the fact. For do but ask yourself, my dear Charlie," lovingly leaning over towards him, "I rest it with your own heart now, whether such a forereaching motive as Charlemont hinted he had acted on in his change—whether such a motive, I say, were a sort of one at all justified by the nature of human society? Would you, for one, turn the cold shoulder to a friend—a convivial one, say, whose pennilessness should be suddenly revealed to you?"

"How can you ask me, my dear Frank? You know I would scorn such meanness." But rising somewhat disconcerted—"really, early as it is, I think I must retire; my head," putting up his hand to it, "feels unpleasantly; this confounded elixir of logwood, little as I drank of it, has played the deuce with me."

"Little as you drank of this elixir of logwood? Why, Charlie, you are losing your mind. To talk so of the genuine, mellow old port. Yes, I think that by all means you had better away, and sleep it off. There—don't apologize—don't explain—go, go—I understand you exactly. I will see you to-morrow."

Chapter 36 *In Which the Cosmopolitan Is Accosted By A MYSTIC, whereupon Ensues Pretty Much Such Talk as Might Be Expected* ૐ

As, not without some haste, the boon companion withdrew, a stranger advanced, and touching the cosmopolitan, said: "I think I heard you say you would see that man again. Be warned; don't you do so."

He turned, surveying the speaker; a blue-eyed man, sandy-haired, and Saxon-looking; perhaps five and forty; tall, and, but for a certain angularity, well made; little touch of the drawing-room about him, but a look of plain propriety of a Puritan sort, with a kind of farmer dignity. His age seemed betokened more by his brow, placidly thoughtful, than by his general aspect, which had that look of youthfulness in maturity, peculiar sometimes to habitual health of body, the original gift of nature, or in part the effect or reward of steady temperance of the passions, kept so, perhaps, by constitution as much as morality. A neat, comely, almost ruddy cheek, coolly fresh, like a red clover-blossom at coolish dawn —the color of warmth preserved by the virtue of chill. Toning the whole man, was one-knows-not-what of shrewdness and mythiness, strangely jumbled; in that way, he seemed a kind of cross between a Yankee peddler and a Tartar priest, though it seemed as if, at a pinch, the first would not in all probability play second fiddle to the last.

"Sir," said the cosmopolitan, rising and bowing with slow dignity, "if I cannot with unmixed satisfaction hail a hint pointed at one who has just been clinking the social glass with me, on the other hand, I am not disposed to underrate the motive which, in the present case, could alone hve prompted such an intimation. My friend, whose seat is still warm, has retired for the night, leaving more or less in his bottle here. Pray, sit down in his seat, and partake with me; and then, if you choose to hint aught further unfavorable to the man, the genial warmth of whose person in part passes into yours, and whose genial hospitality meanders through you—be it so."

"Quite beautiful conceits," said the stranger, now scholastically and artistically eying the picturesque speaker, as if he were a statue in the Pitti Palace; "very beautiful"; then with the gravest interest, "yours, sir, if I mistake not, must be a beautiful soul—one full of all love and truth; for where beauty is, there must those be."

"A pleasing belief," rejoined the cosmopolitan, beginning with an even air, "and to confess, long ago it pleased me. Yes, with you and Schiller, I am pleased to believe that beauty is at bottom incompatible with ill, and therefore am so eccentric as to have confidence in the latent benignity of that beautiful creature the rattle-snake, whose lithe neck and burnished maze of tawny gold, as he sleekly curls aloft in the sun, who on the prairie can behold without wonder?"

As he breathed these words, he seemed so to enter into their spirit—as some earnest descriptive speakers will—as unconsciously to wreathe his form and sidelong crest his head, till he all but seemed the creature described. Meantime, the stranger regarded him with little surprise, apparently, though with much contemplativeness of a mystical sort, and presently said: "When charmed by the beauty of that viper, did it never occur to you to change personalities with him? to feel what it was to be a snake? to glide unsuspected in grass? to sting, to kill at a touch; your whole beautiful body one iridescent scabbard of death? In short, did the wish never occur to you to feel yourself exempt from knowledge, and conscience and revel for a while in the care-free, joyous life of a perfectly instinctive, unscrupulous, and irresponsible creature?"

"Such a wish," replied the other, not perceptibly disturbed, "I must confess, never consciously was mine. Such a wish, indeed, could hardly occur to ordinary imaginations, and mine I cannot think much above the average."

"But now that the idea is suggested," said the stranger, with infantile intellectuality, "does it not raise the desire?"

"Hardly. For though I do not think I have any uncharitable prejudice against the rattle-snake, still, I should not like to be one. If I were a rattle-snake now, there would be no such thing as being genial with men—men would be afraid of me, and then I should be a very lonesome and miserable rattle-snake."

"True, men would be afraid of you. And why? Because of your rattle, your hollow rattle—a sound, as I have been told, like the shaking together of small, dry skulls in a tune of the Waltz of Death. And here we have another beautiful truth. When any creature is by its make inimical to other creatures, nature in effect labels that creature, much as an apothecary does a poison. So that whoever is destroyed by a rattle-snake, or other harmful agent, it is his own fault. He should have respected the label. Hence that significant passage in Scripture, 'Who will pity the charmer that is bitten with a serpent?' "

"*I* would pity him," said the cosmopolitan, a little bluntly, perhaps.

"But don't you think," rejoined the other, still maintaining his passionless air, "don't you think, that for a man to pity where nature is pitiless, is a little presuming?"

"Let casuists decide the casuistry, but the compassion the heart decides for itself. But, sir," deepening in seriousness, "as I now for the first realize, you but a moment since introduced the word irresponsible in a way I am not used to. Now, sir, though, out of a tolerant spirit, as I hope, I try my best never to be frightened at any speculation, so long as it is pursued in honesty, yet, for once, I must acknowledge that you do really, in the point cited, cause me uneasiness; because a proper view of the universe, that view which is suited to breed a proper confidence, teaches, if I err not, that since all things are justly presided over, not very many living agents but must be some way accountable."

"Is a rattle-snake accountable?" asked the stranger with such a preternaturally cold, gemmy glance out of his pellucid blue eye, that he seemed more a metaphysical merman than a feeling man; "is a rattle-snake accountable?"

"If I will not affirm that it is," returned the other, with the caution of no inexperienced thinker, "neither will I deny it. But if we suppose it so, I need not say that such accountability is neither to you, nor me, nor the Court of Common Pleas, but to something superior."

He was proceeding, when the stranger would have interrupted him; but as reading his argument in his eye, the cosmopolitan, without waiting for it to be put into words, at once spoke to it: "You object to my supposition, for but such it is, that the rattle-snake's accountability is not by nature manifest; but might not much the same thing be urged against man's? A *reductio ad absurdum*, proving the objection vain. But if now," he continued, "you consider what capacity for mischief there is in a rattle-snake (observe, I do not charge it with being mischievous, I but say it has the capacity), could you well avoid admitting that that would be no symmetrical view of the universe which should maintain that, while to man it is forbidden to kill, without judicial cause, his fellow, yet the rattle-snake has an implied permit of unaccountability to murder any creature it takes capricious umbrage at—man included?—But," with a wearied air, "this is no genial talk; at least it is not so to me. Zeal at unawares embarked me in it. I regret it. Pray, sit down, and take some of this wine."

"Your suggestions are new to me," said the other, with a kind of condescending appreciativeness, as of one who, out of devotion to knowledge, disdains not to appropriate the least crumb of it, even from a pauper's board; "and, as I am a very Athenian in hailing a new thought, I cannot consent to let it drop so abruptly. Now, the rattle-snake—"

"Nothing more about rattle-snakes, I beseech," in distress; "I must positively decline to reënter upon that subject. Sit down, sir, I beg, and take some of this wine."

"To invite me to sit down with you is hospitable," collectedly acquiescing now in the change of topics; "and hospitality being fabled to be of oriental origin, and forming, as it does, the subject of a pleasing Arabian romance, as well as being a very romantic thing in itself—hence I always hear the expressions of hospitality with pleasure. But, as for the wine, my regard for that beverage is so extreme, and I am so fearful of letting it sate me, that I keep my love for it in the lasting condition of an untried abstraction. Briefly, I quaff immense draughts of wine from the page of Hafiz, but wine from a cup I seldom as much as sip."

The cosmopolitan turned a mild glance upon the speaker, who, now occupying the chair opposite him, sat there purely and coldly radiant as a prism. It seemed as if one could almost hear him vitreously chime and ring. That moment a waiter passed, whom, arresting with a sign, the cosmopolitan bid go bring a goblet of ice-water. "Ice it well, waiter," said he; "and now," turning to the stranger, "will you, if you please, give me your reason for the warning words you first addressed to me?"

"I hope they were not such warnings as most warnings are," said the stranger; "warnings which do not forewarn, but in mockery come after the fact. And yet something in you bids me think now, that whatever latent design your impostor friend might have had upon you, it as yet remains unaccomplished. You read his label."

"And what did it say? 'This is a genial soul.' So you see you must either give up your doctrine of labels, or else your prejudice against my friend. But tell me," with renewed earnestness, "what do you take him for? What is he?"

"What are you? What am I? Nobody knows who anybody is. The data which life furnishes, towards forming a true estimate of any being, are as insufficient to that end as in geometry one side given would be to determine the triangle."

"But is not this doctrine of triangles someway inconsistent with your doctrine of labels?"

"Yes; but what of that? I seldom care to be consistent. In a philosophical view, consistency is a certain level at all times, maintained in all the thoughts of one's mind. But, since nature is nearly all hill and dale, how can one keep naturally advancing in knowledge without submitting to the natural inequalities in the progress? Advance into knowledge is just like advance upon the grand Erie canal, where, from the character of the country, change of level is inevitable; you are locked up and locked down with perpetual inconsistencies, and yet all the time you get on; while the dullest part of the whole route is what the boatmen call the 'long level'—

a consistently-flat surface of sixty miles through stagnant swamps."

"In one particular," rejoined the cosmopolitan, "your simile is, perhaps, unfortunate. For, after all these weary lockings-up and lockings-down, upon how much of a higher plain do you finally stand? Enough to make it an object? Having from youth been taught reverence for knowledge, you must pardon me if, on but this one account, I reject your analogy. But really you some way bewitch me with your tempting discourse, so that I keep straying from my point unawares. You tell me you cannot certainly know who or what my friend is; pray, what do you conjecture him to be?"

"I conjecture him to be what, among the ancient Egyptians, was called a——" using some unknown word.

"A——! And what is that?"

"A——is what Proclus, in a little note to his third book on the theology of Plato, defines as—— ——" coming out with a sentence of Greek.

Holding up his glass, and steadily looking through its transparency, the cosmopolitan rejoined: "That, in so defining the thing, Proclus set it to modern understandings in the most crystal light it was susceptible of, I will not rashly deny; still, if you could put the definition in words suited to perceptions like mine, I should take it for a favor."

"A favor!" slightly lifting his cool eyebrows; "a bridal favor I understand, a knot of white ribands, a very beautiful type of the purity of true marriage; but of other favors I am yet to learn; and still, in a vague way, the word, as you employ it, strikes me as unpleasingly significant in general of some poor, unheroic submission to being done good to."

Here the goblet of iced-water was brought, and, in compliance with a sign from the cosmopolitan, was placed before the stranger, who, not before expressing acknowledgments, took a draught, apparently refreshing—its very coldness, as with some is the case, proving not entirely uncongenial.

At last, setting down the goblet, and gently wiping from his lips the beads of water freshly clinging there as to the valve of a coral-shell upon a reef, he turned upon the cosmopolitan, and, in a manner the most cool, self-possessed, and matter-of-fact possible, said: "I hold to the metempsychosis; and whoever I may be now, I feel that I was once the stoic Arrian, and have inklings of having been equally puzzled by a word in the current language of that former time, very probably answering to your word *favor*."

"Would you favor me by explaining?" said the cosmopolitan, blandly.

"Sir," responded the stranger, with a very slight degree of severity, "I like lucidity, of all things, and am afraid I shall hardly be able to converse satisfactorily with you, unless you bear it in mind."

The cosmopolitan ruminatingly eyed him awhile, then said: "The best way, as I have heard, to get out of a labyrinth, is to retrace one's steps. I will accordingly retrace mine, and beg you will accompany me. In short, once again to return to the point: for what reason did you warn me against my friend?"

"Briefly, then, and clearly, because, as before said, I conjecture him to be what, among the ancient Egyptians—"

"Pray, now," earnestly deprecated the cosmopolitan, "pray, now, why disturb the repose of those ancient Egyptians? What to us are their words or their thoughts? Are we pauper Arabs, without a house of our own, that, with the mummies, we must turn squatters among the dust of the Catacombs?"

"Pharaoh's poorest brick-maker lies proudlier in his rags than the Emperor of all the Russias in his hollands," oracularly said the stranger; "for death, though in a worm, is majestic; while life, though in a king, is contemptible. So talk not against mummies. It is a part of my mission to teach mankind a due reverence for mummies."

Fortunately, to arrest these incoherencies, or rather, to vary them, a haggard, inspired-looking man now approached—a crazy beggar, asking alms under the form of peddling a rhapsodical tract, composed by himself, and setting forth his claims to some rhapsodical apostleship. Though ragged and dirty, there was about him no touch of vulgarity; for, by nature, his manner was not unrefined, his frame slender, and appeared the more so from the broad, untanned frontlet of his brow, tangled over with a disheveled mass of raven curls, throwing a still deeper tinge upon a complexion like that of a shriveled berry. Nothing could exceed his look of picturesque Italian ruin and dethronement, heightened by what seemed just one glimmering peep of reason, insufficient to do him any lasting good, but enough, perhaps, to suggest a torment of latent doubts at times, whether his addled dream of glory were true.

Accepting the tract offered him, the cosmopolitan glanced over it, and, seeming to see just what it was, closed it, put it in his pocket, eyed the man a moment, then, leaning over and presenting him with a shilling, said to him, in tones kind and considerate: "I am sorry, my friend, that I happen to be engaged just now; but, having purchased your work, I promise myself much satisfaction in its perusal at my earliest leisure."

In his tattered, single-breasted frock-coat, buttoned meagerly up to his chin, the shatter-brain made him a bow, which, for courtesy, would not have misbecome a viscount, then turned with silent appeal to the stranger. But the stranger sat more like a cold prism than ever, while an expression of keen Yankee cuteness, now replacing his former mystical one, lent added icicles to his aspect. His whole air said: "Nothing from me." The repulsed petitioner threw a look full of resentful pride and cracked disdain upon him, and went his way.

"Come, now," said the cosmopolitan, a little reproachfully, "you ought to have sympathized with that man; tell me, did you feel no fellow-feeling? Look at his tract here, quite in the transcendental vein."

"Excuse me," said the stranger, declining the tract, "I never patronize scoundrels."

"Scoundrels?"

"I detected in him, sir, a damning peep of sense—damning, I say; for sense in a seeming madman is scoundrelism. I take him for a cunning vagabond, who picks up a vagabond living by adroitly playing the madman. Did you not remark how he flinched under my eye?"

"Really," drawing a long, astonished breath, "I could hardly have divined in you a temper so subtly distrustful. Flinched? to be sure he did, poor fellow; you received him with so lame a welcome. As for his adroitly playing the madman, invidious critics might object the same to some one or two strolling magi of these days. But that is a matter I know nothing about. But, once more, and for the last time, to return to the point: why sir, did you warn me against my friend? I shall rejoice, if, as I think it will prove, your want of confidence in my friend rests upon a basis equally slender with your distrust of the lunatic. Come, why did you warn me? Put it, I beseech, in few words, and those English."

"I warned you against him because he is suspected for what on these boats is known—so they tell me—as a Mississippi operator."

"An operator, ah? he operates, does he? My friend, then, is something like what the Indians call a Great Medicine, is he? He operates, he purges, he drains off the repletions."

"I perceive, sir," said the stranger, constitutionally obtuse to the pleasant drollery, "that your notion, of what is called a Great Medicine, needs correction. The Great Medicine among the Indians is less a bolus than a man in grave esteem for his politic sagacity."

"And is not my friend politic? Is not my friend sagacious? By your own definition, is not my friend a Great Medicine?"

"No, he is an operator, a Mississippi operator; an equivocal character. That he is such, I little doubt, having had him pointed out to me as such by one desirous of initiating me into any little novelty of this western region, where I never before traveled. And, sir, if I am not mistaken, you also are a stranger here (but, indeed, where in this strange universe is not one a stranger?) and that is a reason why I felt moved to warn you against a companion who could not be otherwise than perilous to one of a free and trustful disposition. But I repeat the hope, that, thus far at least, he has not succeeded with you, and trust that, for the future, he will not."

"Thank you for your concern; but hardly can I equally thank you for so steadily maintaining the hypothesis of my friend's objection-ableness. True, I but made his acquaintance for the first to-day, and know little of his antecedents; but that would seem no just reason why a nature like his should not of itself inspire confidence. And since your own knowledge of the gentleman is not, by your account, so exact as it might be, you will pardon me if I decline to welcome any further suggestions unflattering to him. Indeed, sir," with friendly decision, "let us change the subject."

"Both, the subject and the interlocutor," replied the stranger rising, and waiting the return towards him of a promenader, that moment turning at the further end of his walk.

"Egbert!" said he, calling.

Egbert, a well-dressed, commercial-looking gentleman of about thirty, responded in a way strikingly deferential, and in a moment stood near, in the attitude less of an equal companion apparently than a confidential follower.

"This," said the stranger, taking Egbert by the hand and leading him to the cosmopolitan, "this is Egbert, a disciple. I wish you to know Egbert. Egbert was the first among mankind to reduce to practice the principles of Mark Winsome—principles previously accounted as less adapted to life than the closet. Egbert," turning to the disciple, who, with seeming modesty, a little shrank under these compliments, "Egbert, this," with a salute towards the cosmopolitan, "is, like all of us, a stranger. I wish you, Egbert, to know this brother stranger; be communicative with him. Particularly if, by anything hitherto dropped, his curiosity has been roused as to the precise nature of my philosophy, I trust you will not leave such curiosity ungratified. You, Egbert, by simply setting forth your practice, can do more to enlighten one as to my theory, than I myself can by mere speech. Indeed, it is by you that I myself best understand myself. For to every philosophy are certain rear parts, very important parts, and these, like the rear of one's head, are best seen by reflection. Now, as in a glass, you, Egbert, in your life, reflect to me the more important part of my system. He, who approves you, approves the philosophy of Mark Winsome."

Though portions of this harangue may, perhaps, in the phraseology seem self-complaisant, yet no trace of self-complacency was perceptible in the speaker's manner, which throughout was plain, unassuming, dignified, and manly; the teacher and prophet seemed to lurk more in the idea, so to speak, than in the mere bearing of him who was the vehicle of it.

"Sir," said the cosmopolitan, who seemed not a little interested in this new aspect of matters, "you speak of a certain philosophy, and a more or less occult one it may be, and hint of its bearing upon practical life; pray, tell me, if the study of this philosophy tends to the same formation of character with the experiences of the world?"

"It does; and that is the test of its truth; for any philosophy that, being in operation contradictory to the ways of the world, tends to produce a character at odds with it, such a philosophy must necessarily be but a cheat and a dream."

"You a little surprise me," answered the cosmopolitan; "for, from an occasional profundity in you, and also from your allusions to a profound work on the theology of Plato, it would seem but natural to surmise that, if you are the originator of any philosophy, it must needs so partake of the abstruse, as to exalt it above the comparatively vile uses of life."

"No uncommon mistake with regard to me," rejoined the other. Then meekly standing like a Raphael: "If still in golden accents old Memnon murmurs his riddle, none the less does the balance-sheet of every man's ledger unriddle the profit or loss of life. Sir," with calm energy, "man came into this world, not to sit down and muse, not to befog himself with vain subtleties, but to gird up his loins and to work. Mystery is in the morning, and mystery in the night, and the beauty of mystery is everywhere; but still the plain truth remains, that mouth and purse must be filled. If, hitherto, you have supposed me a visionary, be undeceived. I am no one-ideaed one, either; no more than the seers before me. Was not Seneca a usurer? Bacon a courtier? and Swedenborg, though with one eye on the invisible, did he not keep the other on the main chance? Along with whatever else it may be given me to be, I am a man of serviceable knowledge, and a man of the world. Know me for such. And as for my disciple here," turning towards him, "if you look to find any soft Utopianisms and last year's sunsets in him, I smile to think how he will set you right. The doctrines I have taught him will, I trust, lead him neither to the mad-house nor the poor-house, as so many other doctrines have served credulous sticklers. Furthermore," glancing upon him paternally, "Egbert is both my disciple and my poet. For poetry is not a thing of ink and rhyme, but of thought and act, and, in the latter way, is by any one to be found anywhere, when in useful action sought. In a word, my disciple here is a thriving young merchant, a practical poet in the West India trade. There," presenting Egbert's hand to the cosmopolitan, "I join you, and leave you." With which words, and without bowing, the master withdrew.

Chapter 38 THE DISCIPLE UNBENDS, *and Consents to* *Act a Social Part* ❧

In the master's presence the disciple had stood as one not ignorant of his place; modesty was in his expression, with a sort of reverential depression. But the presence of the superior withdrawn, he seemed lithely to shoot up erect from beneath it, like one of those wire men from a toy snuff-box.

He was, as before said, a young man of about thirty. His countenance of that neuter sort, which, in repose, is neither prepossessing nor disagreeable; so that it seemed quite uncertain how he would turn out. His dress was neat, with just enough of the mode to save it from the reproach of originality; in which general respect, though with a readjustment of details, his costume seemed modeled upon his master's. But, upon the whole, he was, to all appearances, the last person in the world that one would take for the disciple of any transcendental philosophy; though, indeed, something about his sharp nose and shaved chin seemed to hint that if mysticism, as a lesson, ever came in his way, he might, with the characteristic knack of a true New-Englander, turn even so profitless a thing to some profitable account.

"Well," said he, now familiarly seating himself in the vacated chair, "what do you think of Mark? Sublime fellow, ain't he?"

"That each member of the human guild is worthy of respect, my friend," rejoined the cosmopolitan, "is a fact which no admirer of that guild will question; but that, in view of higher natures, the word sublime, so frequently applied to them, can, without confusion, be also applied to man, is a point which man will decide for himself; though, indeed, if he decide it in the affirmative, it is not for me to object. But I am curious to know more of that philosophy of which, at present, I have but inklings. You, its first disciple among men, it seems, are peculiarly qualified to expound it. Have you any objections to begin now?"

"None at all," squaring himself to the table. "Where shall I begin? At first principles?"

"You remember that it was in a practical way that you were represented as being fitted for the clear exposition. Now, what you call first principles, I have, in some things, found to be more or less vague. Permit me, then, in a plain way, to suppose some common case in real life, and that done, I would like you to tell me how you, the practical disciple of the philosophy I wish to know about, would, in that case, conduct."

"A business-like view. Propose the case."

"Not only the case, but the persons. The case is this: There are two friends, friends from childhood, bosom-friends; one of whom, for the first time, being in need, for the first time seeks a loan from the other, who, so far as fortune goes, is more than competent to grant it. And the persons are to be you and I: you, the friend from whom the loan is sought—I, the friend who seeks it; you, the disciple of the philosophy in question—I, a common man, with no more philosophy than to know that when I am comfortably warm I don't feel cold, and when I have the ague I shake. Mind, now, you must work up your imagination, and, as much as possible, talk and behave just as if the case supposed were a fact. For brevity, you shall call me Frank, and I will call you Charlie. Are you agreed?"

"Perfectly. You begin."

The cosmopolitan paused a moment, then, assuming a serious and care-worn air, suitable to the part to be enacted, addressed his hypothesized friend.

Chapter 39 THE HYPOTHETICAL FRIENDS &

"Charlie, I am going to put confidence in you."

"You always have, and with reason. What is it, Frank?"

"Charlie, I am in want—urgent want of money."

"That's not well."

"But it *will* be well, Charlie, if you loan me a hundred dollars. I would not ask this of you, only my need is sore, and you and I have so long shared hearts and minds together, however unequally on my side, that nothing remains to prove our friendship than, with the same inequality on my side, to share purses. You will do me the favor, won't you?"

"Favor? What do you mean by asking me to do you a favor?"

"Why, Charlie, you never used to talk so."

"Because, Frank, you on your side, never used to talk so."

"But won't you loan me the money?"

"No, Frank."

"Why?"

"Because my rule forbids. I give away money, but never loan it; and of course the man who calls himself my friend is above receiving alms. The negotiation of a loan is a business transaction. And I will transact no business with a friend. What a friend is, he is socially and intellectually; and I rate social and intellectual friendship too high to degrade it on either side into a pecuniary make-shift. To be sure there are, and I have, what is called business friends; that is, commercial acquaintances, very convenient persons. But I draw a red-ink line between them and my friends in the true sense—my friends social and intellectual. In brief, a true friend has nothing to do with loans; he should have a soul above loans. Loans are such unfriendly accommodations as are to be had from the soulless corporation of a bank, by giving the regular security and paying the regular discount."

"An *unfriendly* accommodation? Do those words go together handsomely?"

"Like the poor farmer's team, of an old man and a cow—not handsomely, but to the purpose. Look, Frank, a loan of money on

220

interest is a sale of money on credit. To sell a thing on credit may
be an accommodation, but where is the friendliness? Few men in
their senses, except operators, borrow money on interest, except
upon a necessity akin to starvation. Well, now, where is the friendliness of my letting a starving man have, say, the money's worth
of a barrel of flour upon the condition that, on a given day, he shall
let me have the money's worth of a barrel and a half of flour; especially if I add this further proviso, that if he fail so to do, I shall
then, to secure to myself the money's worth of my barrel and his
half barrel, put his heart up at public auction, and, as it is cruel to
part families, throw in his wife's and children's?"

"I understand," with a pathetic shudder; "but even did it come
to that, such a step on the creditor's part, let us, for the honor of
human nature, hope, were less the intention than the contingency."

"But, Frank, a contingency not unprovided for in the taking beforehand of due securities."

"Still, Charlie, was not the loan in the first place a friend's act?"

"And the auction in the last place an enemy's act. Don't you see?
The enmity lies couched in the friendship, just as the ruin in the
relief."

"I must be very stupid to-day, Charlie, but really, I can't understand this. Excuse me, my dear friend, but it strikes me that in going into the philosophy of the subject, you go somewhat out of
your depth."

"So said the incautious wader-out to the ocean; but the ocean
replied: 'It is just the other way, my wet friend,' and drowned
him."

"That, Charlie, is a fable about as unjust to the ocean, as some
of Æsop's are to the animals. The ocean is a magnanimous element,
and would scorn to assassinate a poor fellow, let alone taunting him
in the act. But I don't understand what you say about enmity
couched in friendship, and ruin in relief."

"I will illustrate, Frank. The needy man is a train slipped off the
rail. He who loans him money on interest is the one who, by way
of accommodation, helps get the train back where it belongs; but
then, by way of making all square, and a little more, telegraphs to

an agent, thirty miles ahead by a precipice, to throw just there, on his account, a beam across the track. Your needy man's principal-and-interest friend is, I say again, a friend with an enmity in reserve. No, no, my dear friend, no interest for me. I scorn interest."

"Well, Charlie, none need you charge. Loan me without interest."

"That would be alms again."

"Alms, if the sum borrowed is returned?"

"Yes: an alms, not of the principal, but the interest."

"Well, I am in sore need, so I will not decline the alms. Seeing that it is you, Charlie, gratefully will I accept the alms of the interest. No humiliation between friends."

"Now, how in the refined view of friendship can you suffer yourself to talk so, my dear Frank. It pains me. For though I am not of the sour mind of Solomon, that, in the hour of need, a stranger is better than a brother; yet, I entirely agree with my sublime master, who, in his Essay on Friendship, says so nobly, that if he want a terrestrial convenience, not to his friend celestial (or friend social and intellectual) would he go; no: for his terrestrial convenience, to his friend terrestrial (or humbler business-friend) he goes. Very lucidly he adds the reason: Because, for the superior nature, which on no account can ever descend to do good, to be annoyed with requests to do it, when the inferior one, which by no instruction can ever rise above that capacity, stands always inclined to it—this is unsuitable."

"Then I will not consider you as my friend celestial, but as the other."

"It racks me to come to that; but, to oblige you, I'll do it. We are business friends; business is business. You want to negotiate a loan. Very good. On what paper? Will you pay three per cent a month? Where is your security?"

"Surely, you will not exact those formalities from your old schoolmate—him with whom you have so often sauntered down the groves of Academe, discoursing of the beauty of virtue, and the grace that is in kindliness—and all for so paltry a sum. Security?

Our being fellow-academics, and friends from childhood up, is security."

"Pardon me, my dear Frank, our being fellow-academics is the worst of securities; while, our having been friends from childhood up is just no security at all. You forget we are now business friends."

"And you, on your side, forget, Charlie, that as your business friend I can give you no security; my need being so sore that I cannot get an indorser."

"No indorser, then, no business loan."

"Since then, Charlie, neither as the one nor the other sort of friend you have defined, can I prevail with you; how if, combining the two, I sue as both?"

"Are you a centaur?"

"When all is said then, what good have I of your friendship, regarded in what light you will?"

"The good which is in the philosophy of Mark Winsome, as reduced to practice by a practical disciple."

"And why don't you add, much good may the philosophy of Mark Winsome do me? Ah," turning invokingly, "what is friendship, if it be not the helping hand and the feeling heart, the good Samaritan pouring out at need the purse as the vial!"

"Now, my dear Frank, don't be childish. Through tears never did man see his way in the dark. I should hold you unworthy that sincere friendship I bear you, could I think that friendship in the ideal is too lofty for you to conceive. And let me tell you, my dear Frank, that you would seriously shake the foundations of our love, if ever again you should repeat the present scene. The philosophy, which is mine in the strongest way, teaches plain-dealing. Let me, then, now, as at the most suitable time, candidly disclose certain circumstances you seem in ignorance of. Though our friendship began in boyhood, think not that, on my side at least, it began injudiciously. Boys are little men, it is said. You, I juvenilely picked out for my friend, for your favorable points at the time; not the least of which were your good manners, handsome dress, and your parents' rank and repute of wealth. In short, like any grown man, boy though I was, I went into the market and chose me my mutton, not for its leanness, but its fatness. In other words, there seemed in you, the schoolboy who always had silver in his pocket, a reasonable probability that you would never stand in lean need of fat succor; and if my early impression has not been verified by the event, it is only because of the caprice of fortune producing a fallibility of human expectations, however discreet."

"Oh, that I should listen to this cold-blooded disclosure!"

"A little cold blood in your ardent veins, my dear Frank, wouldn't do you any harm, let me tell you. Cold-blooded? You say that, because my disclosure seems to involve a vile prudence on my side. But not so. My reason for choosing you in part for the points I have mentioned, was solely with a view of preserving inviolate the delicacy of the connection. For—do but think of it—what more distressing to delicate friendship, formed early, than your friend's eventually, in manhood, dropping in of a rainy night for his little loan of five dollars or so? Can delicate friendship stand that? And, on the other side, would delicate friendship, so long as it retained its delicacy, do that? Would you not instinctively say of your dripping friend in the entry, 'I have been deceived, fraudulently deceived, in this man; he is no true friend that, in platonic love to demand love-rites?'"

"And rites, doubly rights, they are, cruel Charlie!"

"Take it how you will, heed well how, by too importunately claiming those rights, as you call them, you shake those foundations I hinted of. For though, as it turns out, I, in my early friendship, built me a fair house on a poor site; yet such pains and cost have I lavished on that house, that, after all, it is dear to me. No, I would not lose the sweet boon of your friendship, Frank. But beware."

"And of what? Of being in need? Oh, Charlie! you talk not to a god, a being who in himself holds his own estate, but to a man who, being a man, is the sport of fate's wind and wave, and who mounts towards heaven or sinks towards hell, as the billows roll him in trough or on crest."

"Tut! Frank. Man is no such poor devil as that comes to—no poor drifting sea-weed of the universe. Man has a soul; which, if he will, puts him beyond fortune's finger and the future's spite. Don't whine like fortune's whipped dog, Frank, or by the heart of a true friend, I will cut ye."

"Cut me you have already, cruel Charlie, and to the quick. Call to mind the days we went nutting, the times we walked in the woods, arms wreathed about each other, showing trunks invined like the trees:—oh, Charlie!"

"Pish! we were boys."

"Then lucky the fate of the first-born of Egypt, cold in the grave ere maturity struck them with a sharper frost.—Charlie?"

"Fie! you're a girl."

"Help, help, Charlie, I want help!"

"Help? to say nothing of the friend, there is something wrong about the man who wants help. There is somewhere a defect, a want, in brief, a need, a crying need, somewhere about that man."

"So there is, Charlie.—Help, Help!"

"How foolish a cry, when to implore help, is itself the proof of undesert of it."

"Oh, this, all along, is not you, Charlie, but some ventriloquist who usurps your larynx. It is Mark Winsome that speaks, not Charlie."

"If so, thank heaven, the voice of Mark Winsome is not alien but congenial to my larynx. If the philosophy of that illustrious teacher find little response among mankind at large, it is less that they do not possess teachable tempers, than because they are so unfortunate as not to have natures predisposed to accord with him."

"Welcome, that compliment to humanity," exclaimed Frank with energy, "the truer because unintended. And long in this respect may humanity remain what you affirm it. And long it will; since humanity, inwardly feeling how subject it is to straits, and hence how precious is help, will, for selfishness' sake, if no other, long postpone ratifying a philosophy that banishes help from the world. But Charlie, Charlie! speak as you used to; tell me you will help me. Were the case reversed, not less freely would I loan you the money than you would ask me to loan it."

"*I* ask? *I* ask a loan? Frank, by this hand, under no circumstances would I accept a loan, though without asking pressed on me. The experience of China Aster might warn me."

"And what was that?"

"Not very unlike the experience of the man that built himself a palace of moon-beams, and when the moon set was surprised that his palace vanished with it. I will tell you about China Aster. I wish I could do so in my own words, but unhappily the original story-teller here has so tyrannized over me, that it is quite impossible for me to repeat his incidents without sliding into his style. I forewarn you of this, that you may not think me so maudlin as, in some parts, the story would seem to make its narrator. It is too bad that any intellect, especially in so small a matter, should have such power to impose itself upon another, against its best exerted will, too. However, it is satisfaction to know that the main moral, to which all tends, I fully approve. But, to begin."

Chapter 40 *In Which* THE STORY OF CHINA ASTER *Is at Second-hand Told By One Who, While Not Disapproving the Moral, Disclaims the Spirit of the Style*

"China Aster was a young candle-maker of Marietta, at the mouth of the Muskingum—one whose trade would seem a kind of subordinate branch of that parent craft and mystery of the hosts of heaven, to be the means, effectively or otherwise, of shedding some light through the darkness of a planet benighted. But he made little money by the business. Much ado had poor China Aster and his family to live; he could, if he chose, light up from his stores a whole street, but not so easily could he light up with prosperity the hearts of his household.

"Now, China Aster, it so happened, had a friend, Orchis, a shoemaker; one whose calling it is to defend the understandings of men from naked contact with the substance of things: a very useful vocation, and which, spite of all the wiseacres may prophesy, will hardly go out of fashion so long as rocks are hard and flints will gall. All at once, by a capital prize in a lottery, this useful shoemaker was raised from a bench to a sofa. A small nabob was the shoemaker now, and the understandings of men, let them shift for themselves. Not that Orchis was, by prosperity, elated into heartlessness. Not at all. Because, in his fine apparel, strolling one morning into the candlery, and gayly switching about at the candle-boxes with his gold-headed cane—while poor China Aster, with his greasy paper cap and leather apron, was selling one candle for one penny to a poor orange-woman, who, with the patronizing coolness of a liberal customer, required it to be carefully rolled up and tied in a half sheet of paper—lively Orchis, the woman being gone, discontinued his gay switchings and said: 'This is poor business for you, friend China Aster; your capital is too small. You must drop this vile tallow and hold up pure spermaceti to the world. I tell you what it is, you shall have one thousand dollars to extend with. In fact, you must make money, China Aster. I don't like to see your little boy paddling about without shoes, as he does.'

" 'Heaven bless your goodness, friend Orchis,' replied the candle-maker, 'but don't take it illy if I call to mind the word of my uncle, the blacksmith, who, when a loan was offered him, declined it, saying: "To ply my own hammer, light though it be, I think best, rather than piece it out heavier by welding to it a bit off a neighbor's hammer, though that may have some weight to spare; otherwise, were the borrowed bit suddenly wanted again, it might not split off at the welding, but too much to one side or the other." '

" 'Nonsense, friend China Aster, don't be so honest; your boy is barefoot. Besides, a rich man lose by a poor man? Or a friend be the worse by a friend? China Aster, I am afraid that, in leaning over into your vats here, this morning, you have spilled out your wisdom. Hush! I won't hear any more. Where's your desk? Oh, here.' With that, Orchis dashed off a check on his bank, and off-handedly presenting it, said: 'There, friend China Aster, is your one thousand dollars; when you make it ten thousand, as you soon enough will (for experience, the only true knowledge, teaches me that, for every one, good luck is in store), then, China Aster, why, then you can return me the money or not, just as you please. But, in any event, give yourself no concern, for I shall never demand payment.'

"Now, as kind heaven will so have it that to a hungry man bread is a great temptation, and, therefore, he is not too harshly to be blamed, if, when freely offered, he take it, even though it be uncertain whether he shall ever be able to reciprocate; so, to a poor man, proffered money is equally enticing, and the worst that can be said of him, if he accept it, is just what can be said in the other case of the hungry man. In short, the poor candle-maker's scrupulous morality succumbed to his unscrupulous necessity, as is now and then apt to be the case. He took the check, and was about carefully putting it away for the present, when Orchis, switching about again with his gold-headed cane, said: 'By-the-way, China Aster, it don't mean anything, but suppose you make a little memorandum of this; won't do any harm, you know.' So China Aster gave Orchis his note for one thousand dollars on demand. Orchis took it, and looked at it a moment, 'Pooh, I told you, friend China

Aster, I wasn't going ever to make any *demand*.' Then tearing up the note, and switching away again at the candle-boxes, said, carelessly; 'Put it at four years.' So China Aster gave Orchis his note for one thousand dollars at four years. 'You see I'll never trouble you about this,' said Orchis, slipping it in his pocket-book, 'give yourself no further thought, friend China Aster, than how best to invest your money. And don't forget my hint about spermaceti. Go into that, and I'll buy all my light of you,' with which encouraging words, he, with wonted, rattling kindness, took leave.

"China Aster remained standing just where Orchis had left him; when, suddenly, two elderly friends, having nothing better to do, dropped in for a chat. The chat over, China Aster, in greasy cap and apron, ran after Orchis, and said: 'Friend Orchis, heaven will reward you for your good intentions, but here is your check, and now give me my note.'

" 'Your honesty is a bore, China Aster,' said Orchis, not without displeasure. 'I won't take the check from you.'

" 'Then you must take it from the pavement, Orchis,' said China Aster; and, picking up a stone, he placed the check under it on the walk.

" 'China Aster,' said Orchis, inquisitively eying him, 'after my leaving the candlery just now, what asses dropped in there to advise with you, that now you hurry after me, and act so like a fool? Shouldn't wonder if it was those two old asses that the boys nickname Old Plain Talk and Old Prudence.'

" 'Yes, it was those two, Orchis, but don't call them names.'

" 'A brace of spavined old croakers. Old Plain Talk had a shrew for a wife, and that's made him shrewish; and Old Prudence, when a boy, broke down in an apple-stall, and that discouraged him for life. No better sport for a knowing spark like me than to hear Old Plain Talk wheeze out his sour old saws, while Old Prudence stands by, leaning on his staff, wagging his frosty old pow, and chiming in at every clause.'

" 'How can you speak so, friend Orchis, of those who were my father's friends?'

" 'Save me from my friends, if those old croakers were Old Honesty's friends. I call your father so, for every one used to. Why did they let him go in his old age on the town? Why, China Aster, I've often heard from my mother, the chronicler, that those two old fellows, with Old Conscience—as the boys called the crabbed old quaker, that's dead now—they three used to go to the poor-house when your father was there, and get round his bed, and talk to him for all the world as Eliphaz, Bildad, and Zophar did to poor old pauper Job. Yes, Job's comforters were Old Plain Talk, and Old Prudence, and Old Conscience, to your poor old father. Friends? I should like to know who you call foes? With their everlasting croaking and reproaching they tormented poor Old Honesty, your father, to death.'

"At these words, recalling the sad end of his worthy parent, China Aster could not restrain some tears. Upon which Orchis said: 'Why, China Aster, you are the dolefulest creature. Why don't you, China Aster, take a bright view of life? You will never get on in your business or anything else, if you don't take the bright view of life. It's the ruination of a man to take the dismal one.' Then, gayly poking at him with his gold-headed cane, 'Why don't you, then? Why don't you be bright and hopeful, like me? Why don't you have confidence, China Aster?'

" 'I'm sure I don't know, friend Orchis,' soberly replied China Aster, 'but may be my not having drawn a lottery-prize, like you, may make some difference.'

" 'Nonsense! before I knew anything about the prize I was gay as a lark, just as gay as I am now. In fact, it has always been a principle with me to hold to the bright view.'

"Upon this, China Aster looked a little hard at Orchis, because the truth was, that until the lucky prize came to him, Orchis had gone under the nickname of Doleful Dumps, he having been beforetimes of a hypochondriac turn, so much so as to save up and put by a few dollars of his scanty earnings against that rainy day he used to groan so much about.

" 'I tell you what it is, now, friend China Aster,' said Orchis, pointing down to the check under the stone, and then slapping his pocket, 'the check shall lie there if you say so, but your note shan't keep it company. In fact, China Aster, I am too sincerely your friend to take advantage of a passing fit of the blues in you. You *shall* reap the benefit of my friendship.' With which, buttoning up his coat in a jiffy, away he ran, leaving the check behind.

"At first, China Aster was going to tear it up, but thinking that this ought not to be done except in the presence of the drawer of the check, he mused a while, and picking it up, trudged back to the candlery, fully resolved to call upon Orchis soon as his day's work was over, and destroy the check before his eyes. But it so happened that when China Aster called, Orchis was out, and, having waited for him a weary time in vain, China Aster went home, still with the check, but still resolved not to keep it another day. Bright and early next morning he would a second time go after Orchis, and would, no doubt, make a sure thing of it, by finding him in his bed; for since the lottery-prize came to him, Orchis, besides becoming more cheery, had also grown a little lazy. But as destiny would have it, that same night China Aster had a dream, in which a being in the guise of a smiling angel, and holding a kind of cornucopia in her hand, hovered over him, pouring down showers of small gold dollars, thick as kernels of corn. 'I am Bright Future, friend China Aster,' said the angel, 'and if you do what friend Orchis would have you do, just see what will come of it.' With which Bright Future, with another swing of her cornucopia, poured such another shower of small gold dollars upon him, that it seemed to bank him up all round, and he waded about in it like a maltster in malt.

"Now, dreams are wonderful things, as everybody knows—so wonderful, indeed, that some people stop not short of ascribing them directly to heaven; and China Aster, who was of a proper turn of mind in everything, thought that in consideration of the dream, it would be but well to wait a little, ere seeking Orchis again. During the day, China Aster's mind dwelling continually upon the dream, he was so full of it, that when Old Plain Talk dropped in to see him, just before dinner-time, as he often did, out of the interest he took in Old Honesty's son, China Aster told all about his vision, adding that he could not think that so radiant an angel could deceive; and, indeed, talked at such a rate that one would have thought he believed the angel some beautiful human philanthropist. Something in this sort Old Plain Talk understood him, and, accordingly, in his plain way, said: 'China Aster, you tell me that an angel appeared to you in a dream. Now, what does that amount to but this, that you dreamed an angel appeared to you? Go right away, China Aster, and return the check, as I advised you before. If friend Prudence were here, he would say just the same thing.' With which words Old Plain Talk went off to find friend Prudence, but not succeeding, was returning to the candlery himself, when, at distance mistaking him for a dun who had long annoyed him, China Aster in a panic barred all his doors, and ran to the back part of the candlery, where no knock could be heard.

"By this sad mistake, being left with no friend to argue the other side of the question, China Aster was so worked upon at last, by musing over his dream, that nothing would do but he must get the check cashed, and lay out the money the very same day in buying a good lot of spermaceti to make into candles, by which operation he counted upon turning a better penny than he ever had before in his life; in fact, this he believed would prove the foundation of that famous fortune which the angel had promised him.

"Now, in using the money, China Aster was resolved punctually to pay the interest every six months till the principal should be returned, howbeit not a word about such a thing had been breathed by Orchis; though, indeed, according to custom, as well as law, in such matters, interest would legitimately accrue on the loan, nothing to the contrary having been put in the bond. Whether Orchis at the time had this in mind or not, there is no sure telling; but, to all appearance, he never so much as cared to think about the matter, one way or other.

"Though the spermaceti venture rather disappointed China Aster's sanguine expectations, yet he made out to pay the first six months' interest, and though his next venture turned out still less prosperously, yet by pinching his family in the matter of fresh meat, and, what pained him still more, his boys' schooling, he contrived to pay the second six months' interest, sincerely grieved that integrity, as well as its opposite, though not in an equal degree, costs something, sometimes.

"Meanwhile, Orchis had gone on a trip to Europe by advice of a physician; it so happening that, since the lottery-prize came to him, it had been discovered to Orchis that his health was not very firm, though he had never complained of anything before but a slight ailing of the spleen, scarce worth talking about at the time. So Orchis, being abroad, could not help China Aster's paying his interest as he did, however much he might have been opposed to it; for China Aster paid it to Orchis' agent, who was of too business-like a turn to decline interest regularly paid in on a loan.

"But overmuch to trouble the agent on that score was not again to be the fate of China Aster; for, not being of that skeptical spirit which refuses to trust customers, his third venture resulted, through bad debts, in almost a total loss—a bad blow for the candle-maker. Neither did Old Plain Talk, and Old Prudence neglect the opportunity to read him an uncheerful enough lesson upon the consequences of his disregarding their advice in the matter of having nothing to do with borrowed money. 'It's all just as I predicted,' said Old Plain Talk, blowing his old nose with his old bandana. 'Yea, indeed is it,' chimed in Old Prudence, rapping his staff on the floor, and then leaning upon it, looking with solemn forebodings upon China Aster. Low-spirited enough felt the poor candle-maker; till all at once who should come with a bright face to him but his bright friend, the angel, in another dream. Again the cornucopia poured out its treasure, and promised still more. Revived by the vision, he resolved not to be downhearted, but up and at it once more—contrary to the advice of Old Plain Talk, backed as usual by his crony, which was to the effect, that, under present circumstances, the best thing China Aster could do, would be to wind up his business, settle, if he could, all his liabilities, and then go to work as a journeyman, by which he could earn good wages, and give up, from that time henceforth, all thoughts of rising above being a paid subordinate to men more able than himself, for China Aster's career thus far plainly proved him the legitimate son of Old Honesty, who, as every one knew, had never shown much business-talent, so little, in fact, that many said of him that he had no business to be in business. And just this plain saying Plain Talk now plainly applied to China Aster, and Old Prudence never disagreed with him. But the angel in the dream did, and, maugre Plain Talk, put quite other notions into the candle-maker.

"He considered what he should do towards reëstablishing himself. Doubtless, had Orchis been in the country, he would have aided him in this strait. As it was, he applied to others; and as in the world, much as some may hint to the contrary, an honest man in misfortune still can find friends to stay by him and help him, even so it proved with China Aster, who at last succeeded in borrowing from a rich old farmer the sum of six hundred dollars, at the usual interest of money-lenders, upon the security of a secret bond signed by China Aster's wife and himself, to the effect that all such right and title to any property that should be left her by a well-to-do childless uncle, an invalid tanner, such property should, in the event of China Aster's failing to return the borrowed sum on the given day, be the lawful possession of the money-lender. True, it was just as much as China Aster could possibly do to induce his wife, a careful woman, to sign this bond; because she had always regarded her promised share in her uncle's estate as an anchor well to windward of the hard times in which China Aster had always been more or less involved, and from which, in her bosom, she never had seen much chance of his freeing himself. Some notion may be had of China Aster's standing in the heart and head of his wife, by a short sentence commonly used in reply to such persons as happened to sound her on the point. 'China Aster,' she would say, 'is a good husband, but a bad business man!' Indeed, she was a connection on the maternal side of Old Plain Talk's. But had not China Aster taken good care not to let Old Plain Talk and Old Prudence hear of his dealings with the old farmer, ten to one they would, in some way, have interfered with his success in that quarter.

"It has been hinted that the honesty of China Aster was what mainly induced the money-lender to befriend him in his misfortune, and this must be apparent; for, had China Aster been a different man, the money-lender might have dreaded lest, in the event of his failing to meet his note, he might some way prove slippery—more especially as, in the hour of distress, worked upon by remorse for so jeopardizing his wife's money, his heart might prove a traitor to his bond, not to hint that it was more than doubtful how such a secret security and claim, as in the last resort would be the old farmer's, would stand in a court of law. But though one inference from all this may be, that had China Aster been something else than what he was, he would not have been trusted, and, therefore, he would have been effectually shut out from running his own and wife's head into the usurer's noose; yet those who, when everything at last came out, maintained that, in this view and to this extent, the honesty of the candle-maker was no advantage to him, in so saying, such persons said what every good heart must deplore, and no prudent tongue will admit.

"It may be mentioned, that the old farmer made China Aster take part of his loan in three old dried-up cows and one lame horse, not improved by the glanders. These were thrown in at a pretty high figure, the old money-lender having a singular prejudice in regard to the high value of any sort of stock raised on his farm. With a great deal of difficulty, and at more loss, China Aster disposed of his cattle at public auction, no private purchaser being found who could be prevailed upon to invest. And now, raking and scraping in every way, and working early and late, China Aster at last started afresh, nor without again largely and confidently extending himself. However, he did not try his hand at the spermaceti again, but, admonished by experience, returned to tallow. But, having bought a good lot of it, by the time he got it into candles, tallow fell so low, and candles with it, that his candles per pound barely sold for what he had paid for the tallow. Meantime, a year's unpaid interest had accrued on Orchis' loan, but China Aster gave himself not so much concern about that as about the interest now due to the old farmer. But he was glad that the principal there had yet some time to run. However, the skinny old fellow gave him some trouble by coming after him every day or

two on a scraggy old white horse, furnished with a musty old sad-
dle, and goaded into his shambling old paces with a withered old
raw hide. All the neighbors said that surely Death himself on the
pale horse was after poor China Aster now. And something so it
proved; for, ere long, China Aster found himself involved in troubles mortal enough.

"At this juncture Orchis was heard of. Orchis, it seemed, had returned from his travels, and clandestinely married, and, in a kind
of queer way, was living in Pennsylvania among his wife's relations,
who, among other things, had induced him to join a church, or
rather semi-religious school, of Come-Outers; and what was still
more, Orchis, without coming to the spot himself, had sent word
to his agent to dispose of some of his property in Marietta, and re-
mit him the proceeds. Within a year after, China Aster received a
letter from Orchis, commending him for his punctuality in paying
the first year's interest, and regretting the necessity that he (Orchis)
was now under of using all his dividends; so he relied upon China
Aster's paying the next six months' interest, and of course with the
back interest. Not more surprised than alarmed, China Aster
thought of taking steamboat to go and see Orchis, but he was
saved that expense by the unexpected arrival in Marietta of Orchis
in person, suddenly called there by that strange kind of capricious-
ness lately characterizing him. No sooner did China Aster hear of
his old friend's arrival than he hurried to call upon him. He found
him curiously rusty in dress, sallow in cheek, and decidedly less
gay and cordial in manner, which the more surprised China Aster,
because, in former days, he had more than once heard Orchis, in his
light rattling way, declare that all he (Orchis) wanted to make
him a perfectly happy, hilarious, and benignant man, was a voyage
to Europe and a wife, with a free development of his inmost nature.

"Upon China Aster's stating his case, his rusted friend was silent
for a time; then, in an odd way, said that he would not crowd China
Aster, but still his (Orchis') necessities were urgent. Could not
China Aster mortgage the candlery? He was honest, and must have
moneyed friends; and could he not press his sales of candles?
Could not the market be forced a little in that particular? The

profits on candles must be very great. Seeing, now, that Orchis had the notion that the candle-making business was a very profitable one, and knowing sorely enough what an error was here, China Aster tried to undeceive him. But he could not drive the truth into Orchis—Orchis being very obtuse here, and, at the same time, strange to say, very melancholy. Finally, Orchis glanced off from so unpleasing a subject into the most unexpected reflections, taken from a religious point of view, upon the unstableness and deceitfulness of the human heart. But having, as he thought, experienced something of that sort of thing, China Aster did not take exception to his friend's observations, but still refrained from so doing, almost as much for the sake of sympathetic sociality as anything else. Presently, Orchis, without much ceremony, rose, and saying he must write a letter to his wife, bade his friend good-bye, but without warmly shaking him by the hand as of old.

"In much concern at the change, China Aster made earnest inquiries in suitable quarters, as to what things, as yet unheard of, had befallen Orchis, to bring about such a revolution; and learned at last that, besides traveling, and getting married, and joining the sect of Come-Outers, Orchis had somehow got a bad dyspepsia, and lost considerable property through a breach of trust on the part of a factor in New York. Telling these things to Old Plain Talk, that man of some knowledge of the world shook his old head, and told China Aster that, though he hoped it might prove otherwise, yet it seemed to him that all he had communicated about Orchis worked together for bad omens as to his future forbearance—especially, he added with a grim sort of smile, in view of his joining the sect of Come-Outers; for, if some men knew what was their inmost natures, instead of coming out with it, they would try their best to keep it in, which, indeed, was the way with the prudent sort. In all which sour notions Old Prudence, as usual, chimed in.

"When interest-day came again, China Aster, by the utmost exertions, could only pay Orchis' agent a small part of what was due, and a part of that was made up by his children's gift money (bright tenpenny pieces and new quarters, kept in their little money-boxes), and pawning his best clothes, with those of his wife and children, so that all were subjected to the hardship of staying away from church. And the old usurer, too, now beginning to be obstreperous, China Aster paid him his interest and some other pressing debts with money got by, at last, mortgaging the candlery.

"When next interest-day came round for Orchis, not a penny could be raised. With much grief of heart, China Aster so informed Orchis' agent. Meantime, the note to the old usurer fell due, and nothing from China Aster was ready to meet it; yet, as heaven sends its rain on the just and unjust alike, by a coincidence not unfavorable to the old farmer, the well-to-do uncle, the tanner, having died, the usurer entered upon possession of such part of his property left by will to the wife of China Aster. When still the next interest-day for Orchis came round, it found China Aster worse off than ever; for, besides his other troubles, he was now weak with sickness. Feebly dragging himself to Orchis' agent, he met him in the street, told him just how it was; upon which the agent, with grave enough face, said that he had instructions from his employer not to crowd him about the interest at present, but to say to him that about the time the note would mature, Orchis would have heavy liabilities to meet, and therefore the note must at that time be certainly paid, and, of course, the back interest with it; and not only so, but, as Orchis had had to allow the interest for good part of the time, he hoped that, for the back interest, China Aster would, in reciprocation, have no objections to allowing interest on the interest annually. To be sure, this was not the law; but, between friends who accommodate each other, it was the custom.

"Just then, Old Plain Talk with Old Prudence turned the corner, coming plump upon China Aster as the agent left him; and whether it was a sun-stroke, or whether they accidentally ran against him, or whether it was his being so weak, or whether it was everything together, or how it was exactly, there is no telling, but poor China Aster fell to the earth, and, striking his head sharply, was picked up senseless. It was a day in July; such a light and heat as only the midsummer banks of the inland Ohio know. China Aster was taken home on a door; lingered a few days with a wandering mind, and kept wandering on, till at last, at dead of night, when nobody was aware, his spirit wandered away into the other world.

"Old Plain Talk and Old Prudence, neither of whom ever omitted attending any funeral, which, indeed, was their chief exercise— these two were among the sincerest mourners who followed the remains of the son of their ancient friend to the grave.

"It is needless to tell of the executions that followed; how that the candlery was sold by the mortgagee; how Orchis never got a penny for his loan; and how, in the case of the poor widow, chastisement was tempered with mercy; for, though she was left penniless, she was not left childless. Yet, unmindful of the alleviation, a spirit of complaint, at what she impatiently called the bitterness of her lot and the hardness of the world, so preyed upon her, as ere long to hurry her from the obscurity of indigence to the deeper shades of the tomb.

"But though the straits in which China Aster had left his family had, besides apparently dimming the world's regard, likewise seemed to dim its sense of the probity of its deceased head, and though this, as some thought, did not speak well for the world, yet it happened in this case, as in others, that, though the world may for a time seem insensible to that merit which lies under a cloud, yet, sooner or later, it always renders honor where honor is due; for, upon the death of the widow, the freemen of Marietta, as a tribute of respect for China Aster, and an expression of their conviction of his high moral worth, passed a resolution, that, until they attained maturity, his children should be considered the town's guests. No mere verbal compliment, like those of some public bodies; for, on the same day, the orphans were officially installed in that hospitable edifice where their worthy grandfather, the town's guest before them, had breathed his last breath.

"But sometimes honor may be paid to the memory of an honest man, and still his mound remain without a monument. Not so, however, with the candle-maker. At an early day, Plain Talk had procured a plain stone, and was digesting in his mind what pithy word or two to place upon it, when there was discovered, in China Aster's otherwise empty wallet, an epitaph, written, probably, in one of those disconsolate hours, attended with more or less mental aberration, perhaps, so frequent with him for some months prior to his end. A memorandum on the back expressed the wish that it might be placed over his grave. Though with the sentiment of the epitaph Plain Talk did not disagree, he himself being at times of a hypochondriac turn—at least, so many said—yet the language struck him as too much drawn out; so, after consultation with Old Prudence, he decided upon making use of the epitaph, yet not without verbal retrenchments. And though, when these were made, the thing still appeared wordy to him, nevertheless, thinking that, since a dead man was to be spoken about, it was but just to let him speak for himself, especially when he spoke sincerely, and when, by so doing, the more salutary lesson would be given, he had the retrenched inscription chiseled as follows upon the stone:

HERE LIE

THE REMAINS OF

CHINA ASTER THE CANDLE-MAKER,

WHOSE CAREER

WAS AN EXAMPLE OF THE TRUTH OF SCRIPTURE, AS FOUND

IN THE

SOBER PHILOSOPHY

OF

SOLOMON THE WISE;

FOR HE WAS RUINED BY ALLOWING HIMSELF TO BE PERSUADED,

AGAINST HIS BETTER SENSE,

INTO THE FREE INDULGENCE OF CONFIDENCE,

AND

AN ARDENTLY BRIGHT VIEW OF LIFE,

TO THE EXCLUSION OF

THAT COUNSEL WHICH COMES BY HEEDING

THE

OPPOSITE VIEW.

"This inscription raised some talk in the town, and was rather severely criticised by the capitalist—one of a very cheerful turn

—who had secured his loan to China Aster by the mortgage; and though it also proved obnoxious to the man who, in town-meeting, had first moved for the compliment to China Aster's memory, and, indeed, was deemed by him a sort of slur upon the candle-maker, to that degree that he refused to believe that the candle-maker himself had composed it, charging Old Plain Talk with the authorship, alleging that the internal evidence showed that none but that veteran old croaker could have penned such a jeremiad—yet, for all this, the stone stood. In everything, of course, Old Plain Talk was seconded by Old Prudence; who, one day going to the graveyard, in great-coat and over-shoes—for, though it was a sunshiny morning, he thought that, owing to heavy dews, dampness might lurk in the ground—long stood before the stone, sharply leaning over on his staff, spectacles on nose, spelling out the epitaph word by word; and, afterwards meeting Old Plain Talk in the street, gave a great rap with his stick, and said: 'Friend Plain Talk, that epitaph will do very well. Nevertheless, one short sentence is wanting.' Upon which, Plain Talk said it was too late, the chiseled words being so arranged, after the usual manner of such inscriptions, that nothing could be interlined. 'Then,' said Old Prudence, 'I will put it in the shape of a postscript.' Accordingly, with the approbation of Old Plain Talk, he had the following words chiseled at the left-hand corner of the stone, and pretty low down:

THE ROOT OF ALL WAS A FRIENDLY LOAN."

"With what heart," cried Frank, still in character, "have you told
me this story? A story I can no way approve; for its moral, if accepted, would drain me of all reliance upon my last stay, and, therefore, of my last courage in life. For, what was that bright view of
China Aster but a cheerful trust that, if he but kept up a brave
heart, worked hard, and ever hoped for the best, all at last would
go well? If your purpose, Charlie, in telling me this story, was to
pain me, and keenly, you have succeeded; but, if it was to destroy
my last confidence, I praise God you have not."

"Confidence?" cried Charlie, who, on his side, seemed with his
whole heart to enter into the spirit of the thing, "what has confidence to do with the matter? That moral of the story, which I am
for commending to you, is this: the folly, on both sides, of a friend's
￫lping a friend. For was not that loan of Orchis to China Aster the
￫ step towards their estrangement? And did it not bring about
what in effect was the enmity of Orchis? I tell you, Frank,
true friendship, like other precious things, is not rashly to be med-
dled with. And what more meddlesome between friends than a
loan? A regular marplot. For how can you help that the helper must
turn out a creditor? And creditor and friend, can they ever be one?
no, not in the most lenient case; since, out of lenity to forego one's
claim, is less to be a friendly creditor than to cease to be a creditor
at all. But it will not do to rely upon this lenity, no, not in the
best man; for the best man, as the worst, is subject to all mortal
contingencies. He may travel, he may marry, he may join the Come-
Outers, or some equally untoward school or sect, not to speak of
other things that more or less tend to new-cast the character. And
were there nothing else, who shall answer for his digestion, upon
which so much depends?"

"But Charlie, dear Charlie—"

"Nay, wait.—You have hearkened to my story in vain, if you do
not see that, however indulgent and right-minded I may seem to
you now, that is no guarantee for the future. And into the power of

242

that uncertain personality which, through the mutability of my humanity, I may hereafter become, should not common sense dissuade you, my dear Frank, from putting yourself? Consider. Would you, in your present need, be willing to accept a loan from a friend, securing him by a mortgage on your homestead, and do so, knowing that you had no reason to feel satisfied that the mortgage might not eventually be transferred into the hands of a foe? Yet the difference between this man and that man is not so great as the difference between what the same man be to-day and what he may be in days to come. For there is no bent of heart or turn of thought which any man holds by virtue of an unalterable nature or will. Even those feelings and opinions deemed most identical with eternal right and truth, it is not impossible but that, as personal persuasions, they may in reality be but the result of some chance tip of Fate's elbow in throwing her dice. For, not to go into the first seeds of things, and passing by the accident of parentage predisposing to this or that habit of mind, descend below these, and tell me, if you change this man's experiences or that man's books, will wisdom go surety for his unchanged convictions? As particular food begets particular dreams, so particular experiences or books particular feelings or beliefs. I will hear nothing of that fine babble about development and its laws; there is no development in opinion and feeling but the developments of time and tide. You may deem all this talk idle, Frank; but conscience bids me show you how fundamental the reasons for treating you as I do."

"But Charlie, dear Charlie, what new notions are these? I thought that man was no poor drifting weed of the universe, as you phrased it; that, if so minded, he could have a will, a way, a thought, and a heart of his own? But now you have turned everything upside down again, with an inconsistency that amazes and shocks me."

"Inconsistency? Bah!"

"There speaks the ventriloquist again," sighed Frank, in bitterness.

Illy pleased, it may be, by this repetition of an allusion little flattering to his originality, however much so to his docility, the disciple sought to carry it off by exclaiming: "Yes, I turn over day and night, with indefatigable pains, the sublime pages of my master, and unfortunately for you, my dear friend, I find nothing *there* that leads me to think otherwise than I do. But enough: in this matter the experience of China Aster teaches a moral more to the point than anything Mark Winsome can offer, or I either."

"I cannot think so, Charlie; for neither am I China Aster, nor do I stand in his position. The loan to China Aster was to extend his business with; the loan I seek is to relieve my necessities."

"Your dress, my dear Frank, is respectable; your cheek is not gaunt. Why talk of necessities when nakedness and starvation beget the only real necessities?"

"But I need relief, Charlie; and so sorely, that I now conjure you to forget that I was ever your friend, while I apply to you only as a fellow-being, whom, surely, you will not turn away."

"That I will not. Take off your hat, bow over to the ground, and supplicate an alms of me in the way of London streets, and you shall   a sturdy beggar in vain. But no man drops pennies into t   f a friend, let me tell you. If you turn beggar, then, for the hon   of noble friendship, I turn stranger."

"Enough," cried the other, rising, and with a toss of his shoulders seeming disdainfully to throw off the character he had assumed. "Enough. I have had my fill of the philosophy of Mark Winsome as put into action. And moonshiny as it in theory may be, yet a very practical philosophy it turns out in effect, as he himself engaged I should find. But, miserable for my race should I be, if I thought he spoke truth when he claimed, for proof of the soundness of his system, that the study of it tended to much the same formation of character with the experiences of the world.—Apt disciple! Why wrinkle the brow, and waste the oil both of life and the lamp, only to turn out a head kept cool by the under ice of the heart? What your illustrious magian has taught you, any poor, old, broken-down, heart-shrunken dandy might have lisped. Pray, leave me, and with you take the last dregs of your inhuman philosophy. And here, take this shilling, and at the first wood-landing buy yourself a few chips to warm the frozen natures of you and your philosopher by."

With these words and a grand scorn the cosmopolitan turned on his heel, leaving his companion at a loss to determine where exactly the fictitious character had been dropped, and the real one, if any, resumed. If any, because, with pointed meaning, there occurred to him, as he gazed after the cosmopolitan, these familiar lines: ·

> *All the world's a stage,*
> *And all the men and women merely players,*
> *Who have their exits and their entrances,*
> *And one man in his time plays many parts.*

"Bless you, barber!"

Now, owing to the lateness of the hour, the barber had been all alone until within the ten minutes last passed; when, finding himself rather dullish company to himself, he thought he would have a good time with Souter John and Tam O'Shanter, otherwise called Somnus and Morpheus, two very good fellows, though one was not very bright, and the other an arrant rattlebrain, who, though much listened to by some, no wise man would believe under oath.

In short, with back presented to the glare of his lamps, and so to the door, the honest barber was taking what are called cat-naps, and dreaming in his chair; so that, upon suddenly hearing the benediction above, pronounced in tones not unangelic, starting up, half awake, he stared before him, but saw nothing, for the stranger stood behind. What with cat-naps, dreams, and bewilderments, therefore, the voice seemed a sort of spiritual manifestation to him; so that, for the moment, he stood all agape, eyes fixed, and one arm in the air.

"Why, barber, are you reaching up to catch birds there with salt?"

"Ah!" turning round disenchanted, "it is only a man, then."

"*Only* a man? As if to be but man were nothing. But don't be too sure what I am. You call me *man*, just as the townsfolk called the angels who, in man's form, came to Lot's house; just as the Jew rustics called the devils who, in man's form, haunted the tombs. You can conclude nothing absolute from the human form, barber."

"But I can conclude something from that sort of talk, with that sort of dress," shrewdly thought the barber, eying him with regained self-possession, and not without some latent touch of apprehension at being alone with him. What was passing in his mind seemed divined by the other, who now, more rationally and gravely, and as if he expected it should be attended to, said: "Whatever else you may conclude upon, it is my desire that you conclude to give me a good shave," at the same time loosening his neck-cloth. "Are you competent to a good shave, barber?"

"No broker more so, sir," answered the barber, whom the business-like proposition instinctively made confine to business-ends his views of the visitor.

"Broker? What has a broker to do with lather? A broker I have always understood to be a worthy dealer in certain papers and metals."

"He, he!" taking him now for some dry sort of joker, whose jokes, he being a customer, it might be as well to appreciate, "he, he! You understand well enough, sir. Take this seat, sir," laying his hand on a great stuffed chair, high-backed and high-armed, crimson-covered, and raised on a sort of dais, and which seemed but to lack a canopy and quarterings, to make it in aspect quite a throne, "take this seat, sir."

"Thank you," sitting down; "and now, pray, explain that about the broker. But look, look—what's this?" suddenly rising, and pointing, with his long pipe, towards a gilt notification swinging among colored fly-papers from the ceiling, like a tavern sign, "*No Trust?* No trust means distrust; distrust means no confidence. Barber," turning upon him excitedly, "what fell suspiciousness prompts this scandalous confession? My life!" stamping his foot, "if but to tell a dog that you have no confidence in him be matter for affront to the dog, what an insult to take that way the whole haughty race of man by the beard! By my heart, sir! but at least you are valiant; backing the spleen of Thersites with the pluck of Agamemnon."

"Your sort of talk, sir, is not exactly in my line," said the barber, rather ruefully, being now again hopeless of his customer, and not without return of uneasiness; "not in my line, sir," he emphatically repeated.

"But the taking of mankind by the nose is; a habit, barber, which I sadly fear has insensibly bred in you a disrespect for man. For how, indeed, may respectful conceptions of him coexist with the perpetual habit of taking him by the nose? But, tell me, though I, too, clearly see the import of your notification, I do not, as yet, perceive the object. What is it?"

"Now you speak a little in my line, sir," said the barber, not un-relieved at this return to plain talk; "that notification I find very use-ful, sparing me much work which would not pay. Yes, I lost a good deal, off and on, before putting that up," gratefully glancing to-wards it.

"But what is its object? Surely, you don't mean to say, in so many words, that you have no confidence? For instance, now," flinging aside his neck-cloth, throwing back his blouse, and reseating him-self on the tonsorial throne, at sight of which proceeding the bar-ber mechanically filled a cup with hot water from a copper vessel over a spirit-lamp, "for instance, now, suppose I say to you, 'Bar-ber, my dear barber, unhappily I have no small change by me to-night, but shave me, and depend upon your money to-morrow'—suppose I should say that now, you would put trust in me, wouldn't you? You would have confidence?"

"Seeing that it is you, sir," with complaisance replied the bar-ber, now mixing the lather, "seeing that it is *you*, sir, I won't an-swer that question. No need to."

"Of course, of course—in that view. But, as a supposition—you would have confidence in me, wouldn't you?"

"Why—yes, yes."

"Then why that sign?"

"Ah, sir, all people ain't like you," was the smooth reply, at the same time, as if smoothly to close the debate, beginning smoothly to apply the lather, which operation, however, was, by a motion, protested against by the subject, but only out of a desire to rejoin, which was done in these words:

"All people ain't like me. Then I must be either better or worse than most people. Worse, you could not mean; no, barber, you could not mean that; hardly that. It remains, then, that you think me better than most people. But that I ain't vain enough to be-lieve; though, from vanity, I confess, I could never yet, by my best wrestlings, entirely free myself; nor, indeed, to be frank, am I at bottom over anxious to—this same vanity, barber, being so harm-less, so useful, so comfortable, so pleasingly preposterous a passion."

"Very true, sir; and upon my honor, sir, you talk very well. But the lather is getting a little cold, sir."

"Better cold lather, barber, than a cold heart. Why that cold sign? Ah, I don't wonder you try to shirk the confession. You feel in your soul how ungenerous a hint is there. And yet, barber, now that I look into your eyes—which somehow speak to me of the mother that must have so often looked into them before me—I dare say, though you may not think it, that the spirit of that notification is not one with your nature. For look now, setting business views aside, regarding the thing in an abstract light; in short, supposing a case, barber; supposing, I say, you see a stranger, his face accidentally averted, but his visible part very respectable-looking; what now, barber—I put it to your conscience, to your charity—what would be your impression of that man, in a moral point of view? Being in a signal sense a stranger, would you, for that, signally set him down for a knave?"

"Certainly not, sir; by no means," cried the barber, humanely resentful.

"You would upon the face of him—"

"Hold, sir," said the barber, "nothing about the face; you remember, sir, that is out of sight."

"I forgot that. Well then, you would, upon the *back* of him, conclude him to be, not improbably, some worthy sort of person; in short, an honest man; wouldn't you?"

"Not unlikely I should, sir."

"Well now—don't be so impatient with your brush, barber—suppose that honest man meet you by night in some dark corner of the boat where his face would still remain unseen, asking you to trust him for a shave—how then?"

"Wouldn't trust him, sir."

"But is not an honest man to be trusted?"

"Why—why—yes, sir."

"There! don't you see, now?"

"See what?" asked the disconcerted barber, rather vexedly.

"Why, you stand self-contradicted, barber; don't you?"

"No," doggedly.

"Barber," gravely, and after a pause of concern, "the enemies of our race have a saying that insincerity is the most universal and inveterate vice of man—the lasting bar to real amelioration, whether of individuals or of the world. Don't you now, barber, by your stubbornness on this occasion, give color to such a calumny?"

"Hity-tity!" cried the barber, losing patience, and with it respect; "stubbornness?" Then clattering round the brush in the cup, "Will you be shaved, or won't you?"

"Barber, I will be shaved, and with pleasure; but, pray, don't raise your voice that way. Why, now, if you go through life gritting your teeth in that fashion, what a comfortless time you will have."

"I take as much comfort in this world as you or any other man," cried the barber, whom the other's sweetness of temper seemed rather to exasperate than soothe.

"To resent the imputation of anything like unhappiness I have often observed to be peculiar to certain orders of men," said the other pensively, and half to himself, "just as to be indifferent to that imputation, from holding happiness but for a secondary good and inferior grace, I have observed to be equally peculiar to other kinds of men. Pray, barber," innocently looking up, "which think you is the superior creature?"

"All this sort of talk," cried the barber, still unmollified, "is, as I told you once before, not in my line. In a few minutes I shall shut up this shop. Will you be shaved?"

"Shave away, barber. What hinders?" turning up his face like a flower.

The shaving began, and proceeded in silence, till at length it became necessary to prepare to relather a little—affording an opportunity for resuming the subject, which, on one side, was not let slip.

"Barber," with a kind of cautious kindliness, feeling his way, "barber, now have a little patience with me; do; trust me, I wish not to offend. I have been thinking over that supposed case of the man with the averted face, and I cannot rid my mind of the impression that, by your opposite replies to my questions at the time, you showed yourself much of a piece with a good many other men—that is, you have confidence, and then again, you have none. Now, what I would ask is, do you think it sensible standing for a sensible man, one foot on confidence and the other on suspicion? Don't you think, barber, that you ought to elect? Don't you think consistency requires that you should either say 'I have confidence in all men,' and take down your notification; or else say, 'I suspect all men,' and keep it up?"

This dispassionate, if not deferential, way of putting the case, did not fail to impress the barber, and proportionately conciliate him. Likewise, from its pointedness, it served to make him thoughtful; for, instead of going to the copper vessel for more water, as he had purposed, he halted half-way towards it, and, after a pause, cup in hand, said: "Sir, I hope you would not do me injustice. I don't say, and can't say, and wouldn't say, that I suspect all men; but I   y that strangers are not to be trusted, and so," pointing
        sign, "no trust."

"But look, now, I beg, barber," rejoined the other deprecatingly, not presuming too much upon the barber's changed temper; "look, now; to say that strangers are not to be trusted, does not that imply something like saying that mankind is not to be trusted; for the mass of mankind, are they not necessarily strangers to each individual man? Come, come, my friend," winningly, "you are no Timon to hold the mass of mankind untrustworthy. Take down your notification; it is misanthropical; much the same sign that Timon traced with charcoal on the forehead of a skull stuck over his cave. Take it down, barber; take it down to-night. Trust men. Just try the experiment of trusting men for this one little trip. Come now, I'm a philanthropist, and will insure you against losing a cent."

The barber shook his head dryly, and answered, "Sir, you must excuse me. I have a family."

"So you are a philanthropist, sir," added the barber with an illuminated look; "that accounts, then, for all. Very odd sort of man the philanthropist. You are the second one, sir, I have seen. Very odd sort of man, indeed, the philanthropist. Ah, sir," again meditatively stirring in the shaving-cup, "I sadly fear, lest you philanthropists know better what goodness is, than what men are." Then, eying him as if he were some strange creature behind cage-bars, "So you are a philanthropist, sir."

"I am Philanthropos, and love mankind. And, what is more than you do, barber, I trust them."

Here the barber, casually recalled to his business, would have replenished his shaving-cup, but finding now that on his last visit to the water-vessel he had not replaced it over the lamp, he did so now; and, while waiting for it to heat again, became almost as sociable as if the heating water were meant for whisky-punch; and almost as pleasantly garrulous as the pleasant barbers in romances.

"Sir," said he, taking a throne beside his customer (for in a row there were three thrones on the dais, as for the three kings of Cologne, those patron saints of the barber), "sir, you say you trust men. Well, I suppose I might share some of your trust, were it not for this trade, that I follow, too much letting me in behind the scenes."

"I think I understand," with a saddened look; "and much the same thing I have heard from persons in pursuits different from yours—from the lawyer, from the congressman, from the editor, not to mention others, each, with a strange kind of melancholy vanity, claiming for his vocation the distinction of affording the surest inlets to the conviction that man is no better than he should be. All of which testimony, if reliable, would, by mutual corroboration, justify some disturbance in a good man's mind. But no, no; it is a mistake—all a mistake."

"True, sir, very true," assented the barber.

"Glad to hear that," brightening up.

"Not so fast, sir," said the barber; "I agree with you in thinking that the lawyer, and the congressman, and the editor, are in error, but only in so far as each claims peculiar facilities for the sort of knowledge in question; because, you see, sir, the truth is, that every trade or pursuit which brings one into contact with the facts, sir, such trade or pursuit is equally an avenue to those facts."

"*How* exactly is that?"

"Why, sir, in my opinion—and for the last twenty years I have, at odd times, turned the matter over some in my mind—he who comes to know man, will not remain in ignorance of man. I think I am not rash in saying that; am I, sir?"

"Barber, you talk like an oracle—obscurely, barber, obscurely."

"Well, sir," with some self-complacency, "the barber has always been held an oracle, but as for the obscurity, that I don't admit."

"But, pray, now, by your account, what precisely may be this mysterious knowledge gained in your trade? I grant you, indeed, as before hinted, that your trade, imposing on you the necessity of functionally tweaking the noses of mankind, is, in that respect, unfortunate, very much so; nevertheless, a well-regulated imagination should be proof even to such a provocation to improper conceits. But what I want to learn from you, barber, is, how does the mere handling of the outside of men's heads lead you to distrust the inside of their hearts?"

"What, sir, to say nothing more, can one be forever dealing in macassar oil, hair dyes, cosmetics, false moustaches, wigs, and toupees, and still believe that men are wholly what they look to be? What think you, sir, are a thoughtful barber's reflections, when, behind a careful curtain, he shaves the thin, dead stubble off a head, and then dismisses it to the world, radiant in curling auburn? To contrast the shamefaced air behind the curtain, the fearful looking forward to being possibly discovered there by a prying acquaintance, with the cheerful assurance and challenging pride with which the same man steps forth again, a gay deception, into the street, while some honest, shock-headed fellow humbly gives him the wall. Ah, sir, they may talk of the courage of truth, but my trade teaches me that truth sometimes is sheepish. Lies, lies, sir, brave lies are the lions!"

"You twist the moral, barber; you sadly twist it. Look, now; take it this way: A modest man thrust out naked into the street, would he not be abashed? Take him in and clothe him; would not his confidence be restored? And in either case, is any reproach involved? Now, what is true of the whole, holds proportionably true of the part. The bald head is a nakedness which the wig is a coat to. To feel uneasy at the possibility of the exposure of one's nakedness at top, and to feel comforted by the consciousness of having it clothed—these feelings, instead of being dishonorable to a bold man, do, in fact, but attest a proper respect for himself and his fellows. And as for the deception, you may as well call the fine roof of a fine chateau a deception, since, like a fine wig, it also is an artificial cover to the head, and equally, in the common eye, decorates the wearer.—I have confuted you, my dear barber; I have confounded you."

"Pardon," said the barber, "but I do not see that you have. His coat and his roof no man pretends to palm off as a part of himself, but the bald man palms off hair, not his, for his own."

"Not *his*, barber? If he have fairly purchased his hair, the law will protect him in its ownership, even against the claims of the head on which it grew. But it cannot be that you believe what you say, barber; you talk merely for the humor. I could not think so of you as to suppose that you would contentedly deal in the impostures you condemn."

"Ah, sir, I must live."

"And can't you do that without sinning against your conscience, as you believe? Take up some other calling."

"Wouldn't mend the matter much, sir."

"Do you think, then, barber, that, in a certain point, all the trades and callings of men are much on a par? Fatal, indeed," raising his hand, "inexpressibly dreadful, the trade of the barber, if to such conclusions it necessarily leads. Barber," eying him not without emotion, "you appear to me not so much a misbeliever, as a man misled. Now, let me set you on the right track; let me restore you to trust in human nature, and by no other means than the very trade that has brought you to suspect it."

"You mean, sir, you would have me try the experiment of taking down that notification," again pointing to it with his brush; "but, dear me, while I sit chatting here, the water boils over."

With which words, and such a well-pleased, sly, snug, expression, as they say some men have when they think their little stratagem has succeeded, he hurried to the copper vessel, and soon had his cup foaming up with white bubbles, as if it were a mug of new ale.

Meantime, the other would have fain gone on with the discourse; but the cunning barber lathered him with so generous a brush, so piled up the foam on him, that his face looked like the yeasty crest of a billow, and vain to think of talking under it, as for a drowning priest in the sea to exhort his fellow-sinners on a raft. Nothing would do, but he must keep his mouth shut. Doubtless, the interval was not, in a meditative way, unimproved; for, upon the traces of the operation being at last removed, the cosmopolitan rose, and, for added refreshment, washed his face and hands; and having generally readjusted himself, began, at last, addressing the barber in a manner different, singularly so, from his previous one. Hard to say exactly what the manner was, any more than to hint it was a sort of magical; in a benign way, not wholly unlike the manner, fabled or otherwise, of certain creatures in nature, which have the power of persuasive fascination—the power of holding another creature by the button of the eye, as it were, despite the serious disinclination, and, indeed, earnest protest, of the victim. With this manner the conclusion of the matter was not out of keeping; for, in the end, all argument and expostulation proved vain, the barber being irresistibly persuaded to agree to try, for the remainder of the present trip, the experiment of trusting men, as both phrased it. True, to save his credit as a free agent, he was loud in averring that it was only for the novelty of the thing that he so agreed, and he required the other, as before volunteered, to go security to him against any loss that might ensue; but still the fact remained, that he engaged to trust men, a thing he had before said he would not do, at least not unreservedly. Still the more to save his credit, he now insisted upon it, as a last point, that the agreement should be put in black and white, especially the security part. The other made no demur; pen, ink, and paper were provided, and grave as any notary the cosmopolitan sat down, but, ere taking the pen, glanced up at the notification, and said: "First down with that sign, barber—Timon's sign, there; down with it."

This, being in the agreement, was done—though a little reluctantly—with an eye to the future, the sign being carefully put away in a drawer.

"Now, then, for the writing," said the cosmopolitan, squaring himself. "Ah," with a sigh, "I shall make a poor lawyer, I fear. Ain't used, you see, barber, to a business which, ignoring the principle of honor, holds no nail fast till clinched. Strange, barber," taking up the blank paper, "that such flimsy stuff as this should make such strong hawsers; vile hawsers, too. Barber," starting up, "I won't put it in black and white. It were a reflection upon our joint honor. I will take your word, and you shall take mine."

"But your memory may be none of the best, sir. Well for you, on your side, to have it in black and white, just for a memorandum like, you know."

"That, indeed! Yes, and it would help *your* memory, too, wouldn't it, barber? Yours, on your side, being a little weak, too, I dare say. Ah, barber! how ingenious we human beings are; and how kindly we reciprocate each other's little delicacies, don't we? What better proof, now, that we are kind, considerate fellows, with responsive fellow-feelings—eh, barber? But to business. Let me see. What's your name, barber?"

"William Cream, sir."

Pondering a moment, he began to write; and, after some corrections, leaned back, and read aloud the following:

AGREEMENT

Between

FRANK GOODMAN, *Philanthropist, and Citizen of the World,*

and

WILLIAM CREAM, *Barber of the Mississippi steamer, Fidèle.*

The first hereby agrees to make good to the last any loss that may come from his trusting mankind, in the way of his vocation, for the residue of the present trip; PROVIDED *that William Cream keep out of sight, for the given term, his notification of "*NO TRUST," *and by no other mode convey any, the least hint or intimation, tending to discourage men from soliciting trust from him, in the way of his vocation, for the time above specified; but, on the contrary, he do, by all proper and reasonable words, gestures, manners, and looks, evince a perfect confidence in all men, especially strangers; otherwise, this agreement to be void.*

Done, in good faith, this 1st day of April, 18——, at a quarter to twelve o'clock, P. M., *in the shop of said William Cream, on board the said boat, Fidèle.*

"There, barber; will that do?"

"That will do," said the barber, "only now put down your name."

Both signatures being affixed, the question was started by the barber, who should have custody of the instrument; which point, however, he settled for himself, by proposing that both should go together to the captain, and give the document into his hands—the barber hinting that this would be a safe proceeding, because the captain was necessarily a party disinterested, and, what was more, could not, from the nature of the present case, make anything by a breach of trust. All of which was listened to with some surprise and concern.

"Why, barber," said the cosmopolitan, "this don't show the right spirit: for me, I have confidence in the captain purely because he is a man; but he shall have nothing to do with our affair; for if you have no confidence in me, barber, I have in you. There, keep the paper yourself," handing it magnanimously.

"Very good," said the barber, "and now nothing remains but for me to receive the cash."

Though the mention of that word, or any of its singularly numerous equivalents, in serious neighborhood to a requisition upon one's purse, is attended with a more or less noteworthy effect upon the human countenance, producing in many an abrupt fall of it—in others, a writhing and screwing up of the features to a point not undistressing to behold, in some, attended with a blank pallor and fatal consternation—yet no trace of any of these symptoms was visible upon the countenance of the cosmopolitan, notwithstanding nothing could be more sudden and unexpected than the barber's demand.

"You speak of cash, barber; pray in what connection?"

"In a nearer one, sir," answered the barber, less blandly, "than I thought the man with the sweet voice stood, who wanted me to trust him once for a shave, on the score of being a sort of thirteenth cousin."

"Indeed, and what did you say to him?"

"I said, 'Thank you, sir, but I don't see the connection.' "

"How could you so unsweetly answer one with a sweet voice?"

"Because, I recalled what the son of Sirach says in the True Book: 'An enemy speaketh sweetly with his lips'; and so I did what the son of Sirach advises in such cases: 'I believed not his many words.' "

"What, barber, do you say that such cynical sort of things are in the True Book, by which, of course you mean the Bible?"

"Yes, and plenty more to the same effect. Read the Book of Proverbs."

"That's strange, now, barber; for I never happen to have met with those passages you cite. Before I go to bed this night, I'll inspect the Bible I saw on the cabin-table, to-day. But mind, you mustn't quote the True Book that way to people coming in here; it would be impliedly a violation of the contract. But you don't know how glad I feel that you have for one while signed off all that sort of thing."

"No, sir; not unless you down with the cash."

"Cash again! What do you mean?"

"Why, in this paper here, you engage, sir, to insure me against a certain loss, and—"

"Certain? Is it so *certain* you are going to lose?"

"Why, that way of taking the word may not be amiss, but I didn't mean it so. I meant a *certain* loss; you understand, a CERTAIN loss; that is to say, a certain loss. Now then, sir, what use your mere writing and saying you will insure me, unless beforehand you place in my hands a money-pledge, sufficient to that end?"

"I see; the material pledge."

"Yes, and I will put it low; say fifty dollars."

"Now what sort of a beginning is this? You, barber, for a given time engage to trust man, to put confidence in men, and, for your first step, make a demand implying no confidence in the very man you engage with. But fifty dollars is nothing, and I would let you have it cheerfully, only I unfortunately happen to have but little change with me just now."

"But you have money in your trunk, though?"

"To be sure. But you see—in fact, barber, you must be consist-ent. No, I won't let you have the money now; I won't let you vio-late the inmost spirit of our contract, that way. So good-night, and I will see you again."

"Stay, sir"—humming and hawing—"you have forgotten some-thing."

"Handkerchief?—gloves? No, forgotten nothing. Good-night."

"Stay, sir—the—the shaving."

"Ah, I *did* forget that. But now that it strikes me, I shan't pay you at present. Look at your agreement; you must trust. Tut! against loss you hold the guarantee. Good-night, my dear barber."

With which words he sauntered off, leaving the barber in a maze, staring after.

But it holding true in fascination as in natural philosophy, that nothing can act where it is not, so the barber was not long now in being restored to his self-possession and senses; the first evidence of which perhaps was, that, drawing forth his notification from the drawer, he put it back where it belonged; while, as for the agree-ment, that he tore up; which he felt the more free to do from the impression that in all human probability he would never again see the person who had drawn it. Whether that impression proved well-founded or not, does not appear. But in after days, telling the night's adventure to his friends, the worthy barber always spoke of his queer customer as the man-charmer—as certain East Indians are called snake-charmers—and all his friends united in thinking him QUITE AN ORIGINAL.

Chapter 44 *In Which* THE LAST THREE WORDS OF
THE LAST CHAPTER *Are Made the Text of Discourse,
Which Will Be Sure of Receiving More or Less Attention from
Those Readers Who Do Not Skip It* ଏ≥

"QUITE AN ORIGINAL": A phrase, we fancy, rather oftener used by
the young, or the unlearned, or the untraveled, than by the old, or
the well-read, or the man who has made the grand tour. Certainly,
the sense of originality exists at its highest in an infant, and probably at its lowest in him who has completed the circle of the
sciences.

As for original characters in fiction, a grateful reader will, on
meeting with one, keep the anniversary of that day. True, we sometimes hear of an author who, at one creation, produces some two
or three score such characters; it may be possible. But they can
hardly be original in the sense that Hamlet is, or Don Quixote, or
Milton's Satan. That is to say, they are not, in a thorough sense,
original at all. They are novel, or singular, or striking, or captivating, or all four at once.

More likely, they are what are called odd characters; but for
that, are no more original, than what is called an odd genius, in his
way, is. But, if original, whence came they? Or where did the novelist pick them up?

Where does any novelist pick up any character? For the most
part, in town, to be sure. Every great town is a kind of man-show,
where the novelist goes for his stock, just as the agriculturist goes
to the cattle-show for his. But in the one fair, new species of quad-
rupeds are hardly more rare, than in the other are new species of
characters—that is, original ones. Their rarity may still the more
appear from this, that, while characters, merely singular, imply but
singular forms so to speak, original ones, truly so, imply original
instincts.

In short, a due conception of what is to be held for this sort of
personage in fiction would make him almost as much of a prodigy

there, as in real history is a new law-giver, a revolutionizing philosopher, or the founder of a new religion.

In nearly all the original characters loosely accounted such in works of invention, there is discernible something prevailingly local, or of the age; which circumstance, of itself, would seem to invalidate the claim, judged by the principles here suggested.

Furthermore, if we consider, what is popularly held to entitle characters in fiction to being deemed original, is but something personal—confined to itself. The character sheds not its characteristic on its surroundings, whereas, the original character, essentially such, is like a revolving Drummond light, raying away from itself all round it—everything is lit by it, everything starts up to it (mark how it is with Hamlet), so that, in certain minds, there follows upon the adequate conception of such a character, an effect, in its way, akin to that which in Genesis attends upon the beginning of things.

For much the same reason that there is but one planet to one orbit, so can there be but one such original character to one work of invention. Two would conflict to chaos. In this view, to say that there are more than one to a book, is good presumption there is none at all. But for new, singular, striking, odd, eccentric, and all sorts of entertaining and instructive characters, a good fiction may be full of them. To produce such characters, an author, beside other things, must have seen much, and seen through much; to produce but one original character, he must have had much luck.

There would seem but one point in common between this sort of phenomenon in fiction and all other sorts: It cannot be born in the author's imagination—it being as true in literature as in zoology, that all life is from the egg.

In the endeavor to show, if possible, the impropriety of the phrase, *Quite an Original,* as applied by the barber's friends, we have, at unawares, been led into a dissertation bordering upon the prosy, perhaps upon the smoky. If so, the best use the smoke can be turned to, will be, by retiring under cover of it, in good trim as may be, to the story.

In the middle of the gentlemen's cabin burned a solar lamp, swung
from the ceiling, and whose shade of ground glass was all round
fancifully variegated, in transparency, with the image of a horned
altar, from which flames rose, alternate with the figure of a robed
man, his head encircled by a halo. The light of this lamp, after
dazzlingly striking on marble, snow-white and round—the slab of
a centre-table beneath—on all sides went rippling off with ever-
diminishing distinctness, till, like circles from a stone dropped in
water, the rays died dimly away in the furthest nook of the place.

Here and there, true to their place, but not to their function,
swung other lamps, barren planets, which had either gone out from
exhaustion, or been extinguished by such occupants of berths as
the light annoyed, or who wanted to sleep, not see.

By a perverse man, in a berth not remote, the remaining
lamp would have been extinguished as well, had not a steward forbade, saying that the commands of the captain required it to be
kept burning till the natural light of day should come to relieve it.
This steward, who, like many in his vocation, was apt to be a little
free-spoken at times, had been provoked by the man's pertinacity to
remind him, not only of the sad consequences which might, upon
occasion, ensue from the cabin being left in darkness, but, also, of
the circumstance that, in a place full of strangers, to show one's
self anxious to produce darkness there, such an anxiety was, to say
the least, not becoming. So the lamp—last survivor of many—
burned on, inwardly blessed by those in some berths, and inwardly
execrated by those in others.

Keeping his lone vigils beneath his lone lamp, which lighted his
book on the table, sat a clean, comely, old man, his head snowy
as the marble, and a countenance like that which imagination
ascribes to good Simeon, when, having at last beheld the Master of
Faith, he blessed him and departed in peace. From his hale look
of greenness in winter, and his hands ingrained with the tan, less,
apparently, of the present summer, than of accumulated ones past,

the old man seemed a well-to-do farmer, happily dismissed, after a thrifty life of activity, from the fields to the fireside—one of those who, at three-score-and-ten, are fresh-hearted as at fifteen; to whom seclusion gives a boon more blessed than knowledge, and at last sends them to heaven untainted by the world, because ignorant of it; just as a country man putting up at a London inn, and never stirring out of it as a sight-seer, will leave London at last without once being lost in its fog, or soiled by its mud.

Redolent from the barber's shop, as any bridegroom tripping to the bridal chamber might come, and by his look of cheeriness seeming to dispense a sort of morning through the night, in came the cosmopolitan; but marking the old man, and how he was occupied, he toned himself down, and trod softly, and took a seat on the other side of the table, and said nothing. Still, there was a kind of waiting expression about him.

"Sir," said the old man, after looking up puzzled at him a moment, "sir," said he, "one would think this was a coffee-house, and it was war-time, and I had a newspaper here with great news, and the only copy to be had, you sit there looking at me so eager."

"And so you *have* good news there, sir—the very best of good news."

"Too good to be true," here came from one of the curtained berths.

"Hark!" said the cosmopolitan. "Some one talks in his sleep."

"Yes," said the old man, "and you—*you* seem to be talking in a dream. Why speak you, sir, of news, and all that, when you must see this is a book I have here—the Bible, not a newspaper?"

"I know that; and when you are through with it—but not a moment sooner—I will thank you for it. It belongs to the boat, I believe—a present from a society."

"Oh, take it, take it!"

"Nay, sir, I did not mean to touch you at all. I simply stated the fact in explanation of my waiting here—nothing more. Read on, sir, or you will distress me."

This courtesy was not without effect. Removing his spectacles, and saying he had about finished his chapter, the old man kindly presented the volume, which was received with thanks equally kind. After reading for some minutes, until his expression merged from attentiveness into seriousness, and from that into a kind of pain, the cosmopolitan slowly laid down the book, and turning to the old man, who thus far had been watching him with benign curiosity, said: "Can you, my aged friend, resolve me a doubt —a disturbing doubt?"

"There are doubts, sir," replied the old man, with a changed countenance, "there are doubts, sir, which, if man have them, it is not man that can solve them."

"True; but look, now, what my doubt is. I am one who thinks well of man. I love man. I have confidence in man. But what was told me not a half-hour since? I was told that I would find it written—'believe not his many words—an enemy speaketh sweetly with his lips'—and also I was told that I would find a good deal more to the same effect, and all in this book. I could not think it; and, coming here to look for myself, what do I read? Not only just what was quoted, but also, as was engaged, more to the same purpose, such as this: 'With much communication he will tempt thee; he will smile upon thee, and speak thee fair, and say What wantest thou? If thou be for his profit he will use thee; he will make thee bear, and will not be sorry for it. Observe and take good heed. When thou hearest these things, awake in thy sleep.'"

"Who's that describing the confidence-man?" here came from the berth again.

"Awake in his sleep, sure enough, ain't he?" said the cosmopolitan, again looking off in surprise. "Same voice as before, ain't it? Strange sort of dreamy man, that. Which is his berth, pray?"

"Never mind *him*, sir," said the old man anxiously, "but tell me truly, did you, indeed, read from the book just now?"

"I did," with changed air, "and gall and wormwood it is to me, a truster in man; to me, a philanthropist."

"Why," moved, "you don't mean to say, that what you repeated is really down there? Man and boy, I have read the good book this seventy years, and don't remember seeing anything like that. Let me see it," rising earnestly, and going round to him.

"There it is; and there—and there"—turning over the leaves, and pointing to the sentences one by one; "there—all down in the 'Wisdom of Jesus, the Son of Sirach.'"

"Ah!" cried the old man, brightening up, "now I know. Look," turning the leaves forward and back, till all the Old Testament lay flat on one side, and all the New Testament flat on the other, while in his fingers he supported vertically the portion between, "look, sir, all this to the right is certain truth, and all this to the left is certain truth, but all I hold in my hand here is apocrypha."

"Apocrypha?"

"Yes; and there's the word in black and white," pointing to it. "And what says the word? It says as much as 'not warranted'; for what do college men say of anything of that sort? They say it is apocryphal. The word itself, I've heard from the pulpit, implies something of uncertain credit. So if your disturbance be raised from aught in this apocrypha," again taking up the pages, "in that case, think no more of it, for it's apocrypha."

"What's that about the Apocalypse?" here, a third time, came from the berth.

"He's seeing visions now, ain't he?" said the cosmopolitan, once more looking in the direction of the interruption. "But, sir," resuming, "I cannot tell you how thankful I am for your reminding me about the apocrypha here. For the moment, its being such escaped me. Fact is, when all is bound up together, it's sometimes confusing. The uncanonical part should be bound distinct. And, now that I think of it, how well did those learned doctors who rejected for us this whole book of Sirach. I never read anything so calculated to destroy man's confidence in man. This Son of Sirach even says—I saw it but just now: 'Take heed of thy friends'; not, observe, thy seeming friends, thy hypocritical friends, thy false friends, but thy *friends*, thy real friends—that is to say, not the truest friend in the world is to be implicitly trusted. Can Rochefoucault equal that? I should not wonder if his view of human nature, like Machiavelli's, was taken from this Son of Sirach. And to call it wisdom—the Wisdom of the Son of Sirach! Wisdom, indeed! What an ugly thing wisdom must be! Give me the folly that dimples the cheek, say I, rather than the wisdom that curdles the blood. But no, no; it ain't wisdom; it's apocrypha, as you say, sir. For how can that be trustworthy that teaches distrust?"

"I tell you what it is," here cried the same voice as before, only more in less of mockery, "if you two don't know enough to sleep, don't be keeping wiser men awake. And if you want to know what wisdom is, go find it under your blankets."

"Wisdom?" cried another voice with a brogue; "arrah, and is't wisdom the two geese are gabbling about all this while? To bed with ye, ye divils, and don't be after burning your fingers with the likes of wisdom."

"We must talk lower," said the old man; "I fear we have annoyed these good people."

"I should be sorry if wisdom annoyed any one," said the other; "but we will lower our voices, as you say. To resume: taking the thing as I did, can you be surprised at my uneasiness in reading passages so charged with the spirit of distrust?"

"No, sir, I am not surprised," said the old man; then added: "from what you say, I see you are something of my way of thinking—you think that to distrust the creature, is a kind of distrusting of the Creator. Well, my young friend, what is it? This is rather late for you to be about. What do you want of me?"

These questions were put to a boy in the fragment of an old linen coat, bedraggled and yellow, who, coming in from the deck barefooted on the soft carpet, had been unheard. All pointed and fluttering, the rags of the little fellow's red-flannel shirt, mixed with those of his yellow coat, flamed about him like the painted flames in the robes of a victim in *auto-da-fé*. His face, too, wore such a polish of seasoned grime, that his sloe-eyes sparkled from out it like lustrous sparks in fresh coal. He was a juvenile peddler, or *marchand*, as the polite French might have called him, of travelers' conveniences; and, having no allotted sleeping-place, had, in his wanderings about the boat, spied, through glass doors, the two in the cabin; and, late though it was, thought it might never be too much so for turning a penny.

Among other things, he carried a curious affair—a miniature mahogany door, hinged to its frame, and suitably furnished in all respects but one, which will shortly appear. This little door he now meaningly held before the old man, who, after staring at it a while, said: "Go thy ways with thy toys, child."

"Now, may I never get so old and wise as that comes to," laughed the boy through his grime; and, by so doing, disclosing leopard-like teeth, like those of Murillo's wild beggar-boy's.

"The divils are laughing now, are they?" here came the brogue from the berth. "What do the divils find to laugh about in wisdom, begorrah? To bed with ye, ye divils, and no more of ye."

"You see, child, you have disturbed that person," said the old man; "you mustn't laugh any more."

"Ah, now," said the cosmopolitan, "don't, pray, say that; don't let him think that poor Laughter is persecuted for a fool in this world."

"Well," said the old man to the boy, "you must, at any rate, speak very low."

"Yes, that wouldn't be amiss, perhaps," said the cosmopolitan; "but, my fine fellow, you were about saying something to my aged friend here; what was it?"

"Oh," with a lowered voice, coolly opening and shutting his little door, "only this: when I kept a toy-stand at the fair in Cincinnati last month, I sold more than one old man a child's rattle."

"No doubt of it," said the old man. "I myself often buy such things for my little grandchildren."

"But these old men I talk of were old bachelors."

The old man stared at him a moment; then, whispering to the cosmopolitan: "Strange boy, this; sort of simple, ain't he? Don't know much, hey?"

"Not much," said the boy, "or I wouldn't be so ragged."

"Why, child, what sharp ears you have!" exclaimed the old man.

"If they were duller, I would hear less ill of myself," said the boy.

"You seem pretty wise, my lad," said the cosmopolitan; "why don't you sell your wisdom, and buy a coat?"

"Faith," said the boy, "that's what I did to-day, and this is the coat that the price of my wisdom bought. But won't you trade?

See, now, it is not the door I want to sell; I only carry the door round for a specimen, like. Look now, sir," standing the thing up on the table, "supposing this little door is your state-room door; well," opening it, "you go in for the night; you close your door behind you—thus. Now, is all safe?"

"I suppose so, child," said the old man.

"Of course it is, my fine fellow," said the cosmopolitan.

"All safe. Well. Now, about two o'clock in the morning, say, a soft-handed gentleman comes softly and tries the knob here—thus; in creeps my soft-handed gentleman; and hey, presto! how comes on the soft cash?"

"I see, I see, child," said the old man; "your fine gentleman is a fine thief, and there's no lock to your little door to keep him out"; with which words he peered at it more closely than before.

"Well, now," again showing his white teeth, "well, now, some of you old folks are knowing 'uns, sure enough; but now comes the great invention," producing a small steel contrivance, very simple but ingenious, and which, being clapped on the inside of the little door, secured it as with a bolt. "There now," admiringly holding it off at arm's-length, "there now, let that soft-handed gentleman come now a' softly trying this little knob here, and let him keep a' trying till he finds his head as soft as his hand. Buy the traveler's patent lock, sir, only twenty-five cents."

"Dear me," cried the old man, "this beats printing. Yes, child, I will have one, and use it this very night."

With the phlegm of an old banker pouching the change, the boy now turned to the other: "Sell you one, sir?"

"Excuse me, my fine fellow, but I never use such blacksmiths' things."

"Those who give the blacksmith most work seldom do," said the boy, tipping him a wink expressive of a degree of indefinite knowingness, not uninteresting to consider in one of his years. But the wink was not marked by the old man, nor, to all appearances, by him for whom it was intended.

"Now then," said the boy, again addressing the old man. "With

your traveler's lock on your door to-night, you will think yourself
all safe, won't you?"

"I think I will, child."

"But how about the window?"

"Dear me, the window, child. I never thought of that. I must
see to that."

"Never you mind about the window," said the boy, "nor, to be
honor bright, about the traveler's lock either, (though I ain't sorry
for selling one), do you just buy one of these little jokers," producing a number of suspender-like objects, which he dangled before
the old man; "money-belts, sir; only fifty cents."

"Money-belt? never heard of such a thing."

"A sort of pocket-book," said the boy, "only a safer sort. Very
good for travelers."

"Oh, a pocket-book. Queer looking pocket-books though, seems
to me. Ain't they rather long and narrow for pocket-books?"

"They go round the waist, sir, inside," said the boy; "door open
or locked, wide awake on your feet or fast asleep in your chair, im.
possible to be robbed with a money-belt."

"I see, I see. It *would* be hard to rob one's money-belt. And I
was told to-day the Mississippi is a bad river for pick-pockets. How
much are they?"

"Only fifty cents, sir."

"I'll take one. There!"

"Thank-ee. And now there's a present for ye," with which, drawing from his breast a batch of little papers, he threw one before the
old man, who, looking at it, read "*Counterfeit Detector*."

"Very good thing," said the boy, "I give it to all my customers
who trade seventy-five cents' worth; best present can be made
them. Sell you a money-belt, sir?" turning to the cosmopolitan.

"Excuse me, my fine fellow, but I never use that sort of thing;
my money I carry loose."

"Loose bait ain't bad," said the boy, "look a lie and find the
truth; don't care about a Counterfeit Detector, do ye? or is the
wind East, d'ye think?"

"Child," said the old man in some concern, "you mustn't sit up any longer, it affects your mind; there, go away, go to bed."

"If I had some people's brains to lie on, I would," said the boy, "but planks is hard, you know."

"Go, child—go, go!"

"Yes, child,—yes, yes," said the boy, with which roguish parody, by way of congé, he scraped back his hard foot on the woven flowers of the carpet, much as a mischievous steer in May scrapes back his horny hoof in the pasture; and then with a flourish of his hat— which, like the rest of his tatters, was, thanks to hard times, a belonging beyond his years, though not beyond his experience, being a grown man's cast-off beaver—turned, and with the air of a young Caffre, quitted the place.

"That's a strange boy," said the old man, looking after him. "I ler who's his mother; and whether she knows what late hours eps?"

The probability is," observed the other, "that his mother does not know. But if you remember, sir, you were saying something, when the boy interrupted you with his door."

"So I was.—Let me see," unmindful of his purchases for the moment, "what, now, was it? What was that I was saying? Do *you* remember?"

"Not perfectly, sir; but, if I am not mistaken, it was something like this: you hoped you did not distrust the creature; for that would imply distrust of the Creator."

"Yes, that was something like it," mechanically and unintelligently letting his eye fall now on his purchases.

"Pray, will you put your money in your belt tonight?"

"It's best, ain't it?" with a slight start. "Never too late to be cautious. 'Beware of pick-pockets' is all over the boat."

"Yes, and it must have been the Son of Sirach, or some other morbid cynic, who put them there. But that's not to the purpose. Since you are minded to it, pray, sir, let me help you about the belt. I think that, between us, we can make a secure thing of it."

"Oh no, no, no!" said the old man, not unperturbed, "no, no, I wouldn't trouble you for the world," then, nervously folding up the belt, "and I won't be so impolite as to do it for myself, before you, either. But, now that I think of it," after a pause, carefully taking a little wad from a remote corner of his vest pocket, "here are two bills they gave me at St. Louis, yesterday. No doubt they are all right; but just to pass time, I'll compare them with the Detector here. Blessed boy to make me such a present. Public benefactor, that little boy!"

Laying the Detector square before him on the table, he then, with something of the air of an officer bringing by the collar a brace of culprits to the bar, placed the two bills opposite the Detector, upon which, the examination began, lasting some time, prosecuted with no small research and vigilance, the forefinger of the right hand proving of lawyer-like efficacy in tracing out and pointing the evidence, whichever way it might go.

After watching him a while, the cosmopolitan said in a formal voice, "Well, what say you, Mr. Foreman; guilty, or not guilty?— Not guilty, ain't it?"

"I don't know, I don't know," returned the old man, perplexed, "there's so many marks of all sorts to go by, it makes it kind of uncertain. Here, now, is this bill," touching one, "it looks to be a three dollar bill on the Vicksburgh Trust and Insurance Banking Company. Well, the Detector says—"

"But why, in this case, care what it says? Trust and Insurance! What more would you have?"

"No; but the Detector says, among fifty other things, that, if a good bill, it must have, thickened here and there into the substance of the paper, little wavy spots of red; and it says they must have a kind of silky feel, being made by the lint of a red silk handkerchief stirred up in the paper-maker's vat—the paper being made to order for the company."

"Well, and is—"

"Stay. But then it adds, that sign is not always to be relied on; for some good bills get so worn, the red marks get rubbed out. And that's the case with my bill here—see how old it is—or else it's a counterfeit, or else—I don't see right—or else—dear, dear me—I don't know what else to think."

"What a peck of trouble that Detector makes for you now; believe me, the bill is good; don't be so distrustful. Proves what I've always thought, that much of the want of confidence, in these days, is owing to these Counterfeit Detectors you see on every desk and counter. Puts people up to suspecting good bills. Throw it away, I beg, if only because of the trouble it breeds you."

"No; it's troublesome, but I think I'll keep it.—Stay, now, here's another sign. It says that, if the bill is good, it must have in one corner, mixed in with the vignette, the figure of a goose, very small, indeed, all but microscopic; and, for added precaution, like the figure of Napoleon outlined by the tree, not observable, even if magnified, unless the attention is directed to it. Now, pore over it as I will, I can't see this goose."

"Can't see the goose? why, I can; and a famous goose it is. There" (reaching over and pointing to a spot in the vignette).

"I don't see it—dear me—I don't see the goose. Is it a real goose?"

"A perfect goose; beautiful goose."

"Dear, dear, I don't see it."

"Then throw that Detector away, I say again; it only makes you purblind; don't you see what a wild-goose chase it has led you? The bill is good. Throw the Detector away."

"No; it ain't so satisfactory as I thought for, but I must examine this other bill."

"As you please, but I can't in conscience assist you any more; pray, then, excuse me."

So, while the old man with much painstakings resumed his work, the cosmopolitan, to allow him every facility, resumed his reading. At length, seeing that he had given up his undertaking as hopeless, and was at leisure again, the cosmopolitan addressed some gravely interesting remarks to him about the book before him, and, presently, becoming more and more grave, said, as he turned the large volume slowly over on the table, and with much difficulty traced the faded remains of the gilt inscription giving the name of the society who had presented it to the boat, "Ah, sir, though every one must be pleased at the thought of the presence in public places of such a book, yet there is something that abates the satisfaction. Look at this volume; on the outside, battered as any old valise in the baggage-room; and inside, white and virgin as the hearts of lilies in bud."

"So it is, so it is," said the old man sadly, his attention for the first directed to the circumstance.

"Nor is this the only time," continued the other, "that I have observed these public Bibles in boats and hotels. All much like this—old without, and new within. True, this aptly typifies that internal freshness, the best mark of truth, however ancient; but then, it speaks not so well as could be wished for the good book's esteem in the minds of the traveling public. I may err, but it seems to me that if more confidence was put in it by the traveling public, it would hardly be so."

With an expression very unlike that with which he had bent over the Detector, the old man sat meditating upon his companion's remarks a while; and, at last, with a rapt look, said: "And yet, of all people, the traveling public most need to put trust in that guardianship which is made known in this book."

"True, true," thoughtfully assented the other.

"And one would think they would want to, and be glad to," continued the old man kindling; "for, in all our wanderings through this vale, how pleasant, not less than obligatory, to feel that we need start at no wild alarms, provide for no wild perils; trusting in that Power which is alike able and willing to protect us when we cannot ourselves."

His manner produced something answering to it in the cosmopolitan, who, leaning over towards him, said sadly: "Though this is a theme on which travelers seldom talk to each other, yet, to you, sir, I will say, that I share something of your sense of security. I have moved much about the world, and still keep at it; nevertheless, though in this land, and especially in these parts of it, some stories are told about steamboats and railroads fitted to make one a little apprehensive, yet, I may say that, neither by land nor by water, am I ever seriously disquieted, however, at times, transiently uneasy; since, with you, sir, I believe in a Committee of

Safety, holding silent sessions over all, in an invisible patrol, most alert when we soundest sleep, and whose beat lies as much through forests as towns, along rivers as streets. In short, I never forget that passage of Scripture which says, 'Jehovah shall be thy confidence.' The traveler who has not this trust, what miserable misgivings must be his; or, what vain, short-sighted care must he take of himself."

"Even so," said the old man, lowly.

"There is a chapter," continued the other, again taking the book, "which, as not amiss, I must read you. But this lamp, solar-lamp as it is, begins to burn dimly."

"So it does, so it does," said the old man with changed air, "dear me, it must be very late. I must to bed, to bed! Let me see," rising and looking wistfully all round, first on the stools and settees, and then on the carpet, "let me see, let me see;—is there anything I ha forgot,—forgot? Something I sort of dimly remember. S thing, my son—careful man—told me at starting this morning, this very morning. Something about seeing to—something before I got into my berth. What could it be? Something for safety. Oh, my poor old memory!"

"Let me give a little guess, sir. Life-preserver?"

"So it was. He told me not to omit seeing I had a life-preserver in my state-room; said the boat supplied them, too. But where are they? I don't see any. What are they like?"

"They are something like this, sir, I believe," lifting a brown stool with a curved tin compartment underneath; "yes, this, I think, is a life-preserver, sir; and a very good one, I should say, though I don't pretend to know much about such things, never using them myself."

"Why, indeed, now! Who would have thought it? *that* a life-preserver? That's the very stool I was sitting on, ain't it?"

"It is. And that shows that one's life is looked out for, when he ain't looking out for it himself. In fact, any of these stools here will float you, sir, should the boat hit a snag, and go down in the dark. But, since you want one in your room, pray take this one," handing it to him. "I think I can recommend this one; the tin part," rapping it with his knuckles, "seems so perfect—sounds so very hollow."

"Sure it's *quite* perfect, though?" Then, anxiously putting on his spectacles, he scrutinized it pretty closely—"well soldered? quite tight?"

"I should say so, sir; though, indeed, as I said, I never use this sort of thing, myself. Still, I think that in case of a wreck, barring sharp-pointed timbers, you could have confidence in that stool for a special providence."

"Then, good-night, good-night; and Providence have both of us in its good keeping."

"Be sure it will," eying the old man with sympathy, as for the moment he stood, money-belt in hand, and life-preserver under arm, "be sure it will, sir, since in Providence, as in man, you and I equally put trust. But, bless me, we are being left in the dark here. Pah! what a smell, too."

"Ah, my way now," cried the old man, peering before him, "where lies my way to my state-room?"

"I have indifferent eyes, and will show you; but, first, for the good of all lungs, let me extinguish this lamp."

The next moment, the waning light expired, and with it the waning flames of the horned altar, and the waning halo round the robed man's brow; while in the darkness which ensued, the cosmopolitan kindly led the old man away. Something further may follow of this Masquerade.

Rinehart Editions

RAVE REVIEWS FOR RICHARD LAYMON!

"I've always been a Laymon fan. He manages to raise serious gooseflesh."
—Bentley Little

"Laymon is incapable of writing a disappointing book."
—*New York Review of Science Fiction*

"Laymon always takes it to the max. No one writes like him and you're going to have a good time with anything he writes."
—Dean Koontz

"If you've missed Laymon, you've missed a treat!"
—Stephen King

"A brilliant writer."
—*Sunday Express*

"I've read every book of Laymon's I could get my hands on. I'm absolutely a longtime fan."
—Jack Ketchum, Author of *Old Flames*

"One of horror's rarest talents."
—*Publishers Weekly*

"Laymon is, was, and always will be king of the hill."
—*Horror World*

"Laymon is an American writer of the highest caliber."
—*Time Out*

"Laymon is unique. A phenom the gro
—Joe Citr

BEWARE

RICHARD LAYMON

LEISURE BOOKS NEW YORK CITY

A LEISURE BOOK®

November 2008

Published by

Dorchester Publishing Co., Inc.
200 Madison Avenue
New York, NY 10016

ISBN 10: 0-8439-6137-6
ISBN 13: 978-0-8439-6137-9

10 9 8 7 6 5 4 3 2 1

Visit us on the web at www.dorchesterpub.com.

BEWARE

Had you been rags or wood
I could have stuffed you and burned you.
But you were some bad breed of blood and bone
With arms that stretched an entire room,
Eyes without end and a heart of stone.

from "The Bogeyman"
by R. S. Stewart

CHAPTER ONE

On the night it began, Frank and Joan Bessler left the stifling heat of their home and walked four blocks to Hoffman's Market. Frank wanted a six-pack.

"Doesn't look open," Joan said.

"It has to be." Frank checked his wristwatch. "I've got nine fifteen."

"Why aren't the lights on?"

"Maybe she's saving on electricity," he said. He hoped he was right, but didn't believe it. For as far back as he could remember—and he'd spent all of his twenty-nine years in Oasis—the market had remained brightly lighted until closing time.

Closing time was ten o'clock to keep an edge on the Safeway that shut at nine. When Elsie Hoffman's husband died, three years ago, there'd been talk she might sell out, or at least close down earlier. But she'd held onto the tiny market and kept it open till the usual hour.

"I do think it's closed," Joan said as they stopped by its deserted parking lot.

The store sign was dark. The only light in the windows was a dim glow from the bulb Elsie always left on overnight.

"I can't believe it," Frank muttered.

"She must've had a reason."

"Maybe she changed hours on us."

Joan waited on the sidewalk, and Frank stepped up to the wooden door. Crouching, he squinted at the window sticker. Not enough light for him to read the times.

He tried the knob.

No go.

He peered through the window, and saw no one. "Damn," he muttered. He knocked on the glass. Couldn't hurt. Maybe Elsie was in the back someplace, out of sight.

"Come on, Frank. She's closed."

"I'm *thirsty*." He rapped harder on the window.

"We'll go over to the Golden Oasis. I'd rather have a margarita, anyway."

"Yeah, well, okay."

He took a final look into the dimly lighted store, then turned away. Behind him, the door banged and shook.

Frank jumped. Whirling around, he stared at the door, at its four glass panes.

"What was that?" Joan asked in a whisper.

"I don't know."

"Come on, let's go."

He backed away, staring at the windows, and decided he would have a heart attack, then and there, if a face should suddenly appear. He turned away fast before it could happen.

"Who's minding the mint?" Red asked.

Elsie sipped her whisky sour. It was sweet and

3

tart. Nobody could make whisky sours like Red. "I closed up a little early," she said.

"Must get lonely in there."

"I tell you, Red, I'm not as young as I used to be, not by a long shot, but I've still got my senses. I haven't gone mush-brained. Not yet. Wouldn't you say so?"

"You're sharp as a tack, Elsie. Always have been."

"Now, I went through pure hell when Herb passed on. Miserable old skinflint that he was, I did love the man. But that was three years ago, come October. I've perked up pretty well, since then. Even at my worst, though—right after I lost him—I never cracked up."

"You were solid as a rock, Elsie." He glanced down the bar. "Right back," he said, and went away to serve a new customer.

Elsie sipped her drink. She looked both ways. To her left was Beck Ramsey, his arm around the Walters girl. A pity on her, Elsie thought. Beck would bring her nothing but trouble. To her right, separated from Elsie by an empty stool, sat the newspaper gal, Lacey Allen. A pretty thing. The men say she's a cold fish, but they'll say that about any gal who won't drop her pants first time you smile at her. She always seemed pleasant enough in the store. A pity to see her sitting all alone at the bar like she didn't have a friend in the world.

"You're an educated lady."

Lacey looked over at her. "Me?"

"Sure. Went to Stanford and all. You're a doctor of something."

4

"English lit."

"Right. Probably one of the best educated folks in town. So you tell me something, if you don't mind my asking."

She shrugged. "All right. I'd be happy to try."

"Is there such a thing as ghosts?"

"Ghosts?"

"You know. Ghosts, spirits of dead folks, haunts."

Lacey shook her head. "You've got me. I've never seen one. All through history, though, people have claimed they exist." She looked away from Elsie, picked up her wineglass, and raised it to her lips. But she didn't drink. Her eyes suddenly opened wide. She gazed at Elsie, and set down her glass. "Did *you* see one?"

"Don't know what I saw. Not sure I saw anything."

"Mind if I . . . ?" Lacey looked at the empty stool between them.

"Help yourself."

She slid off her stool and climbed onto the one beside Elsie.

"This is just between us. I don't want to be written up in the *Trib*, everyone in town saying Elsie's got cards gone."

"I promise."

"Okay then."

A hand from behind patted her shoulder. She jumped, splashing her dress.

"Jeez, I'm sorry!"

"Lord!" She looked around. "Frank, you scared the daylights outa me!"

"I'm really sorry. Gosh, I . . ."

"Well, that's all right."

"Let me get you another drink."

"I won't argue with that."

He nodded a greeting to Lacey, then smiled at Elsie. "I guess I owed you a scare, though, after the one I just got at your store."

"What do you mean?"

"Have you got a watchdog in there, or something?"

"What happened?"

"We were over at your place a few minutes ago. I looked in the door, you know, to see if you were in, and something gave it a bash you wouldn't believe. Scared the socks off me."

"Did you see what it was?" Lacey asked.

"I didn't see anything. It sure gave me a start, though. Did you get yourself a dog, Elsie?"

"I don't keep animals. All they do is die on you."

"What was it, then?"

"I wish I knew," Elsie said. "Heard something, myself, around nine. Sounded like someone walking. I looked everywhere—up and down the aisles, back in the storage room. I even checked the meat locker. No one in the store but yours truly. Then the cash register opened on its own accord, and that did it. I closed up."

"Maybe you've got a ghost," Frank said, half grinning.

"That's what I wonder," Elsie said. "What do you think, Lacey?"

"I think we should drive over to your store and take a look."

Lacey swung her car into the parking lot of Hoffman's Market.

"Why don't you wait here," Frank told his wife.

"And miss the fun?" She flung open a rear door, climbed out, and smiled at Lacey. "You think we'll make the paper?"

"That depends on what's inside," she said, and followed Elsie to the door.

"We'll make the paper for sure," said Frank, "if we all get slaughtered in there."

Elsie frowned over her shoulder. "You do talk, Frank."

"If you're so nervous," Joan told him, "maybe *you* should wait in the car."

"And let you get slaughtered without me? How would that look?"

Elsie peered through a window. "I don't see anything. Course, I didn't before."

"Let's go in," Lacey whispered. She rubbed her arms. In spite of the night's heat, she had goose bumps. Maybe this wasn't such a great idea, she decided as Elsie pushed the key into the lock. But it had been *her* idea. She could hardly back out now. Besides, she did want to find out what had caused the trouble.

Elsie pushed open the door and entered. Lacey followed her in. The hardwood floor creaked under their footsteps. They stopped near the counter.

Except for the light from a ceiling fixture near the door, the store was dark. Lacey could see only a short distance up the aisles.

"Maybe you could turn on some . . ."

"Holy shit!"

She swung around. Frank's hand was still on the door. He'd stopped in the midst of shutting it. He and Joan stood motionless, staring.

"I'll be . . ." said Elsie.

Lacey walked to the door and crouched. "Wicked-looking thing," she said. The meat cleaver was buried deep in the wood only inches beneath the lower windows.

"A little higher . . ." Frank muttered.

"That's what hit the door!" Joan cried.

"That's right."

"God, you could've been killed!"

Lacey stood up. "I think we'd better get out of here."

"Yeah," Frank said. "And quick. Whoever threw that sucker isn't fooling around."

"Shouldn't we call the police?" Elsie asked.

"From the bar. Come on."

Oasis Tribune

Saturday, July 12

BURGLAR ATTACKS LOCAL MAN

Frank Bessler, local T.V. repairman, narrowly escaped injury last night when he interrupted a burglary in progress at Hoffman's Market.

BEWARE

Bessler and his wife, Joan, arrived at the market shortly after it was closed for the night by its proprietor, Elsie Hoffman. As Bessler peered inside, the front door was shaken by a cleaver thrown by an unseen assailant.

Police were summoned after Bessler notified Mrs. Hoffman of the occurrence. The responding patrolman, Ralph Lewis, searched the market and determined that the assailant had fled.

No signs of forced entry were found. According to Mrs. Hoffman, no money was taken. The empty wrappers of two T-bone steaks were discovered behind the meat counter, along with an empty bottle of wine.

Elsie Hoffman, who has operated the market alone since the demise of her husband, admits she is troubled by the burglary and the assault on Bessler, but has no plans to change the store's hours of operation. "Fear can run your life if you let it," she states. "I won't let it run mine."

Says Bessler, "I went in for a beer and almost bought a farm."

Oasis Tribune

Tuesday, July 15

MARKET HIT AGAIN

Hoffman's Market, over the weekend, was again the target of an unknown vandal. Opening her store for business, Monday morning, proprietor Elsie Hoffman found the empty wrappings of beef, potato chips, and other edibles scattered about the floor.

"Looks like someone had another feast," commented Mrs. Hoffman, whose store was the scene of a similar invasion on Friday night. On that occasion, local T.V. repairman Frank Bessler barely escaped serious injury when the surprised vandal hurled a meat cleaver at his head.

Police believe that both incidents are the work of the same individual. To date, nobody has seen the perpetrator. Nor is it known how he gains entry to the store.

Red Peterson, bartender at the Golden Oasis and a long-standing friend of Mrs. Hoffman, has offered his German shepherd, Rusty, to guard the market's premises. "I'll put Rusty up against any ten hooligans, and we'll just see who takes a bite out of what," says Red.

Mrs. Hoffman has agreed to use the dog in hopes of preventing further losses.

CHAPTER TWO

Dusk settled over Bayou Lafourche, and the participants began to arrive. They came in dinghies and skiffs and canoes, silently paddling or poling their way around the bend, landing on the high ground and dragging their vessels ashore.

The man's black, sweaty face looked grim in the telescopic sight of Matthew Dukane's rifle. "Smile," Dukane said. Though his whisper seemed loud, he doubted anyone would hear him. He was sitting astraddle a branch high in the tree. Even in total silence, those below would be unlikely to catch his whisper; in all this din, they didn't stand a chance.

A Chicago boy, Dukane didn't know what the hell was causing such a racket. The place sounded like the Brookfield Zoo gone manic. Or the jungles of Vietnam.

He sighted in an old, white crone. A teenaged girl with cornrows. A fat white man who looked like a good ol' boy. A bony red-haired gal. A strikingly beautiful mulatto woman. A black fellow with the build of a Sumo wrestler.

Quite a congregation, Dukane thought. But then,

Laveda was quite a woman. Hard to imagine anyone so beautiful could be so damned evil.

She hadn't shown herself yet. That was her style, though. Like most ladies who thought too highly of themselves, she had a fondness for dramatic entrances.

The drums began. Dukane glanced at the three drummers. They were all black men, naked to the waist, squatting at the edge of the clearing with their drums between their legs. They thumped the skins with their open hands.

Dukane looked away, and saw another skiff land. Its lone occupant climbed out. A white girl in cut-offs and a T-shirt. Quite attractive. He found her in the scope. The girl was Alice Donovan, no doubt about it. Though her hair was longer now, she still bore a striking resemblance to the graduation photo given to Dukane by her parents when they hired him.

Even as she walked toward the clearing, she began to sway with the low throb of the drumbeats.

The ceremonial fire was lighted.

The drumbeats quickened, and the dancing began.

Resting the weapon across his lap, he watched. The tempo was picking up, the drummers pounding out a frenzied beat. The dancers twirled and leapt in the firelight. Several were already naked. As he watched, Alice skinned off her T-shirt. She whirled, waving it like a banner while her other hand opened her cut-offs. She didn't pull the shorts down. She danced as if forgetting them. They hung in place, at first, then slowly slipped lower and lower until they

were halfway down her bare rump. They suddenly dropped. Dukane thought they might hobble the girl and trip her, but she jumped gracefully free. He turned his gaze to the mulatto woman with skin the color of tea. She was glossy with sweat, writhing as she rubbed her breasts.

Plenty of guys, Dukane thought, would pay through the nose for a show like this. He was slightly aroused, himself, but frightened. He'd heard people say fear is an aphrodisiac. Maybe it was, for them. In Dukane's experience, he'd found fear to be a great shrinker of erections.

Erections. Plenty of them down there. No coupling, though. Not yet. Nobody was even touching— not each other, anyway. They danced alone, jerking to the wild race of the drums, stroking themselves as if no one else existed.

Suddenly, the drums stopped. The dancers dropped to their knees.

A single, low voice said, "Laveda." Other voices joined it in a slow chant. "Laveda, Laveda, Laveda . . ."

Dukane flinched as something dropped onto his head. It moved in his hair, scurried down his forehead. He brushed it away. Probably a goddamn spider. The swamp was full of them.

The group kneeling around the fire continued to chant.

Out of the darkness behind the drummers stepped Laveda. Dukane had kept her under surveillance for two weeks in New Orleans hoping she would lead him to Alice—but he'd never seen her like this. He stared.

She wore a sheathed dagger at her side, suspended from a belt of gold chain. She wore a gold band on each upper arm. She wore a necklace of claws. And nothing else.

Her thick, blonde hair hung past her shoulders. Her skin glistened as if rubbed with oil. Dukane couldn't take his eyes off her. She was six-foot-one of the most stunning woman he had ever seen.

The chanting stopped as she walked among her congregation.

"The river flows," she said.

In unison, the others chanted, "The river is red."

"The river flows."

"Flows from the heart."

"The river flows."

"All powerful is the river."

"Its water is the water of life," she said.

"All powerful is he who drinks at its shore."

"Who, among us, would be all powerful?"

"I," answered the chorus.

Dukane spotted Alice. She looked ecstatic.

Laveda drew out her dagger. Standing near the fire, she raised it high and slowly turned in a circle. "Who, among us, would drink at the river?"

"*I.*"

"For he who partakes of the flowing river shall inherit all powers."

"The power of life, the power of death . . ."

". . . shall vanquish all enemies . . ."

"The strong and the weak shall perish at his command!"

". . . shall do what he will!"

"What thou wilt shall be the law!"

"Who shall drink at the river?"

"*I!*" they roared.

The drums rumbled. The congregation, still kneeling, swayed to the rhythm.

"The river flows!" Laveda yelled, wandering among her people. "It flows and winds. We shall drink from its shores, this night. We shall drink its all powerful waters and take its power into ourselves. The river is endless. Its waters flow forever. Eternal power shall be ours!"

She stopped and placed her open hand on the head of the beautiful young mulatto. The woman rose to her feet.

"We shall drink at the river!"

Dukane winced as Laveda jerked the woman's head back by the hair and flicked her knife across the throat. She pressed her mouth to the spouting wound.

Two men held the convulsing mulatto from behind, and Laveda stepped back. Her face was smeared with blood. It streamed down her body.

"Drink, all of you, at the river!"

As the drums roared, the whole mob rushed forward. Including Alice. They caught the blood in their mouths and hurried off, smearing their bodies, dancing with sudden fury as if they'd all gone mad. Laveda, herself, leapt and spun like the others, her golden hair flying, flesh shimmering in the firelight, breasts slick with blood. A huge, black man fell to the ground at her feet. She dropped onto him, impaling herself. As she rode him, she took a man into her mouth.

Everywhere Dukane looked, bodies were falling upon each other, mounting and thrusting to the thunder of the drums.

Alice, on her back near the center of the group, was barely visible under the pale body of a middle-aged man.

Slinging the rifle across his back, Dukane climbed down from the tree. He propped his rifle against its trunk. He tried to ignore the lump of fear in his belly as he disrobed.

A piece of cake, he told himself.

Cakes get eaten.

Screw that analogy, he thought, and managed a smile.

When he was naked, he mussed up his hair until it hung over his eyes. Then he slipped his Buck knife from its sheath.

The things I'll do for money.

Even as he cut into his forearm, though, he knew this wasn't just for money. Now that he'd located the girl, he could think of several less hazardous ways to snatch her from the cult. But none were this daring, this exciting. None would give him the same thrill.

Gonna get myself killed one of these days.

With a trembling hand, he smeared blood over his cheeks and mouth and chin.

He stabbed his knife into the trunk of the cypress, then made his way toward the clearing. His heart pounded with the thudding drums. His mouth was parched. Licking his lips, he tasted his own blood.

16

From behind a bush, he studied the fire-lit congregation. No one was standing, no one keeping watch. All were busy writhing in groups of two or more, or crawling off to join new partners.

Six feet from where he stood, two women were entwined, faces buried between wide-spread thighs. The one on top was a lean, white woman with a strawberry birthmark on her rump. Dukane crawled forward and nipped it. Her buttocks clenched and she yelped with surprise. Twisting her head around, she gazed at him with wild eyes. Dukane leered. He threw himself onto her sweaty back. Together, they rolled off to the side. She squirmed on top of him, moaning as he nibbled the side of her neck and fondled her breasts. The other woman scurried to join in. She pried apart their legs and knelt between them, her mouth going to the girl, her hand groping Dukane.

It squeezed him, massaged him, stroked him. He grew hard, his erection rising and pressing against the groin of the girl on top of him. He felt a tongue.

Then the woman tumbled away, sprawling as a burly black man fell upon her and rammed in.

Dukane threw himself over, rolling onto the girl who'd been on top of him. She clawed at the grass as he wedged her legs apart. Kneeling behind her, he stroked her wet opening. Then he clutched her hips and thrust into her. His quick, hard lunges soon brought her to a quaking orgasm. He withdrew, rigid and aching, concentrating to prevent his own body from finding its release. With a pat on her rump, he crawled away from the girl.

He spotted Alice. She was several yards away, on her back, her heels embedded in the rump of a fat man, pressing him down deeper. As Dukane crawled toward her, a hand darted from behind and gripped his erection. Lowering his head, he looked between his legs.

A chill swept up his spine.

Lying on her back, one hand clutching him, was Laveda. She licked her lips. Her eyes looked dull and glazed.

Maybe she's too far gone, Dukane thought, to realize I don't belong.

He started to crawl backward as Laveda pulled him.

There are thirty others here, he told himself. At least thirty. She couldn't know them all on sight.

Could she?

No. The New Orleans group was only one of a hundred. She had followers all over the country. Several thousand. New members all the time. She couldn't possibly keep track.

Her face appeared between his legs. Lifting her head, she sucked him into her mouth. He felt her tight lips, her pressing tongue, the edges of her teeth.

If she knows, Dukane thought, she'll bite. Or ram that dagger . . .

But she didn't. Her mouth held him tightly, sucking.

At least she can't see my face, he thought.

And then he was lost in the growing ache of need. Images flashed through his mind of Laveda writhing in the firelight, her skin glossy, her firm breasts tipped with rigid nipples.

18

Her hands spread his buttocks. She pushed a finger in, and he burst with release. She sucked hard as he pumped inside the tight wetness of her mouth. After he was done, she continued to tug at him for a few moments.

Then her head lowered. Her eyes were shut. She licked her lips.

Dukane crawled forward. Looking back, he saw her curl onto her side and reach out for the foot of a nearby girl. The girl, astraddle an older man, freed herself from his embraces and scurried toward Laveda.

He looked for Alice, and found her in the same place, still gasping under the fat man. He hurried to them. The fat man was grunting and pumping, his rump shaking like Jell-O.

Dukane pinched his carotid artery, felt him go rigid for a moment, then limp. He rolled the man off Alice, and took his place.

She smiled languidly. Her hands stroked his back. Her heels caressed his rump. She was hot and slick beneath him. She shivered as Dukane gnawed the side of her neck.

He pushed himself to his hands and knees. Alice clung to his neck, at first, when he started to crawl forward. Then her grip loosened. She fell to the ground and he kept crawling. Her hands trailed down his belly as he passed over her. They fondled his penis.

Dukane lowered his head to look at her. "Ride me," he said.

Alice made a husky laugh. Then she rolled over

and climbed onto Dukane. She straddled him, thighs hugging his hips, breasts against his back, arms wrapping his chest. "Giddyap," she whispered.

He crawled past several squirming piles of bodies. Once, Alice reached out to squeeze a looming breast and fell from Dukane's back. She quickly remounted.

Dukane continued forward.

"My turn," Alice whispered in his ear.

"Huh?"

"You ride me."

Dukane dropped to his elbows. She slid forward. Dukane climbed onto her back, but kept his feet on the ground for support. With one hand, he gripped her hair. He raised her head and pointed her toward the bushes. With his other hand, he slapped her rump. She whinnied and started to move.

Dukane walked, keeping most of his weight off her back while he guided her away from the group. At the edge of the clearing, she halted. She began to chew the leaves of a nearby bush.

Hunching low, Dukane pressed himself to her back. His right arm reached under her and caressed a breast. His left hand pinched her carotid. She started to collapse. He threw her over and they rolled together under the sheltering bushes.

For a long time, Dukane lay motionless on top of the girl. He watched the crowd.

Apparently, the disappearing act had drawn no attention.

He climbed off Alice. Staying low, he dragged her deeper into the undergrowth. When they were

well away from the clearing, he hoisted her over his shoulder and ran.

Oasis Tribune

Wednesday, July 16

GUARD DOG SLAIN

The dismembered body of Rusty, bartender Red Peterson's German shepherd, was found yesterday morning inside Hoffman's Market where the dog had been left, overnight, to guard the store against recurrent vandalism and grocery thefts.

Says proprietor Elsie Hoffman, who found the slain canine, "I'm just sick about it, just sick. We shouldn't have left that poor dog in here. I just knew he'd come to no good." In tears, she added, "That dog was the world to Red."

Red Peterson, owner of the dog and bartender at the Golden Oasis, was unavailable for comment.

CHAPTER THREE

Lacey climbed onto a bar stool. She tapped a cigarette out of its pack, and pressed it between her lips.

George O'Toole swiveled toward her. His ruddy, broad face crinkled with a smile, and he struck a match.

"Thank you."

"And what'll it be you're drinking tonight?" he asked, with a lilt Lacey assumed he had picked up from Barry Fitzgerald movies.

"A little red wine."

"A dainty drink for a dainty lady," he said. He raised a thick, weathered hand and caught the bartender's eye.

The bartender was Will Glencoe.

"A spot of red for the lady, Will. And another Guinness for himself." The bartender turned away. "You did Red a fine turn, writing up your story the way you did. He was almighty ashamed of the way he carried on about Rusty. I can understand a grown man weeping over the loss of a good dog—done it myself more than once. But it's a private thing, and a man doesn't want it blatted about. You did him a fine turn."

"He's right, there," said Will, setting down the drinks. "Take your average reporter, he'd have a field day. Bunch of bloodsuckers, that's what they are."

"But not our Lacey. You did yourself proud, young lady."

She reached into her purse.

"You put that away."

"Thank you, George."

He paid, and Will stepped away to take an order down the bar.

"Where *is* Red tonight?" Lacey asked.

George narrowed one eye. "Now where would *you* be, if a heartless so-and-so had done your dog that way?"

"Elsie's?"

He turned his wrist over, and peered at his watch. "She'll be closing up in ten minutes. Red's there with his twelve gauge. He'll be camping there tonight, hoping the filthy beggar shows up again. I offered my services—two guns are twice one—but he's after doing it alone, and I can't say I blame the man." George lifted his stein. "To your health," he toasted.

"And yours, George."

He winked at her, and drank.

Lacey sipped her wine. "What's Red planning to do, shoot the man?"

"The beggar cut down his dog, Lacey."

"I know, I saw it."

"And was it as bad as they say?"

"My God, George. I've never seen anything like . . ." She gagged. Tears filled her eyes.

23

"Now, now." George patted her shoulder.

She wiped the tears away, and took a deep breath. "I'm sorry." She managed a smile. "I don't normally go around gagging in public. Just thinking about that . . ." She did it again.

"Careful there. Say now, do you know how to tell the groom at a Kerryman's wedding?"

She shook her head.

"He's the one in the pin-striped Wellingtons."

She wiped her eyes, and sighed.

"Feeling better, now? Have another wine, and we'll talk of other things. I've a raft of Kerryman jokes. They're sure to gladden your heart."

"Thanks, George. I really should be going, though."

Outside in the warm night air, she felt better. She climbed into her car and rolled down the window. Her hand paused on the ignition. She wanted to go home, take a long bath, and get to bed. But she couldn't. Maybe it was none of her business. Knowing Red's plan, though, she wouldn't feel right if she didn't at least talk to him, warn him of the possible consequences.

You don't blow a man apart with a shotgun because he killed your dog. Not unless you want a prison stretch. Even shooting an intruder, unless the man is armed, could mean more trouble than Red probably bargained for.

She started her car and drove the three blocks to Hoffman's Market. Its sign was brightly lighted;

it hadn't closed yet. She pulled into the parking lot, and stopped beside Red's pickup truck. In the past, she'd rarely seen the pickup without Rusty pacing its bed, tail wagging, fur ruffled by the wind. She used to fear for the dog's safety. Suppose it leapt over the low panel as the truck sped along? Once, she'd voiced her fear to Red. "Would *you* jump off a moving truck?" he'd asked. "No, but I'm not a dog." Red grinned at that. "You can say that again."

Lacey ran her hand along the tailgate and looked into the empty truck bed, then hurried away.

The door of the market wasn't locked. She pushed it open, and stepped inside. Nobody at the counter.

"Hello," she called.

Swinging the door shut, she glanced at the pale gash left by the meat cleaver.

"Elsie? Red?"

She looked down a bright aisle. At the far end, just in front of the meat counter, a shotgun lay on the floor. An icy chill washed over Lacey, raising goose bumps. Even the skin of her forehead felt stiff and prickly. She rubbed it as she walked between the grocery shelves, eyes fixed on the shotgun.

The air, she noticed, had the faint but pungent odor she knew from shooting skeet with her father.

Only when she was standing over the shotgun did she lift her gaze to the meat counter and see Elsie's head wrapped in cellophane.

Lacey's mouth jerked open. Her scream came out voiceless, a quiet explosion of breath.

She dropped to a crouch, grabbed the shotgun,

and pivoted. Nobody coming up behind her. She worked the pump action. It made a loud metallic *snick-snack*, and a blue shell tumbled to the floor.

Keeping her eyes averted from Elsie, she walked along the meat counter. Just ahead, a display of Diet Rite had been blasted apart. Cans lay in all directions, half of them pierced by shot. The floor was slippery with a thin layer of cola.

Beyond the display, barely hidden by the shelves of the next aisle, she found Red. He lay on his back, alive, reaching across his chest, trying to fit his severed left arm into place.

"Oh boy," he whispered. "Oh boy."

"Red?"

He glanced up at Lacey, then looked back at his arm. "Oh boy," he mumbled.

"I'll get help," she said. Keeping the shotgun ready, she ran for the front. Elsie, she knew, kept a phone on a shelf behind the cash register. Should she go for that, or . . .

She was tackled from behind. She hit the floor flat-out and hard. The wind burst from her lungs. She tried to push herself up, but a weight on her rump and legs held her down. Her collar jerked back, choking her. Then something struck the side of her head.

She opened her eyes and saw the ceiling. On either side were shelves of groceries: cans of soup and chili on the left, cookies and crackers on the right.

Even without moving, she knew what had been done to her. She could feel the gritty, cool wood

under her bare skin. She could feel hot areas where her skin had been mauled. Her nipples burned and itched. So did her vagina. She felt stretched and battered inside. Her eyes filled with tears.

Raising her head, she looked down at herself. Her breasts were red as if they had been wrung. She saw teethmarks on both nipples. Fingernail scratches trailed down her belly. Propping herself up with stiff arms, she felt a slow trickle inside her.

At the end of the aisle lay Red. His severed arm lay across his chest. He was motionless.

With tissues from her handbag, she cleaned herself. She wasn't afraid. She felt dirty and sick and ashamed. When she used her last tissue, she picked all of them up off the floor and stuffed them into her bag.

She started to dress, watching the door, worried that someone might enter before she could finish. Her panties were torn apart; she put them in her bag. Both straps of her bra were broken, the catches in back ripped loose. She pushed it into her bag, and stepped into her jeans. She struggled to pull them up. They encased her, snug and protective. She wished her blouse were as sturdy and tight as her jeans, but she felt bare even after putting it on.

The walk to the checkout counter seemed to take a long time. She moved slowly, carefully, feeling that the slightest jostle might shake something loose inside her body.

Finally, she reached the counter. She picked up the phone.

CHAPTER FOUR

"Okay, Lacey. If you remember anything else, though, give me a call."

"I will."

Rex Barrett drew a thumb along the handlebar moustache that he'd raised since becoming chief of the Oasis Police Department. To Lacey, it made the lean lawman look like a twin of Wyatt Earp. She often suspected that he'd grown it for that reason.

"You'll be writing this up for the *Trib*?" he asked.

"Yes."

"I'd appreciate your not mentioning specifics about the way he did Elsie."

"Fine," she said, leaning back against the counter. There were other specifics she planned not to mention.

"Now, if I were you, I'd drag my doctor out of bed for a quick once-over. You took some good knocks tonight and you just never know, with a head injury."

"I'll do that," she lied.

"I would, if I were you."

"Is it all right if . . . ?" Two men wheeled a stretcher down the aisle. One hurried ahead to open

the door. She looked at the body bag. The contours of the black plastic resembled a human. Had they pieced Elsie back together?

Shutting her eyes, she tried to think about something else. Her shoulder was touched. She flinched and snapped open her eyes.

"It's okay," Barrett said. He squeezed her shoulder.

"Sure."

"You go on, now. See your doctor. Get a good night's sleep."

"I will. Thanks."

Outside, she saw the stretcher being slid into the rear of the coroner's van. She hurried past Red's pickup, and opened her car door. The ceiling light came on. As she started to climb in, goose bumps prickled her skin.

She snapped her head sideways. Nobody in the backseat.

But she couldn't see the rear floor.

Silly, she thought. Like a kid checking under the bed.

Silly or not, she had to make sure nobody was hunched out of sight behind the front seats. Planting a knee on the cushion, she grabbed the headrest and eased herself forward. Her breast hurt as it pushed against the vinyl upholstery. She peered over the top of the seat. Nobody down there.

Of course not.

But she'd had to make sure.

She twisted around, sat down, and pulled her door shut. She locked it. With a glance to the right, she saw that the passenger door wasn't locked. Stretching

across the seat, she jabbed the button down with her forefinger. She checked the rear doors. Their lock buttons looked low and snug.

She sighed. With a slick, sweaty hand, she rubbed the back of her neck. Then she pushed the key into the ignition, and started the car.

A cigarette. She wanted a cigarette. A little treat for herself, an indulgence, a comfort that didn't have to wait till she reached her home on the outskirts of town. The drink and the bath had to wait: not the cigarette.

She opened her handbag. With a glance around the parking lot to be sure no one would see, she pulled out her ruined bra and panties. She tossed them onto the passenger seat. Then she reached into the bag, looking down into its darkness, hoping to find her pack of Tareytons without touching the sodden wads of tissue. Her body jerked as she fingered a cool, slippery ball and gagged. The pack of cigarettes was beneath the mess. She pulled it out, gagging again as her hand came out wet and sticky. She rubbed her hand on her jeans.

"God," she muttered.

Her whole body ached, as if the pressure of the spasms had burst open all her injuries. She pressed her legs together, and held her breasts gently until the pain subsided.

Then she shook out a cigarette. She held it in her lips and lit it, staring at the glowing red coils of the car's lighter. The smoke was as soothing as she'd hoped. With a sigh of satisfaction, she turned on

the headlights and backed her car out of the parking space.

The coroner's van was gone. Three police cars remained, as did Red's pickup. She supposed the pickup would be towed away before morning.

The road was deserted. She turned her radio on, and listened to a country station from Tucson. Ronnie Milsap was singing "What a Difference You Made in My Life." When his song ended, Anne Murray came on with "Can I Have This Dance?" Nice of them to play a couple of her favorites. The songs helped to soothe her shattered nerves.

As she reached her block, she took a final, deep drag on her cigarette. She held the smoke in, stubbed out her cigarette, and let the smoke ease out of her mouth.

From behind her came a muffled cough.

Her eyes snapped to the rearview mirror. A slice of ceiling. The back window. The empty road.

Had it been the radio?

No, the cough had come from behind. She was sure. It sounded like someone in the backseat. Impossible. She'd looked so carefully.

The muffler? A simple backfire? No.

Lacey swerved across the road, shot up her driveway, and hit the brakes. The car lurched to a stop. She shut it off. Grabbing her handbag, she threw open the door and leapt out. She slammed the door.

Fighting an urge to run, she stepped close to the rear window and peered inside. Nobody there. Of course not.

Under the car? Could a man hang on, down there? It seemed impossible. But now that the idea had entered her mind, she had to check. She dropped to her knees, planted her hands on the cool concrete, and lowered herself until she could see under the carriage. She scanned the dark space.

Nobody.

The trunk? She stood up, brushing off her hands, and stared at the trunk's sloping hood.

How could anyone get in? Pick the lock? Child's play, probably, for someone who knew how. And if he could get in, he could get out just as easily.

What if it's not even latched?

Holding her breath, Lacey stepped softly toward the rear of the car. The edges of the trunk's hood were not perfectly flush with the bordering surfaces. Slightly higher. Less than a quarter of an inch, though. Maybe that was normal.

Maybe not.

Maybe the killer, the slug who raped her, was hunched inside the trunk, holding it shut.

She lunged at the trunk, slapped both hands on its top, shoved down and threw herself forward. The car rocked under her weight. But no *clack* of the trunk's lock. She lay there, thinking. No clack. The trunk had been locked, after all. Probably. But that didn't mean the killer wasn't inside, didn't mean he couldn't get out.

He can't get out if I stay like this, she thought. But she couldn't stay that way, sprawled on the trunk with her face pressing the back window, her legs hanging off. Her belly, on the trunk's rim, took most

of her weight so she could hardly breathe. And the pain of lying on her injuries was almost unbearable.

She squirmed backward until her feet found the driveway, then pushed herself off and ran for her house. She leapt onto the stoop. Sliding her key into the lock, she glanced over her shoulder. Her blue Granada stood in the driveway, looking as it should, as if nothing were wrong. For an instant, Lacey questioned herself. Had she imagined the cough?

No.

He's in there. In the trunk.

She shoved open the front door, shut and bolted it behind her, and rushed across the living room. She dropped her handbag on the dining room table. Skirting the table, she entered her bedroom and flicked on a light. She rushed to her bed. Jerked open a nightstand drawer. Took out a Smith & Wesson .38-caliber revolver.

Then she ran from the house. She started to leave the front door open in case she needed a quick escape. But the man could've already left the trunk. Not likely—Lacey had been in the house no more than half a minute. That could be time enough, though. He might be out of the trunk, hiding nearby, ready to jump her or sneak inside the house. So she closed the front door and locked it.

She stood on the Welcome mat, holding the revolver close to her belly. Its weight felt good in her hand. She felt safer than before, as if she'd been joined by a powerful trusted friend—a brother who would nail the bastard for her.

Just point and fire.

The only real danger, now, lay in being caught from behind. *Like before. That's how he got me before.*

Not this time.

He might be in the geraniums.

He's probably still in the trunk.

Lacey sprang from the stoop, past the geranium bushes, and raced into the center of her lawn. She spun around, revolver ready. No one.

Okay.

Still in the trunk.

She ran to her car. Standing behind it, she studied the keys in her left hand. She found the trunk key. Revolver ready, she stabbed the key into the lock and twisted it. The latch clicked.

She jumped back, and aimed. The springs groaned as the trunk began to open. The lid inched upward. Lacey stared at the dark, widening gap. Her finger was tense on the trigger. The lid gathered speed, stopped abruptly at its apex, and quivered for a moment.

In the darkness of the trunk, nothing moved.

Lacey stepped closer. She saw her spare tire, a pack of road flares, and an old towel she sometimes used for wiping the car windows. There was certainly no man in the trunk.

She sighed. She felt weary, disappointed. She'd been sure she would find the killer there.

The rapist.

The man who tore her and bit her and pumped his foul seed into her.

He would be in the trunk and Lacey would pump him full of a different kind of seed—the kind that

grows death—the lead kind. He would never hurt anyone again.

"Damn," she muttered.

Reaching up with her left hand, she slammed the trunk shut. The car rocked slightly with its impact.

She remembered her torn undergarments on the front seat. Better pick them up.

Stepping around the end of the car, she saw that the rear door jutted out an inch. Its lock button stood high.

"My God," Lacey said. She covered her mouth, and staggered backward.

CHAPTER FIVE

She refused to run. Back in the market, she had run and he'd taken her down from behind. It was a mistake she would not repeat.

Cautiously, turning to check every side, she made her way to the front door. She stood against its cool wood, the handle near her hip, and reached behind her with the key. It clicked and skidded against the lockface. Finally, it slid in. She turned it. The lock tongue snapped back.

Through the bushes to her left, she saw a quick pale movement. She jerked her revolver toward it. The shape rushed clear of the bushes and appeared in the open ahead of her, just across the lawn.

A man. Cliff Woodman. Out for a run.

He glanced toward Lacey, waved, and suddenly stopped.

"That you, Lacey?"

"It's me."

"Is that a gun?"

"Yeah."

"Trouble?"

"I don't know."

Lacey stepped away from the door and lowered

her revolver as Cliff jogged toward her. She immediately felt better. Cliff, a gym teacher at the high school, was forty years old and an ex-marine. Tonight, in his running shoes, shorts, and a bandanna knotted around his head as a sweatband, he looked almost savage.

"What's the problem?" he asked.

"I think I've got a prowler."

"Where?" He squinted at the bushes in front of the house.

"I don't know. I think he was in my car."

"Your car?" Cliff strode toward it, hunched slightly, arms away from his sides like a wrestler about to do battle. Lacey hurried after him. He jerked the handle of the passenger door.

Thank God it's locked, Lacey thought, hoping he wouldn't discover her torn bra and panties.

He tugged open the back door. "Nobody there now," he announced, and flung the door shut. "I'll look around the back."

Lacey held out the revolver. "You'd better take this."

"Couldn't hurt." He took it, and started up the driveway toward the rear of the house.

Lacey followed. "I'll go with you."

He nodded.

She hurried forward until she was beside him. "You've got to know, Cliff," she whispered. "I think he's a murderer."

"For real?"

"I just came back from Hoffman's Market. Elsie was killed there tonight. So was Red Peterson."

37

Cliff's heavy brows lowered. "Fella that offed Red's dog?"

"I guess so. I think he hid in my car when I left there."

"Maybe he hightailed it."

"I don't know."

"Well, if he's around here, we'll get him." Cliff grinned. "Save the taxpayers the expense of a trial."

They followed the driveway past the back of the house. Cliff stared ahead at the garage.

"It's padlocked," Lacey said. "The laundry room's open, though."

"Let's have a look."

Walking near the front of the garage, Lacey scanned her yard, the lounge chairs and barbecue, the hedge along the far side.

Cliff took her arm. He pushed her against the wall, close to the laundry room door. "Don't move," he whispered. He knelt in front of her. Reaching up, he slowly turned the knob. He threw open the door and leaned forward to peer in. Then he rose to his feet. He entered the laundry room, crouching. Lacey stepped in after him.

"Do you want the light on?" she asked.

"It'd wreck our night vision."

He went to the far end, then hurried back. Together, they cut across the yard. They walked single-file through the narrow space between the side of the house and the hedge. Then he led her to the front door.

"Any chance he got inside?"

"No, I don't . . ."

Cliff opened the front door.

"Oh no," Lacey sighed. "I unlocked it just as you came along."

"I'd better have a look."

"Yeah, please. Damn, that was stupid."

They entered the house, and she locked the door. Cliff walked ahead of her, glancing behind furniture, lifting draperies. In the lamplight, his back was glossy. The band of his gray shorts was dark with sweat, and Lacey caught herself wondering what— if anything—he wore beneath them. She suddenly became very aware of her own nakedness inside her jeans and flimsy blouse, a body beaten, soiled by another man's filth.

She tried not to think about it.

She followed Cliff around the dining room table, and into her bedroom. The lamp was still on, the nightstand drawer still open. She stood against the door frame, watching him. On the far side of the bed, he dropped to his knees and lifted the coverlet. Then he got to his feet again, and came back. His eyes met Lacey's, and he smiled as if to reassure her. When he looked toward the closet, Lacey lowered her gaze. His chest was muscular, his belly flat. His shorts hung low on his hips. They fit snugly. She glimpsed his bulge, and quickly looked away, a warm thickness of revulsion in her stomach.

He opened the closet door and looked inside.

"So far," he said, "so good."

Lacey backed out of the doorway. She followed him into the kitchen. He walked through, glancing to each side, ducking to peer under the heavy wooden

table that barely fit into the breakfast nook, opening the utility closet door and shutting it again after a quick inspection. He checked the back door. Locked.

Glancing at Lacey, he shook his head.

He had, she realized, a dangerous face: deep-set, dark eyes, jutting cheekbones, thin lips, a blocky jaw. A somewhat handsome face, but not a face to inspire any special feeling of tenderness.

He stepped past her, his arm brushing against her breast. She flinched away from the unwanted contact. Had he done it on purpose? Staying farther away from Cliff, she followed him around the corner and into her study. He walked past its bookshelves, checked behind an easy chair, and looked in the closet.

"I really appreciate your helping me like this," Lacey said.

"Glad I came by when I did."

"I guess it's just a wild-goose chase."

"Not yet," he said, stepping toward her. She quickly backed out of range. He went past, pulled open the linen closet door, then entered the bathroom and turned on its light. He walked past the toilet and sink. At the tub, he slid back the frosted glass door. Then he turned to Lacey and smiled. Not an open friendly smile: it was guarded and sardonic. "*Now,*" he said, "it's a wild-goose chase."

"Well, thanks an awful lot."

"I'm just sorry we didn't bag him. For your peace of mind. If you'd like me to stick around for a while, I'd be happy to."

"Thanks. I think I'll be all right."

"Suit yourself."

He handed the revolver to Lacey. "If you ever have to use this, go for the torso and don't settle for one hit. Put three or four in him, but save a shot or two, just in case."

Lacey nodded. Strange advice, she thought, but coming from Cliff it sounded perfectly natural.

"And remember I'm just three houses away, if you need me. Let me give you my number." He wrote it on a pad by the kitchen telephone. "If you have any trouble, give me a ring. I can get here a lot quicker than the cops."

"All right." She walked ahead of him to the door.

"Sure you won't feel better if I hang around for a bit?"

"I'm sure. Thanks anyway." She opened the front door for him. "Have a good run."

He jumped off the stoop, and raced across the lawn.

Lacey shut the door and locked it, relieved that he was gone. Had it been intentional, touching her breast? Probably. He'd been so insistent on staying. More than likely, he'd hoped she would fall into his protective arms and . . .

Hell, he was just being a good neighbor.

She tried to push the revolver into her waistband, but the jeans were too tight. She shoved its barrel down a front pocket. It wouldn't go in past the cylinder, so she pulled it out and carried it into the kitchen and held it while she poured herself a glass of pinot noir. She took the revolver and wine into her study and sat at her desk.

Her back felt exposed. Turning her chair, she could see the open door. That was better, though she still felt vulnerable. She placed the revolver on her lap. With a trembling hand, she lit a cigarette.

Then she sipped her wine and picked up the phone. She dialed.

On the other end, the phone rang twice.

"*Tribune*," said James, the night editor.

"It's Lacey. I've got a story for you. There were two killings at Hoffman's tonight."

"Ahhh." He sounded disgusted. "Okay, you want to give it to me?"

"*Tribune* reporter Lacey Allen last night discovered the mutilated body of Elsie Hoffman and fatally injured Red Peterson when she entered Hoffman's Market shortly before closing time."

"*You* found them?"

"Afraid so."

"Christ!"

"Before she could summon authorities, Miss Allen was herself assaulted and rendered unconscious by an unseen assailant. Paragraph. Police, arriving on the scene, found that Red Peterson had succumbed to his injuries. A thorough search of the premises revealed that the killer had fled."

For the next five minutes, she continued to tell her story to James and the *Tribune*'s tape recorder, filling in details, never mentioning her rape or the specifics about the killings or her suspicion that the assailant had escaped in her car, finally recapping the earlier incidents at the market. "That about

does it," she finished. "Except for one thing. I'd like some time to recuperate. Tell Carl I won't be in to-morrow, okay?"

"Sure thing. You all right?"

"Just beat up a little. I'll be in Friday."

"Fine. Great work, Lacey."

"Just happened to be at the right place at the right time."

"I detect a note of irony."

"Only a note?"

"Take care of yourself, kid."

"I will. Night, James."

"See ya."

She hung up. With the revolver and empty wine-glass, she returned to the kitchen for a refill. Then she went into the bathroom. She shut the door and thumbed down its lock button. A feeble measure. Any pointed instrument turned in the keyhole, she knew, would pop open the lock. But the little pre-caution was better than none at all.

She set her pistol and glass on the floor beside the tub, and started the water running. When it felt hot enough, she stoppered the drain.

She turned to the medicine cabinet mirror. The face looking back at her was a bad copy of the one she was used to: slack and pallid, dark under the eyes, the eyes themselves wide and vacant. Turning her head, she fingered back the hair draping her right temple and studied the patch of swollen, red-blue skin. The ear, too, was slightly puffed and discolored.

"A shadow of her former self," she muttered. It

brought a slight smile. Part of the strangeness left her eyes.

She took off her blouse. Then she unfastened her jeans, tugged them down, and kicked them off. She tossed the blouse and jeans into the hamper.

She looked down at herself. Fingers had left red-blue impressions on both her breasts.

Must've grabbed them and squeezed.

The teeth indentations had disappeared, but her nipples were purple. She touched one and winced.

Her body was seamed with fingernail scratches: her shoulders and upper arms, her sides, her belly, her thighs. At least he hadn't raked her breasts, and none of the scratches would show when she was clothed—the silver lining.

She tested the water with a foot. Hot, but not burning. She climbed in and slowly lowered herself, clenching rigid with pain as the water seared the raw lips of her vagina. The pain faded, and she let herself down the rest of the way. She gritted her teeth as the water scorched her torn thighs. But that pain soon faded, like the other. She took a deep breath. Leaning forward, she turned off the faucet.

The house was silent except for the slow plop of water drops near her feet.

Bracing herself against the shock, she splashed water onto her scratches. At first, it felt like lava running down her open flesh. Then it wasn't so bad. After a sip of wine, she lathered herself with soap and rinsed.

She picked up her wineglass again, and lay back. Head propped against the rear of the tub, she sipped the wine. It felt warm and good going down. Hold-

ing the glass in one hand, she reached down with the other, down through the hot water between her open legs. Tenderly, she fingered herself.

He must've chewed her there, too.

Filthy bastard!

At least he didn't kill me—another silver lining?

Fuck the silver linings.

Lacey blinked tears away, and reached for the bar of soap. She rubbed herself gently.

And the bathroom lights went out.

She threw herself against the side of the tub. She clawed the rug, trying to find the revolver.

Where *was* it?

Then she touched its cool steel. She picked it up by the barrel, found its handle, and gripped it tight.

She stood up. She lifted one foot out of the water and stepped over the tub's wall. With that foot firm on the rug, she leaned out. In the vague light from the window, she searched the bathroom. She saw no one. The door appeared to be shut.

Must be shut. Still locked. I'd have heard the button pop . . .

Okay, maybe the bulbs in the fixture blew. *Three* bulbs? Fat chance. How about a general power failure? Sure thing. No, it had to be the fuse box.

He's in the house!

Slowly, she raised her other foot out of the water. She stepped clear of the tub and stood aiming at the door.

Naked and wet, she felt more vulnerable than ever before in her life. She backed up, and knelt beside the hamper. Switching the pistol to her left

hand, she reached in. She pulled out her jeans, her blouse.

The blouse was easy. She got it on without letting go of the gun. But she needed two hands for the jeans. She set the pistol on the counter by the sink, within easy reach.

Stupid, she thought as she fumbled with her pants. This is just the moment he'll choose to bust the door in. But she heard nothing. Only a car speeding along, somewhere far away. If he'd just hold off for a few seconds, she would be dressed and ready for him. She had to be dressed.

She was bent over, balanced on one leg, her other foot high and pushing into the jeans, when she felt fingers clutch her ankle and jerk it out from under her.

She hit the floor.

Rough hands jerked her pants off. She tried to scramble up, but the weight of a man drove her against the floor, forced her legs apart. Her blouse was ripped off her back. Then he was lying on her, pinning her arms to the floor. She felt his hardness against her rump.

"Scream, cunt, and I'll rip off your head."

She pressed her face to the rug. She cried, she whimpered with pain, she bit her lips until she tasted their blood, but she didn't scream. At some point, with the man grunting and thrusting in the darkness above her, Lacey passed out.

CHAPTER SIX

Dukane landed his Cessna Bonanza, that night, at Santa Monica airport. He stepped into the passenger cabin.

Alice smiled at him. "Hello, dead man."

"Pleasant flight?" he asked.

"Very nice. I spent it thinking about what they'll do to you."

"Nothing too drastic, I hope." He bent down and unlocked the cuffs chaining her left wrist to the seat's armrest.

"You messed with Laveda, man. You're good as dead."

"*Better* than dead, at the moment."

"Sure, joke. You'll be laughing outa the other side of your face when they catch up with you. And they will. And I'll be with 'em, you can count on it. I'll be the one with the knife, cutting out your eyes."

"Such talk," he said.

"You can't hide from us. We're everywhere. We know all. We're all powerful."

"Yep. Okay, stand up." He backed away. Alice stepped into the aisle. She looked good in the yellow sundress—fresh, and even younger than her

47

nineteen years. Dukane had bought it at a Penny's in Houma, leaving Alice drugged in the passenger seat of his rented car. After buying the dress, he drove to a deserted stretch of road. He braced her against the side of the car, stripped off the oversized shirt he'd earlier used to clothe her, and wrestled her limp body into the dress.

"Are we getting outa this plane, or you just gonna stare at me all night?"

"We need to make a decision. I can either take you out of here handcuffed, as a prisoner, or you can agree to cooperate and we'll go to my car like friends. Which do you prefer?"

"You don't need the cuffs."

"If you try to get away, you'll be hurt."

"I know, I know. You proved that back in the bayou, didn't you? Well, I'll tell you something. I don't have to get away from you. They'll come for me. Wherever you take me, they'll come. I don't have to lift a finger—just wait and use my powers to call them."

"Fancy car," Alice said as Dukane climbed into the Jaguar beside her. "Kidnapping must pay good."

"Yep." The car grumbled to life.

"How much did my folks pay you?"

"Enough."

"Enough to die for?"

"That's not in my plans."

"It's in mine. They'll have to die, too. Can't go messing with Laveda."

"You're a sweetheart," Dukane said. He backed out of the parking space, and headed for the exit.

"Wouldn't want to be in your shoes, man."

"I know. You're all powerful. You've drunk at the river."

"Fuckin' right."

"Imagine. All that from drinking a gal's blood."

"The blood is the life."

"Where've I heard that before," he said, and switched the radio on. He turned left onto Ocean Park Blvd.

"This isn't the way home."

"I'm not taking you home. You've got a date with a certain Dr. T. R. Miles. He specializes in deprogramming screwed up kids."

"Deprogramming?" She made a quiet, nasal laugh. "What do you think I am, a Moonie?"

"I didn't hire him, your parents did. Far as I'm concerned, you and the rest of Laveda's gang ought to be burned at the stake."

Her head jerked toward him.

"That's how the old-timers dealt with witches, I believe."

"We're not witches," she muttered.

"Near enough. Laveda's got her own set of rules and rituals, but it boils down to the same thing—you're a bunch of homicidal lunatics on a power trip. You need to be stopped."

"We can't be stopped," she said, but the earlier tone of scornful confidence was gone from her voice. "We're everywhere."

"Put the torch to Laveda, and the whole gang would fall apart."

"Shut up."

A layer of fog hung over the road as they neared the ocean. It swirled in the headlights, rolled off the windshield. Dukane slowed down. He squinted ahead, searching for the dim glow of traffic lights.

In the silence, he thought about Alice's bluster falling away at the mention of fire. She seemed to have an exaggerated fear of burning.

He'd noted the same dread in the man named Walter. The muscular fellow had acted brazen, at first, during Dukane's interrogation three nights before the bayou gathering. Like Alice, he'd claimed to be invulnerable. He'd refused to talk. But he broke down, whimpering and pleading, when Dukane doused him with gasoline. In short order, he told about Laveda's group, its structure and purposes, the extent of its membership, the time and location of the meeting. What Dukane learned had scared the hell out of him, but it gave him all he needed to know in his search for Alice.

At the blur of a red light just ahead, Dukane eased down on the brake. He hit the arm of the turn signal, hoping this was Main, and turned left when the light changed. He drove slowly, gazing into the fog, seeking a landmark. When he saw the Boulangerie, off to the right, he knew where he was. He continued down Main, glimpsed a cluster of vague figures at the entrance to the Oar House, and kept going until he reached the traffic signal at Rose. A pair of

dim lights appeared ahead. He waited for the car to pass, then turned left and parked at the curb.

"Let's go," he said.

They climbed from the car. Alice followed him up the street, hunched slightly and moving fast, her bare arms crossed against her breasts.

"We're almost there," Dukane told her, his chin shaking. He clenched his teeth, then made a conscious effort to relax his muscles and stop the shivering. Alice, he knew, must be freezing in her thin sundress. He put an arm across her shoulders, but she whirled away.

"Don't touch me," she said.

"Just trying to help."

"I can live without it."

They crossed a dark street, and hurried up the sidewalk. "This is it," he said, nodding toward the lighted porch of a small, wood-frame house. He opened the gate. They rushed up a narrow walkway. Dukane took the porch stairs two at a time, and rang the doorbell.

Alice waited beside him, legs tight together, arms hugging herself, teeth chattering.

The door was opened as far as the guard chain allowed. A black-haired, attractive woman studied them through her wire-rimmed glasses.

"We're here to see Dr. Miles," Dukane said.

"Yes?"

"I'm Dukane."

The woman nodded. She shut the door briefly, then swung it open. "Please come in."

They stepped into the warm house. The woman shut the door, took a sip of coffee from her Snoopy mug, and turned to them. "You must be Alice," she said.

Alice curled her nose.

"You both look chilled to the bone. Let's go in by the fire, and I'll get you some coffee."

They followed her into the living room. It was wood paneled and cozy, with the feel of a summer cottage. Alice crossed toward the fireplace. She stopped two yards from its screen, and held out her hands.

"Cream or sugar?"

Alice didn't respond.

"I'll take mine black," Dukane said.

"Back in a jiff," the woman said, and left.

Dukane stepped past Alice. He stood close to the fire, feeling its heat through his trouser legs, then crouching to warm his upper body and face. He turned around, still squatting, and smiled up at Alice. "Nothing like a nice, crackling fire."

"Get fucked."

The woman came back, carrying a coffee mug in each hand. Dukane noticed the way her breasts jiggled slightly under the cashmere of her white turtleneck. Below the hem of her tweed skirt, her calves looked trim and well defined. Probably, Dukane thought, she jogs on the beach—just like half the other residents of Venice.

He stood, and accepted a hot mug. This one came from the Hearst Castle gift shop. She held out a Big Apple mug to Alice.

Alice swatted it from her hand. The mug flipped away, exploding coffee, and bounced off the rug.

The woman slapped her face.

Alice leaped at her, snarling, hands out like claws. As Dukane set his mug on the mantel, he saw that the woman needed no help. She grabbed Alice's right arm, jerked it toward her, and swiveled around. Her rump caught Alice low. The girl flew over her back and hit the floor with a grunt.

"Sorry about that, but I won't allow intemperate behavior." Her sweater had pulled up, revealing lightly tanned skin above her belt. She adjusted her sweater, and stared down at Alice. "Is that understood?"

Alice gazed at the ceiling. "You're gonna die."

"Not before I've straightened you out."

"You're Dr. Miles?" Dukane asked.

Her smile caught him off-guard; he'd expected a condescending smirk. "Don't be embarrassed," she said. "A doctor with a name like Teri Miles is begging for erroneous assumptions of gender. You thought I was the good doctor's receptionist?"

"Or wife. I was starting to envy him."

She smiled, and surprised him again—this time by blushing.

Dukane took a sip of hot coffee. "I see you can handle yourself well."

"One has to, in this line of work. I've had patients a lot rougher than Alice."

"She seems to think she'll get away in short order."

"I have a locked room for her, grates on the windows. So far, I haven't lost anyone."

"She thinks she'll have help."

"You made sure you weren't followed?"

"In that fog, it would've taken Rudolph to follow us."

Dr. Miles grinned. "Any red noses in the rearview mirror?"

"Not a one."

"We should be all right, then. Nobody knows where she is except you and her parents."

"*They'll* know," Alice said from the floor.

"She thinks they'll find her through telepathy."

"I'd say that's remote."

"Hope so," Dukane said. "Laveda's gang believes in all sorts of hogwash, but if they have any special power, I haven't seen it in action. I observed one of their meetings, infiltrated it, even had contact with Laveda herself. If she's some kind of mind reader, I think she would've known I didn't belong. She acted as if I were just another member of the group. They all did. So I think their magic is a lot of talk, not much else. It's a dangerous bunch, though. They *think* they've got a handle on magical powers, so they act as if they do. They're basically fearless, think they're invulnerable."

"We are," Alice said. She sat up, crossed her legs, and looked up at them, smirking.

"They do fear burning."

"Fire," said Dr. Miles, "has traditionally been associated with purification. I've dealt with satanists who actually exhibit a phobic response to it."

"There's something else I should tell you. They practice human sacrifice. I saw a young woman mur-

dered at their meeting. The others drank her blood. Even Alice, here."

Dr. Miles stiffened slightly.

"So it's a bloodthirsty group."

"You could be in a great deal of danger if they do find out, somehow, that Alice is here."

"Well . . ."

"It might be wise for me to stick around."

"I'm sure that won't be necessary."

"I'd feel easier about it."

"I don't think you realize—the process could take weeks, depending on the depth of her conditioning. Besides, I really don't imagine there's much cause for concern. Her location's secret. As for telepathy, I agree with you that it's hogwash. I've been involved with these matters for several years, and haven't lost a patient yet."

"All right," Dukane said. He felt a bit rebuffed, and realized his offer had been motivated by more than simple concern for her safety. He was attracted to her, wanted to spend more time in her presence. "Well, I'll check in occasionally."

"Better that you don't. We wouldn't want to compromise her location."

"Whatever you say. But be careful, all right?"

"I always am."

"For all the good it'll do," said Alice.

CHAPTER SEVEN

Lacey woke up, and wished she hadn't. She lay on her back, eyes shut. Her arms, stretched overhead, were numb. Moving slightly, she felt a sheet beneath her. She wasn't covered: a mild breeze stirred against her skin, probably from the window above her bed.

She tried to lower her arms, but a tightness around the wrists held them in place. They were tied.

She moved her feet. They, at least, were free.

She licked her lips. No gag.

But she was blindfolded. She could feel it. She tried to open her eyes, but couldn't raise the lids. From the sticky stiffness against them, she guessed they were taped shut.

Lying motionless, she listened. The only sound in the bedroom was the hum of her electric clock. Through the open window came sounds of birds, a car door banging shut, a power mower somewhere in the distance.

So it's morning.

And I told James I wouldn't be coming in. Neat play. Somebody'd come by to check on me, if I hadn't told him that.

Just as well. This maniac would only kill him.
If he's here!

Lacey realized, with a dizzying sense of relief, that he might very well have departed—tied her up, took her car, and headed for distant places. Why not?

Because, as David Horowitz always says, if it sounds too good to be true, it usually is.

He's still here. Probably watching me right this second. Does he know I'm awake?

Lacey tried to breathe slowly and deeply, feigning sleep.

What does he want? she wondered. *Why the hell hasn't he killed me like he did the others? Don't worry, he probably will.*

Unless I get him first.

Fat chance.

You can't kill a man you never see.

She hadn't spotted him in the car, though he'd been in the backseat on her way home from Hoffman's. She and Cliff had missed him when they searched the house—unless he sneaked in later.

But how, in God's name, did he get into the bathroom? That door never opened, she was almost positive. And he sure didn't climb in through the window. He was just suddenly there. A magician, a regular Houdini.

How do you kill a guy like that?
Easy, you don't.
But maybe he is gone.
No, he's here. Still here.
But why?
Because he likes *you.*

Scream, cunt, and I'll rip off your head. Sure he likes me.

The doorbell rang.

Footsteps raced toward her.

She opened her mouth to yell, and a hand slapped across it.

"Don't make a sound," whispered the low, scratchy voice from last night.

The bell rang again, loud in the silent house. Who was there? James or Carl coming by to check on her, after all? Cliff? It rang again. She kicked her legs high, twisting to swing them off the bed, but an arm hooked them behind the knees and stopped them. She bucked and writhed. The powerful arm pressed, curling her back, raising her rump off the bed, forcing her legs down until her knees mashed her breasts.

She shook her head, tried to bite the hand. But it stayed tight on her mouth. Her teeth couldn't find flesh to bite, only scraping it without doing damage.

Mouth covered, compressed as she was, she couldn't bring in enough air through her nostrils. She stopped struggling and tried to breathe. Her lungs burned.

The doorbell rang again.

Go away!

She sucked air in through her nostrils, but couldn't draw it in deeply enough, couldn't seem to get it to her lungs. She felt as if she were drowning. The man seemed to realize this, and pressed his hand slightly upward to block her nose.

No!

A roar filled her head. She sucked against the hand. No air came through. She kicked, but the man pressed her knees harder against her chest. Her heart thundered as if it might explode.

Then the arm stopped pushing at her legs. As she lowered them, the hand left her mouth. She gulped in air.

"I oughta kill you," the man whispered.

Lacey kept gasping.

He shoved her legs apart, and she felt his mouth. Then he was on top of her, pushing inside her, ramming. Lacey didn't struggle. She lay still, trying to catch her breath, trying not to think, to build a wall in her head that she could hide behind, away from the pain and filth and terror.

"I'll untie your hands," he said when he was finally through.

Lacey nodded.

"You can't hurt me. You can't get away from me. Don't try."

"I won't."

He removed the bonds. Lacey tried to lower her arms. At first, they wouldn't move. They burned and tingled as feeling slowly returned to them. At last, she was able to bring them down. She rubbed the deep indentations on her wrists.

"What do you want?" she asked.

He made a nasty laugh. "I've got what I want. You. And your house."

Reaching to her face, she touched the adhesive tape over her eyes. Her hands were slapped away.

"Leave it."

"Who are you?"

"If I told you that, you'd know."

What kind of answer was that? "Do I know you?" she asked.

"Damn right."

"What did I do? Did I *do* something to you?"

"It's what you didn't do. But we've taken care of that, haven't we?" Lacey flinched as he put a hand on her breast. She didn't try to remove it, didn't dare. "I've always wanted you. Now I've got you. Want to know what's next?"

She nodded.

"I'm gonna be your guest for a while. For a long, long while. This is a lot better than the market. The market stinks. No bed, no pussy to curl up with. This is just what I want, and I'm gonna stay."

"Are you . . . hiding out?"

"Oh yes. And they're a sharp pack of bastards. They'll come looking. Might even check here, but we're too smart for 'em. Lacey's gonna answer the phone, Lacey's gonna answer the door, Lacey's even gonna go to work after today, just like everything's normal. But she won't let no one in, and she won't tell our little secret, and she won't try to run away. 'Cause if she does, I'll do horrible disgusting things to her."

She couldn't believe it! He would actually let her leave the house? "All right," she said.

"I know what you're thinking. You're thinking, soon as I let you free, you'll run off to the cops. If the cops don't get me, you'll leave town. Either way,

you'll be safe from me. But you're wrong. Wrong wrong wrong. You can't escape."

The hand went away from her breast, picked at the side of her face, and ripped the tape away. It came off with a sound like tearing cloth, stinging her skin, uprooting brows and lashes. Lacey clutched her eyes until the pain subsided. Then she lowered her hands. She opened her eyes. Squinting against the light, she looked up. Then to the sides.

The man was gone!

She bolted upright, and studied the sunlit room. He was not there! She swung her legs off the bed, knocking the wadded tape to the floor, and stood up. Dizzy. She grabbed the top of the dresser for support. When her head cleared, she lunged for the doorway.

The door slammed shut. She rushed against it, grabbed the knob.

A hand clutched her shoulders and swung her around.

Nobody there.

She felt hands on both her breasts. They squeezed. She saw depressions the fingers made in her flesh, but not the fingers themselves.

"Get the idea?" the man asked.

"Oh my God," Lacey muttered. "You're invisible!"

"Fuckin' right."

Reaching to her breasts, she touched his hands. Their surface stopped her fingers like a layer of hard air—but air with the texture of skin. She shook her head. "How?"

"A little miracle."

"No, really," she said, trying to sound eager, as if suddenly overcome with curiosity. She touched his hairy wrists, his thick, heavily muscled forearms: he was standing directly in front of her. "Who did it to you? How?"

"If I told you that, you'd know."

"I want to know."

"Then you'd . . ."

Lacey clenched his forearms and kicked, shooting her leg up high through the space in front of her. Her instep smacked flesh. The man's arms jerked away and he bellowed. Lacey tugged open the door. She dashed out and across the dining room to her kitchen. Grabbing the knob of the back door, she hesitated. What use to run away? How do you hide from an invisible man? You don't. Sooner or later, he'd get her.

She slid a carving knife out of its rack, and dashed toward the breakfast nook. She rushed alongside the table, swinging a chair out behind her to block the narrow passage. Spinning around, she shoved the other chair out. Now she stood behind the table, both sides blocked, knife in front of her, ready.

Almost ready.

She opened a cupboard behind her. She lifted out a heavy bag. Clamping the knife in her teeth, she unrolled its top.

With a skidding rumble, the table scooted toward her. She lurched backward. The edge of the counter caught her rump. She leapt, throwing herself backward, drawing up her knees. Her buttocks hit the

countertop, and the table crashed against the cupboards.

Lacey dropped her feet to the table. Lunging forward, she flung out the contents of the sack. A cloud of flour filled the air.

The man dived through it, an empty shape in the white powder.

Jerking the knife from her mouth, Lacey plunged it into his back. He shrieked. His head drove into her belly, slamming her backward. Grabbing his shaggy, powdered hair, Lacey tugged away his head. She saw the hazy image of a face, and smashed her fist into its nose. Then she kicked and shoved at the writhing figure until it slid to the floor.

She crawled to the table's edge, and looked down. He was on his knees, head to the floor, growling, reaching behind him with dusty white arms, groping for the knife. His back was half-clear where his blood had swept the flour off.

Lacey jumped, landed beyond him, and fell. Scurrying to her feet, she ran from the kitchen. She grabbed her handbag and keys off the dining room table, and raced into her bedroom. She yanked her bathrobe off the closet hook. Pulling it on, she ran for the front door. Got outside. Sprinted to her car and locked herself inside and shot it backward out of the driveway. She hit the brakes. Shifted to Drive. And sped up the road away from her house and the man and the horror.

My God, she thought, I did it!

CHAPTER EIGHT

Lacey rolled a clean sheet of paper into her type-writer at the *Tribune* office, and rushed through her story:

> *Tribune* reporter Lacey Allen warded off a masked assailant in her home, Thursday morning, and escaped with minor injuries after stabbing him with a kitchen knife.
>
> According to Miss Allen, the attacker likely concealed himself in the trunk of her car the previous night, after brutally murdering Elsie Hoffman and Red Peterson at Hoffman's Market. "Some time during the night," remarks Allen, "he must have sneaked out of the trunk and broken into my house."
>
> Awakened in the early morning hours, the young reporter was subdued by the intruder and told that he wished to use her home as a temporary refuge. She was warned of severe consequences if she refused to cooperate.
>
> Later in the morning, while preparing coffee at his request, Miss Allen surprised the suspected killer by flinging flour into his face. Wielding a

butcher knife, she attacked and wounded the man, enabling herself to escape.

She sped from the scene in her car. Pulled over by Officer Donald Martin of the Oasis PD, Miss Allen blurted out her story. The officer radioed for backup units. Minutes later, officers Martin, Grabowski and Lewis rushed the house, only to find it deserted. A thorough search of the premises and surrounding neighborhood proved fruitless.

Though authorities are baffled by the suspect's disappearance, the incident at Miss Allen's home provides the first clues to his identity. Full sets of fingerprints were discovered at the scene, and have been wired to the FBI headquarters in Washington, D.C., for possible identification. Also, impressions of his bare feet were found on the floury kitchen floor, and photographed for later comparisons.

According to Miss Allen, the suspect was a white male in his late twenties, six feet tall, weighing 180 pounds, with long hair. From bits of conversation, Miss Allen feels certain that he is, or has been, a resident of Oasis.

Citizens are urged to exercise extreme caution until the suspect has been apprehended.

Lacey reread her story, then got up from her desk and took the two typewritten pages to Carl Williams. She handed them to the lanky editor, and hiked up her loose corduroys. The rest of the clothes fit no better. Somebody might've at least asked her sizes before sending Alfred out for a new wardrobe. At the time, she'd been too upset to care.

Carl finished reading the story. He rolled back his chair, and frowned. "Left something out, didn't you?"

"Do *you* believe the guy was invisible?"

"That's what you told me. And the police."

"But do you believe it?"

He sighed, and rubbed a hand through his short curly hair. "Hell no," he said. "I don't believe it. Not for a second."

"You figure I imagined it."

"Well Lace, you've gone through a lot of . . ."

"Slipped a cog or two?"

"I'm not saying that. But it's not unusual for someone—in a car accident, say—to lose her memory of what happened. Goes on all the time."

"I remember everything."

"I'm not saying you don't. I'm just saying that, under the circumstances, your sense of reality might've taken a beating."

"Okay, and that's basically what the cops thought. And it's what our readers will think, too. I have to go on living in this town, Carl. If I claim this guy was invisible, I'll be a joke."

"Word'll get out, anyway."

"It'll only be rumor, if it does. I can deny it. But I can't deny something in a story I've written for the *Trib*. Besides, it's not really a lie; I'm pretty sure my description is accurate—as far as it goes. I just can't admit he's invisible, though. I can't. Not in public."

"Yeah." He rubbed his face. "Guess it wouldn't do the *Trib*'s credibility any good, either. Can't have a reporter who *sees* things—or doesn't, as the case may be." He gave her a weary smile. "We'll run it this way."

"Thanks."

"You'll give me a call when you get to Tucson?"

"Right away."

"Fine Take care of yourself, Lace. I'll keep you posted on any new developments."

"Thanks. See you in two weeks. Sooner, if they get him."

Lacey went out the rear door to the *Tribune*'s small parking lot. After the air-conditioning, the heat outside felt like the breath of an oven. Too bad Alfred didn't buy shorts instead of these corduroys. Squinting against the brilliant glare, she stopped at the rear of her car.

Her stomach fluttered a bit as she opened the trunk. She swept a hand through its emptiness, touched her spare tire, her towel, her flares. Then, satisfied, she shut the trunk and went to the driver's door. She unlocked it, opened it, and reached around to flip up the lock button of the back door.

She opened the door. Crawling over the seat, she reached down and ran her hand along the floor. Then she climbed out, locked and shut the door.

She slid in behind the steering wheel, and locked herself in. Leaning sideways across the seat, she raked the floor with her fingertips.

Okay.

No passenger.

She started the car, and drove from the parking lot. Her tank was full. She drove for two hours, and didn't stop until she reached the Desert Wind hotel in Tucson.

CHAPTER NINE

"Alfred, go on over to Harry's and pick me up some lunch."

With a nod, Alfred fumbled among half a dozen pens safely clipped inside his plastic pocket shield. He plucked out a Bic, and slipped a notepad from his trousers. "What'll it be?"

"Pastrami on a sourdough roll, hold the onions. Fries, and a Bud." Carl waited for the young man to finish scribbling, then gave him a five-dollar bill.

"Want a doughnut or something?"

"Nope."

"Back in a jiff."

"No hurry." Carl followed him outside, watched him start down the sidewalk toward the deli three blocks away, and called after him, "Don't forget to bring me back some ketchup."

"Oh, I'll remember."

He watched Alfred slip the notepad out of his seat pocket. He stepped back inside the office. He shut and locked the door, then hurried through the deserted room to his desk. His hands were sweaty and trembling. He wiped them on his pants legs. He took a deep breath, and picked up the telephone.

On the first try, his finger slipped and he had to dial again.

At the other end, the phone rang six times before it was picked up. A woman's pleasant voice said, "Spiritual Development Foundation, Miss Prince speaking."

"This is Carl Williams, number 68259385."

"Just a moment, please."

He waited for her to punch the code number into her terminal.

"Level?" she asked.

"Red."

"Very good. What can we do for you, Mr. Williams?"

"I have an urgent message for section three."

"Just a moment, please. I'll put you through to the section three coordinator."

Carl heard the faint ringing of a phone. Then a strong male voice said, "Farris, here. What have you got for us?"

"This is Carl Williams, publisher of the *Oasis Tribune*. That's Oasis, Arizona."

"Right." He sounded impatient.

"We've had a series of incidents here that I suspect might be related to the SDF—a couple of nasty murders and an assault on one of my reporters, a Miss Lacey Allen."

"I see. And what makes you think they may be connected to SDF?"

"Oasis is the home town of Samuel Hoffman. Also, Hoffman's mother was one of the murder victims."

"You think Hoffman may have been the perpetrator?"

"My reporter, Miss Allen, claims that her attacker was invisible."

"Sounds like our man," Farris said, sounding pleased. "Any knowledge of his present whereabouts?"

"Miss Allen wounded him this morning—about four hours ago—at her home here in town. The police couldn't find any trace of him, but I imagine he isn't far from here."

"Excellent."

"I may be wrong about this, sir, but I think he's still after the Allen woman. While she was his prisoner, he threatened to hunt her down if she ever escaped."

"I see. Where is Allen now?"

"She's on her way to Tucson. She took his threat seriously, and plans to hide out there for a while."

"Her exact location?"

"I don't know. She's promised to give me a call, though, once she's found a room. I suspect she'll check into a hotel."

"Very good. I'll alert our Tucson personnel. Now. This Allen woman, does she trust you?"

"Yes."

"As soon as she gives you her location, I want you to do two things. First, inform me immediately. Second, drive to Tucson and meet her. Stay with her, and keep us informed of her movements. If Hoffman goes for her, we want to be there."

"What if . . . suppose he attacks while I'm there?"

"Any sacrifice you make on our behalf will be rewarded."

"I mean, do you want me to kill him?"

"Laveda would prefer him alive. It's a moot point, however; you probably couldn't kill him if you tried."

CHAPTER TEN

A quiet, rumbling sound entered Dukane's mind. He realized, vaguely, that the sliding glass door to his balcony was being opened. Suddenly alarmed, he tensed and opened his eyes.

It was morning. He stared at the nightstand, thought about jerking open the drawer and grabbing his automatic. Then he remembered bringing a woman home last night from the bar at La Dome. Rolling over, he saw that the other side of the king-size bed was empty.

"Cindy?" he asked.

"Out here."

He crawled across the bed, climbed off, and saw her standing naked on the sunlit balcony. Her back was toward him, her hands on the railing. He stepped out. The sun felt warm on his bare skin. She looked around and smiled. Kissing her cheek, Dukane pressed himself lightly against her back. He slipped his hands up the smoothness of her sides, and held her breasts.

"It's a lovely day for a swim," she said.

"If you're planning a dive from here, don't. I tried it once. Broke my ankle."

"Yuck. I guess I won't."

"It's farther than it looks, and the concrete is very hard."

"Were you drunk?"

"When I jumped? Cold sober."

She sighed as he fingered her rigid nipples. She squirmed, her buttocks rubbing him. Then she turned around. She leaned back against the railings. "Right here," she said.

"A bit awkward."

"Consider it a challenge."

"I'm always up for a challenge."

She gripped the railing with both hands and spread her legs. Dukane clutched her hips. Crouching slightly, he found her wet slit. He thrust upward into her. Her head went back and she moaned.

When they were done, they left the balcony. Cindy disappeared into the bathroom. Dukane put on his robe, and went downstairs. He started to prepare coffee. As its thin stream trickled into the pot, Cindy entered the kitchen. She was wearing one of his short-sleeved plaid shirts, and nothing else.

"Okay if I borrow this?" she asked, raising her arms and turning around.

"Wish it looked that good on me." As he spoke, he remembered Alice wearing one of his spare shirts before he bought the dress for her. He wondered how Dr. Teri Miles was faring with her. He didn't envy the woman, spending days alone with the little bitch. Thinking about it, a familiar worry whispered in his mind. He pushed it away. They're all right, he told himself.

"What's your drothers for breakfast?" Cindy asked. "I make a mean Spanish omelet, if you've got the makings."

"Hmmm?"

"Spanish omelet. Hello? You tuned in?"

"Yeah. That sounds great. There're chilis in the refrigerator."

"Cheese, eggs?"

"Them too. You go ahead and get started, I'll bring in the paper."

"*News*paper?" She wrinkled her nose. "How dreary."

"I just read the funnies."

"Liar liar, pants on fire."

"Not at the moment."

With a laugh, she pulled open the refrigerator. She bent over, the tail of the shirt riding up. Dukane glimpsed her pale rump, then turned away.

Outside, he spotted the *Times* halfway up his long driveway. He crossed the lawn, its grass cool and dewy under his feet. The driveway felt pleasantly warm and dry. He picked up the paper. Heading back to the house, he pulled off its plastic ribbon.

The bold letters near the bottom corner of the front page made his heart lurch. KABC ANCHORMAN AND WIFE SLAIN.

He stopped in the wet grass:

KABC news anchorman Ron Donovan and his wife, Ruth, were found brutally murdered last evening in their Hollywood Hills home. The bodies . . .

He didn't read more. He ran to the front door, flung the paper down in the foyer, and raced upstairs. In his bedroom, he grabbed his trousers. He tugged his wallet from the rear pocket, flipped it open, and searched the bill compartment. He pinched out a business card: Dr. T. R. Miles, MD. At the telephone beside his bed, he dialed.

The phone rang fifteen times before he hung up.

In less than a minute, he was dressed. He rushed downstairs.

Cindy was on her knees, reaching into a cupboard, when he entered the kitchen. He patted her bare rump. "Come on."

"Huh?"

He held out her panties and skirt. "Put 'em on, quick. I've gotta get somewhere fast."

"What's wrong?"

"Just hurry."

Looking puzzled and worried, she started to get dressed. "Where're we going?"

"Venice. I have to check on someone."

She zipped the side of her skirt and followed him to the side door. "My shoes."

"You can stay in the car." He rushed into the connecting garage, climbed into his Jaguar, and pressed the remote button to raise the door. Cindy slid onto the passenger seat as he gunned the engine to life.

"Are you going to tell me what's up?" she asked.

"No," he said, and sped backward up the driveway.

"That's a hell of a note."

"It's business. It's dangerous. You're better off not knowing." He glanced back to make sure the road

was clear, then swung onto it, hit the brakes, and shifted to first gear.

"Then why are you taking me with you?"

"Wouldn't be safe to leave you behind."

"Safe for who?"

"You."

"Oh wonderful."

"It'd probably be all right," he said, "but I don't want to take the chance, so it's better if you just stick with me for now."

"God, what've I got myself into?"

"Consider it an adventure."

"Maybe you could just drop me off at my apartment, huh?"

"No time." He sped down the wooded hillside, stopped at Laurel Canyon Boulevard to wait for a break in the traffic, then shot out.

"Look, I'm really not up for an adventure."

"I'm sorry. Believe me, I was looking forward to your Spanish omelet, a day of swimming and lying in the sun, passionate embraces . . ."

"Me too, damn it."

"Things go wrong."

"Yeah. How about letting me out?"

"Barefoot and purseless?"

"Just stop down here at Ventura, and I'll hop out."

"That's a long hike to Hollywood."

"I've got a girlfriend. She's only a few blocks away. I'll be fine, thank you."

Dukane thought it over. He didn't like the idea of dumping her out, but he saw no point in dragging her to Venice, possibly into danger. Steering with

one hand, he slipped the wallet from his pocket. He gave it to her. "Keep that until I get your purse back to you. Collateral."

"Oh Matt, that's not necessary."

"There's some cash in it. Use whatever you like."

She laughed. "Are you joking?"

"Not at all. Pick up a pair of shoes, treat your friend to lunch, whatever. I'll get your purse and stuff back to you tonight. You'll be home?"

"I'll be there."

"The address on your driver's license, right?"

"Yep."

The traffic light at the intersection with Ventura Boulevard was red when they reached it. Cindy leaned across the seat, kissed Dukane quickly on the mouth, and sprang from the car.

It took him three freeways and twenty minutes to reach the Lincoln exit in Santa Monica. The traffic on Lincoln was heavy. He finally reached Rose, turned right, and sped up the street for several blocks. He parked on Rose. He ran to the other side, then walked.

Approaching Dr. Miles's house, he saw that the gate of its low picket fence stood open. His stomach knotted.

Maybe the mailman had left the gate open.

Wishful thinking.

They got to Alice's parents, found out where she was being kept. No telepathy necessary. No magical powers. Just a check of their records, a visit to the girl's home, an interrogation.

Shit! He'd known, damn it, that something like

this could happen. He should've insisted on staying. He'd let the lady talk him out of it, he'd gone against his better judgment, and . . .

The front door stood ajar. Grabbing his automatic, Dukane toed it open. The foyer, the hallway, were deserted. The house was silent.

With his elbow, he eased the door shut. He stepped forward, silent except for the groan of the hardwood floor. At the edge of the living room entry, he stopped. He listened, but heard nothing. Holding his breath, he peered around the corner.

The naked, headless body of a woman was sprawled on the floor, her flesh carved, a fire poker protruding from between her spread legs.

Alice smiled at him. "I knew you'd come," she said. She sat cross-legged near the body, her face and yellow sundress smeared with blood. The head of Teri Miles lay in her lap. She lifted it with both hands. The wire-rimmed glasses were in place, one lens webbed with cracks. The eyes were open, staring. Alice grinned.

From behind the couch and easy chair, three figures rose into view.

"These are my friends. I told you they'd find me."

"Drop your weapon," said the man behind the chair. He wore a three-piece suit and a confident smile. In his hand was an automatic, probably .25 caliber, small enough to be concealed easily in a pocket. Too small for much accuracy.

Neither of the others held a gun.

The one on the left, a fat bearded man dressed

like a biker, climbed over the back of the couch. He stepped down, his belly swinging, and waved a bloody bowie knife in front of his smile.

The one on the right stepped around an end of the couch. He wore grease-stained coveralls. He held a pipe wrench.

Dukane took a step into the living room.

"I told you to . . ."

"You drop yours," he said, raising his .45. "Mine's bigger."

The man's eyes flicked to the side. Catching the movement, Dukane whirled around, flung up his left arm, and blocked the knife. The woman wielding it hissed and jerked the blade back, tearing open his forearm. Dukane swung his heavy Colt. It slammed across her cheek and she stumbled backward, grabbing her face.

Dukane started to turn. He heard a quick flat *bam* like a screen door slamming shut. The bullet punched through his jacket sleeve, but he felt no hit. The clean-cut man tried again as Dukane brought up his automatic and fired. The man's chin dissolved in a burst of red.

Even as the gun bucked, the biker chopped down with his knife. He missed Dukane's wrist, but the powerful blow against the barrel knocked his pistol free. Alice grabbed his ankles. He fell backward as the huge knife slashed at his belly. Hitting the floor, he jerked a foot free. Alice reached for it. His heel smashed her face aside.

He kicked out at the legs of the biker, but the

bulky man lunged forward, kicking back, slashing at his shins.

The grease monkey, at the biker's side, hurled the wrench down at Dukane's head. It almost missed. It numbed his ear and brought tears to his eyes. Dukane grabbed the wrench. He sat up, swinging it to keep away the knife. It clanked against the blade. Before the knife could slash back, he leaned far forward and hammered the man's knee. With a cry of pain, the biker hobbled and fell.

The mechanic was bending down, reaching for Dukane's automatic. Dukane threw the wrench. It bounced off his shoulder, knocking him off balance. As he dropped to one knee, Dukane scrambled toward him. He saw the man pick up the gun, swing its barrel toward him. His fist cut upward. Hit the man's hand. The barrel jumped with the impact, tipped high and blasted a hole through the mechanic's upper teeth. The bullet exited the top of his head, splashing gore at the ceiling.

Dukane jerked the pistol from his dead fingers. He stood as the biker limped toward him, snarling, waving the knife like a pirate's cutlass.

He shot the man in the chest.

The woman who'd caught Dukane's barrel with her cheek was on her hands and knees, spitting blood and bits of broken teeth. She was wearing a tennis dress. Across the seat of her panties was printed "DON'T POACH."

Alice lay on the floor, curled up, blood spilling out between the fingers holding her face.

Dukane went to her.

He snapped a handcuff around her left wrist and dragged her across the floor. He cuffed her to the tennis player.

Then he searched for a telephone and called the police.

CHAPTER ELEVEN

Lacey was awakened by maids giggling and chattering in the hallway. They spoke Spanish, a language she had picked up as a child in Oasis. She grinned as she listened.

Two of the women had gone on a double-date to the drive-in, last night. Infuriated by their drunken boyfriends, they'd insisted on sitting together. The boyfriends climbed out of the car and went stumbling away, at which point the girls grandly drove off.

Lacey wondered who owned the car.

She flung the sheet aside, and groaned as she sat up. All over her body, her muscles ached with stiffness. She felt better than before, though. Waking up in the hotel room yesterday morning, she'd felt like the loser in a scrimmage with the Dallas Cowboys. Today, by comparison, was great.

Getting off the bed, she hobbled into the bathroom. She studied herself in the full-length mirror. Though her hair was a mess, her face had lost its haggard, haunted look. The bruises mottling her body had turned a sickly, greenish yellow. Hard ridges of scab had formed on her scratches.

"Won't be posing for a centerfold," she muttered. "But not bad."

She took a shower in the huge, glass-sided stall, then dried herself and got dressed in the same baggy clothes Alfred had bought on Thursday.

This was Saturday.

Escape day. Thursday and Friday, she'd been afraid to leave her room. She'd sat around reading paperbacks from the hotel gift shop, watching television, smoking, indulging herself in incredibly expensive food and wine from room service. After two days of it, she was ready to get out. More than ready.

She intended to buy several items, but the sun felt wonderful so she left her car in the hotel parking lot and walked. Three blocks away, in a sporting goods store just off Stone, she found most of what she wanted: a web belt to hold up her corduroys, a tank top and gym shorts, a one-piece bathing suit, suntan oil, a pocket knife, and a sheath knife with a six-inch blade. After purchasing the items, she shut herself into a dressing room and changed into the shorts and top.

She wandered the downtown area, enjoying the feel of the sun, pleased but slightly nervous with the stares of passing men.

Near noon, she entered a hardware store. She bought a spray can of "aluminum"-colored paint. She ate lunch at a McDonald's, then returned to her hotel.

She put on the swimsuit. With its high neckline, it concealed the worst of her injuries. Scratches and

bruises showed on her thighs, her shoulders, her arms. But that couldn't be helped. She was determined to use the pool, no matter how she looked. Turning, she studied her back. The suit left it bare almost to the rump. Her back, at least, looked reasonably unmarred.

She emptied her handbag on the bed, and filled it with what she needed: suntan oil, an Ed McBain paperback, the can of spray paint and her sheath knife. With a bath towel draping her shoulders, she left the room.

The pool, in the hotel's center courtyard, was nearly deserted: a young man was swimming lengths in a steady crawl; a deeply tanned woman lay face-down on a lounge with the top of her black bikini untied; and a middle-aged couple sat beneath an umbrella, sipping Bloody Marys. Lacey spread her towel on a lounge far from the others, and sat down.

She slicked herself with coconut oil, breathing deeply of its aroma, a rich sweet fragrance that reminded her of other, better times.

Of Will Rogers State Park, near Pacific Palisades where she stayed with Tom and his family that week in spring, six years ago. Her senior year at Stanford. They spent every day at the beach, swimming far out, body surfing, walking the shoreline, or just stretching out on their towels. Tom would trickle coconut oil onto her back. His hands would glide over her, sometimes slipping down between her legs.

Brian used to do that, too, but she never loved Brian. Never loved anyone after Tom. But Brian came along at a time when she needed a man, and

she'd never had such sex; Brian cared about nothing else.

Lying back, Lacey sighed and remembered those times by his pool when she lay on her back with her eyes shut and the sun on her naked body—the sun, the oil, and Brian's sliding, searching hands.

Now, she wondered if she could ever allow another man to have her. She knew her desire was strong: it always had been. But could she let herself be touched without recoiling, entered without shuddering in revulsion?

Sprawled on the bathroom floor. The rug against her face. Fingers clamping her shoulders. Erection ramming her.

Hurt by the sudden shock of memory, she opened her eyes, groped inside her handbag, and took out the book. She struggled to read, but her mind soon strayed from the words. She saw herself tied to the bed and she heard the scratchy voice—"I oughta kill you"—and felt him jerk her legs apart, felt his mouth. She shut the book.

The pool was deserted. The man who'd been swimming lengths now lay on the concrete, dripping, hands folded under his head. Lacey took off her sunglasses. She got up from the lounge and stepped to the pool's edge.

She dived in, jerking rigid at the cold blast of water, gliding through its silence and finally curving upward to the surface. She swam to the far end, turned, and swam back with all her might. Then she turned again and raced to the other end and back. She sidestroked two lengths, then breast-stroked

two lengths, then climbed exhausted from the pool. She lowered the back of her lounge and flopped on it facedown, gasping.

She heard the slap of footsteps.

"You're quite a swimmer."

Raising her head, she looked up at the man—the one who'd been in the pool before her. "Thanks," she told him.

"I'm Scott."

"Hi."

He was slim and muscular and tanned. His tight bikini trunks covered little of him, and concealed less. He sat on the concrete beside Lacey, facing her. "Do you have a name?" he asked.

"Doesn't everyone?"

"Oooh. Touchy."

"Sorry. I'm just not in the mood for company."

"That's the time when you *need* company the most."

"Wrong." She lowered her head, and shut her eyes.

"Can't get rid of me that easily. Nothing I enjoy more than a challenge."

"Climb a mountain."

"Too rough. I prefer smoother terrain."

"Leave me alone, all right?"

"Your back will burn. Would you like me to apply a dab of oil?"

"I wouldn't. I'd like to be left alone. Why don't you go try someone else?"

"Because you're beautiful and lonely."

Lacey sighed. "I really don't need this. If you won't leave, I will."

"Ah, say no more. I can take a hint."

She opened one eye enough to see him stand. Scott smiled and waved as he backed away.

Resting her head on her crossed arms, Lacey tried to sleep. Her mind replayed the encounter. The guy had been arrogant and pushy. But, damn it, she could've at least been polite. She'd acted like a bitch. She felt herself blushing at the memory.

Well, what's done is done.

She tried not to think about it.

She lay motionless, concentrating on the hot pressure of the sun.

"A libation for the lady."

Lifting her head, she saw Scott above her, a Bloody Mary in each hand. "You don't give up, do you?"

"That's why I seldom fail."

Lacey turned over, stared at the grinning man, and finally sat up. "I'm Lacey," she said. "And I apologize for acting creepy."

"Creepy is a fair first-line of defense," he said, sitting down on the concrete. "Only fair, though. Total complacency works better. It reduces the woman's guilt factor. Much more difficult to penetrate."

"You've studied the subject."

"Women fascinate me." He took the dripping celery stalk from his drink and licked it.

Intentional symbolism? More than likely. Holding back a smile, Lacey removed her own stalk and tapped off its drops on the rim of her glass. She set it down beside her lounge. Scott placed his beside it.

"To our fortunate encounter," he said.

"Okay."

He clinked his glass against hers, and they both drank. Her Bloody Mary was hot with Tabasco. It made her eyes water, her nose start to run. She sniffed.

"So tell me, Lacey, what is a lovely young lady doing alone at this fashionable resort hotel?"

"What makes you think I'm alone?"

"I have an unerring nose for such things."

"Unerring?" she asked, somewhat surprised that he had used the correct pronunciation—err as in purr.

"*Seldom* erring. But it's hit the mark this time, hasn't it?"

"Isn't 'mark' a con man term for a sucker?"

"Do you see yourself as a sucker?"

"Do you see yourself as a con man?"

He grinned—a boyish, disarming grin. Lacey wondered how much time he spent at mirrors, practicing it. "A confidence man? Of course. Here I am, trying to win your confidence."

"When's the pitch?"

"Later. I haven't won yet, have I?"

"Far from it."

"Are you always this distrustful?"

"Only of strangers who approach me uninvited."

"Ah. You assume I have mischief on my mind."

"Do you?"

"That would be telling."

If I told you that, you'd know. The low, rough voice. She suddenly trembled as if a cloud had smothered the sun, an icy wind blown across her.

"What's wrong?"

"Nothing."

"Hey, I was only joking about the mischief."

"I know."

"Are you all right?"

"I just . . . what you said, it reminded me of something."

"Must've been something unpleasant."

"It was."

"Want to talk about it?"

"No."

"A chance like this doesn't come along every day, you know: a friendly, willing ear, the sunlight beating down, a Bloody Mary in your hand. Besides, I might be able to help."

"How could you help?"

"How will I know unless you tell me your problem? Let me guess, though: it involves a man."

She took a drink, and stared at the glistening pool.

"He did something to you."

The bantering tone was gone from Scott's voice. Lacey glanced at him. He was staring at his drink, his face solemn.

"Yes," she said.

"He didn't jilt you, nothing like that. Whatever he did, you're frightened of him. He hurt you, didn't he? Beat you up."

"You're very observant," Lacey muttered, glancing down at her bruises and scratches.

"You came here to get away from him. You're hiding out, probably even registered under a fake name in case he comes looking for you."

"I couldn't," she said. "I had to use a credit card to get the room."

"But the rest is right?"

"Close enough." Lacey sipped her drink and set the glass on her belly. Its cold wetness soaked through her damp swimsuit. It felt good.

"Husband, boyfriend, or stranger?"

"Stranger."

"Did you go to the police?"

"He got away."

"And you're afraid he'll come after you?"

"He'll kill me, if he can."

"We won't let him."

"We?"

He winked. "You and me, kid."

"Thanks for the offer, but I don't want anyone else involved in this. Besides, I don't think he'll find me here."

"It doesn't take a genius to find someone hiding out at a major hotel—particularly if she's using her real name."

"Thanks."

"How long have you been here?"

"This is the third day. I got in Thursday afternoon."

"Then you've been here much too long. You're lucky he hasn't already shown up."

"He doesn't even know what city I'm in, Scott."

"You're not from Tucson?"

"No."

"But I'll wager this is the nearest large city, and the place he'll look first."

"I guess so," she admitted.

"If I were you, I'd get out of here today and check into a different hotel. Better still, head for another town."

"It's past check-out time. Besides, I don't want to. I like this one."

Scott shrugged. "In that case, I think you should allow me to act as your escort."

"No. Really, Scott . . ."

"I'd be happy to do it. After all, you're a beautiful woman, and we're both alone in the city. How could I spend my time better than by keeping company with a creature like you?"

"A creature?" she asked, smiling.

"A damsel in distress."

"It might be dangerous."

"I'm good with my dukes. Besides, I pack heat."

"A gun?"

"A Colt .45 automatic. Never go anywhere without it. Except, of course, to the swimming pool."

"What are you, a bank robber?"

"You ever hear of Charlie Dane?"

"*San Francisco Hit, Manhattan Mayhem* . . . ?"

"*Tucson Death Squad.* That's to be his latest battle against the forces of evil. The galleys are up in my suite this very moment."

Lacey stared at him, frowning. "But those are written by Max Carter."

"Otherwise known as Scott Bradley."

"You."

"Me."

"That still doesn't explain the gun."

"Max keeps the rod at his side when he sits at the old typewriter. It puts him in touch with Charlie Dane."

Lacey grinned. "Does Max also wear Charlie's trench coat?"

"Too hot. But he does don the battered fedora."

"Not while he's escorting me, I hope."

"I'll leave Max in the room, and borrow his piece."

"He won't mind?"

"He's always eager to please."

CHAPTER TWELVE

Carl grabbed the phone before its second ring. "*Tribune.*"

"Carl?"

His heart began to hammer. "How's it going, Lace?"

"So far, so good. He hasn't found me yet. Any activity on your end?"

"Nope. There haven't been any incidents since you left."

"Damn. I almost wish . . . At least I'd know he's still there."

"Well, maybe he's just lying low. Or maybe your knife did the trick."

"Don't I wish."

"So, how are you feeling?"

"Scared. Other than that, I guess I'm all right. Recuperating."

"That's good. Look, you'd better let me know where you're staying. If something breaks, up this way, I'll want to let you know."

"Sure. I'm at the Desert Wind, room three sixty-two."

Carl wrote it down.

"I meant to call you yesterday, but . . . couldn't get myself to do anything. Felt like crawling under a rock."

"That's all right, Lace. Perfectly understandable."

"Anyway, I'm better now."

"Glad to hear it. Look, is there anything I can do for you?"

"Just keep me posted, is all."

"Sure thing. Take care of yourself, now."

"I'll try. So long, Carl."

He hung up. Across the room, one of his reporters hunched over a typewriter working on the lead story for tomorrow's edition. Otherwise, the office was deserted. "Jack?"

The reporter looked up, raising his eyebrows.

"See if you can't hunt down Chief Barrett. Try to talk him into letting us release the details of the Hoffman and Peterson murders."

"He's already refused, Carl."

"Try him again. Tell him a blow-by-blow description would be in the public interest, make them more aware of the danger. Maybe he'll go for it."

"Okay," Jack said, sounding reluctant. He pushed his chair back, stood up, and stretched. Then he headed for the door.

The moment he was gone, Carl dialed the telephone.

"Spiritual Development Foundation."

He gave his name, number and level.

"Very good, Mr. Williams."

"Let me talk to Farris. It's urgent."

Farris's voice came over the phone. "We've been waiting for your call," he said.

"Sorry. I just received the information. Miss Allen's at the Desert Wind Hotel in Tucson. Room number three six two."

"Excellent. I'll notify our personnel in the area. Your next step is to join her."

"Right."

"Do that at once."

"I'll leave right away."

As he hung up, a voice from behind asked, "What was that all about?"

Carl swiveled around. Alfred, standing in front of the restroom door, looked at him with suspicion. "You told where Lacey is. Who'd you tell?"

"Chief Barrett."

"What'd you want to do that for?"

"She asked me to." Turning back to his desk, Carl pulled open the top drawer and removed a letter opener. "Bring me Jack's story," he said.

Alfred walked toward Jack's desk, his head low and shaking. "I don't think you should've done that," he said.

"You're not paid to think."

"Well . . ." He gathered two pages from the desktop, and walked slowly back toward Carl.

Carl got up from his chair. With the letter opener behind his back, he reached out his left hand for the papers.

"Here they . . ."

Carl grabbed Alfred's wrist, jerked him forward, and plunged the slim blade into his belly.

CHAPTER THIRTEEN

A strolling guitarist stopped at their table. "A song?"

Scott nodded. "How about 'Cielito Lindo'?" he asked Lacey.

She dipped a tortilla chip into hot sauce. "Fine."

With a smile, the white-clothed Mexican began to strum chords and sing. Lacey sat back, munching her chip and sipping her margarita as she watched him. He stood with his back arched, his head thrown back, his dark face writhing as if the song called up unbearable sorrow. His plaintive voice pushed Lacey's mind back to a strolling minstrel in Nogales, only a few days before her breakup with Brian. One of their last good times together. The next week, back in Oasis, he brought a man to the house and insisted the three of them go at each other. Lacey refused, and he beat her. No more Brian. No more men, at all, after that.

For a moment, she felt the void and sank into it. No man, no love, no babies, only empty darkness. She was cut loose and drifting. Starting to panic.

She took a long drink from her margarita, and managed a smile for Scott.

Get off it, kiddo, she told herself. A hell of a time

to worry about becoming an old maid. You should live so long.

The singer finished his song, and Scott handed him a dollar.

"*Gracias*," the man said. With a slight bow, he turned away.

"Are you all right?" Scott asked.

"Just beweeping my outcast state."

Scott raised an eyebrow. "Troubling deaf heaven with your bootless cries?"

Lacey grinned. "Yup."

The waitress set down plates in front of them. They had both ordered Dinner #6: a chimichanga, refried beans, rice, and a taco. Lacey took a deep breath of the steam rising from her meal. Her mouth watered.

"Plates are hot," warned the waitress. "Will there be anything else for you?"

"Want a beer?" Scott asked.

"I'll stick with margaritas."

"That'll be it for now," he told the waitress, and she left.

Across the candlelit room, the singer began "The Rose of San Antone" for two lean men in business suits. One of them saw Lacey watching. He met her gaze, looked her over, then turned away and spoke to his friend. The other man glanced at her. She looked away, embarrassed, certain they were wondering about her appearance. In her plaid blouse and corduroys, she felt shabby: all right for McDonald's, but barely good enough for a restaurant of Carmen's quality.

She should've found time to buy a dress. When Scott escorted her back to her suite that afternoon, though, he gave her strict orders not to leave it without calling him. She hadn't wanted to drag him around Tucson in search of evening wear, so she'd simply stayed in her room until he picked her up for dinner. Now, she regretted it.

She swallowed a mouthful of rice, and said, "What's next?"

"Find a good piano bar . . ."

"I mean, tomorrow and the next day and the day after that."

"Depends on you."

"Are we just going to *wait*? I mean, I could stay at the hotel for two weeks, as I planned, and nothing happen, and the minute I step into my house back in Oasis, *wham*."

"You think he's at your house?"

"He could be anywhere: in my house, at the hotel, even here. He might even be dead, but I think that's too good to hope for."

"So you don't want to wait around? You'd rather go on the offensive? Good. That's just what Charlie Dane would suggest."

"Are you willing?" she asked.

"I was planning to suggest it, myself."

She cut into the chimichanga with her fork, and scooped a bite into her mouth. The fried tortilla crunched. She chewed slowly, savoring its spicy meat and cheese.

"So tomorrow, we'll go to your house."

"That'd be great." Lacey took another bite. Then

she picked up her handbag and set it on her lap. She opened it. She took out the can.

"What's that, paint?"

"There's something you have to know. You may decide I'm crazy and call the whole thing off, but I have to tell you the truth. This afternoon, when I explained the whole situation to you, I left something out. It's why I have this paint. I told you the man was wearing a mask. That's my story for public consumption, but it's not quite the truth. I told the truth to the police and my editor, and they didn't believe me. I don't really expect you to believe me, either. But here goes. The man who killed Elsie Hoffman and Red Peterson, the man who attacked me—he's invisible."

Scott stared at his plate. He forked a huge bite of chimichanga into his mouth, and chewed slowly, frowning. He swallowed. He finished his margarita and refilled the glass and took another sip. "Invisible?" he asked, as if he thought he'd misunderstood.

"Not a ghost or apparition or hallucination," Lacey said. "It's a man. But you can look right at him and see right through him and never know he's even there. He's invisible."

"How?" Scott asked.

"He didn't tell me. 'A little miracle,' he said."

"A miracle, all right."

"That's what the paint is for. It'll adhere to him, and he won't be invisible again till he gets it off his skin."

"Invisible," Scott said, shaking his head.

"Do you believe me?"

"Let me put it this way: we'll proceed as if I do. Hell, if it's true, I might get a whizz-bang story out of this. Another *Amityville Horror*. Who knows?"

Back at the hotel, Scott drew a Colt .45 automatic from the shoulder holster under his sport coat.

They searched Lacey's suite, walking behind chairs, feeling inside closets and under the beds, stepping into the shower stall. At last, Scott sighed and sat on the couch. "If the guy's invisible," he said, "there's no way we can be sure he isn't here."

"He hasn't attacked," Lacey said.

"Maybe he's waiting for me to leave. So I guess I'd better stay." He patted the couch. "This'll do fine."

"You're really going to stay?"

"I can't do much protecting from the end of the hall."

"Well, I guess it's all right. I won't let you sleep on the couch, though, with two beds in the other room."

"You sure?"

"It'd be ridiculous."

Grinning, Scott drawled, "Mighty grateful, ma'am. I accept your hospitality."

Lacey went to bed first. Though she usually slept in the nude, tonight she wore her jogging shorts and tank top in case her sheet should slip off during the night. She lay wide awake. From the other room came quiet TV voices. She listened, but couldn't make out their words.

Had it been a mistake, offering the other bed? It might've sounded like an invitation for something

more. Had Scott taken it that way? God, what if he came over to her bed and climbed in?

He would say something cute. "I'm here to guard your body at close range."

She rolled onto her belly, and forced her mind away from the possibility. How'll we work it in the morning? Each drive our own cars, I suppose. Meet at my house. We'll park in front. Go in together? Sneak in? And search the place. Spread flour around so we can see footprints? God, what a clean-up job. Would it come out of the carpet?

The television voices stopped.

Lacey heard quiet footsteps. She expected Scott to enter the bathroom just off the hallway, but the steps kept coming. The doorknob rattled a bit. Then the door swung open.

She pressed her face against the pillow and shut her eyes.

Please, let him go straight to his own bed.

I'm here to guard your body at close range.

The footsteps stopped between the beds. She heard the squeak of springs, followed by a whispered "damn" as if he were angry about the noise. Obviously, he thought she was asleep and didn't want to disturb her. So he had no intention of coming to her bed, after all.

Lacey remained motionless, listening to his breathing, to the quiet sounds the bed made as he shifted to remove his shoes, to the single link of his belt buckle and the whisper of his zipper. Then the springs squawked.

He's standing up.

Coming here, after all? Lacey's heart began to thunder.

Turning her head slightly, she opened one eye and saw him in the darkness only a yard away. He stepped out of his pants, folded them once, and placed them on the floor beside his bed. He took off his shoulder holster, then his shirt. His tanned skin looked very dark against his white briefs. Crouching, he folded his shirt and set it on top of the pants. Then he turned away to pull down the bedcovers. He climbed in without taking off his shorts.

Lacey shut her eye. Her heart was still racing, and she realized that she'd barely been breathing since Scott entered the room.

She was parched. She tried to work up enough saliva to moisten her mouth, but couldn't.

She waited.

I'll die if I don't get a drink of water. Probably those margaritas.

Slipping her sheet aside, she swung her legs off the bed and stood up. She rushed through the darkness to the bathroom, and turned on a light. Squinting against its glare, she ran cold water. She filled a glass and drank. In the mirror, she saw hair clinging to her sweaty forehead. She shook her head at the image. She drank another glassful of cold water, then turned off the faucet and used the toilet. The flush sounded very loud. If Scott heard it . . . *No, he's all right. He'll stay in bed. If he'd wanted to try anything tonight, he would've done it by now.*

She flicked off the light and opened the door.

Scott clutched her shoulders. He was wearing

only his briefs. In his right hand, upraised to his shoulder, he held the pistol. It smelled oily and metallic.

"What . . . ?"

"Shhhh. We've got company."

CHAPTER FOURTEEN

Standing close to Scott in the dark hallway, Lacey heard the quiet rap of knuckles on wood. "Where's it coming from?" she asked.

"Our door."

"You sure?"

Scott nodded.

"My God."

"Come on." Holding her by the elbow, Scott led her into the main room. They stood motionless. After a moment of silence, the knocking resumed. "I'll watch from the closet," Scott whispered. "You get the door."

"What if it's *him*?"

"Then we're in luck."

As Scott hurried to the coat closet, Lacey turned on a lamp. "Right there," she called. She scanned the room, and found her handbag on the coffee table. Rushing to it, she took out the can of spray paint and the knife. She pulled off the leather sheath, and slid the knife under the waistband at the back of her shorts. The blade was cool and flat against her rump. She felt the scrape of its edges as she walked to the door.

She peered through the peephole. Though the man in the bright hallway looked shrunken and distorted as if viewed in a distant funhouse mirror, Lacey recognized his lanky build, his haggard face and short, curly hair.

"Carl?"

She flicked off the guard chain, and pulled the door open. Carl gazed at her with grim, red-rimmed eyes. "Hi, Lace."

"Carl, what's going on? What're you doing here?"

"I'm sorry. Did I wake you?"

"No. Come on in."

Lacey stepped aside to let him enter. Then she shut and chained the door. She turned to him. "Did something happen? What's wrong?"

"Our man paid a visit to the *Trib*. He . . . he killed Alfred."

"Oh my God!"

"I came back from lunch, and . . . Alfred was on the floor." Reaching into a pocket of his baggy slacks, Carl pulled out a folded sheet of paper. "The police have the original. It was pinned to him, to his belly . . . with my letter opener." He handed the paper to Lacey.

She set the spray can on the coffee table, and unfolded the paper, and stared. The photocopy was stained as if it had been used to mop up a spill of black ink. But the typing was legible. She read it in silence. "Can't get rid of me that easy. Better come home, bitch, or your editor's next." With a trembling hand, she gave the note back to Carl.

"I thought I'd call you, but . . . Hell, I remembered what you said about him being invisible. Still not sure I can believe that, but I figured I'd better be careful. If he *is* like you say, he might've been right behind me, watching me dial. If he got the hotel's number . . . Well, I figured I'd drive on out to be on the safe side."

"He could've been in your car!" Lacey blurted, suddenly alarmed.

"No. I checked it over."

"Your trunk?"

"Checked that, too."

"Maybe he followed you."

"I don't think so. Wasn't much traffic. The only car behind me much had a couple in it—a man driving, a woman passenger." He made a grim smile. "Neither one was invisible. So I think we're okay on that score."

"You saw the man's face?" Lacey asked.

"Not up close, but he had one. It's all right, Lace. Now stop worrying. I wasn't followed."

"He could've put something on. A mask, make-up . . ."

Carl shook his head. "We've gotta figure out what to do about this guy. Seems to me, we're both in the same boat, now. I don't think I want to hang around Oasis and just wait for him to slit my gullet. I figure, if we stick together on this . . ."

"What about the woman passenger?" Lacey asked.

"Huh?"

"In the car that followed you."

"It wasn't *following* me. It was just *behind* me."

"All the way?"

"I don't know." He sounded annoyed. "I didn't keep track. It was just some clown and his wife."

"How do you know it was his wife?"

" 'Cause," Carl said, smiling slightly, "she was asleep the whole way."

"*Asleep?*"

"Sure. Slumped over, her head against the side window . . . Oh, for Christsake, Lace, don't turn paranoid on me. Don't start telling me she was dead, and the driver was your invisible man decked out in a Stetson and mask."

"You think that's not possible?"

"I think you're jumping to some mighty big conclusions."

"He figured you would know where to get in touch with me. Killing Alfred, leaving the note, he did it so you'd lead him here. For Godsake, he's probably . . ."

"Now don't get all worked up. Calm down. There's nothing to . . ."

Lacey jerked stiff as her knife turned, the blade slicing a white-hot line up her buttock. She clutched the wound and spun around. The suspended knife slashed through the air, barely missing her face, and jerked toward Carl.

"*Scott!*"

The closet door burst open. Scott crouched, pistol forward, but his face was twisted with confusion. "*Where?*"

Even as Lacey pointed, the blade punched into Carl's throat. Blood shot out. It spurted a few inches,

then splattered as if hitting a sheet of glass. It sprayed and sheathed the surface—the face and shoulders and chest of a six-foot man.

Scott gazed, his mouth agape.

"Shoot him!"

The figure, vague as a patch of floating red cellophane, raised Carl off his feet and flung him at Scott. Scott leapt sideways. The body hit the closet door, crashed it shut, and thudded to the floor. The knife, Lacey saw, was still embedded in Carl's throat.

Scott aimed at the film of blood rushing toward him. "Stop!"

Lacey braced herself for the roar of gunfire. It didn't come.

A yard in front of Scott, the figure halted.

"Fuckin' blood," muttered a scratchy voice.

The layer of red shifted as if a child were finger-painting on his face.

"Hands on your head," Scott ordered.

The top of the head wasn't there, but Lacey saw two hand-shaped images of blood suspended above the concave face—a face like the back of a translucent red Halloween mask.

Lacey grabbed her can of silver paint from the coffee table and tugged off its plastic top. Tossing the cap aside, she shook the can. It rattled as if a marble were trapped inside. She stepped close to the dripping, red veil in front of Scott's automatic.

"Don't do it," the man muttered.

As her forefinger lowered to the plastic nozzle, the red membrane shifted like a flag struck by wind. Something struck Lacey's hand. The can tumbled

away. Then a tightness clenched her wrist and swung her toward Scott. He jumped out of the way, rushed in front of her, and dived. He landed flat on the floor, his hands grabbing only air.

The door flew open, ripping the guard chain from its mounting, and slammed shut.

Scott pushed himself to his knees. His eyes met Lacey's. He shook his head.

Lacey stepped over to Carl's body. She knelt down beside him. Blood no longer pumped from his torn throat. She covered her face with both hands, and started to cry.

CHAPTER FIFTEEN

Lacey lay facedown on the living room floor, her shorts around her knees, Scott patting her cut buttock with a cool, damp washcloth. "Not much bleeding," he said. "You don't have bandages or anything, do you?"

"Afraid not."

"Have any sanitary napkins?"

She felt heat flood her face, and wondered if the blush extended to her rump. "Not with me."

"Well, it's not much more than a scratch, but . . ."

"Oh, I think there *is* a pad in the medicine cabinet. The hotel variety. Right behind some kind of shower cap and shoeshine rag."

"Advantages of a first-rate hotel," Scott said, and left her. He returned, seconds later, tearing open the white wrapper. He knelt down, and pressed the soft pad against her wound. "The tape's on the wrong side," he muttered.

"Supposed to be. My underwear'll hold it in place."

"Oh." He went for her panties, and hurried back.

"Thanks," Lacey said. "I can take care of the rest."

While she pulled on her panties and shorts, Scott

went into the hallway. He came back with a blanket.

He used it to cover the body of Carl Williams. Dots of blood darkened the fuzzy pink blanket, bloomed, and grew together. Lacey turned away.

She got to her feet. Wandering to a far corner of the room, she picked up the can of spray paint. She sat gently on the couch, clutching the can with both hands.

Scott sat beside her. "I screwed up," he said. "I'm sorry. I thought everything was okay until you yelled. Then I couldn't find a target." Shaking his head, he sighed. "Christ, what a screwup. I'm sorry about your friend. If I'd just been . . ."

"Don't blame yourself. Nobody could've stopped it, at that point."

"Charlie Dane could've," he mumbled.

"Charlie would've shot the bastard when he had the chance," Lacey said.

"Yeah."

"The bastard's out there, now. He's had time to get the blood off."

"Yeah."

"Why didn't *you* shoot him?"

For a long time, Scott stared at the coffee table.

"Scott?"

"I thought we had him. I figured we'd tie him up. I've got a cassette recorder in my room. I thought . . . well, I'd get his story. You know, before calling in the cops. Interview him, find out how he got that way, what he's been doing, if there are others like him."

"Others?"

"If one man can be made invisible, why not more? Christ, can you imagine an army of them? Think what they could do. They could turn the world upside down."

"I suppose so," Lacey said. "But there's only one here, and he's probably figuring a way, right now, to get at us. You aren't going to have much luck writing a book about him if we're both killed, so next time . . . My God!" Jumping to her feet, she rushed to the desk and grabbed a straight-backed chair.

"What?"

She ran to the door with it, tipped it backward and braced it under the knob. "Maybe that . . ." she muttered. She turned to Scott. "A passkey. He could get one so easily."

Scott sighed. "Damn, I should've thought of that. Afraid I'm not helping much." He looked at her with despair. "Sorry. I'm really not good enough for this kind of thing. Living it isn't quite the same as writing it." He propped his elbows on his knees, and rubbed his face.

Lacey went to him. Crouching, she placed a hand on his back. "Hey, it's all right. Don't feel bad. If you hadn't been here, he would've had me."

Scott raised his head and looked at her. "Thanks."

"It's the truth. You saved my life."

He smiled slightly. "You're right."

"Of course I am."

"But I'm right, too," he said. His face changed, turning hard and determined. "This is out of my league. I'm not going to let my inexperience jeop-

ardize you any longer." He touched her cheek, stood up, and walked toward the desk.

"What are you doing?"

"Calling in reinforcements," he said, and picked up the telephone. He set his automatic on the desk, then dialed with quick, sure strokes of his forefinger. Eleven numbers.

Long distance?

CHAPTER SIXTEEN

The bedside telephone woke Dukane, and he saw a naked woman bending over him in the darkness. Her head jerked toward the phone. In the moments between the clamors of the first and second rings, Dukane realized that the woman—a stranger before he brought her home tonight—had been interrupted in the process of tying his left wrist to the headboard.

He yanked both arms. The headboard shook and a cord bit into his right wrist, but his left pulled free.

The woman grabbed it, tried to force it down.

"Thanks," Dukane said, "but I'm not into bondage."

He twisted his arm out of her grip. As the woman reached for it again, he clutched her neck and thrust her forward, ramming her head against the oak of his headboard. She slumped. He shoved her off the bed, rolled to his right, and picked up the phone.

"Hello?"

"Dukane? It's Scott. I'm in deep trouble, pal."

"What's the problem?"

"There's a killer after me. An invisible killer."

"Invisible?"

"I know it sounds ridiculous, but believe me, it's true. He just murdered a guy here in the room."

"Okay. Where are you?"

"The Desert Wind hotel in Tucson. Room three sixty-two."

"Where's this killer?"

"Probably right outside the door."

"Okay. Hang tough, kid, I'm on my way. It'll take me about four hours, though. Maybe less, but don't count on it."

"Hurry."

"Right." Dukane hung up. He slid open a drawer of the nightstand, took out a switchblade knife, and severed the cord binding his right hand to the headboard. Then he turned on a light. He climbed across the bed and knelt over the unconscious woman.

She lay on her back, breathing deeply as if asleep, her arms and legs outflung. A beautiful, slim, small-breasted blonde. Just his type. Too much his type, perhaps. But he'd known a lot of women over the years, and only a handful had turned out to be plants. He should've been a lot more careful, after Friday's disaster. He should've expected something like this.

Confidence kills.

She began to stir, her eyelids squeezing tight with a stab of pain, a hand rising to her head. She pursed her lips and said, "Oooh." Then her eyelids fluttered open. She gazed at Dukane with confusion for a moment before her memory apparently returned and she bolted upright.

Dukane clutched her throat and slammed her down. "Who sent you?"

She sneered. "No one."

"I don't have time for games." He jabbed his knife down. Her body jerked as if jolted by a cattle prod, mouth springing open to scream. He stopped the point of his knife above her bulging right eye. An eighth of an inch above it. She blinked, her lashes flicking over the steel tip. "Who sent you?"

She said nothing. Slowly, the panic left her face. Her body relaxed. Even the straining tendons and muscles of her neck went slack under Dukane's hand. She smirked up at him. "Do as you like," she said. "Cut out my eye, if that's what pleases you. Take whatever you wish. My breasts?" Her hands moved, stroking them. The dark nipples stood rigid. "I am all powerful," she whispered. "I am immortal."

"Have you drunk at the river?" Dukane asked.

"Oh yes, oh yes."

He eased the blade away from her eye.

"Immortal," she said. "All powerful."

He removed his right hand from her throat. "Okay, get up." As he inched the knife away, her fingers caught his wrist. Dukane tensed, expecting an upward thrust. But she tugged down. He wasn't ready for that. The blade punched into the pale flesh between her breasts.

Dukane snatched it free.

The woman bucked, clutched the wound, and sat up with a look of sudden terror on her face.

Blood spilled out between her fingers. She glanced

at it, then gazed at Dukane with eyes like a hurt child.

"Shit," Dukane muttered, suddenly feeling sorry for her. "Don't worry, you missed your heart. I'll call an ambulance." He rushed around the end of the bed. "Press down hard on the wound." He picked up the phone.

As he started to dial, the woman grabbed the bed and pushed herself to her feet.

"Lie down, damn it!"

She suddenly ran.

"Hey!" Dukane dropped the phone and scrambled over the bed, hoping to stop her before she reached the sliding door to the balcony.

She was too quick.

Her forehead rammed the door. The plate glass burst. She lunged through a spray of tumbling shards that slashed her bare skin, and disappeared onto the balcony. Dukane rushed after her. As he ducked through the smashed door, she threw herself headfirst over the railing. Dukane lunged, reached for her foot, and touched its heel with his forefinger. Then all he could do was watch.

She kicked and twisted for a second that seemed like minutes even to Dukane, then threw out her arms to break her fall. The concrete slab of the pool's apron smashed her arms out of the way, and she hit it with her face.

Dukane looked down at her body, and sighed. He knew he shouldn't feel sorry for her; she'd probably planned to kill him tonight. But Christ, the waste . . .

a beautiful girl . . . Why the hell did she ever get mixed up in such . . .

He clutched the railing, frozen by a sudden chill as a huge, black-robed man darted from behind bushes beside the pool. The man crouched at the broken body, flung it over his shoulder, and lumbered away.

Dukane pried his fingers off the railing. His skin was crawly with goose bumps. He stared down at the dark figure and knew he should give chase, but he couldn't move.

Besides, he told himself, Scott has priority. He watched, rubbing his prickly arms and thighs, thinking it strange that he should be so spooked. Whoever the bastard was, Dukane could probably nail him in unarmed combat, even with one hand tied behind his back. Probably. The thought didn't give him much comfort.

He picked bits of glass out of his feet, then hobbled down the long balcony to its guest room entrance. He slid open the door and stared at the pale carpet.

"Shit," he muttered.

One ruined carpet was enough for one night.

On hands and knees, keeping his feet elevated, he crawled across the carpet. In the guest bathroom, he found iodine, adhesive tape, and gauze. He quickly bandaged his feet.

Ignoring the slight pain, he rushed back to his bedroom. He glanced at the clock. Less than five minutes had passed since Scott's call.

A long time, five minutes.

A long time for that dumb woman. A long time for a guy like Scott, waiting to get bailed out.

It took him under a minute to dress.

Then he ran downstairs, through the dark house, and out to his garage. He jumped into his Jaguar. Thumbed the garage door switch. Keyed the ignition. The engine thundered, shaking the car.

In his rearview mirror, he watched the door rise. The gap widened. He saw the dark-robed man looking in at him, the naked body of the girl still over his shoulder.

Dukane jammed the shift to reverse and floored the gas pedal. He popped the clutch. The car leapt backward. He gripped the wheel, expecting an impact, but the car shot past the figure. Caught in the headlight, the man turned slowly to face him.

Dukane's foot hovered over the brake. He could easily stop and have another try.

But Scott was waiting.

He'd already wasted too many minutes.

So he sped backward to the street, leaving the strange man alone in the driveway with the corpse.

CHAPTER SEVENTEEN

"What was that about?" Lacey had asked as soon as Scott put down the phone.

"Saving our hides."

"Dukane? Who's he?"

"The real-life Charlie Dane. Excuse me a minute, I want to get dressed." He left her alone in the room.

Lacey got up and followed him. When she reached the bedroom, Scott was stepping into his pants. "There really *is* a Charlie Dane?"

Scott fastened his trousers and picked up his shirt. "Sure is. No trench coat and battered fedora, and he operates now instead of the forties, but the rest is pretty close. A hell of a guy. He'll get us out of here. We just have to stay alive for the next four hours, till he arrives."

"Maybe we should call the police."

"What good would they be against an invisible maniac?"

"What good will this Dukane be?"

Scott grinned, for the first time since the attack looking calm and confident. "Good enough."

* * *

"What time is it?" Lacey asked.

"Eleven forty."

"Is that all?" Only twenty minutes had passed since Scott's talk with Dukane. For the past ten, Lacey had been sitting cross-legged beside the barricaded door, her pocket knife open on her lap, the paint can beside her ready to spray if the door should be forced open.

Scott had spent much of the time wandering the suite. He'd looked out the windows and determined that no ledges ran over from adjacent rooms. He'd shoved the couch against a locked, connecting door. Then he'd knelt down to remove the knife from Carl's throat.

"Should you do that?" Lacey had asked. "What about fingerprints?"

"We need it."

"But the police. My God, we don't want them thinking we killed Carl."

"Don't worry."

"Thanks, but I can't help it."

"The police are the least of our problems, right now."

Lacey had looked away when he pulled out the knife. He arranged the blanket again over Carl's head, then took the knife into the bathroom and cleaned it.

Now Scott was turning over the coffee table.

"What're you doing?"

"Clubs," he said, and began to unscrew one of

the short, tapering legs. When it came free, he tossed it underhand. It thumped the floor near Lacey, and rolled toward her. She picked it up by the narrow end. It felt like a small baseball bat. A thick, inch-long bolt protruded from the top.

As Scott twisted another leg off the table, Lacey heard voices in the hallway.

"Six fifty for a Piña Colada," said a man. "You believe it?"

"That's not so bad," a woman said. "It included the glass."

"Sixty cents' worth of glass. A nickle worth of booze."

"They're awfully cute glasses."

"Maybe we should get a few more."

"It would be nice to have a complete set." The woman's sudden yelp made Lacey jump. Her mind flashed an image of the two under attack, and she grabbed the spray can, tensing, ready to unblock the door and rush out to help. But the yelp led into a giggle. A different kind of attack. "Jimmy, *don't*! Christ, I almost dropped the glasses."

"Anything but that."

Lacey heard a key ratchet into a lock. A knob turned. A door swung open with a barely audible squeak, and banged shut.

"Hope they got in alone," Scott said, starting on a third leg.

"I sure hope so. They sounded nice."

"The guy's a cheapskate."

"He was just kidding around."

"Yeah. On the surface. Underneath, he's a cheap-skate."

"He did buy two of those drinks."

"At six fifty a whack. Not only a cheapskate, but he likes to play martyr."

Lacey looked at Scott, and saw he was smiling.

The door's lock button snapped out. Lacey turned, saw the door lurch, the chair tip forward a fraction. She thrust herself to her knees. The knife fell from her lap. She grabbed it. Scott threw himself against the wall on the other side of the door. He held a table leg in one upraised hand, the knife in the other. The automatic remained tucked in his belt.

The door eased back silently, then rammed the chair again, this time forcing the legs to scoot an inch across the carpet.

"Shoot him through the door," Lacey whispered.

Scott shook his head. "Louder," he mouthed.

"Shoot through the door!"

"Right." Clamping the club between his legs, he pulled out the automatic. He held it close to the door and worked its slide, jacking a live cartridge out.

The door settled back into place.

Lacey waited, holding her breath, expecting an-other thrust. Scott picked up his bullet and dropped it into his shirt pocket.

Nothing happened.

"Whatever he is," Scott whispered, "he doesn't like bullets." Tucking away the pistol, he shoved the

chair more firmly under the knob. "I think we're all right for a while . . . till he figures a new way to get at us."

"What'll he do?"

Scott shrugged.

"What time is it now?"

Scott glanced at his wristwatch. "Five minutes later than the last time you asked."

"Encouraging," she muttered.

"Three and a half hours to go."

"If your man's on time."

"Knowing Dukane, he'll be early."

"I hope so." Lacey sat down again, feeling a slight pain as her shorts drew taut across her wound. Raising herself for a moment, she tugged the shorts to loosen them. Fortunately, the cut was high enough so that she didn't rest on it, sitting upright. It hurt very little, except for a frequent, achy itch. It itched now. She scratched it gently with her fingernails. "What makes you think this Dukane will do us any good?"

"He's brilliant, innovative, a crack shot . . ."

"Able to leap tall buildings in a single bound?"

"Damn near. Won the Medal of Honor in Vietnam. Dropped in behind the lines, killed God-knows how many gooks, freed two dozen POWs and led them all back. Alone."

Scott shook his head, looking astonished by the feat. "He's been a private investigator and bodyguard for nine years. An amazing guy. He's actually lived the Charlie Dane stories. Most of them are based on incidents from Dukane's past."

"Hope I live long enough to meet him."

"I keep trying to figure out what he'd do, if he were here instead of me."

"What would he do?"

Scott shook his head. One corner of his mouth smiled. "He'd make clubs out of the table legs."

"Would he shoot through the door?"

"More than likely."

"I wish you had."

"Don't tell anyone, but my shooting has been limited to pistol ranges. I've never killed a man."

"That would've been a good time to start."

"Well . . ." Scott sighed. "I'm not against it—morally, I mean. Sort of a big step, though. Besides, I'd still rather take him alive. I mean, can you imagine the *story*? It'd be terrific! Do it up nonfiction. A hardbound sale. Major advertising and promotion. Whammo, a best seller!"

"Give *me* your gun," Lacey said, scrambling to her feet. She held out her hand. "Come on, give it. If you aren't willing to shoot him, I sure am."

He held onto it. "Sorry."

"Sorry won't get us out of a coffin. Now come on! You've missed two big chances to blast this bastard to hell. Let *me* do it."

"Lacey, don't get . . ."

She lunged, reaching for the automatic. Scott knocked her arm away. He shoved her backward with the table leg, its bolt biting into her chest. "Calm down!"

"You'll get us killed!" she blurted, and suddenly started to cry. She turned away. She wanted to run for the bedroom or bathroom, to let out her despair

in private, but was afraid to leave him. So she faced the wall, crying into her hands. She heard Scott approach. His arms reached forward and folded lightly across her belly.

"I won't let anything happen to you," he said, his breath warm through her hair. "I promise."

"What about your best seller?"

"I won't let him get you."

Lacey turned around. Blinking tears away, she stared up into his serious eyes. "You could shoot to wound," she said, and tried to smile.

"That's it." His fingers brushed the tears off her cheeks.

Lacey put her arms around him and shut her eyes. If she could only keep on holding him, feeling his strong body against her, the easy rise and fall of his chest, the gentle stroke of his hands on her back, then maybe nothing bad would happen.

The handle of his automatic felt flat and hard against Lacey's belly.

She might reach for it. But that would end the closeness, the trust. Better to keep that, to stay with him, than to risk losing it by going for the gun.

She felt another hardness, lower down.

Scott plucked the tails of her tank top from her shorts, and reached up inside it, caressing her back, then easing her away and moving gently to her breasts. He held them in each hand, his palms gliding against her turgid nipples. Lacey moaned. The hands continued to caress her for nearly a full second after she heard the crash of shattering glass.

Scott looked at her, stunned. "The windows!"

CHAPTER EIGHTEEN

The noise of the bursting window came from a distance, from the bathroom or bedroom. Lacey broke for the door. Dropping to a crouch, she grabbed her spray can and pocket knife. She glanced back. Scott was at the hallway entrance, pistol out.

"Let's run!" she snapped.

Scott glanced at her, frowning.

She kicked the chair. It dropped backward to the floor, and she tugged the door open.

"Come on!"

Scott whirled around and ran. He scooped up a table leg and dashed after her through the door. He jerked it shut. "Get ready. When he comes out, we'll . . ."

Lacey raced up the corridor. When she reached a corner, she looked back. Scott glanced from the door to her. She motioned for him. He muttered something through his teeth, then ran to join her.

"We had a chance . . ."

"We've got a better chance if he can't find us." She shoved open a fire door.

They entered a dimly lighted stairwell. Scott thrust the door shut and leaned against it.

"Come on," Lacey said. She started up the concrete stairs. "He'll expect us to head down."

"Where we going?"

"I don't know." She turned at the first landing, and started up the next flight of stairs. Above her, she saw the blue metal door to the fourth floor. She raced up, Scott close behind her, and grabbed the knob. As she pushed the door open, Scott patted her arm. He pressed his forefinger to his lips. They stood motionless, listening.

For a moment, Lacey heard nothing. Then the metallic sound of a springing latch echoed quietly up the stairwell.

Scott shoved the door hard. It flew open, and he pointed to the upper steps. The door banged against the outside wall as they turned away and leapt up the stairs three at a time. In seconds, they reached the landing. Lacey charged up the remaining stairs. Halfway to the top, she heard the lower door clump shut.

Would it fool him? If so, he would only be delayed long enough to leave the stairwell and glance down the fourth floor corridor.

Scott, slightly above her, was first to reach the door. He held it open for Lacey. She raced through. Scott eased it shut, turning the knob to prevent the latch from snapping back into place.

With a few steps, they passed an ice machine and rounded a corner. Scott stopped, looking each way.

To the right, the corridor led past the doors of only half a dozen rooms, then abruptly ended. To the left, it seemed to stretch on forever.

"This way," Scott muttered. He ran to the left.

Past rooms. Past a fire hose and ax. Past swinging doors of staff rooms.

Lacey, sprinting to stay beside him, saw a bank of elevators ahead. "Let's try those," she gasped.

They ran for them. The doors of all four elevators were shut. Scott threw himself against the nearest panel and jammed fingers into both buttons. Double disks of light appeared between each of the door sets: one with an arrow pointing up, the other down.

Lacey pressed herself to the wall beside him. Craning her neck, she gazed at the dark arrows above the doors. She gasped for air. The spray can and knife were slippery in her hands. She could feel the vibrations of the elevators against her back, hear the distant, quiet bells as they stopped at other floors. She looked up the corridor, squinting as if that might help her see the man's approach, then glanced again at the arrows above her. They stayed dark.

"This is no good," she whispered.

With a nod of agreement, Scott flung himself away from the wall. They left the elevators behind and dashed down the corridor. Their feet thudded on the carpet. From behind came the quiet ding of an elevator bell. Lacey looked back. They were too far away to return in time. She ran hard to catch up with Scott.

Just ahead, a hallway led off to the left. Scott slowed and turned the corner. He stopped, and Lacey halted beside him. She leaned back against an ice machine, panting for breath.

"What now?" she gasped.

Scott pointed with the club in his left hand. A yard away was a fire door.

"Might as well."

Across the hall, a door opened. A slight, young man in blue pajamas and a satin robe stepped out backward. He pulled his door shut gently so it stopped against the frame. Turning around, he smiled a surprised greeting. In his hands, he held a cardboard ice bucket.

"Cheerio," he said.

Scott lunged across the hall, grabbed the front of his robe, and thrust him into the room. Lacey followed. She shut the door quickly and silently.

"Hey now!" the man said. He seemed more offended than afraid. "What . . . ?"

Scott snarled and raised the club. The man's mouth snapped shut. He looked from Scott to Lacey, eyes narrowing behind his oversized glasses.

"We're Nick and Nora Charles," Scott said. "Asta's back in our room."

"Oh?"

Scott let go of him. The man offered a small, pale hand. "Hamlin Alexander."

After shaking hands, they moved away from the door. One of the double beds was mussed, the other neatly made.

"You alone?" Scott asked.

"I just shooed away a nymphet. I don't expect her to return in the immediate future." He set the ice bucket on the dresser beside a full bottle of Stolichnaya. "Room service didn't provide ice. Expected me

to fetch it myself, obviously. I don't suppose we might venture out for some, now that we're acquainted?"

"I don't think so," Scott said.

"If you're indeed Nick and Nora, I doubt you intend to rob or mutilate me. Would you care for a warm drink?"

They nodded, and he opened the bottle.

"I don't suppose you caught my concert tonight? Really first-rate."

"Sorry," Scott said.

Hamlin poured vodka into three glasses. "To a warm and *healthy* relationship," he toasted.

Lacey sipped her vodka. Its strong taste made her cringe, but it felt warm and pleasant going down.

"Now," said Hamlin. "To what do I owe your presence? You're not a pair of lunatic fans, obviously. Am I a hostage of choice or opportunity?"

"Opportunity," Scott told him. "You came out your door at the right time."

"The right time for you, perhaps."

Though they were talking softly, Lacey worried that their voices might carry through the door. She crossed the room and turned on the television.

"Oh please," Hamlin muttered. "Ah, I see," he said as Lacey increased the volume. "Background noise. That's about all the cyclops is good for. Now, what brings you into my august presence?"

"We're being pursued by a killer."

Hamlin raised his eyebrows, sat on his rumpled bed, and crossed his legs. "I see you're well armed."

"He has an Ingram, a small assault weapon capable of firing twenty rounds per second."

"Nasty."

"Extremely. So you can see that we'd prefer to avoid a confrontation. If he didn't see us come in, we'll be all right. Even if he knows which floor we're on, I don't think he'll take the chance of barging into every room."

"I hate to appear simplistic, but have you considered bringing in the gendarmes?"

"A special team is flying in from Washington," Scott told him. "We expect it to arrive," he checked his watch, "in roughly three, three and a quarter hours."

"Washington? So we're embroiled in a cloak-and-dagger scheme? I should have guessed; you have that clean-cut, boy-next-door, FBI look about you." He peered at Lacey as she sat down beside Scott on the other bed. "Nora, however, is not an agent. No no. Too delicate, feminine, vulnerable. I should think Nora is an innocent bystander cast by mischance into the role of heroine." He nodded shrewdly. "Perhaps a witness?"

"Very observant," Scott said.

"The fellow with the nasty weapon, a Ruskie agent?"

"Can't tell you."

"The solution to your problem is makeup. I just happen to have, in my possession, an elaborate makeup kit complete with hair, teeth, blood, and Dick Smith's Flex-Flesh. I don't *just happen* to have it—very deliberate. I often travel incognito. For security and privacy, you understand. The kit has many uses, however. The nymphets blush and cream

at the chance to be transformed into the monsters they are: zombies, hags with oozing pustules, vampires. The vampire is my specialty. Those submoronic sexpots throw themselves into the role with such abandon—snarling, baring their fangs—and it's rarely my neck they insist upon sucking. Quite delightful. I'd be more than happy to transform the two of you. Not into monsters, perhaps, but with a few deft touches and a change of clothes you might walk right past the murderous Ruskie without being recognized."

"Thanks anyway," Scott said.

"On the other hand, I might apply a multitude of wounds: bullet holes, slash marks, quantities of artificial blood. I'm superb at corpses. I'll arrange you on the floor. If your maniacal Soviet should burst through the door, he'll assume you've already been dispatched. No need to repeat the process. *Voila!*"

"That's ridiculous," Scott told him.

"It's genius. A subtle but profound difference."

"Maybe. But I still think . . ." The deafening clamor of a bell in the corridor stopped his words.

Hamlin jumped, spilling his drink.

The high-pitched ringing went on.

"Fire alarm!" Scott shouted.

"You don't think . . . ?"

Grabbing his makeshift club, Scott scurried off the bed and raced toward the door. Lacey picked up her spray can, her knife. Hurrying after him, she saw him touch the knob. "Not warm," he said. He looked back. "Hamlin," he yelled over the din. "Get over here!"

The small man rushed to them. His face, so confident before, now looked drawn and pale.

"Look out the door. See if there's smoke."

They stepped aside so they couldn't be viewed from the hallway, and Hamlin opened the door. "Appears fine," he said.

"Check around the corner."

He stepped out. Scott held the door open a crack. A moment later, Hamlin shoved through it and gazed at them. "Jesus H. Christ! The other end of the hall—all kinds of smoke. People spilling out of their rooms like . . . Christ, my horn!" He hurried past them. Seconds later, he returned with a black leather case. "Don't know about you, but I'm getting the fuck out of here!" Flinging open the door, he dashed across the hallway to the fire door.

Lacey stepped out beside Scott. Half a dozen people were now in the short hall, most in night clothes, rushing for the door. Hamlin threw it open. He coughed as dark smoke bellowed into his face. He started to shut it, but the door knocked him backward and a flaming man stumbled from the stairwell. His fiery arms reached for Hamlin, but the little man smashed them aside with his instrument case and leapt out of the way.

Screams mixed with the blaring alarm bells as the burning man staggered toward the onrushing group of guests. They scattered. Falling among them, he clutched the negligee of a horrified young woman. She lurched away, but flames were already starting to curl up her white gown. A nearby man ripped it from

her shoulders. She kicked free of the garment and threw herself into his arms.

Scott grabbed Lacey's wrist. He jerked her after him, around the corner to the long corridor. Hamlin was far ahead of them, dashing through stunned guests, dodging some, stiff-arming others aside, the black case hugged under one arm like a football. Though the far end of the corridor was gray with rolling smoke, Lacey saw no flames.

"This way's blocked," Scott yelled to an elderly couple heading toward them. The couple stopped, looking at each other with confusion as Scott and Lacey hurried by.

The greatest number of people was gathered in front of the elevator bank, screaming and shoving in a frenzy to get closer to the doors.

As Scott and Lacey reached the edge of the crowd, an elevator arrived. Its double doors slid open, but the small enclosure was already packed. A roar of protest bellowed from those inside as the mob pressed forward. Through a gap in the crowd, Lacey saw one of the men in the elevator jerked out. Amid darting fists, a new man took his place. The doors rolled halfway shut, then slid open again. A tiny, dark-haired man leapt high, clambering over the shoulders and heads of those inside, his right hand clasping a black leather case. A moment later, the doors closed.

"What'll we do?" Lacey asked.

"Forget the elev . . ."

A woman's shriek rose above the tumult. Lacey

looked, couldn't see her, then saw the bloody head of a fire ax rise above the figures at the far side of the crowd. It swung down. The mob parted, people stumbling out of the way, yelling and screaming. The ax chopped down, knocking through the up-raised arm of a man staggering backward, and split his head. As he fell, the ax swung sideways, biting into the belly of a naked woman—the one whose nightgown had caught fire earlier.

Lacey gaped as the slaughter continued, the ax chopping from side to side, catching people in the chest and belly and throat. They fought and tripped over each other, trying to get away. For an instant, Lacey glimpsed the length of the weapon. It swung, held by no one—no one she could see. It hacked through a man's neck. His severed head tumbled through the air, spraying blood.

Lacey clutched Scott's arm. "It's him!" she shouted.

"Come on!"

"Where?"

Side by side, they raced down the corridor. As they neared the corner, Lacey looked back. The ax had finished hacking its way through the mob. Splatters of blood hung suspended in the air behind it. Abruptly, it lurched forward.

Lacey gasped, and rounded the corner after Scott. He threw himself against the door of Hamlin's room—locked.

"Come on!"

They rushed farther down the short hall, leaping past the small fire spreading around the dead man like a pool of strange, burning blood.

The next door, too, was locked.

Only three remained. Scott glanced at them, apparently decided they would offer no more than this one, and drew out his automatic. He blasted a single shot through the area where the lock tongue entered the frame, and kicked the door open.

Lacey looked back.

The ax flew at her, flipping end over end.

Scott jerked her inside and slammed the door. He threw himself against it.

"Get a chair!" he yelled.

Lacey dashed across the room, grabbed a straight-backed chair from beneath the table, and ran with it to Scott. He braced it under the knob.

An instant later, the door thundered. An ax head burst through it, high up, throwing out a shower of splinters.

"You're mine!" a man's voice cried out. "Mine, cunt!"

The ax crashed again through the door, this time lower, smashing the chair down from the knob. The door flew open.

Gunfire shocked Lacey's ears, and she gazed at Scott. He was crouched and snarling, the automatic bucking in his grip as he fired shot after shot at the doorway.

Lacey covered her ears against the gun's endless roar.

The ax lunged forward, jerking in midair, and dropped to the floor.

CHAPTER NINETEEN

"Spray him," Scott snapped as he braced the door shut.

Kneeling, Lacey aimed the paint can toward the ax. She pressed down the nozzle. A fine, silvery cloud sprayed out and drifted down, spreading into a layer half a foot above the carpet. As she moved the can back and forth, the surface took on features. She saw the heavily muscled, jutting slopes of shoulder blades, and realized she must be kneeling at his head. She gave it a quick blast. The paint misted his thick hair and sprayed cool against her own thighs. With a quick sweep to the right, she coated one of his arms. Then she sprayed the other. Its thick hand still gripped the haft of the ax.

Scott crouched and pried the fingers loose. He held the wrist. "Still has a pulse," he muttered. "Hit lower, let's find the wounds."

Lacey sprayed down the long, tapering expanse of his back. She hesitated at his waist, but only for a moment. Invisibility was his greatest weapon: painting him was like cutting Samson's hair. The hell with modesty. She sprayed his buttocks.

Then she took her finger off the nozzle and stared at his shiny back, at its three gaping, ragged wounds. Looking into them, she saw the green carpet several inches down. Clear, silver-dusted fluid overflowed the holes.

At the shoulder, she saw the crater of a healed gunshot wound. Near the center of his back was a narrow, inch-long ridge. The knife wound from Wednesday night? She touched it, feeling an edge of hardness. A scab? Her finger came away wet with paint. As she wiped it on her shorts, the fire alarm stopped blaring.

She looked at Scott. He shrugged.

In the quiet, she heard distant voices.

"Maybe it's out," Scott said, his voice sounding odd in the stillness.

His hands moved from wound to wound. "I missed the heart, thank God. Not much flow. If I didn't hit a major vessel . . ." He took off his shirt, and ripped its sleeves off. Folding one of the sleeves into a thick pad, he pressed it tightly to a wound near the side of the back. "Hold it there," he said. "Hard."

While Lacey kept the pad in place, he folded his other sleeve and pressed it to a second wound, lower down. Lacey held that one for him. He tore his shirt up the back, and used one of the halves to make another compress. He pushed it against the final wound.

"Right back," he said. He hurried away and returned seconds later, holding a suitcase. He dropped

it to the floor and threw it open. Crouching, he rummaged through it. He flung out a pair of panty hose, a half slip, several pairs of briefs. "Those'll do," he muttered. He took out a leather case, jerked open its zipper, and upended it. Out fell scissors, a plastic container of rubber bands and safety pins, a tiny sewing kit, a tube of Krazy Glue, a Swiss Army knife, and a roll of adhesive tape. "Fantastic!" he blurted. He snapped open the metal canister of tape.

Tearing off a strip, he tried to secure one of the bandages in place. The tape slid on the wet paint. Scott cursed under his breath, then grabbed the torn remnant of his shirt from the floor and swabbed the man's back, clearing off excess paint around the compresses until each was surrounded by no more than a vague, translucent stain. He tested the tape: it held.

Working together, Scott and Lacey quickly secured the pads to his back.

"Let's turn him."

They rolled him onto his back.

"Don't paint him yet. I'll work by touch." He picked up a pair of nylon briefs, scowled, and tossed them aside. Then he pulled a cotton blouse from the suitcase and started to tear off its sleeves. As he folded them into pads, Lacey gazed down at the strange, sprawled shape of the man.

He looked like a legless, one-sided sculpture molded of aluminum foil. Circles of carpet were visible around his bandages. The unreality of the sight made Lacey nervous. "I want to spray him," she said. "I'll stay away from the chest."

Scott nodded. He bent over, a compress in one hand, reaching down with his other hand like a mime pretending to examine a make-believe patient.

Lacey aimed the paint can at the silver half-shell of the man's nearest arm, and sprayed. The paint wrapped over it, and the arm was suddenly human. Crawling past Scott, she sprayed the other arm. Then she scurried alongside the body. Using the concave globes of his rump as a guide, she sprayed the tops of both legs. Then she lifted them at the ankles and coated their undersides.

Scott was busy applying the final compress as Lacey shot spray from hip to hip, spreading a silver layer over the man's groin.

She stared at his penis. It lay to one side. Even flaccid, it looked thick and heavy, much larger than others she'd seen. No wonder it had felt so enormous inside her—ramming painfully, stretching her, making her bleed.

Disgusted, she looked away.

Scott met her eyes. "Are you okay?" he asked.

"Yeah."

Down the hall, someone knocked roughly on wood. "Fire's out," called a strong voice.

"Quick," Scott said. "Get the ax."

Lacey picked it up. Scott grabbed the man's hands and raised his back off the floor. He dragged him away from the door. He pulled him around a corner of the room, and let him down alongside a wall. Then he took the ax from Lacey. He lifted a corner of the mattress, and hid the ax beneath it.

"Okay," he said. "Let's go see."

"Just . . . leave him here?"

"Come on." Scott slid his automatic under the bed, and hurried to the door. As they stepped into the smoky corridor, a policeman came out of the first room—Hamlin's room. He pivoted, bringing up his service revolver.

"Thank God you're here," Scott blurted. "Some maniac . . ."

"I know." The cop holstered his pistol.

A fireman with a smudged face stepped out of the room.

"Came after us with a goddam ax," Scott said. "We were over by the elevators, and . . . Christ, did you see what he did to those people? He came after us—my wife and I . . ." Scott put an arm around Lacey. "We barely got away. He tried to bash our door down."

"What did he look like? Couldn't get a decent description from the others."

The fireman walked past them, past their broken door, and knocked on the next door down. "Fire's out," he called. "Anybody here?"

"Describe him," the cop said. Glancing at the fireman, he called, "Don't go in there without me."

"Tall, maybe six-two. Long dark hair."

"Caucasian?" the cop asked, writing on his notepad.

"Yes. Maybe thirty years old. He was wearing pajamas. Striped pajamas. Blue and white. I'm not sure, but I think he went out there." Scott pointed at the fire door across from Hamlin's room. "Didn't see

him, but the door made a metal sound, you know, like it was closing."

"ID?"

"Ours?" Scott asked.

"Please."

Scott slipped a wallet from his hip pocket. He pulled out the driver's license and handed it to the officer.

"Name?"

"Scott Bradley."

"This is your current address?"

"Yes."

He copied the information, then returned the license. "Thank you, Mr. Bradley, missus. Now you two go on downstairs, see one of the officers in the lobby."

"Can we get some things from the room?"

"Go ahead." The policeman stepped past them.

Scott and Lacey entered the room. Scott shut the door.

"Now what?" Lacey asked.

"I don't know. I've got to think. They're clearing the building. We have to get him out of here, somehow."

"Why don't we turn him over to the police?"

"Now? Are you joking? I've got to have a few hours alone with him."

"But . . ."

"We could make a million bucks off the guy. Nobody's going to get a crack at him till I've had a chance to get his story."

"If he dies . . ."

"Bite your tongue," Scott said.

They stepped around the corner and Lacey looked down at the man. His chest and face were still unpainted. The chest bandages seemed to hang in space above his silver back.

"Okay," Scott said. "Let's leave him. We'll come back and pick him up later."

Together, they pushed the body under the nearest bed. Scott retrieved his automatic. He shoved it into a front pocket, but the grips protruded. In the suitcase by the door, he found a pink bathrobe. He put it on and belted it. "How do I look?"

The robe was much too small, his shoulders straining the fabric, the sleeves reaching only halfway down his forearms.

"Pink's your color," Lacey said.

"We'd better make sure we get back here before the lady," he muttered, and turned off the lights.

CHAPTER TWENTY

Dukane brought his Cessna Bonanza in for a landing in Tucson, rented an Oldsmobile from Hertz, then sped toward the city.

He pressed a switch to lower the window, and put an arm out to catch the air. The night felt warm and dry.

Tuning in a country music station, he pressed the gas pedal to the floor. A straight, deserted road like this, no reason he shouldn't get it up to eighty. Cut off a few extra minutes. Might mean the difference to Scott.

Up against an invisible man? The more he thought about it, the crazier it sounded.

How the hell do you make a man invisible?

Even better, how do you nail him?

We shall see, Dukane thought, and began to sing along with Tom T. Hall.

When he reached downtown Tucson, he knew there was too much commotion for 3 A.M. He swung the Olds onto Garfield Street. A block ahead of him, a fire truck and a dozen police cars filled the road. Their spinning domes flung red and blue lights over the crowd of onlookers, splashed their

colors against walls and store windows. Most of the crowd's attention was focused on the hotel. The Desert Wind. Peering up through the windshield, Dukane saw no trace of fire or smoke. Except for a few broken windows, the hotel looked fine. Whatever had happened was over.

That explained why there was only a single fire truck. The others had already left. This one remained for the mop-up. Its crew might stay for a few hours, checking around, making sure the fire wasn't still burning secretly inside a wall, ready to blaze up the minute they took off.

But why all the police cars?

Easy. Because more must've happened than a fire.

He hadn't been in time to prevent it. From the look of things, whatever happened must've been an hour ago. At least. No way he could've arrived in time to help. Christ, he just hoped Scott was all right.

He turned the corner, and found an empty stretch of curb. He pulled over, took his attaché case from the backseat, and walked back to Garfield Street. Crossing to the left side, he made his way through the crowd. Many of the people were dressed in nightclothes, obviously hotel guests who'd been evacuated.

"What happened here?" he asked a man in a bathrobe.

"*Some* excitement, huh? Fire. And I hear some nut went after folks with an ax. Panicked, I guess. Killed half a dozen folks. I saw 'em cart out the bodies."

"How long ago?"

"Seems like hours. All over, now. You should've got here sooner. Brought 'em out in body bags, just like in the news. All over, now. Hope they're gonna let us in pretty soon. Got a conference at nine. Can't very well go dressed like this, can I?"

Dukane shook his head, and moved on.

A hand clapped his shoulder from behind. He whirled around and looked into the haggard, boyish face of Scott.

"Glad you made it," Scott said.

"Glad *you* did."

"Dukane, this is Lacey Allen."

She nodded a greeting. Her hair was mussed, her face dirty or bruised, the tail of her tank top half untucked.

"Let's go to my car," he said. "We can talk there."

"So he's still in that room," Scott finished, "unless he walked off."

"Or the police found him," said Dukane.

"If they did, they haven't brought him out."

"Not that we saw," Lacey added, and stubbed out her cigarette in the car's ashtray.

"What'll we do?" Scott asked.

"If you're so determined to get his life story, I suppose we'll have to go up there and bring him out. Lacey, you'd better wait here. They'll have found the editor's body in your room. They'll be looking for you, and we can't have you pulled in for questioning just now. Scott, take off that silly robe."

"But my Colt . . ."

"Leave it with Lacey."

In the hotel lobby, Dukane showed a false FBI credential to the officer in charge, explaining he needed to retrieve paperwork from his room. He and Scott were allowed to pass.

As they stepped into an elevator, two men in plain clothes joined them. Dukane pushed a button for the fifth floor.

"Which floor?" he asked the men.

"Same."

The door closed, and the elevator started upward.

"Are you gentlemen guests of the hotel?" asked the taller of the two. He was about forty, with neatly trimmed black hair and the weary, cynical eyes common to cops. He appeared in better shape than his younger buddy. From the thickness of his neck, Dukane guessed that he worked out with weights.

"We're on official business," Dukane said.

"ID?"

Dukane showed it.

"FBI, huh? I'm impressed. Aren't we impressed, Arthur?"

"I know I am," said Arthur.

"What about you?" he asked Scott.

"Me?" Grinning, Scott scratched his bare chest. "I'm impressed, too."

The man didn't look amused. "Got an ID?"

"He's with me," said Dukane.

The doors opened, and all four left the elevator.

A uniformed cop nodded to the other pair. He glanced at Dukane and Scott.

"Let them pass," said the tall one. "FBI." He pointed to a dark pool of blood. "Try not to step in it."

"We'll be careful," Dukane said.

Scott nodded to the left.

"Hope you catch him," Dukane told the men, and started away.

"We're not the FBI, but we sometimes do get our man."

"I'm sure you do."

"Come along, Arthur." The pair turned to the right and started up the corridor.

Dukane and Scott walked the other way. As they reached the corner, Dukane glanced back. The uniformed cop was still near the elevator bank. The two in plain clothes had nearly arrived at the far end of the corridor.

"Lucky they didn't come with us," Scott said.

"We're not out of here yet."

Halfway up the short hall, Dukane spotted the battered door. He entered first, stepping over the strewn contents of a suitcase. Women's clothing.

Scott pointed to the first bed.

They crouched beside it. Dukane lifted the draping edge of the coverlet. In the space below the bed, he saw a naked, silver-skinned man. He grabbed an arm, and dragged the man out.

"Good Christ," Dukane muttered, staring at the empty face, at the bandages suspended over the hollow chest cavity. He laid a hand on the chest. He

felt the texture and warmth of skin where none was visible, felt the slow rise and fall of breathing. "I'll be damned," he said. "I never would've believed it."

"Thought I was kidding you?"

"Not exactly. Just figured you were mistaken, somehow. But he's invisible, all right."

"How'll we get him out of here?"

"Won't be easy. Especially the way he looks." Dukane swiped a finger over the paint. It was dry. "Got any turpentine?"

Scott made a feeble laugh.

"Too bad he's not completely invisible when it would do us some good. Where's your room?"

"Third floor."

"You still have the key?"

"Sure."

"Go downstairs and bring up your luggage. You have extra clothes?"

Scott nodded.

"They'll be a tight fit on this guy, but we can't haul him out of here looking like this."

"What about his face?"

"I don't know. Go get your stuff, though. Take the stairs. I don't want you running into more cops."

Scott stood up. He started to turn away, but hesitated. "You know, Matt . . . those cops. The plain clothes guys? They looked familiar to me. I can't quite place them, but . . ." He chewed his lower lip. "They worry me."

"Think about it. In the meantime, get your stuff up here."

"Right."

While Scott was gone, Dukane searched the suit-case of the room's occupant. He found no makeup, so he checked the bathroom. There, on a shelf above the sink, was a blue canvas satchel. He un-snapped it, folded it open, and studied the contents neatly arranged inside clear plastic pockets: Q-tips, skin moisturizer, fingernail polish and remover, blush-on, mascara, lipstick, an eyebrow pencil, and a tiny tan bottle of makeup base. He took out the bottle of base, dabbed a bit of the fluid onto his fin-gertip, and tapped it on the mirror. The smudge was opaque, and nearly flesh-colored. A bit too dark, with a reddish tinge, but close enough.

He took the bottle into the bedroom. Kneeling down, he poured the beige fluid onto the man's face and spread it evenly. The face took form under his fingers. He saw the broad forehead, the prominent cheekbones, the hollow cheeks, the long narrow nose. As he progressed, he wished he had shaved the man. The makeup clung to his heavy eyebrows, gave his whiskers the look of spiky, mutated skin.

At the sound of footsteps, Dukane drew his auto-matic from its shoulder holster. Scott came in, swinging his suitcase and attaché case onto the bed.

"Any trouble?" Dukane asked.

"Didn't meet a soul. But I remembered about the cops. I saw them at dinner tonight."

"Where?"

"At Carmen's, a couple of miles from here. They sat at a table across from us. Maybe it's just a coinci-dence . . ."

"A surveillance team."

"Why would cops be watching Lacey and me?"

"Good question."

Scott opened his suitcase. He tossed a sport coat, shirt, and a pair of trousers to the floor.

"Sunglasses?"

"Yeah."

"We could use a hat."

"He'd better not lose it," Scott said, and removed a battered, tan fedora from his suitcase. He took out a shirt for himself. "You did a nice job on his face."

"If those cops were watching you, they might be showing up. Better watch the door. I'll dress our friend."

Scott left.

Dukane slid the brown trousers up the man's legs, tugging to get them over his buttocks. They were a tight fit, but he managed to hook the waist shut. The bulky, silver privates still hung outside the fly. Dukane hesitated, reluctant to touch them. Holding his breath as if he were handling excrement, he tucked the scrotum into the pants, then pushed the penis inside. As he started to withdraw his hand, silver fingers grabbed it and pressed it to the soft flesh.

Dukane jerked his hand away.

The man chuckled.

Backing off, Dukane drew the automatic from his shoulder holster.

"You don't need that," said a quiet, raspy voice. "I'm going with you guys."

"Explain."

"I been listening. Don't know who you are, but

you're not with The Group. You get me out of here, protect me, I won't give you no trouble. I'll do whatever you want. You name it. Just don't let the others take me."

"A deal," he said, but didn't lower the gun. "How are you feeling?"

"Like I got the shit kicked out of me. I been shot before, only not this bad."

"Those wounds should've killed you."

"Not me, man. I'm Sammy Hoffman, Wonder Man. Takes more than a few fuckin' bullets to switch me off."

"Can you sit up?"

Grimacing, he pushed himself off the floor. He raised his arms in front of his face, and turned them. "Fuck, man, I look like the Tin Woodsman."

"Put on this shirt."

He took it. "Where's my pal, Lacey?"

"Waiting outside."

"She going with us?"

"Yes."

"Oh good." He drew the shirt taut across his chest and buttoned it. Dukane gave him the sport coat. "You guys gonna try and walk me out of here?"

"That's the idea." He found a pair of socks in Scott's suitcase, and tossed them to Hoffman.

"Those bastards from the Group'll give us trouble."

"We'll handle it."

"Man, you better. They want my ass." He finished putting on the socks.

"Put your hands on top of your head."

"Hey, come on."

"Do it," Dukane said, and tugged handcuffs out of his rear pocket. He stepped behind Hoffman, pulled one arm down behind him, cuffed it, then brought down the other arm and snapped the second bracelet around its wrist.

He put the sunglasses on Hoffman's face, concealing the empty eye sockets. Then he placed Scott's old fedora on the man's head. "Okay, on your feet."

Hoffman stood up.

Dukane led him to the door, where Scott was crouched and peering through the ax holes.

"Any sign of our friends?"

"Looks clear." Scott turned, glanced at Hoffman, and wrinkled his nose. "He doesn't look like much."

"It's the best I can do. He'll pass, as long as nobody gets a close look."

"Long as they're a mile off."

"Better leave your luggage here."

"Gotta bring my galleys. And recorder." He hurried away, and returned a few seconds later with his attaché case.

They left the room, Dukane holding Hoffman's right arm, Scott his left. Dukane shoved open the fire door.

Two revolvers pointed at his chest. Two men grinned.

"Greetings," said the taller one. "Come in, come in. Don't just stand there."

They stepped onto the landing.

"Well Arthur, looks like the FBI got their man— *our* man. Tough rocks, Sammy. That *is* you, I take it."

"Go fuck yourself, Trankus."

"You're not an easy guy to catch. I must thank you fellows, and of course Miss Allen, for being of such invaluable assistance."

"Glad to help," Dukane said. He glanced at Scott. "Don't try anything."

Scott nodded.

Arthur frisked him, taking his knife. Then he took away Dukane's automatic and switchblade.

"Very good," said Trankus.

"Glad to cooperate with the police."

"Now, let me lay out our alternatives. Arthur and I are, of course, bona fide members of the Tucson Police Department. As such, we'll be able to walk you three gentlemen out of the hotel, no questions asked. We will then transport you to the destination of our choice."

"Not the police station, I assume."

"True. You're a bright fellow, probably not FBI at all."

"Just a regular guy."

"Valuable catches, all three of you. Wonderful bonuses for us, if we deliver you intact. On the other hand, Sammy is top priority. You two are quite expendable, whoever you are. Therefore, if you make any attempt to resist us, we shall cheerfully expend you. Right now, if you prefer."

"We won't resist," Dukane said.

"Excellent. You two hold onto Sammy, and precede us down the stairs. When we reach the lobby, we'll leave by the main door."

"Whatever you say."

Keeping their grips on Hoffman, they started down the stairs.

"You fuckers aren't gonna let these guys have me?" he whispered.

"We don't have much choice."

"You're nuts. You don't know what they'll do to you. You never been questioned by The Group, man. They'll stick an electric wire up your dick . . ."

"Knock it off," Trankus said.

"You guys are better off shot dead here on the stairs. I'm telling you . . ."

"Where there's life, there's hope," said Trankus.

"Not if they get you to the compound."

"Compound?" asked Dukane. "What's that?"

"Get me out of here, and I'll take you. A guided fuckin' tour."

"You always did have stupid ideas," Trankus said. "That's what got you into this mess. How could you have *imagined* you'd get away with it?"

"Done all right, till now."

"Certainly. Our people have been following your progress, Sammy. For an invisible man, you left a wonderfully visible trail. A word of advice, though it's a bit late—always conduct your affairs in such a way as to stay out of the news."

"Thanks."

They reached the door to the lobby. "Stop," Trankus said. He stepped past them, and pushed open the door.

They drew curious glances as they crossed the lobby. "Looters," Trankus explained. That seemed to satisfy the other cops.

In seconds, they were outside.

"What about Lacey?" Dukane asked.

"For Christsake!" Scott snapped.

"Oh, we wouldn't forget Miss Allen." When they reached the side street, Trankus said, "This way." Apparently, he knew just where to find the car.

They walked up the center of the deserted street.

As they neared the car, Dukane saw Lacey watching through a window. He raised a hand as if to scratch his belly, made a fist with his forefinger protruding and worked his thumb up and down.

They reached the car.

"Miss Allen, would you care to join us?" Trankus pressed the muzzle of his revolver against Dukane's ear.

Dukane nodded.

Lacey swung open the driver's door. She held Scott's automatic at her waist.

Dukane threw his arm up, knocking Trankus's pistol back. The blast deafened him, scorched the nape of his neck. A second blast, from the car, caught Trankus in the chest.

Arthur crouched and aimed at Lacey.

Hoffman started to run.

Scott swung his attaché case, smashing aside Arthur's pistol.

Dukane tripped Hoffman. As the man tumbled to the street, Scott drove two fingers into Arthur's eyes, then chopped his throat. Grabbing Trankus's gun off the pavement, Dukane put a bullet into Arthur's head.

They retrieved the other weapons.

Then they dragged Hoffman to the car and flung him into the backseat. Dukane climbed in on top of him. Scott shoved Lacey into the passenger seat, and the car sped away.

CHAPTER TWENTY-ONE

Lacey sat huddled against the passenger door, shaking as her mind replayed the kick of the pistol, the stunned look on the man's face when her bullet slammed into him, the way he flopped backward with his hands groping the air. She told herself it was necessary, she *had* to shoot him. That didn't help. She felt cold and sick.

At first, the car hurled up the street, skidded around a corner, then around another corner. Lacey held tightly to the door handle as the momentum tugged at her.

Then the car slowed to a moderate speed.

"Looks all right behind," Dukane said.

"Where to?"

"The desert?"

"Which way?"

"This way's fine. I'll tell you when to turn."

Scott nodded, then looked over at Lacey. "How are you doing?"

"Rotten."

"You did great."

"Who . . . who were they?"

159

"Apparently from some group that's after Hoffman."

"Hoffman?"

"Our invisible friend," Scott said. "His name is Samuel Hoffman."

"Elsie's son?"

"That's right," Hoffman muttered.

"My God! He did that . . . butchered her that way? His own mother?"

"She was a cunt," came the rough voice from the backseat. "Same as you."

"Shut up," snapped Dukane.

Turning, Lacey looked around at the man beside Dukane. The hat was gone. So were the sunglasses. The eyeless blur of face looked grotesque and unfamiliar, more like a death's head than the face of Sammy Hoffman. She quickly turned away.

She hadn't seen Sammy in nearly ten years, not since the day he attacked Miss Jones. But she remembered the way he always stared at her. Sometimes, he even followed her.

Then came the night in her bedroom. She always liked to open the curtains, after getting into her nightgown, so the sun would fill her room in the morning. This time, when she opened them, she found a monster staring up at her, its nose and cheek mashed crooked against the window screen. She screamed. The hideous face lurched back, its features returning to normal, and she recognized Sammy. "You creep!" she shrieked as he dashed away. "You goddamn creep!"

Her father phoned Sammy's parents, that night.

They were furious, said they would make Sammy wish he'd never been born. They must have carried out their threat, too; the next morning, Sammy showed up in class with a black eye and welts on his arms.

That was the day he attacked Miss Jones. Lacey never heard for sure, but rumor claimed that he raped the young teacher. Afterward, Lacey felt sick when she thought about it. Had she been to blame, somehow? It only made her feel worse to realize how glad she was that Sammy had chosen the teacher to rape, not her.

Well, he'd got her at last. Over and over again. She pressed her thighs tightly together, as if to prevent him from getting between them once more.

Looking out the windshield, she saw that they had left the city behind. The desert road was dark except for a half-moon and the bright tunnel of the headlights. Off to the sides, the terrain looked bleak and rugged. Saguaro cacti stood in the distance like lonely, disfigured men watching them pass. Occasionally, she saw a house. They were few and dark.

She wished she were home and safe, and Sammy Hoffman far away, locked up where he could never get at her again. Locked up or dead.

"Make a left here," Dukane said.

Slowing the car, Scott turned onto a narrow, two-lane road.

"We'll find a place to hole up, get your friend's story."

"Gonna write me up?" Hoffman asked.

"Lacey and I," Scott said, "want to write a book

about you. We want to get your whole story on tape."

"Don't waste your time. Laveda, she'll see you never live to do it."

"Laveda?" Dukane asked, sounding shocked. "She's mixed up in this?"

"Mixed up? Hell, she's it. She's behind the whole fuckin' thing. And you're all on her list, now. They know you've been with me. They've gotta shut you up. Too bad, huh Lacey? I hate to see good quiff get wasted."

Lacey heard Hoffman grunt.

"Just pointing out the facts of life."

Scott glanced at Lacey. "You'll be okay. We'll take care of you."

"Is he right, though? Will they try to kill us?"

"They won't get us," Dukane said.

"What's to stop them?"

"Me and Scott."

"I'm glad *you're* so confident," Lacey said.

"If necessary, we'll set ourselves up with new identities."

"I don't think I'd like that," she said, and stared out the window. A new identity. No more Lacey Allen, no more Oasis. Life in a strange town, always afraid the truth will be uncovered and the hunters will come. On the other hand, she no longer had strong ties to Oasis. After her parents were killed in a car crash, she'd simply stayed on because the town was familiar and comfortable. Most of her childhood friends had moved on. The job at the *Tribune* was pleasant and secure, but she'd often felt rest-

less, had thought of heading out for a more challenging job in LA, or San Francisco. Only inertia held her back. Why abandon the safe, routine life of Oasis for the unknown? Someday, maybe. Someday she would just up and leave. Alone, if she had to. But she always imagined a man would come along, one day, and take her hand, and lead her into a new life.

The man, apparently, was Sammy Hoffman. But he didn't lead her into a new life, he dragged her screaming.

She wished for the old security, the peace she'd known before he came along. But it was gone forever. She'd been terrorized, beaten and raped, she'd seen people butchered, she'd killed a man herself, and now she was faced with a life of hiding.

She suddenly realized, with a mixture of regret and excitement, that she had already lost Lacey Allen. Lacey had died, had been reborn into a new and horrible world. No longer the same person, she deserved a new name.

A natural step, when the rest of your identity has changed so completely. Maybe the new Lacey, whatever her name might be, would make a better life for herself. The old one hadn't done so well, not really. This was a chance to abandon her old ways, to seek out what she had missed.

"Might not be so bad," she said.

"What?" Scott asked.

"Starting over."

"Better than the alternative," said Dukane.

"Don't worry about it, Lacey."

"She better worry about it," Hoffman said. "You all better. Only way I stayed alive, this long, is 'cause I'm invisible."

"There is another solution," Dukane said.

"Yeah? I'd like to hear it."

"Kill Laveda."

Hoffman made a single, husky laugh. "Sure thing. You saw how easy it is to kill me? All those fuckin' bullets and here I am, like nothing happened? Well, Laveda made me that way. And next to her, I'm nothing. I bet I don't have a tenth of her powers. You're crazy if you think you can kill . . ."

"Damn," Dukane muttered. "There's a car behind us. No headlights. About half a mile back."

"How long's it been there?"

"I just spotted it. The moon caught its windshield, I think. Could've been on our tail since Tucson."

"I thought you said we were clear."

"Thought we were."

Looking over her shoulder, Lacey glanced at the grotesque, eyeless face of Hoffman and felt the back of her neck prickle. She quickly turned her attention to the rear window. She saw the red glow of their own taillights, the pale moonlit strip of road, but no other car. "I don't see it," she said.

"It's there."

"Police?" Scott asked.

"Cops wouldn't run blind."

"You guys gotta do something," Hoffman said. He sounded scared. "They got us spotted, they'll start coming out of the fuckin' woodwork."

"Not much woodwork around here," Dukane said.

"You got no idea, man. No idea. You think we've got guys in the cops, we've got 'em *everywhere*. Every fuckin' corner of the country. Man, I'm top priority. There ain't nothing they won't do to nail my ass. They'll swarm us. We'll be dead meat in an hour."

"Calm down."

"You gotta get this *paint* off me!"

"Shut up. Scott, cut the lights as we round this bend, then swing off the road. See if we can't lose 'em."

As the headlights died, Lacey faced front and grabbed her door handle. The car swerved to the left and sped off the road, lurching over the rough ground, slamming down a cactus that stood in the way like a man with upraised arms, bounding over hillocks and landing hard, finally careening down the steep side of a gully. Lacey threw a hand against the dash as the car slid to a stop.

"Watch Hoffman," Dukane said, and leapt from the car.

"I ain't going nowhere."

Lacey saw Dukane scramble to the top of the gully and sprawl flat. She opened the glove compartment. With trembling hands, she took out a cigarette and lit it. She inhaled deeply, held the smoke inside, and slowly blew it out.

Hoffman coughed. "Bad for your health," he said. Then he laughed softly. "Not that it matters. None of us gonna live long enough for cancer."

"Shut up," Scott said.

She was nearly down to the filter by the time Dukane returned.

"It went by," he said through the window.

"It'll be back," said Hoffman. "The fuckers are psychic."

Ignoring him, Dukane stepped to the front of the car and crouched down. "Oh shit," he muttered. "I thought so. Broken axle."

"What'll we do?" Scott asked.

"Walk."

CHAPTER TWENTY-TWO

They traveled parallel to the road, well away from it so they wouldn't be spotted if a car should pass. They only saw the road, themselves, when they sometimes reached higher ground.

Scott carried both attaché cases. Dukane, pistol in hand, walked behind Hoffman. Lacey stayed close to Scott, her eyes on the rough ground.

A long time had passed since Lacey's last hike in the desert. She remembered that time clearly. She was with Brian. They left his car by the road, and walked for nearly an hour in the fresh warmth of early morning. He took photos with his Polaroid: of cacti, of wildflowers, of lizards, of Lacey. They drank wine and ate cheese. The heat and alcohol made her tipsy. When she got tipsy, she got horny. They stripped and took pictures of each other, and that turned her on even more, and finally they spread their clothes on the burning ground and made love.

She looked at Scott, walking slightly ahead and to her right. His shirt clung to his back with sweat. His wallet made a bulge over his left buttock. She remembered the feel of him during those seconds

when they embraced in the hotel room. If only they hadn't been interrupted . . .

Three years, now, since she'd taken a man in her arms, into her body.

Except for Hoffman.

He doesn't count.

She felt his hardness plundering her, and her excitement turned into an icy knot of revulsion. She watched him walking beside Dukane, the back of his head silver in the moonlight, his hands cuffed behind him. He looked undamaged. Why hadn't the bullets killed him, damn it? She should've grabbed Scott's gun, when they had him down, and pumped a few rounds into his head.

Maybe she still could.

But that would end Scott's dream of a best seller.

Besides, she didn't know if she could kill another person—even Hoffman. The look on that man's face when her bullet hit him . . .

A dead saguaro lay at her feet like a rotting corpse. She stepped over it.

"Ah ha!" Dukane said, and pointed.

On a distant rise of land stood a small house. Its windows were dark, its stone walls pale. A pickup truck stood in front of it.

"The gods are smiling on us," Scott said.

Lacey guessed the house was half a mile away, and set far back from the road—far enough, she hoped, so that it hadn't been noticed by those in the other car. Of course, they must've seen its entry drive. Maybe they'd already checked the place and moved on.

The house vanished as she made her way down the side of a gully.

Hoffman grunted. He stumbled, fell headlong, and tumbled to the bottom. "Shit!" he snapped, rolling onto his back. "Fuckin' handcuffs!"

Dukane pulled him to his feet.

"Get these things off me, 'fore I kill myself."

"That's hardly likely."

"Damn it, take 'em off! What do you think I'll do, run for it? Where'll I go? I'm with you guys, now. You're my only chance. I wouldn't break for it if I could, not with The Group on our fuckin' tails. I'm yours. Get me someplace safe. Man, those bastards are gonna roast me. Just let me have my hands so I don't bust my damn neck. That asking too much? I ain't gonna be any good to you guys with a busted neck."

Dukane took a key from his pocket.

"Don't," Lacey warned.

"We'll cuff him in front."

"No! For Christsake, he'll get loose!"

"It's risky," Scott said. "He's stronger than you'd think."

"Okay. I'll lay down. How's that?" Hoffman asked, dropping to his knees. "Can't run if I'm lying down, right?" He fell forward, landing on his side, and rolled to his belly. "Just put the cuffs in front. That'll be okay. You oughta try walking in this fuckin' desert with your hands behind your back, see how you like it."

Dukane crouched over him.

"Wait!" Lacey said. "Maybe he tripped on purpose.

Just so he'd have an excuse for you to take off the cuffs."

"Shut the fuck up," Hoffman snapped.

"He didn't have much trouble before. Now, when we're in easy shot of a pickup truck, he suddenly can't stay on his feet."

"Stupid cunt."

"Lacey's right," Scott said.

"Yeah. Okay, up."

"Up *yours*. I'm not taking one more step till you change the cuffs. You want to drag me? Go ahead. Have fun."

"What happened to your spirit of cooperation?" Dukane asked.

"You can fuckin' carry me."

"Is that your last word on the subject?"

"Damn right."

"Sorry to hear that." Dukane stepped close to Hoffman's head.

"Are we gonna carry him?" Scott asked.

"I think he'll decide to walk."

"Think again, asshole."

Dukane stomped on his head, smashing his face into the gravel floor of the gully. Lacey cringed, shocked by the sudden violence. As she turned away, Scott took her into his arms. She pressed her face to his chest. Behind her, Hoffman's yell of pain became hysterical gasping.

"You . . . you . . . oh you bastard! I'll kill you, I'll kill you!"

"You'll walk with us," Dukane said, his voice quiet and calm.

"I'll tear out your heart, you motherfuckin' . . ."

Lacey heard a thud, a grunt.

"You . . . !"

"Time to go," Dukane said. "You won't like it, if I lose my patience."

"It's all right," Scott whispered. He eased Lacey away, and she saw Dukane jerking the man to his feet.

"My *face*!"

"Not much loss, Hoffman. Nobody can see it, anyway."

Hoffman turned to Lacey. She stared at his moonlit face, its eyeless sockets, its snarling mouth, gaps in its forehead and left cheek where the make-up or skin had been scraped off, a few patches of tinted flesh hanging like torn cloth. "Your fault," he told her. "I'll get you for this."

"You'll get no one," Dukane said, and shoved him toward the slope.

They climbed out of the gully. The house seemed no closer than before. Lacey wondered if its occupants had heard Hoffman's outcries. Noise carries far in the desert, just as it does over water. But the windows were still dark. Perhaps the walls of the gully had contained most of the sound. Or maybe those in the house were heavy sleepers.

Lacey hoped the house was deserted. That seemed unlikely, though, with a pickup parked in front.

Along the way, Hoffman fell several more times as if to prove his point. Each time, he cursed the handcuffs that stopped him from catching himself. But he didn't stay long on the ground. He struggled quickly to his feet, looking around at Dukane.

Finally, they made their way up the low hill to the house. They took a path through the cactus garden at its side.

"Give me your shirt, Scott."

Without hesitation, Scott took off his shirt and handed it over. Dukane draped it over Hoffman's head and used his own belt to cinch it around the neck.

"Want me to go around back?" Scott asked.

Dukane shook his head. "Let's play it straight." Holstering his pistol, he took Hoffman's elbow and led the way to the front door. He pressed the doorbell. From inside the house came a quiet ring of chimes.

They waited.

He rang again.

A light came on above the door.

"State your business," called a voice from inside—the voice of a young woman.

"Our car broke down," Dukane said. "We'd like to use your phone."

"I don't have one. Go on, get out of here."

"We're worn out," Lacey said. "At least let us have some water. We've been walking a long time."

"Use the tap by the garden," she called. "You're not getting in here. I saw you coming. You've got guns."

"We're FBI, ma'am," Dukane told her.

"Sure. And I'm John Edgar Hoover."

"She hasn't got a phone anyway," Lacey whispered.

"Okay, Scott. Get over there and hotwire the pickup."

With a nod, Scott turned away.

"All right, lady," Dukane said. "We'll leave."

"That's just fine."

Lacey turned to follow Scott, and grabbed his arm as a woman with a double-barreled shotgun lurched upright in the pickup's bed.

"No you *don't*!" yelled the woman.

CHAPTER TWENTY-THREE

The front door swung open. A woman stepped out with a revolver. She was slim, no older than twenty, with black hair cropped short. Though she must have had plenty of time to dress, she wore only a short pink nightgown. Apparently, thought Lacey, she'd been determined to keep them out.

"Put down your guns," she said.

Dukane nodded to Scott. They set a total of four pistols on the ground: two of their own, plus the two they'd taken from Trankus and his partner.

"They were planning to make off with the truck," said the other woman, climbing down. "Otherwise, I would've let them go." She was larger than the one in the doorway, with broad hips, and breasts that swung loosely inside her T-shirt.

"What'll we do?" asked the smaller one.

"Let's get them inside and call the police."

"You *do* have a phone," Dukane said.

"Of course."

"Okay, inside."

The small one backed into the house, waving her revolver. The one with the shotgun took up the rear. When they were all inside, she shut the door.

"Okay, Nancy, call the cops."

"Don't do that," Dukane said. "Here, look at my credentials." He handed his wallet to the girl with the pistol.

She slipped it open and stared. "Says he's FBI, Jan."

"Anybody can get a fake ID."

"We were escorting our prisoner to Tucson when our car broke down."

"What's he doing with a shirt on his head?" Jan asked.

"He's deformed," Dukane explained. "We put the shirt over him to spare you the sight."

"Bullshit," Jan said.

"It's true," Lacey told her.

"They covered my head 'cause they kidnapped me and don't want you seeing who they've got. They snatched me this morning. I'm Watson Jones, vice president for Wells Fargo . . ."

"Can it, Hoffman."

"Let him talk," said Jan.

"They're holding me for two million bucks. The three of 'em, they're in it together. Look, get these cuffs off me, huh? Dukane, he's got a key."

"Heard about a kidnapping?" Jan asked Nancy.

"No."

"They ain't released it to the news."

With relief, Lacey saw a wry smile on Jan's face.

"For the vice president of a bank, buster, you ain't got such good grammar."

"He's a rapist and murderer," Dukane said.

"That's a con! Get his fuckin' key before he grabs your guns."

175

"Nobody's going to grab your guns," Dukane said. "This is your house. Fine with us if you want to hold the artillery. As I said before, we just want the use of your telephone. I need to call headquarters so they can pick us up."

"We'd better call the cops. Nancy?"

"You don't want to do that," Dukane said.

"Yes, I think we do."

Nancy walked backward across the red ceramic tile of the living room, and lowered herself onto a couch. She reached out for a telephone on the lamp table.

"Where'd she go?" Hoffman blurted. "What's she doing? Don't let her call!"

"If you make that call," Dukane said, "it's quite possible we'll all be dead by morning."

Nancy looked at Jan.

"Explain yourself," Jan said.

"Our friend here belongs to a certain organization— a cult that wants him back. They have connections inside the Tucson police."

"Suppose we call the Highway Patrol?"

"They may or may not be infiltrated. I don't know about that. But I do know this: if you phone in, they'll dispatch a car to this location by radio. Any joker with a Bearcat scanner will know right where to find us."

"We'll be dead meat," Hoffman said.

"What do you think?" Jan asked her friend.

Nancy shook her head, looking confused.

"It's all too damned fishy for me. Go ahead and call the Highway Patrol."

"Don't," Dukane warned.

Nancy lifted the receiver and dialed for the operator. "Hello? I'd like the number . . ."

"Please," Lacey said, starting forward. "Put it down."

Jan swung the shotgun toward her. At that instant, Dukane leapt. He caught Jan around the hips, throwing her backward. The shotgun fired.

As its roar stunned Lacey's ears, she saw the base of the phone jump from the table, exploding, crashing into the lamp behind it. Phone and lamp flew against the blasted wall. Dukane and Jan hit the floor.

Scott rushed Nancy. The girl, frozen by the blast that barely missed her, offered no resistance. She sat on the couch, phone receiver still in her right hand, gazing at the splintered table surface as Scott freed the revolver from her left hand.

"What happened?" Hoffman yelled. "Somebody take this fuckin' shirt off my head! Who got shot?"

Dukane, on top of Jan, shoved the shotgun across the floor. She stopped struggling. As he pinned her arms, they both gazed toward Nancy.

"She's okay," Dukane said.

"Get off me," Jan muttered.

He climbed off, and went for the shotgun. Jan hurried to the couch. She sat down and put an arm around the girl. "I'm sorry," she said. "I almost . . ." She began to cry. The daze left Nancy's face. Her chin trembled, and she lay her head against Jan's breast.

"Why don't you all just get out of here," Jan

blurted. "Get the hell out. Take the pickup. Just get out of here."

"Where are the keys?" Dukane asked, his voice gentle.

"My purse. In the kitchen."

He went for them, and returned a moment later. "I'll see that the truck's returned to you," he said.

"Just get out."

"Come on," he said.

They went outside, leaving the two women on the couch. Dukane lowered the tailgate. He and Scott lifted Hoffman onto the truck bed. "I'll ride in the back with him," he said, climbing aboard with the shotgun.

They closed the tailgate. Scott lifted the two attaché cases over the side panel. He took the pistols off the ground, and gave two of them to Dukane.

"You take this," he said, handing Nancy's revolver to Lacey.

They climbed into the cab.

As Scott started the truck, Lacey saw Jan gazing out one of the front windows of the house.

"They'll be all right," Scott said.

"Now that we're gone."

"Yeah." He pulled the truck away from the house, with the headlights off, and sped up the long, narrow road. The deep blue of the sky was lighter in the east. Lacey wondered at it, for a moment, then realized the night was nearly over.

She leaned back and shut her eyes. She felt weary and sick, but not sleepy. Taking a deep breath, she was nearly overcome by nausea. Her mind whirled

with images of Nancy's shocked face, the face of the man she had shot, the screams as Hoffman chopped through the crowd at the elevators, little Hamlin Alexander leaping into the packed elevator, the knife plunging into Carl's throat. She snapped open her eyes. "Oh God," she muttered.

"It'll soon be over." Scott patted her leg.

"All this death . . ."

"I know."

And then she saw a dark car ahead of them on the road, its doors open, men crouched behind the doors with guns.

"Down!" Scott yelled, and hit the brakes.

CHAPTER TWENTY-FOUR

Lacey flung herself sideways as the night exploded. Scott dropped in front of her, his back striking her nose, shoving at her breasts. Dazed, she wondered if he'd been hit. But she felt him moving. Then the truck lurched backward. It gained speed. The rear end swerved and she felt the truck bound off the smoothness of the road. It rose. It pounded down. Through the gunfire and roar of the engine, she heard rapid thunks like a dozen hammers pounding metal. The tail of the truck swung back. She felt the smoothness again.

Raising her head, she saw the blasted windshield and Scott's hand gripping the side of the steering wheel. As she looked, a bullet blasted through the top of the wheel. She ducked again.

The truck sped wildly, bumped off the other side of the road, swerved back, stayed on the pavement for a while, then lurched off again.

The shooting stopped. She felt Scott raise himself slightly, perhaps enough to peer out. Then he moved higher. He sat up. Lacey lifted her head. The road had turned. The other car was out of sight.

Scott floored the gas pedal.

"You okay?" he asked.

"Yeah." Sitting up, she realized her nose was bleeding. She licked the blood from her upper lip, wiped it with the back of her hand.

The truck skidded to a stop. They were in front of the house again. Looking down the road, Lacey saw no sign of the car. She jumped from the cab and followed Scott to the house. He unlocked the door. Stepping inside, she scanned the living room. Deserted.

She returned to the truck and grabbed the attaché cases while Scott and Dukane hustled Hoffman to the ground. He fell. As Dukane stood over him, Scott climbed into the pickup. Lacey watched him drive the smoking vehicle along the front of the house and through the cactus garden. At the edge of the slope, he jumped clear. The pickup plunged down. She heard it bang and slam. She expected it to explode, but it didn't.

"Why'd he do that?" she asked Dukane.

"The truck's no good. Too shot up. No point giving the bastards any extra cover."

"At least we don't have the ladies to contend with," Scott said as he returned. "They hightailed it. I saw 'em out there, running like a couple of jackrabbits."

"They're best out of it," Dukane said.

He and Dukane grabbed Hoffman and dragged him into the house. Lacey shut the door, locked it.

"Get the lights," Dukane said.

Lacey switched off the outside light, then stepped to the near end of the couch and turned off the remaining lamp. Darkness filled the room.

"Watch out the window, Lacey. Scott, give me a hand. We'd better secure our friend."

They pulled Hoffman to his feet and led him out of the living room.

Moving a rocker away, Lacey knelt at a front window. The road was deserted. In the east, the sky was a pale blue. She took a deep, shaky breath, and touched the skin beneath her nostrils. The bleeding had stopped. She folded her arms on the windowsill, and rested her chin on her hands.

She thought of Jan and Nancy running through the desert, and wished she were with them. Running. Leaving all this behind. But she couldn't leave Scott. She would stick this out with him, see it through to the end.

She thought of the old movie, *Bonnie and Clyde*— the ambush, bullets ripping into Warren Beattie and Faye Dunaway, making their bodies dance and writhe as if in a horrible orgasm.

Maybe it wouldn't hurt so much. You must go into shock right away. And then it's over.

The glow of the sun reached over the horizon, casting gold across the desert. She lay her forehead down on her folded hands, and wept.

"It's all right," said a voice behind her. Scott's voice. His hands slipped under her armpits, and he lifted her. He turned her around to face him. "It's all right," he said, more softly. His fingertips brushed tears from her cheeks.

"I don't want us to die."

" 'We owe God a death,' as Falstaff says." He kissed her. "But it's not due yet."

She put her arms around him, and held him tightly. She pressed her face to the warm curve of his neck. He rubbed her back, her shoulders. Then he eased her away and led her past Dukane.

"I'll tuck her in," he said.

Dukane nodded.

Scott guided her to a bed of cushions and blankets prepared in a short hallway. The nearby doors were closed.

"Where's Hoffman?" Lacey whispered.

"The bathroom. We cuffed him to the base of the sink. He can't get loose."

"Can we use the bedroom?"

"Safer here. No windows."

He lay down beside her, and held her gently.

Closing her eyes, Lacey felt his mouth on her open lips. His hand stroked her belly and slowly, so slowly, inched upward. Fingers glided over her breast as if seeking out its shape and texture through the fabric of her shirt. She lifted the shirt, and moaned as he touched her bare skin. His fingertips moved lightly, teasing like feathers, making her squirm with pleasure as they brushed circles around one nipple, then the other.

His mouth went away briefly. Then it took a breast, sucking gently, the tongue probing and flicking.

This is how it should be, she thought. Gentle and slow and loving, the desire almost painful, wanting

him so badly that nothing else matters. For an instant, she thought of Hoffman cuffed inside the bathroom, only a few yards away, but the image was washed away with a thrilled tremor as Scott's hand slipped under the waistband of her shorts. A finger traced her panties' elastic strip, moving slowly from side to side, lightly scraping her skin, toying with the band.

Lacey pushed a trembling hand down the front of his pants. Sliding it inside his shorts, she felt his hot erection. As she curled her fingers around it, she felt Scott's hand slip into her panties. She gasped as he found her opening. While she stroked his thick shaft, his fingers glided against her, slipped into her, probing and pushing. Her own hand explored Scott, wanting his penis inside her. He eased away. Kneeling beside her, he tugged her pants down. She kicked them off, reached out for him, and opened his trousers. She pulled them down, freed his erection, fondled it, held its burning flesh as he climbed onto her, then guided it between her spread legs.

It sunk into her, filling her, gently pushing deeper and deeper.

"Oh dear God," she sighed. "Dear Scott."

CHAPTER TWENTY-FIVE

Dukane knelt alone at the window, staring through its open louvers at the area in front of the house. The low, morning sun made his eyes burn. An effect of going too long without sleep. He closed them. The lids shut out the sunlight, felt soothing on the raw tissue.

He saw Nancy. She winked at him, and lifted her pink nightgown. He expected bare skin, a thatch of pubic hair, perky breasts with upthrust nipples. But no. Not yet. Under the nightgown were red gym shorts and a tank top. She pulled the top over her head, and there they were, her breasts, firm creamy mounds with nipples erect. She began to dance, whirling, waving the shirt like a flag as her other hand lowered to her gym shorts. But now they were faded blue cut-off jeans. She opened them, continuing to dance, and they slowly slid down her legs. She skipped out of them.

She lay on her back, knees up, thighs apart, rubbing herself with both hands, then beckoning him. But as he approached, he saw jagged shards of glass embedded in her skin. They protruded from her

185

breasts, belly, thighs—glistening, clear blades waiting to rip him up. With a grin, she opened her mouth. Her tongue slid out, weighted with a jagged triangle of glass. Reaching between her legs, she spread her flesh. Powdered glass spilled like salt from her vagina.

"Fuck me," she said.

"Not till you take the glass out," he told her.

She spat the chunk from her mouth. It shot out like shrapnel, flipping and twisting toward him. He flinched away. His forehead struck the windowsill.

He awoke with a gasp.

"*Christ*," he muttered, angry at himself for dozing off, and shaken by the dream.

He scanned the area in front of the house. Still no sign of the car or any people. Getting to his feet, he crossed the room. He knelt on the couch and parted the curtains behind it. Fifty feet away stood a garage of white stone. Nobody at its corners or visible on its roof. But off to the left, a hundred yards away, a figure was lying prone on a rise among balls of cacti. Dukane saw a rifle in his arms. He ducked away, and hurried into the kitchen. From its window, he saw another distant sniper.

He filled a glass with water. As he sipped it, he entered the hallway. Scott and Lacey were asleep on the floor, holding each other. He carefully stepped around them, and entered the bedroom. From its window, he spotted another man with a rifle.

At least they're not assaulting the place, he thought. Containing us. Maybe waiting for rein-

forcements. That would explain why the car hadn't shown up again. One of them must've taken it to alert others.

If the girls got away all right, they'd go for the authorities. An army of cops might descend on the place any time.

Interesting to see which army arrives first.

Setting down his empty glass, he went into the hallway and shook Scott's foot. The man woke with a start. Lacey moaned, but didn't awaken. Scott gently untangled himself from her, and followed Dukane into the living room.

"I want you to take over the watch. They've got snipers stationed on both sides and the rear. Maybe one in front, but I haven't spotted him."

"All right."

"I don't think they'll rush us, but we can't rule it out."

He left Scott by the front window, and went into the kitchen. He searched a utility closet, a cupboard under the sink, and wasn't surprised at not finding what he wanted. People don't usually store combustibles in the house.

He returned to the living room.

"I'm going out for a second," he said, unholstering his automatic.

Scott frowned.

"We've gotta get the paint off Hoffman."

"What for?"

"Have to make him disappear in case the cops show up. That's assuming you're still hot to get his story for yourself."

"I am. But I don't like the idea of you going out-side."

Dukane slapped his shoulder. "Buck up, boyo, I'll be back."

He led Scott to the window over the couch, and pointed out the rifleman. "I don't expect you to hit him at this range, but put a few rounds close enough to worry him if he starts tracking me."

With a nod, Scott opened the louvered window.

"You have the keys?"

Scott fished Jan's key case out of his pocket. Dukane took it. He went to the front window.

Scanning the area in front of the house, he saw no one. He pushed open the door and stepped out. Back against the wall, he searched the barren terrain. Odd if nobody was covering the front. If there were only four, though, and one had to drive for help . . . Well, the two at the sides could easily pick off anyone trying to break from the front.

He stepped off the edge of the stoop. Pressing his back to the wall, he made his way toward the corner. Prickles stung his legs, and he looked down to see cactus spines clinging to his trousers. The girls had apparently planted "jumping cactus" along the wall, a variety that seems to shoot its quills into anyone venturing too close.

Nice of them, he thought.

At the corner, he blinked sweat from his eyes and crouched down. The spines dug into his calves. Ignoring the pain, he peered around the wall's edge. He glimpsed the sniper, saw the rifle aimed his way.

Two shots blasted at once. As a bullet whined off the wall inches from his face, he sprang up and dashed for the garage. Gunfire erupted from both the house and sniper, a roar that seemed to jolt the air around him as he ran.

A bullet tugged his sleeve near the shoulder.

Abruptly, there was silence. He threw himself against the side door of the garage, and shoved a key at the lock face.

Didn't fit.

He tried another. This one slid in. He turned it, threw open the door, and burst into the stifling heat of the garage.

There were no windows.

Feeling along the wall, his fingertips found a light switch. He flicked it. A single bulb came on.

No car.

But he smiled as he saw what he wanted.

Lacey, shocked awake by the shooting, grabbed her revolver, scrambled off the makeshift bed, and rushed into the living room. She saw Scott kneeling on the couch, aiming through the open slats of a window.

He glanced around at her.

"Come here," he said.

She hurried to the window.

"See that guy out there? Dukane's in the garage. He'll be coming out in a minute, and the guy'll try to nail him. Take my place here. I'll go to the front. When Dukane comes out, start shooting."

"It's too far."

"Doesn't matter. With fire coming from two angles, he won't know whether to . . ."

"Shit or go blind?"

"Exactly."

Lacey nodded, and Scott ran out the front door. She cocked the revolver. She lined up the distant man in the sights, glanced away at the garage door, then back to the man. From his location, it looked as if the garage would give Dukane shelter for the first two or three yards. Then he would be in the open.

Her hand was sweaty on the walnut grips.

Too bad the man's so far away, she thought. If he was half that distance, she'd stand a much better chance of hitting him.

Just as well, maybe. She didn't need another killing on her conscience.

The garage door opened. She sighted on the man and held her breath. Then she glanced again at the door. Dukane stepped out, a large metal container in each hand. But he didn't run. Instead, he set them outside the door and vanished into the garage. Moments later, he reappeared. With a ladder!

He spread the ladder's legs, climbed it, and boosted himself onto the roof of the garage.

He was gone.

Seconds passed. Lacey licked her parched lips.

Then a single gunshot roared in the stillness.

The distant figure of the rifleman lurched as if kicked, and dropped flat.

Dukane climbed down the ladder. He made a thumbs-up gesture toward Lacey, then carried the

ladder back into the garage. He picked up the two containers, and strolled across the open area.

He and Scott came into the house, beaming like boys who'd just won a no-hitter.

"Nice play," Scott said.

"The bastard came too close, first time across. I chickened out of the return run."

"Wonder if we can get his rifle."

"Not worth the risk. The rear man would pick us off. But I got what I wanted." He raised the cans: a two-gallon tin of gasoline and a gallon container of turpentine.

Lacey frowned. "Turpentine? You're going to take the paint off Hoffman?"

"Right."

"Don't."

"Could come in very handy. Lacey, you stay out here and keep an eye on the situation. Scott, get your recorder. No time like the present to get his story."

CHAPTER TWENTY-SIX

Statement of Samuel Hoffman
July 20

Okay. You want me to talk, I'll talk. Give you everything you need to know for your fuckin' book that's gonna get you killed.

I'm Sammy Hoffman. You guys know that, right? Okay. So I'll start with something you don't know. How about this? I banged my English teacher way back in high school. She was a cunt. That's what you do to cunts, bang 'em.

The one I really wanted, it was Lacey. Used to spend all my time looking at her, thinking how she'd look naked, thinking how her tits'd feel, and her ass and her puss. Now I know, now I know. Only wish I'd got her then. She was just sixteen. Should've took her someplace and kept her. But I was chicken-shit. She was too damn beautiful. Scared me off. Yeah, well, got her at last. Well worth the wait, I tell you that. You guys oughta have a sample, if you haven't already.

Okay, so I had this hard-on for Lacey but I was scared to touch her and this English teacher bitch

pissed me off so I did her instead. Right on top of her desk after school. It was a kick.

I was dumb, then. If I was smart, I'd of turned the bitch's switch off so she couldn't put her mouth on me. But I didn't, and she did.

Adiós, Oasis.

So I'm on the road, here and there and everywhere, doing people every chance I get, always on the move. Shit, I've probably got kids from one end of the country to the next, 'less all the hons got themselves scraped. Yeah, well, plenty were probably on the pill.

Left lots of graves, too. Dead men don't yap. Learned my lesson from the English teacher. See, she taught me something, after all. Thought I was stupid.

Stupid, all right. I should've stayed on my own. That was my big mistake.

Klein. Harold Klein. Met him in LA. A bar on La Cienaga. Tiny's Place. We tipped a few, and he saw my piece and we started jabbing and he figures I'm up for some action. Says he needs a driver and he'll pay me a thousand. That sounded good, only he didn't level. Told me he was hitting a Wells Fargo. I park in front of the bank, only he goes in next door to this TV station and blows the face off this anchor gal, Theresa Chung. Remember her?

Okay. We get the fuck out of there and he has me drive up in this canyon and stop. Only instead of pulling out the bucks he owes me, he pulls a Colt automatic. Dead men don't yap, right? Only he didn't figure on Sammy Hoffman, and guess who winds up in the ditch?

Next thing I know, I wake up in the middle of the night with a muzzle up my mouth. Friends of Harold, right? Wrong. Coworkers. They figure, if I'm good enough to put the dark on Harry, I'm good enough for them. Smart fellas.

Too bad I wasn't that smart. I'd of kissed them off.

But I went along, and pretty soon I'm a hot-shot assassin for The Group. They don't want people snooping into their business, you know? Blowing the whistle on them? Snatching off some of their converts for deprogramming? That sort of shit. They set up the hits real good and paid me through the nose and took good care of me. I was living like a fuckin' tycoon.

Who'd I hit? Senator Cramer, for one. Guy was calling for an official investigation. Seems his son got mixed up in the SDF. That's The Group, you know. The Spiritual Development Foundation. Anyway, that's what got me into this piss soup, that bastard from *People* catching a shot of me in the crowd.

Before Cramer was that nigger mayor in Detroit. Jackson? The LA city council explosion, that was me. The New York police commissioner, Barnes. This ain't necessarily in order, you understand. I can give you guys all the details later, when you get me out of this rat trap and take me someplace safe. Give you something to shoot for. If I tell you everything now, you might just let those bastards have me, right? I'm no fool. I'll just whet your appetites a bit, okay?

Remember Dickinson? Heart attack in his office while he was dickin' his secretary? That was me. Tricked up his rubbers. Chavez, the *investigative*

reporter? He put his nose into the SDF. The o.d. that put him away, it wasn't self-inflicted: it was Sammy-inflicted.

That's just scratching the surface. There's plenty more. Shit, I worked six years for The Group.

Anyhow, it was that *People* shot that put me away. They figure I can't show my face around, so I'm the perfect sucker for their experiment. They're gonna make me invisible, they say. Sure. Invisible. And shit smells like Chanel, right?

Only they do.

Lacey knocked on the door.

"Come on in," Dukane said.

Lacey opened it, and stepped into the bathroom. The air was pungent with the smell of turpentine. Scott and Dukane, kneeling over Hoffman, were scouring him with washcloths. The small cassette recorder from Scott's attaché case rested on the toilet seat.

Scott smiled up at her. His face was sweaty, damp hair clinging to his forehead. "How's it going?" he asked.

"One of the men changed positions. He went over to the body. He's still near it."

"They had to correct their field of fire," Dukane said. Tipping the turpentine can, he dampened his washcloth and started working on Hoffman's shoulder. Most of the back was clear, now. The arms, still painted, remained cuffed behind him. One leg was gone, as if it had been amputated below the rump. Scott was busy cleaning the other.

"How about joining the party?" Hoffman asked. "I been entertaining these guys with my exploits. Great stuff, I hate you to miss it."

She ignored him. "There's plenty of food," she said. "Shall I make some breakfast?"

"I'm starving," Scott said.

"Bacon and eggs all right?"

"Can't eat that shit," said Hoffman. "Get me some beef, and don't cook it."

"What about you, Matt?"

"Bacon and eggs sound fine. I could use some coffee, too."

"Gonna get me that meat?"

"It's frozen," she said.

"So unfreeze it."

She left the bathroom, never mentioning why she had come in. She couldn't ask them to move out, and she certainly had no intention of using the toilet in front of them. In a kitchen cupboard, she found a plastic pitcher. She lowered her pants and squatted over it. When she finished, she flung its contents out the front door. Then she washed her hands, and set about preparing breakfast.

Guess she didn't want to hear, huh? I get the feeling she don't like me.

Anyway, The Group's got this lab. It's out in Iowa, looks just like a farm. Even grow stuff there. The lab's underground, all kinds of security. Make up all their shit there: potions, amulets, stuff like that. Witchin' shit.

Okay, they take me to the lab. I figure I'm in for

it. I mean, how they gonna make a guy invisible, you know? I figure I'm in for shots, at least. God only knows. You don't make a guy invisible with food coloring.

But they don't put me in a cell or a dissection room or nothing, they put me up in a nice room aboveground. I've even got my own little enclosed garden right outside my door. This isn't so bad after all, I figure.

And it gets even better. These two gals come in, and they're both fantastic knockouts. One of them, the gal in charge of the project, she's . . . you'd have to see her. Give you wet dreams. But man, I know right off I'd be in deep shit if I crossed her. It's her eyes. She has this look like she wouldn't mind eating your heart. Well, that wasn't what I wanted eaten so I figured I'd keep off her.

The other, her assistant, wasn't any slouch but she didn't have that wicked look so I was hoping to get a piece of her.

Okay, they're in charge. They're witches, and the gorgeous one turns out to be the leader of the whole ball of wax. Laveda herself. I'd worked six years for her, never seen her. Keeps herself a low profile.

They come in one morning before dawn, it's a Wednesday, with a sack. Laveda tells me to open it. I do, and inside is this guy's head. Nothing else, just his head. A fresh one.

"What am I supposed to do?" I say. "Eat it?" They don't even crack smiles. Instead, Laveda hands me these black beans and tells me what to do.

I'm not a squeamish guy, you know? I was okay,

sticking the beans in his mouth and ears and nose. Then it came to the eyes. You oughta try it sometime. I've gouged a few eyes in my time, but I never stuck around to inspect the damage. Anyway, okay, I popped this guy's eyes and stuck the beans in and shut the lids. Made my skin crawl.

Then they give me a shovel and we go out in my little garden and I have to dig a hole. It only has to be a foot deep. When I'm done, we all get naked. I figure, this is getting better and better. Maybe next is an orgy, who knows? I'd heard plenty about Laveda and her orgies.

Okay, the three of us are standing there bare-ass in the dark, with Coral hanging onto the head. Laveda's wearing this gold chain belt with a dagger at one side and a gold flask on the other. She takes out the dagger. Coral gets on her knees and holds out the head.

What Laveda does then, she starts carving a design on the guy's forehead. Looks like a figure-eight with x's in the middle.

Okay. After she's done with the cutting, she takes the flask off her belt and opens it and holds it up at the sky. "The river flows," she says. "Its water is the water of life. All powerful is he who drinks at its shore." She takes two drinks out of the flask, and some of it runs off her chin and I see it ain't Scotch, it's blood. Then she takes a mouthful of the stuff and gets the guy's head from Coral and spits it right into his mouth.

Coral does the same thing. Two gulps for her, one for the goddamn head. Then it's my turn. I've

done a lot of shit, but I'm no fuckin' vampire. You oughta try a swig of blood, sometime. Put you off your appetite for a week. But that wasn't the worst, the worst was putting my mouth up to this guy's mouth. I didn't want to shut my eyes, you know, and have the gals think I couldn't take it. So I stare the poor dead bastard right in the face and hold his mouth open and try to spit in the blood without touching his lips. But I touched them, all right. And his mouth couldn't hold all this blood, you know, so it came slopping back like he was puking.

Shit. Enough of that. So much for my goddamn orgy. We plant the head face-up, and that's it. The gals slip into their clothes again. *Adios*, see you tomorrow.

I brushed my teeth so hard my gums bled and I figured it was more of *his* blood, and the harder I brushed the more blood came out. I figured the only way to get all the blood out was to upchuck. Didn't do that. It might break the spell, or whatever, and we'd have to go through the whole thing again. So I finally quit brushing, and gargled a lot with Irish, and spent the rest of the day killing the bottle.

The next morning, Coral comes in alone. She's got a bottle under one arm, and I'm hoping it isn't blood. It's Remy Martin. Not for me, though. It's for our pal in the garden. She has me water the fuckin' head with it. A whole fifth of cognac. I suggest we save some for ourselves—I mean, is *he* gonna miss a couple of shots? But she doesn't go for it. Doesn't go for me, either, when I try out a few moves on her.

Okay, we keep this up for a week. Every morning, she wakes me up and we go out with a fresh bottle to dump on the ground.

I keep putting moves on her, and she's getting more bitchy all the time. But I figure I'll get her, sooner or later. One way or the other.

The eighth day, Laveda's with her. She tells me to keep my hands off Coral, and I figure it out. They're a couple of dykes, right? Says she'll cut off my cock . . . Yeah, well, she hasn't yet. The cunt.

Anyway, after she lays this on me we go out to the garden and get naked, and Laveda starts this chanting shit, holding up a fifth of Remy. I was cold sober. I never do drugs. Maybe she had me hypnotized or something, who knows? But anyway, pretty soon I hear this other voice—a man's voice. Coming out of nowhere. It says, "What are you doing?"

Laveda hands me the bottle. "Say, 'I'm watering my head.'"

So I say it.

"Let me water the head," the voice says.

"Tell him 'no.'"

So I tell him no.

Then the dirt over the head starts to move, like a finger's drawing in it. It draws the same design, that figure-eight with the x's, like Laveda cut in the guy's forehead.

"Now he may water your head," Laveda tells me.

"Go ahead," I say.

Something snatches the bottle out of my hand

and it falls to the ground and the cognac spills out. That's it. We get dressed, and the gals take off.

I spent a while out there looking for a speaker. Figured there might be one hidden around somewhere. But if there was, I didn't find it.

The next morning, Laveda and Coral come back. First we strip down, then I have to dig up the head. What a fuckin' sight it was. They made me take out the beans, dig 'em right out of his ears and nostrils and mouth and . . . and out of his eyeholes. The beans'd sprouted a little, by then. Laveda held up this mirror and told me to put one of the beans in my mouth. "Don't swallow it," she told me. She didn't have to tell me that.

I put one in my mouth, like she said, and held it in my cheek like a wad of chewing tobacco. Only it didn't taste like tobacco. It tasted like a rotten fuckin' corpse.

Anyway, I look at the mirror and *bango*, I'm gone.

Lacey knocked on the bathroom door and entered. "Breakfast is . . ."

On the floor where Hoffman had been, she saw six bandages: three hovering several inches above the tile, the others pressed against it. And she saw his silver penis and scrotum. He lay on his back, one handcuff around a leg of the sink.

"Just in time," Hoffman said.

Dukane poured turpentine onto a washcloth. The cloth left his hand, moved through the air, and began to stroke the penis.

"He's *free?*"

"Just one hand," Scott told her.

"All I need," said Hoffman, rubbing himself to an erection. "Squeamish guys. Don't want to touch my dick. How about you?" He flung the cloth at Lacey. It slapped her upraised arm, and she knocked it away. "Rather lick me? Wouldn't get the paint off, but it'd get *me* off."

"Shut up!" Scott yelled.

"Touchy touchy. This guy's got a hard-on for you, hon. Don't we all?"

Dukane pounded down, his fist hammering the emptiness near the bandages.

Hoffman grunted.

Lacey hurried from the bathroom. "Breakfast is on the table," she called back.

She rushed into the kitchen, breathing deeply, fighting her revulsion. Afraid she might vomit, she bent over the kitchen sink.

"That guy's an animal," Scott said, stepping up behind her.

"Stop maligning animals."

He laughed softly, and kissed her bare shoulder.

CHAPTER TWENTY-SEVEN

Okay, where was I? Oh yeah, just popped a bean in my mouth. Just like that, I'm gone. I look down and can't see nothing—no legs, no dick, no nothing. I feel myself. I'm all there, just like normal, only I can't see myself. I give Coral's tits a squeeze and watch 'em bunch up, and Laveda stabs me in the back with a fuckin' dagger.

Hurts like shit. I go down, wondering why they went to all the trouble making me invisible if they're gonna kill me.

Laveda says, "I warned you not to touch her." Then she tells me I'll be okay, I can't be killed 'less I'm hit in a vital place like my heart or a big artery or I'm burned, or something; I've drunk at the river and I'm all powerful and I'll heal up in no time flat. She tells me to get up, and I do. I can feel myself bleeding for a while, but pretty soon it stops.

She tells me to take the bean out of my mouth. I do, and *presto* I'm there again.

Long as I've got one of the beans in my mouth, she says, I'll be invisible. When I spit it out, you can see me again. But if I swallow one, it's so long Sammy for weeks, maybe months. It'll digest, see, and some

of it'll get in my system. Long as any's in my system, I stay invisible.

Then Laveda lets me know what it's all about. She's got big plans for me. Tomorrow, I'm supposed to head off for D.C. and do a job on the president, the VP, the speaker of the house. Presto, instant chaos. That's just the thing for Laveda and her bunch. They'll be free to do whatever they want. And it'll be a cinch for me, right? I can go anywhere, do anything. I can't be stopped. I pretend it's a great idea.

Well that night, I get a few ideas of my own. Laveda's right, I can go anywhere and do whatever I please; I could think of plenty of stuff I'd rather do than spend the rest of my life knocking off people for The Group.

So I strip and pop a bean in my mouth, and do a little exploring. I explore my way right into Laveda's room, which turns out to be just down the hall. Coral's there, too. Just like I figured.

They're sitting around gabbing. Turns out, I'm the first guy they've done this number on. Laveda'd tried it herself, a year ago, and Coral's saying how she'd like a crack at being invisible.

Laveda sort of puts her off. I think I know why, too. Reason she hasn't gone around making lots of her people invisible. It gives them too much power. She wants all the power for herself, wants to stay in control. She just made me invisible to get a job done for her. And I figure I'm probably expendable, she'll wipe me out once I get it done.

Well, they finally leave off their jabber and get

down to rolling on the bed. You should've seen those two go at each other. Grunting and groaning, licking, eating each other out. I almost popped my load, just watching. Must've gone on for an hour. I wanted to jump right on 'em and stick it in the nearest hole, but I held off. Didn't want to mess with Laveda. The gal's bad news.

They finally get done. I see Coral making for the john, so I get in quick ahead of her. She starts taking a shower. Okay, I know Laveda's out in the other room and if she gets me, I've had it. But I'm invisible, right? How's she gonna hurt me if she can't find me?

So I climb into the shower with Coral. She suspects something when the door slides open, but before she has a chance to yell I bash her head on the tile and knock her out. More than out, dead. So then I lay her down in the tub and have my fun. You ever let it go after holding back for an hour? Nothing like it. Thought I'd bust, I came so hard.

Okay, I get out of the tub and dry off—don't want to be tracking water, you know. Then I get scared 'cause I see myself in the fuckin' mirror! It isn't me, really. The place is all steamy and there I am, like a hole in it. Bad news! I wanted to get outa there. So I hurried and finished drying, and snuck open the door a crack, just enough to see out. Laveda was on the bed. Looked like she was asleep.

I spent a lot of time watching her, wondering if I oughta turn off her switch. I mean, I knew I should. The bitch and her whole bunch would be after me for doing her playmate, and I'd be up shit creek if

they ever got their hands on me. But I tell you what, I was scared. You'd be scared too. She's not what you'd call normal. I figured, what if I made a try for her and I couldn't kill her no matter what I did? She's got this magic, right? I finally figure I'm not gonna chance it. I'll just pull a vanishing act.

So I sneak out and get back to my room for the rest of the beans. Then it's *adios*.

No sweat at all, getting out of the compound. I walked right past the guards. Nothing there for them to see, except the beans in my hand, and those aren't big enough that anybody'd notice. The one in my mouth, that's invisible. Guess 'cause it's mixed up in my spit. I figured out, after a bit, I could pop 'em all in my mouth when I needed to hide 'em. Smart, huh? Better than leaving the things behind when I wanted to sneak in someplace: lost two, that way.

Okay, so I'm out of the compound and walking down this road. It's three miles, all of it through Group property, till I get to a highway. Remember now, I'm not only bare-ass, I'm bare*foot*. You try walking three miles barefoot, sometime.

I wanted a car bad. You get out in the sticks around midnight and see how many cars go by. Zip. And the ones that did come along, how was I gonna stop 'em? I finally made it to a farmhouse, dog tired. Speaking of dogs, that's where I ran into my first. I don't know if they can see me or what, but they sure as shit know where to find me. This one at the farm raised hell, even took a nip out of my leg before I killed it.

Farmer Joe came out to snoop around, and that gave me a chance to get inside. I waited till he was

back in bed, then got a knife and went upstairs and slit his gullet. Got the wife, too. They had three kids. Just one was a girl. I had a good time with her.

After that, I wanted to sack out. But what am I gonna do with the bean in my mouth? Don't want it falling out while I'm asleep. So I just went ahead and swallowed it.

I woke up, after a couple of hours, when this car pulled up in front. There's Laveda, and half a dozen guys from the compound. The guys are wearing these weird masks. What they are, I figure out later, they're infrared gadgets. Put on one of those suckers, and you can see me. See my heat image. Those bastards from The Group think of everything.

Okay, I figured they wouldn't know for sure I was there. They might think I just did my business and moved on, long as they didn't see me. So I hid. I ran over to the boys' room, and dumped the crap out of their toy box and hid in there. Sure enough, they didn't find me. Spent half an hour turning the house, then gave up.

But the fuckers set the place on fire. Insurance, I guess. Just in case they'd missed me. Tells you something, don't it? Sure told *me* something. Told me they wanted my ass dead.

I just about cooked, but I got out of that place. Their car was gone. Great, I'm home free. Then I catch a slug in the shoulder and go down. This is it, Sammy. They'll move in now, and Laveda'll get your dick just like she said. Except *they* don't move in. Just this one guy comes out from beside the garage, decked out with a rifle and those infrared

goggles. I play dead, and he's dumb enough to come close and it's bye-bye dummy. I grab the rifle out of his hands and ram it through his teeth and blast off the back of his head.

Then I go over to the garage and hot-wire one of Farmer Joe's cars, and get the fuck out of there.

Lacey threw open the bathroom door. "A car's coming!"

"Cops?" Dukane asked.

"I don't think so."

She ran ahead of them, pressing her shirt to her damp breasts.

After cleaning the breakfast dishes, she had given in to her need to clean herself. She filled the sink with warm water, then checked the windows to be certain the snipers remained in their normal positions. Returning to the kitchen, she used liquid detergent to wash her hair. Bent over the sink to rinse, she worried about leaving the house unguarded, imagined the front door bursting open, men with guns rushing in. As soon as the soap was out of her hair, she grabbed a hand towel and again checked the windows.

Everything looked all right.

But she didn't like the kitchen, felt blind at its sink, and vulnerable. So she filled two pans with water and carried them into the living room. Facing the front window, she took off her clothes. She sponged herself with warm soapy water, and wiped the slickness away with cool water from the other pan. It felt very good. Maybe later, once the men

were done in the bathroom, she would ask them to move Hoffman out and she could take a real bath. When was the last time? Yesterday? Just before going out to dinner with Scott. Only yesterday. It seemed like weeks ago.

She squeezed the sponge against the nape of her neck and felt the cool water stream down her back. It slid over her buttocks and between them, and trickled down the backs of her legs. If Scott were here, he could wash her back . . .

She imagined him coming into the room, and smiling with delight when he saw her. She would turn to face him. He would kiss her mouth, her neck, her breasts. His tongue would prod her nipples.

Rather lick me?

The memory of Hoffman's words smashed her fantasy. She tossed the sponge into the water and picked up a dish towel. She patted her legs dry. She rubbed between them. She looked around at the cut on her buttock. It was slightly red at the edges, but scabbed over. It hadn't been much more than a scratch, after all. But it itched more than the others that threaded her body. She resisted an urge to rake it with her fingernails, but rubbed it gently with the towel.

As she started to dry her arms, the sound of a car engine froze her. She glanced out the window. A black Rolls Royce sped up the road toward the house.

Whipping the towel around her waist, she scooped up her shirt and raced for the bathroom.

Now Scott and Dukane were rushing past her,

pistols ready. Scott checked the side window. Dukane kicked over a water pan as he dashed to the front. He crouched at the window.

Scott ran to the hall.

Lacey pulled her shirt on, grabbed her revolver off the rocking chair, and knelt beside Dukane. The car had stopped in front of the door—no more than ten yards away. Through its tinted windows, she saw moving, indistinct shapes.

A door flew open. A naked woman was thrust from the car. She fell facedown, and the door slammed shut.

Her back and rump were striped with raw, bleeding wounds. She pushed herself up. On her knees, she looked at the window. Lacey moaned, cold with sickness as she recognized the swollen, bloody face. Jan. The flesh of her chest and belly was tattered. Blood spilled from open wounds where her nipples should have been, flowed from her vagina, sheathing her thighs, forming a puddle on the ground between her knees.

The rear window slid down three inches. Lacey saw the crown of a bald head inside the car.

"We want Hoffman," a man's voice called through the opening. "Give us Hoffman, and we'll let the rest of you go. If you're . . ."

Dukane fired. With the first shot, the pale scalp erupted and dropped from sight. The second shot smashed into the window, halfway down, blasting out a cone of glass but not breaking through.

The car sprang forward.

Until that instant, Lacey didn't see the cord—the white electrical cord around Jan's left ankle and running up to the crack at the bottom of the car door. It snapped taut. Tugged Jan's leg from under her. Dragged her, spinning and bouncing, alongside the car.

Lacey's own scream drowned out the screams from Jan. Covering her ears, she lowered her head and shut her eyes tight.

Finally, she raised her head. The car had turned around and was now speeding back. Its body hid Jan from her view until it turned right and headed up the entry drive. Then she glimpsed the tumbling carcass.

Throwing herself away from the window, she grabbed the nearer pan and vomited into it. As convulsions wracked her, she realized vaguely that her towel had fallen away. It didn't matter. Her mind reeled at what she'd seen. Would they do the same to Nancy? To her? Lacey's stomach was empty, now, but she strained with dry heaves. Her mouth dripped hot stomach fluids. Her eyes dripped tears.

"You stay with Lacey," Scott told Dukane. "I'd better go in and get the rest of Hoffman's story."

Dukane helped Lacey to the couch. Lying on it, she felt the soft fabric against her buttocks. She pulled a pillow down to cover her bare groin.

"What about Nancy?" she asked.

"There's nothing we can do."

Dukane handed the panties and shorts to Lacey. "We could give them Hoffman," she said.

211

He turned away, and sat on an edge of the coffee table. As Lacey put on her clothes, he said. "They won't let us go."

"Why not?"

"Several reasons. First, we killed some of their people: the cops in Tucson, the sniper, the guy in the car just now. They can't let us get away with that. Second, we've been in contact with Hoffman and they've got to assume he talked, maybe gave out the formula for becoming invisible."

"Did he?"

"He did. That, plus plenty of other information. The Group can't allow that. How many reasons is that?"

"Two."

"Three, even if the other reasons didn't exist, they'd want us for the sport. The people in The Group are evil. I've had some prior experience with them. I know. They love the power, love to make people cringe at their feet, to torture and kill for their own pleasure."

"Doesn't sound good," Lacey said.

"It's not."

CHAPTER TWENTY-EIGHT

Okay, I'm tooling along in Farmer Joe's car, keeping a sharp lookout for the bunch from the compound. But I never do see 'em. The farmhouse was north of the compound, so they must've figured I'd keep going that way. Well, I didn't. I went east. Got clean away.

But it gets to be daylight, and there's some traffic on the highway, and I start getting queer looks from the jerks in the other cars. Doesn't take me long to figure out why. I'm invisible, right? So who's driving my car?

I don't give much shit where I'm going—long as it's not back to the compound—so I pull into a Denny's and climb in back of the first car I find unlocked. Wherever they're going, I'll go. So I'm sitting there in the backseat and along comes not just momma and poppa, but three brats. Being invisible's no cinch. When the door opens, I knock this little bastard on his ass and get out of there. The kid's bawling, tells his dad somebody *pushed* him, and the old man gives him a whack for fibbing. Nice guy.

Next time, I play it safe. A guy comes in the parking lot alone. I make sure he doesn't lock up, then I

213

go in Denny's, in the kitchen there, and heist myself a coke and a couple of burgers and polish 'em off while I wait for the guy.

He takes me into Iowa City, to this university there. I find my way into a girls' dorm. I tell you, thought I'd died and gone to heaven. Plenty of food for the taking, found me an empty room, and *man* the girls! You should've seen those hons in the showers.

There's one in particular, comes in for a shower every night around nine. A real honey, looks like a movie star, tits out to here. I'm sitting down so the steam won't give me away. Front row seat. Watching her rub herself all over with soap. I've got a hard-on feels like it's gonna bust.

Well, this one night I can see she's hot. Not just washing, you know, but feeling herself, rubbing her tits, playing around with her puss. Finally, she gets on her back with her legs up so the water's hitting her quiff. I move in with my mouth. I'm licking and sucking and sticking my tongue in, and she's so far gone she doesn't know, like she thinks the spray's doing it. Maybe she thought she was dreaming, I don't know. Well, she's squirming and moaning and rubbing her tits, and I just go ahead and put my dick right in. Should've seen her eyes bug out. Looks down at herself. Reaches down. I pull it out and give her a handful. She feels it up and down, like trying to figure out if it's what she thinks. She looks real confused and scared, at first. Then she gets this funny little smile on her face, and puts it back in.

I go ahead and hump the daylights out of her. She damn near screams when she comes.

After we're done, she starts drying herself off, frowning like she's trying to figure something out. Then she says, "Are you here?"

I take the towel, and finish drying her.

"What are you?" she asks.

I don't answer.

"Am I . . . imagining you? I've never . . . here I am, talking to myself. Shit." Then she reaches out and touches me, touches my dick. "You sure don't *feel* like an hallucination." She gets this funny smile again, and goes down on her knees and sucks me off. "Don't taste like one, either," she says when she's finished. "Whatever you are, I hope you don't go away."

"I'm the invisible man," I whisper.

"No shit?"

"A government experiment went haywire. They're after me. 'Fraid I'll spill the beans." A good one, right? Spill the beans? Anyway, I tell her I'm hiding out 'cause they'll kill me, which wasn't that far from the truth. If The Group ever got their hands on me . . .

Well, this gal's fascinated. Says I can hide out in her room, and she'll take care of me.

And she does. Man, does she take care of me! A real wild gal. Name was Robin, like the bird. The first couple days, she cut all her classes and stayed in the room with me. Only just left to get us food. Told all her friends she'd come down with something. It was like a fuckin' honeymoon. Didn't do nothing but play games.

That, and talk. A great talker, Robin. Name me a woman that isn't. She wanted to know the story of my life. I just made up a lot of shit, made me sound like a regular sweetheart. Most of all, she wanted to know how I got invisible, and what it was like. Said she wished she was that way, she'd do just what I did except she'd head over to the boys' shower room. I let her know it wasn't all fun and games, like how you freeze your ass off when it's cold out, and how tough it is to get places. Like how do you drive?

So she drags out her makeup and shows me how to put it on so I've got a face. Puts a wig on me. Presto, I've got a head. After a couple of days, I have her go out and buy me some clothes and sunglasses. Now I'm all set. I don't look like much. Look kind of weird, in fact, and even weirder when my mouth's open, but I figure at least I'll be able to get around at night like a human being.

Robin's got other ideas, too. She's full of ideas. It's June, see, and she's got final exams coming up. So she puts me to work hiding out in faculty offices and heisting exams. Stupid stuff, but it gave me something to do and kept her happy.

She also wants to even up a score. Her boyfriend dumped her for some bitch. They're living off campus, so she drives me out there to take care of them. She just wants me to do some tricks, move some furniture around, make stuff float, scare the shit out of 'em. But the gal turns out to be a fox so after I spook 'em for a while, I do the guy, tear him up, chase the gal around with his head, have my own kind of fun.

Well, Robin finds out all about it when she sees the newspaper. Calls me a maniac, shit like that. Frankly, I think she's just pissed 'cause I fucked the gal. But she's also yelling about how the cops'll come looking for her, seeing as she was the jilted lover. I figure she's probably right. The cops'll pull her in and she'll finger me. So it's *adios* Robin. I break her neck and light out.

I take along her makeup, and the clothes she bought me, and my six beans. I hide in a utility closet till night, then get the hell out of the dorm and steal her car. She isn't gonna need it, right?

The car's hot, though. I'm no dummy. I know I've gotta dump it fast. So I drive downtown—what there is of it—and I see where a movie's just getting out. None of the gals coming out of the theater are alone, so I follow this guy. When he gets to his car, I bash him. I scoot him over to the passenger seat, and bring my stuff over to his car.

Smart, huh? Look at it this way: if I heist a car, somebody's gonna miss it and call the cops. Probably by morning. There I am, stuck with another hot car before I hardly get used to it. But if I take the guy with it, he's not gonna tell his car's gone, right? Dead men don't yap. And if a guy goes to the movies alone, you can lay odds he's single. Won't be a wife waiting up for him, worrying her tail off. So I figure I can use the car for a couple of days, at least, maybe longer. You ever need a car for a long haul, kill off the driver.

Anyway, once I've got the guy's car, I drive out in the boondocks, throw him in the trunk, and put on

my makeup and clothes so I'll pass for a normal person.

I'm on the road a long time, after that. I drive at night. Rip off restaurants and houses for food. Sleep in the backseat when daylight hits, either that or take a house. I found one place where the folks were on vacation or something. Stayed there a week. But most of the time, the places weren't deserted and I had to do the people. Couldn't stay more than a day or two, then, 'cause sure enough somebody'd come around snooping.

Then it'd get in the papers. Goddamn papers. I know The Group, see, know they're watching out for stuff like that. Probably sticking pins in a map. Not gonna quit till they've got my ass nailed.

So then I get this bright idea. I grab a camper, an RV, off a couple of old farts I figure are retired and nobody's gonna miss 'em for a while. Then I head west. Keep my hands to myself, don't leave a trail for the fuckin' Group.

First thing you know, I'm in Phoenix. I figure, hey, how about paying a visit to my old friends in Oasis?

CHAPTER TWENTY-NINE

"Give us Hoffman!"

The voice startled Lacey awake. She raised her head off the couch and saw Dukane crouched by the front window.

"Give us Hoffman," the tinny voice continued, "and we'll let you live."

Lacey rushed to Dukane's side. Looking out the window, she saw the black Rolls Royce stopped in front of the house—perhaps thirty feet away. The doors on its far side stood open, but the body of the car hid whatever was being done.

"I warn you," said the amplified voice. Lacey spotted its source: a man on a distant rise of land, speaking into a megaphone. "Give us Hoffman, or you will all be annihilated. There is no escape for you unless you do as we ask. You have seen what we do to our enemies. Each of you will meet a similar end, if you continue to ignore our request." The megaphone was lowered.

Lacey heard the bathroom door open. Scott rushed across the floor and knelt at the other window.

From behind the car came a heavy clank. A

hammer striking metal? The pounding continued with a slow, even rhythm.

"What're they doing?"

Scott frowned at Lacey, and she saw anguish in his eyes. He backhanded speckles of sweat off his upper lip. "Maybe you shouldn't watch."

"You think it's Nancy?"

"Yeah."

Dukane suddenly rushed from the room.

The pounding stopped for a few seconds, then started again. Lacey scurried over to Scott's window.

"Sounds like they're driving in stakes," he said.

"Oh God." Lacey sank down. Turning, she sat beneath the window with her back against the wall. She brought up her legs, hugged them to her breasts, pressed her mouth to one knee.

The slow pounding kept on.

Dukane returned to the room, crouching low, a wine bottle in hand.

"Nobody's moving in," he said, and squatted near the other front window. "Can you tell what they're doing?"

"Driving in stakes, I think."

"Shit," he muttered. He took a handkerchief from his pocket, tore it in half, and twisted one of the pieces into a strip. He stuffed it into the bottle's mouth, and drew it out. The pungent fumes of gasoline stung Lacey's nostrils.

He reversed the rag and stuffed it into the bottle again. Three inches hung out like a wick.

The pounding outside continued.

"Anybody got a match?"

Lacey hurled herself forward, scurried to the coffee table, and grabbed a lighter. She raced back to Dukane.

"When I open the door, light the rag."

Lacey nodded, suddenly excited, eager to be striking back.

Dukane jerked the door open.

Lacey lighted the wick. As fire bloomed from the dripping rag, Dukane pitched the bottle. He slammed the door shut and dived into Lacey, throwing her to the floor as bullets burst through the wood above them. Splinters rained down.

Dukane rolled off, and scrambled to his window. Lacey saw Scott take aim. She rushed to his side as the flaming car lunged forward, its far doors still open, leaving two men behind. One raced after it, yelling, his open Hawaiian shirt fluttering behind him like a cape. He turned a somersault as Scott's bullet smacked the back of his head. The other man, on his knees with a hammer when the car left him unprotected, sprang to his feet. He ran toward the house, waving the hammer overhead like the tomahawk of a demented Apache.

"Let him come!" Dukane yelled. "We can use him."

His naked body, as bony as a starved man, was streaked with blood. Not his own, Lacey assumed. What had he been doing? She was afraid to look away from him. He ran toward the window, shrieking, and looked about to dive through when a dozen bullets hit him from behind.

Scott threw Lacey back.

The man's head drove into the window as if trying

to squeeze itself between two of the flat, open slats of glass. They burst, tearing his scalp, ripping the sides of his face and neck. His chin came to rest on the sill. Blood slid down the inside of the wall.

Lacey scooted backward, unable to look away from the ghastly man's head. "Get . . . get him *out* of here!" she stammered. "Get him OUT!"

"Oh good Christ," Dukane said. He was staring out his window. "My God, those . . . !" Leaping away from the window, he took quick strides toward the dead man's protruding head.

"What did they . . . ?"

"*Bastards!*" Dukane swung up his leg in a vicious kick, catching the man in the face. The head bounded upward. Lacey glimpsed its torn, mashed face. The eyes seemed to glare at her with hatred for an instant as the head smashed through three more louvers. Then it dropped backward out of sight.

Scott ran to the window. He knelt beside it and looked out. "Oh no," he muttered. He turned to Dukane, his face ashen. "What'll we do?"

"Nothing."

"*Nothing?*"

"We can't get to her. They'd nail us before we got a yard."

"We can't just leave her like that!"

"Want to put her out of misery?"

"No! My God, Matt! I don't think she's even hurt."

"Hard to tell."

"I think she's all right. But my God, we can't

just . . . Stop!" he told Lacey, raising his hand like a traffic cop as she crawled forward. "You don't want to see it."

"What? What did they do to her? You said she's all right."

"They've got her staked down. With Jan."

"Jan?"

"What's left of her," Dukane muttered. "They're tied face-to-face."

CHAPTER THIRTY

I'm in the camper, right? I'm not gonna take it to Oasis, though. Suppose somebody digs up the old farts? I don't want their RV popping up where I'm at. So I ditch it at the Phoenix airport, along with my clothes and makeup, and don't take nothing with me but my four beans. I'd lost two, by then. But the one I'd eaten was still doing its job. Still is. That's close to two months, right?

Okay, I take a Greyhound to Oasis. Leave the driving to them. The thing was nearly empty, so I didn't have no trouble.

First thing I do when I get there, I look up my old pal Lacey in the phone book. Only her name ain't in it. I figure she's either unlisted, or she's got herself married, or she's moved on. I can't exactly stop someone on the street and ask, right? If she's in Oasis, though, I'm gonna find her.

So what I do, I head for the old lady's market. Too much going on in the Safeway, people gonna be tripping over me. The market's quiet, I know my way around. Hell, I damn near lived in that dump when I was a kid. After school, weekends. Beat the shit out of me if I gave 'em any lip about it.

Well, this is my chance to pay the old lady back. Spook her up, and do her. But first I'm gonna lay low. If Lacey's still in town, she's gonna pop up in the market sooner or later. Everybody does. Even the Safeway regulars, they show up for a frozen pizza or aspirin or some kind of odds and ends. So I'll just hang out and wait.

Only trouble is, the old bat's got ears like a hawk. I don't even make it through the first day, and she hears me moving around. It's night, about an hour before closing time, when suddenly she perks up and starts acting scared and looking all over for me.

Well, I like seeing her scared. Gives me a kick, throwing a fright into folks, but she's special. I'm thinking of all the times she used to slam me around, whip me with the ironing cord. Her and the old man both. Too bad *he* kicked off before I got a chance at him, the old turd. Anyway, she's plenty scared 'cause of the noises, so I throw another one into her by opening up the cash register. That does it. She closes and hightails it.

I'm pissed, right? There goes my big plan for laying low and waiting for Lacey to show up. So I'm eating a steak and soaking up a bottle of red to make myself feel better when some asshole starts pounding on the door. I toss a fuckin' meat cleaver at him. Too bad I missed.

So what happens next? A whole troop comes piling into the store. The old lady, the jerk that was at the door, some other gal, and guess who? My old pal, Lacey. Things are looking up, right? Only they take

one look at the cleaver stuck in the door, and run off like the joint's haunted.

I go after 'em. By the time I get to the door, though, they're packed in this car and taking off.

Well, at least I know Lacey's still in town.

A cop shows up, a little later. I just stand around and watch him search. When he takes off, I sack out in the storeroom.

That was Friday night. I figured the old cow'd be back in the morning, but she didn't open up all weekend. Spooked her good, I guess. Anyway, she comes in Monday morning and sees the mess I'd made. She always did hate messes. She wasn't so scared, this time. Just pissed off. People came in, she'd tell 'em it was vandals, probably kids. If they come back, she says, she's gonna fix their wagon.

So that night, some pal of hers shows up with a fuckin' watchdog. I get out of there till they leave, 'cause the dog's gonna go for me, you know. Well, once they're gone I sneak in again to take care of the mutt. It damn near got me, but I opened up its head with the meat cleaver and ripped the thing apart. Then I skinned it. Even tried some. I figure, shit, it tried to take a bite out of me. Turn-about's fair play. Didn't taste bad.

I figure all hell's gonna break loose when they find what's left of the dog, so I get out of there before morning.

Head over to the high school. Forgot school's out for the summer, till I got there. But it turns out they've got summer school going, and most of it's athletic stuff. So I'm okay, after all.

Guess where I go? Where else, the girls' shower room. I've got a thing about shower rooms, huh? When I was a kid, I used to always dream about getting into this one, grabbing a peek at all those hons, maybe copping a feel here and there. Used to wish I could turn invisible, and just spend all day with 'em. Well, I knew that was impossible. Impossible, right? So I thought I'd dress up like a girl and sneak in that way. Figured I'd get caught, though. Well, now I'm invisible and I make my dream come true.

These hons are a lot younger than the ones at the university. Some are still flat, some got these tiny little pointed tits that look like they're half nipple, and some got boobs out to here. Some haven't even got a bush, yet.

I have a great time watching, sometimes grabbing a little feel. Tell you how you do it. I worked out a system at the university. You go for where their hands are. They're rubbing soap on their pussy, you can get in a feel without them noticing. See what I mean?

Anyway, around noon, things slow down in the shower department. Only a few in there, rinsing off after their volleyball and stuff. One's this blonde with nifty little pointed tits. I follow her home. The house is empty, which works out nicely. I don't want her knowing my secret, so I bop her on the head. Then I blindfold and gag her. Wait till she comes around before I start the fun and games.

You'll be happy to know I didn't kill her. No point. Just draw attention to myself, right? The way I did it, she maybe kept it to herself. You live in a little

town like Oasis, you don't want it getting around you've been raped. People figure you brought it on yourself, you'll never live it down. So I just left her, and headed on back to the market.

Guess who's there. Not just my old lady, but the asshole that owned the dog. He's got himself a shotgun. And he doesn't go away. He's gonna blow the head off the bastard that put the dark on his pooch. So he says.

The store's full of people. They're all buying one or two things, just for an excuse to visit the scene of the crime. Must be eight o'clock before the joint clears out.

That's when I go to it. Start spooking 'em. The asshole almost gets me with his shotgun, though. Blows apart a coke display. Then I take his shotgun away and knock him on the head. I don't have time to finish the job, 'cause the old lady's screaming her face off and running for the door.

I catch up to her, throw her down, and tell her who I am. It's Sammy, her darling son, come back to give her a taste of what she'd given him.

She's crying and pleading with me, saying she's sorry. Man, is she sorry. Especially when I start snapping her fingers. I have to gag her to stop the screams. Then I drag her back to the meat counter.

She and the old turd taught me how to be a butcher, how to use the bone saw and cleaver. Made me sick. All that blood. But then I got to like it, and they'd catch me eating the raw meat and they'd say I was stealing and knock me around. Well, they got their way. Made me into a butcher.

So here goes the old bag, up on the chopping block. I go at her real slow, wanting to keep her alive for a while so she can see what a good butcher she turned out. I even use tourniquets on her stumps to keep the bleeding down so she'll last a while longer.

Hope she enjoyed it.

Packaged her up real nice in cellophane, and laid her out with the rest of the beef. Then I went over to the guy. He's still out cold. I start with his arm. Hack it right off. And then I hear the front door open.

If it ain't my old pal, Lacey! This, I know, is gonna be a banner day. I let her snoop around some, then I go for her. Knock her out, strip her down, and do what I'd been wanting to do since I was a high school kid. Ah, she was fine, just fine. You oughta know, right? You haven't had a piece yet, you're missing a bet.

I don't kill her. No way. I've got big plans for her. So I leave. Only one car in the lot, that and a pickup truck. I knew the pickup belonged to the dog man, so the car has to be Lacey's. I get in, and lay down on the back floor.

It's a long wait. The cops come. I don't know, it's maybe an hour before she finally comes out. She checks the car real careful, almost like she knows I'm there. Doesn't see me, though. Course not. So she starts up the car and heads for home.

She lights up this cigarette, and I cough. God knows what she must've thought. Scared her plenty, though. Thinks I'm in the trunk, I guess. When she stops, she jumps on the trunk like maybe it isn't

locked. Has her face pressed up against the back window and here I am, looking right at her with her cheek mashed in.

Then she runs off, goes in her house, and I get out of the car. I'm standing there, and out she comes with a revolver. Shit, this gal's got balls. She goes right to the trunk and opens it, planning to blast me to hell. Course, I'm not there. I'm over by her front door, now, waiting for her to come back and open it.

She gets it unlocked, and we're about to go in when this jock shows up. He's gonna play big hero and search around. So they go off together, and she doesn't bother to lock the door up, so I help myself and go inside.

Pretty soon, they come in. The guy looks all over the place. He wants to stay, but Lacey won't bite, so he runs off and she's finally alone.

Almost alone, right?

Gets herself some wine, and makes this call. That's how I find out she works for the paper. Cute call. Doesn't tell what I did to her. That's gonna be her secret. Just between her and me. Like I say, you can't let a thing like that get around, not in a town like Oasis.

So after the call, lo and behold, she locks herself in the john and starts to run the bath. Never even suspects I'm right in there with her. I have myself a great time watching her strip, check herself out in the mirror, lay down in the tub, soap herself up, sip her wine. I just stand there enjoying it for a while. I figure, she's mine now. I own her. I can do what I want with her, as much as I want.

Well, I finally decide it's time to spook her, start

showing her who's running the show. So I turn off the light. I hear her splashing. Then she's out of the tub and pointing this pistol at her door as if I'm gonna come bashing through it. I just stand behind her and enjoy it. She's scared shitless. I can hear her gasping, making little whiny sounds. I leave her alone till she starts to get dressed, then I nail her. This time's better than before. It's better when they're conscious, squirming and crying. Adds a little flavor to the proceedings, you know?

By the time I'm done, I'm beat. Busy day, right? So it's time to hit the sack. I tie her to the bed and blindfold her. Don't want her walking off—or limping, as the case may be. And I don't want her learning my little secret till I'm ready to spring it on her. I want to see her reaction.

Next morning, after some asshole comes to the door, I have another go at her. She's better than ever, squirming and fighting. That should've given me a clue: the bitch has a lot more guts than I counted on. But I figure, once she sees I'm invisible, she's gonna know she can't win. She'll fall in line.

I let her know my plan. She's gonna be like Robin in Iowa, gonna take care of me and keep her mouth shut, and go on about her business just like nothing'd happened. I warn her what'll happen if she screws up. Then I go ahead and untie her and take off the blindfold.

First thing she does, when she sees she can't see me, is give me a kick in the nuts. Then she runs. But she's smart, gotta give her that. She doesn't try to run away, knows she can't get away from someone

she can't see, so instead she goes in the kitchen thinking she'll finish me off. Throws flour on me so she can see where I am, and sticks a knife in my back.

That would've taken care of most guys, just like all the fuckin' bullets you pumped into me. But I'm not most guys, right? I've drunk at the river, all that shit. Got magic powers. So she hurts me and gets away, probably thinks she's killed me.

But she hasn't. I'm out of there and hiding by the time the cops show up. Well, I figure she'll come back sooner or later. I'll just wait her out.

That's what, Thursday? I hang around all day, and she doesn't come back. Then I hang around Friday. When she doesn't show up by Saturday, I figure it's gonna be a long wait if I don't get into action.

I know she works for the paper, right? So I figure somebody there's gonna know where to find her. Turns out, the cops are there. Somebody got offed with a letter opener, and there's a note makes it sound like I done it. Weird, huh? Anyway, I stick around till the cops go. There's only me and the editor. He's acting funny.

I get ready in case I have to follow him. Snatch a shirt and cowboy hat out of the cleaners next door. Hide the stuff out back, then I nail some bitch that's getting in her car. I park it near the *Trib*'s lot, check her purse to see she's got some blush-on for my face—better than nothing—and put my clothes in her car.

I'm all set, right? I just wait a while, and the edi-

tor shows up. He checks his car real careful. Good thing I didn't hide in it, huh?

So I follow him to Tucson, and the rest is history. You know the rest. Except maybe how I got in the room, that second time. Lowered myself on a sheet. Man, that was hairy!

When you got away that time, I figured I'd flush you out with a fire. Used cleaning fluid. Started four fires, in all. Burned real good.

I would've had you and Lacey, only I got overconfident about the gun. Well, shit, can't win 'em all.

CHAPTER THIRTY-ONE

"Might be good for you to listen, Lacey."

"Why?"

"Know your enemy," Scott said.

She nodded. She wished she could leave and avoid the presence of Hoffman—even his voice disgusted and frightened her. But she was curious. "I don't know," she said.

"You'll have to hear him a lot," he said, "if you're going to collaborate on the book with me. Might as well get used to the idea."

"Yeah. All right."

Scott started the tape. "Okay," Hoffman said. "You want me to talk, I'll talk."

Dukane stepped over to a front window. He knelt at its side, and peered out.

Looking at Nancy? Wondering if he could save her?

"The one I really wanted, it was Lacey."

She tried not to listen. She thought about Nancy.

The girl had been out there for nearly an hour now. Dukane had spent most of that time looking at her. "She's gagged," he'd told Lacey. That explained why there were no screams.

He'd discussed shooting at the ropes or stakes that pinioned her spread-eagled to the ground. But even if he could free her that way, he supposed a fusillade would tear her apart before she could make the door—particularly since she was bound fast to Jan's larger body. Maybe after dark . . .

The tape played on. Lacey found herself listening, appalled by the list of Hoffman's victims, by the bragging and insolent tone of his voice. She listened with dread to the ghastly method of transformation, sickened by the image of the severed head, the beans being pushed through its eyes, the drinking of blood. When he described his attack on Coral, she shivered at the memory of herself in the dark bathroom of her home.

His tale of perversion and slaughter went on and on. Lacey thought about going into the kitchen, standing by the sink, running the water full blast to drown out the hideous sound of his voice. But she couldn't force herself to leave. She felt compelled to listen, much as she might be drawn to a grisly accident, horrified and worried about the victims but curious to see their broken remains.

Scott flipped the cassette over.

Then Hoffman was in Oasis, looking for her name in the telephone directory. She remembered the series of obscene midnight calls that had made her life miserable two years ago until she took an unlisted number. Thank God for those calls. The new number had at least postponed Hoffman's attack. If she'd only stayed away from the market . . .

She gagged as Hoffman described eating the dog.

Then he was in the shower room at the high school, secretly touching the girls, following one home to rape her. Lacey knew most of the people in Oasis. She wondered who the girl was. Pitied her. But it could've been so much worse.

When he told of breaking his mother's fingers, Lacey knew what was coming. She didn't want to hear about the butcher job. With a finger in each ear, she blocked the sound. But her mind saw him hacking Elsie apart, wrapping the pieces in cellophane. Scott, sitting only a few feet away, looked at her with sadness in his eyes. Then he blushed and turned away.

Lacey took the fingers from her ears. "Ah, she was fine," Hoffman said. "Just fine." Who did he mean? "You oughta know, right. You haven't had a piece yet, you're missing a bet."

Scott glanced at her, made a shy smile, and lowered his gaze to the floor.

Lacey, suddenly understanding, felt heat rush to her skin. Bad enough that Hoffman should violate her, but to *brag* about it, to suggest that Scott . . . What could she expect from a bastard like Hoffman?

She listened to the way he hid in her car, how he sneaked into the house, how he stood close to her as she phoned James. With growing dread, she waited for his description of the attack. She watched Scott as Hoffman spoke. He sat with his legs crossed, his hands gripping his knees. "This time's better than before. This time she's conscious, at least till the very end." He stared at the floor, his face dark red.

"It's better when they're conscious, squirming and crying." Scott raised his face. He looked at her, and she saw tears shining in his eyes.

My God, she thought, he's crying for me.

She hesitated only a moment, then crawled across the floor to him and sat at his side. He took her hand.

"First thing she does when she sees she can't see me, is give me a kick in the nuts."

Scott squeezed her hand. He looked at her and grinned as Hoffman told how she stabbed him. Then they listened as he described following Carl to the hotel.

At last, it was over.

Scott turned off the machine.

Dukane turned away from the window, a strange pleased look on his face. He sat with his back to the wall. Grinning. "Listening to him . . . I got an idea. I know how we might save Nancy. It's a risk for all of us. It may not even work, but it stands a decent chance. I think we owe it to her."

"What's your idea?" Scott asked.

"Send Hoffman out for her."

Lacey groaned as the words clutched her bowels. She felt numb all over.

"We'd have to let him loose," Scott muttered.

"As I said, it's a risk. He might try to get away, or he might turn on us. In either case, he'd be hard to stop. But he's awfully worried about Laveda. I don't think he'd want to make a break, not with the place surrounded. By now, somebody out there might have a pair of those infrared goggles."

"The goggles could kill his chance of getting to Nancy."

"We'd have surprise on our side. They probably aren't watching constantly with those things—if they have them at all. They certainly won't expect us to send Hoffman out for the girl."

"I don't know."

"Lacey?"

"I . . . He's a monster. He'll try something. He'll try to kill us or . . . if he does get away, all the innocent people he'll kill . . ."

"His chances of escape are remote," said Dukane. "I think he knows that. As long as he sticks with us, he has some firepower on his side. If I were him, I'd stick with us until I'm sure we've had it. *Then* I'd chance a break."

"He's put Lacey through hell," Scott said. "If he does take you and me out . . . God only knows what he'd do to her." He placed a hand on Lacey's knee, held it tightly. "I don't want to risk that."

"All right," Dukane said.

"Wait." Lacey covered Scott's hand and squeezed it. "We can't leave her out there. She . . . as Matt said, we owe her. Let's give it a try."

Lacey sat on the floor, her back to the couch, her legs drawn up protectively as Dukane led Hoffman in. One cuff was attached to Dukane's left wrist; the other stood out sideways.

Scott followed, several paces behind, with Jan's shotgun aimed toward the area above the floating cuff.

Lacey raised her revolver and aimed at the same empty space.

"If it ain't Annie Oakley," Hoffman said. "Don't look so worried, huh? I'm doing you guys a favor."

As they approached the broken front window, Dukane removed the handcuffs. He slid a small carving knife from his rear pocket. "Take this," he said. "But leave it outside once you've cut her free."

The knife left his hand. He backed away.

"I'm supposed to go out the window, right?"

"Right. We'll open the door on your way back."

"*If* I come back, huh?"

"If you don't, you'll end up in Laveda's hands. Sooner or later."

"Yeah yeah."

"Get going."

The knife, hovering several feet off the floor, turned toward the broken window. The end of its handle lowered against the sill.

"Holy fuckin' shit," Hoffman said. He sounded impressed. "Look at them, will you?"

"We've seen."

"You just want the one underneath, right?"

"Right."

"Other's dead as a carp." The knife raised and shot through the opening. "Ha! Right on target. She can't feel it anyway, huh?" After a pause, he said, "Look out, belowwww."

Dukane crouched by the window.

As Scott hurried to the other one, curiosity overcame Lacey's distaste. She joined him, pistol ready, and peered out. Immediately, she regretted it. She

gagged, but managed to swallow the bitter fluid that gushed up her throat.

She forced herself not to look away. The arms and legs of both women were spread wide and bound to metal stakes, but the mangled carcass on top hid most of Nancy from her view. Flies swarmed over the tattered skin of Jan's back and rump. The rear of her head had been scraped bald. A splinter of bone protruded from her left arm. Her left leg was dislocated and stretched far longer than the other; Lacey saw a knife embedded in its buttock.

As she watched, the knife slid out. It moved slowly over the ground to the staked foot, and sawed through the rope. Though Nancy's foot remained bound to Jan's, it was now free of the stake. It didn't move.

The knife crossed the area between the spread legs, and cut the next rope.

It dropped out of sight beside the legs, and reappeared sliding along the ground near Nancy's outstretched left arm. It cut through the rope, then returned over the ground to her side. It appeared again near the feet, crossed the space between them, and moved up the other side. It snaked the length of Nancy's right arm, sawed through the rope.

Dukane stepped to the door.

The women's feet wobbled slightly. Then they rose from the ground and the bodies jerked into motion. Gunfire broke the silence. Bullets kicked up dust around the dragging bodies. Dark matter burst from Jan's back. Her head jumped, pieces exploding away.

Dukane threw open the door.

The bodies bounced up the low stoop. More bullets smacked into Jan, splashing her like pebbles striking water.

Then they were inside. Dukane kicked the door shut. As slugs pounded through it, he lunged toward the raised feet of the women. The feet began to drop. He swung his pistol, but it swept through empty air. Scott raced to help. Dukane's head snapped sideways. He staggered and dropped to his knees. Scott clutched his own belly. As he doubled, his shirt collar and belt jerked taut. He was lifted high off the floor.

Lacey fired twice at the space beneath him.

Then he was slammed down. The tile floor pounded aside his hands and knees. His forehead hit with a thud.

Dukane shot over him. Four bullets hit the far wall, blasting holes in the plaster, knocking down a framed oil of a desert sunset. He came forward slowly, in a crouch, his head turning as if he thought he might see a target. The gun suddenly flew from his twisted hand. He grunted as the front of his pants dented in. His nose jerked sideways, spouting blood. Throwing himself forward, he reached out and fell.

Lacey fired above his back. Her bullet smacked the wall. She aimed over his head and fired again. His head jumped. For a sinking instant, she thought she'd hit Dukane. Then the head snapped down, thudding the floor. He went limp.

Lacey pushed herself to her feet. She stood with her back to the wall, pistol forward. Dukane and

Scott both lay motionless on the red tile floor. She breathed hard. Her heart felt ready to explode.

"My turn," Hoffman said.

From the left.

She shot at his voice. Splinters burst from the hall door frame.

"Time for fun and games."

She aimed again, then hesitated, realizing the six-shot pistol held only one more live cartridge. If she missed with this one . . .

She knew a target she couldn't miss.

With a quaking hand, she raised the pistol and pressed its muzzle to her head.

CHAPTER THIRTY-TWO

"Go on," said the voice in front of Lacey. "I'll fuck you anyway. Only thing is, you won't get a chance to enjoy it."

She tried to force her finger to move, to squeeze the stiff, curved metal of the trigger just a bit, just a quarter inch, just enough. But part of her mind resisted. She wanted to live. She gazed at Scott's unmoving body, and didn't want to leave him. She wanted to see him smile again, to hear his laughter, to feel his gentle arms around her. Even if only one more time. As she stared at Scott, he moved one hand slightly.

She thumbed back the pistol's hammer.

"*Adios*," said Hoffman.

She stabbed the pistol forward, felt its muzzle stop against Hoffman, and jerked the trigger.

"Bitch!" he shrieked through the gun's roar.

Something clubbed her face, knocking her head back against the wall. Her hand stung. The pistol fell. Another blow struck her face. As she sagged, a hand clutched her throat. It held her to the wall. The neck of her tank top jerked out. The fabric stretched taut, popped, and tore down the front. Pain erupted

in her breasts as he grabbed them and tugged her to the floor.

Her knees pounded the tile. He forced her backward. Down beside Nancy. Beside Jan. She tried to raise her head, but had no strength. Warm fluid spilled onto her legs as the gym shorts were yanked down. Hoffman's blood! Her panties were ripped away.

Where's Scott? her mind screamed. He's alive. She'd seen him move. *Why doesn't he stop this!*

She gasped in agony as Hoffman shoved into her. He rammed hard, one hand gripping her breast as if to keep her from being shoved over the floor by the force of his thrusts. A wetness splattered her shoulder as he plunged.

She should've . . . why hadn't she pulled the damn trigger on herself and ended it? Better that than . . .

He pushed her head sideways. As he chewed and sucked the side of her neck, she saw Jan's face inches away from her own. The blank, staring eyes. The flap of dark flesh hanging off her cheek. The torn lips baring her broken teeth.

Dead.

Better this. Hoffman grunting and slobbering, twisting her skin, battering her insides with his vile organ. Better this than like Jan.

She lowered her gaze to the wide, blinking eyes of Nancy. They were filled with terror, but alive.

Where's Scott!

Hoffman's weight was on her now, crushing her chest, his mouth mashing her lips, suffocating her as he pounded down with his pelvis. Then he was rigid.

Lacey felt his jerking throb inside her, the spurt of fluid.

He lay on top of her, breathing heavily. At last, his weight lifted. She felt his organ slide out.

She raised her head enough to see Scott and Dukane still unconscious on the floor.

"Guess what's next," Hoffman hissed.

Lacey shut her eyes and said nothing.

He grabbed her hair and pulled her to her feet. "One guess, cunt." He paused. "No? Well, just watch and see."

The door flew open behind Lacey. A hand squeezed the back of her neck. Another clutched between her legs. She was lifted off her feet and hurled outside.

She hit the ground hard, tumbling, gasping as gravel and cactus tore her skin. Then she lay still and awaited the hail of bullets.

CHAPTER THIRTY-THREE

Dukane's head throbbed with fire. He lay motionless, feeling the floor under him, wondering what had happened. Slowly, he remembered. Guilt hit him like a club.

What have I done!

He forced himself to open one eye. The living room was bright with sunlight. Nearby was the sprawled body of Scott, hands cuffed behind him.

Dukane was tied with electrical cord. As he struggled to free himself, he heard a quiet sob.

"Scott?" he whispered.

The body rolled over. "Matt?" His face was wet with tears. "I thought you were dead."

"Where's Hoffman?"

"I . . . I don't know. He took Nancy into the bedroom a few minutes ago. Probably in there. Matt, Lacey's . . ." He choked back a sob. "Lacey's gone."

"Where?"

Scott shook his head. "I came to . . . asked Hoffman. He just laughed."

"Shit."

"Oh God, Matt . . ."

"Take it easy." He jerked his hands free. Grimacing as pain cut into his head like a lance, he rolled onto his side and untied the knotted cord at his feet. He scanned the room, and flinched. In the rocking chair facing the broken front window sat Jan. The shotgun rested over the sill, aiming outside.

"Beau Geste," Scott muttered.

"Maybe the shotgun's loaded." Dukane forced himself to stand. He took one step.

A tinny, amplified voice said, "We want Hoffman. You've got five minutes. Bring him out, and we'll let you go. If not, you'll all die. The girl first."

"Lacey," Scott whispered.

Dukane rushed to the window. As he reached for the shotgun, he looked out.

He saw Lacey. A hundred yards away. Sprawled across the hood of the Rolls Royce. Her arms and legs were outstretched and tied.

A dozen men and women stood near the car, watching as a woman lashed her once with a thin, golden chain.

The woman was naked. Glossy, blonde hair draped her back. Her gold arm bands glinted sunlight.

Laveda!

In spite of the heat, gooseflesh prickled Dukane's skin.

Lacey's quiet gasp of pain came through the silence as the chain struck again.

Dukane grabbed the double-barreled shotgun. He broke it open. The chambers were empty. Turning from the window, he looked for other weapons.

The pistols were nowhere in sight. He quietly closed the breach.

"Four minutes," the distant voice announced.

Dukane hurried to Scott. He fished a key from his pocket and knelt to unlock the cuffs.

"Is it Lacey?"

"Yes."

"Oh God."

"Come on." Dukane tiptoed into the hallway, Scott close behind him. The bathroom door stood open. The bedroom door was shut. Almost.

He stepped quietly toward it. Stopped.

From inside came muffled grunting sounds, the creak of bedsprings.

Nancy lay on the bed, her sweat-slick body pounding against the mattress, arms stretched overhead, breasts oddly mashed, legs wide open and twitching, the lips of her vagina spread far apart like an open, sucking mouth. Dukane heard the slap of flesh, and wet, smacking sounds.

"Three minutes," announced the amplified voice.

Dukane shouldered open the door. He ran for the bed, reversing the shotgun, raising it high by its barrels.

Nancy's wet eyes looked up at him. She turned her head away as he swung the shotgun down.

It stopped before hitting her, stopped six inches above her face, stopped with a crashing thud like a coconut hurled against concrete. The stock of the shotgun split on impact. Teethmarks appeared in Nancy's cheek—empty, ragged holes that quickly filled with blood.

Scott dived onto her. He groped above her left arm, grabbed, snapped a handcuff in place, closed the other bracelet around his own wrist.

"Got him!" Scott cried.

CHAPTER THIRTY-FOUR

"You have two minutes," said the man with the megaphone.

Even as he spoke, the thin chain twirled over the head of the woman beside Lacey, its gold links flashing sunlight, and whistled down. She cried out as it cut fire across her breasts. A smile trembled on the woman's lips. Her nipples stood erect on her sweaty breasts.

She's getting off, Lacey thought.

It must've been at her command that the rifles hadn't opened up on Lacey, that instead the Rolls had come for her. She'd watched it approach, too frightened to move, thinking *it's dead*, Dukane got it with a Molotov cocktail, how can it be coming? It bore down on her, its grill blinding in the sunlight. She thought it might crush her into the gravel, but it slipped sideways and its black front tire missed by inches. A door flew open. She was dragged inside the chilly, air-conditioned car.

Two men held her across their laps, pawing her as the car sped away.

The chain whipped down, lashing her belly.

The woman was breathing hard. But not from the

exertion. She licked her lips, and struck again. Lacey jerked rigid as the chain cut her thighs.

It was the woman who ordered her tied to the car's hood. The sun-baked metal had scorched her, but the pain of the burned flesh faded when the whipping started.

The chain whished down, biting into her shoulder and breast.

A man suddenly threw himself onto her, licking the blood from her breast.

The woman lashed him. "Not yet!" she snapped. Others jerked him away.

"One minute," said the man with the megaphone.

"They won't come," said a stocky, red-faced man. The chain slashed her belly.

"I did not expect them to come," the woman said in a trembling voice. "They threw her out. She's ours."

"Will we drink?" asked a voice.

"When I am done with her." Again, the chain whipped down.

Lacey bucked as it tore her.

"The dagger."

A teenaged girl in a bikini and Dodger cap handed a knife to her. Lacey stared at its thin, tapering blade.

"The river flows," said the woman.

"The river is red," chanted the others.

"The river flows!"

"Flows from the heart."

"The river . . ."

"They're coming out!" a man cried.

Lifting her head, Lacey stared over her torn body.

Dukane and Scott were out of the house, walking slowly forward, tugging at the open space between them.

She glanced at the woman, saw a fierce smile on her face.

"Tell the snipers not to shoot. I want all three alive."

A man spoke over his megaphone, ordering everyone to hold fire.

On both sides of the car, men and women lowered their weapons.

Lacey gazed at Scott, watched him struggle to hold his invisible, silent captive. The pain of her wounds was forgotten as gratitude and despair brought tears to her eyes.

They're doing this for me, she realized.

Sacrificing themselves.

If only she'd had the courage to end her life back at the house when she had the chance . . .

They were thirty yards away.

"Go back!" she yelled, but she knew it was too late.

The men kept coming, jerking and swaying as if the beast between them fought to free himself.

Twenty yards.

She could see the grim, determined look on Scott's face.

Ten yards.

A low laugh came from the woman. "Bring him to me," she called. "I have waited a long time for Samuel Hoffman. And for you, Matthew Dukane. This will be a great day for me."

"Every dog has its day," Dukane said. One side of his mouth curled into a smile.

He and Scott sprang apart, diving sideways and rolling through the dust. Four pistols appeared from behind them. They stopped rolling, and their gunfire stuttered through the stillness in a deafening roar.

Bodies whirled and flopped. Dirt exploded around Scott and Dukane as their fire was returned. Screams tore through the din. A man clutched his belly and sat down hard. The ball cap and bloody matter flew from the head of the teenaged girl as she fired at Dukane. He tossed a pistol aside and kept firing his automatic. A man spun, crashed into the side of the car, and fell.

Dukane yelled as he was hit.

Scott rose to one knee, not even glancing at him, shoving a fresh magazine into the handle of his .45. Gravel kicked up beside his foot, but he didn't flinch. He worked the slide and resumed firing.

Dukane was on his knees, his left arm hanging limp, firing with his right.

A man raced forward, shooting. A bullet slammed him down.

Abruptly, there was silence.

Jerking her head from side to side, Lacey saw no one still standing. On both sides of the car lay crumpled bodies.

Scott ran forward in a crouch. Far off, a rifle cracked. Dirt spouted in front of him.

As Dukane dropped and crawled forward, Scott dived to the ground near a fat man. He grabbed the

man's rifle. It had a telescopic sight. Settling himself in a prone position, he aimed toward the far left of the house.

A distant shot. The top of a cactus near Dukane exploded. Scott fired, then made a thumbs-up sign at Dukane. He swung the barrel to his right.

Dukane scurried forward. He reached the front of the car, and began to cut the rope at Lacey's foot.

A shot thunked the grill.

Scott fired. "Watch it," he called. "Still one out there."

Dukane freed Lacey's left hand, then rushed around the rear of the car and came up at her other side. As he sliced through the rope, a shot rang out. The bullet smacked the windshield inches above her head.

He scurried to the front.

Scott fired. "Got him!" he yelled. "That oughta be it."

Lacey sat up. As soon as her right foot was loose, she scooted off the hood. Scott, hurrying toward her, passed the rifle to Dukane and pulled off his shirt. He draped the shirt over Lacey's back. Holding her by the shoulders, he looked down at her torn body. "Oh God, Lacey," he murmured. "I'm sorry. I'm so sorry."

With blurry, tear-filled eyes, she stared at his tormented face. She kissed him. Then she managed a smile. "Who do you think you are, James Bond?"

"Max Carter and Charlie Dane."

Dukane came up behind him. "I think I deserve a kiss, too."

He got one. Lacey hugged him, ignoring the pain of her own wounds, and kissed his dry lips.

"You guys are nuts, coming out like that."

"The best defense . . ." Dukane said.

Lacey gasped, her joy suddenly turning to cold fear. "Hoffman! You let him . . ." She staggered back, clutching the shirt tight to hide her nakedness, looking behind her as if she might somehow see him sneaking up.

"Hoffman isn't with us," Dukane said.

"I know. You let him . . ."

"He's still in the house," Scott interrupted. "Securely handcuffed in the bathroom."

"You mean . . . ?"

"Pretty good act, huh?"

"Now," said Dukane, "how about attending to my arm before I bleed to death?"

"Oh," Scott muttered. "Forgot about that."

"I didn't."

CHAPTER THIRTY-FIVE

The bullet had smashed a bone in Dukane's forearm. Scott broke the stock off a rifle, and made ungainly splints from it. He used strips of Dukane's shirt to bandage the wound and lash the splints into place.

"We'd better get you to a hospital," he said. "Both of you, and Nancy."

"All in good time. See if the car works."

Scott helped Lacey inside.

"Right with you," Dukane said.

As Scott climbed into the driver's seat, Dukane wandered from body to body, crouching over several of the women for a closer inspection.

Scott turned the ignition key. The car came to life, blowing cool, welcome air onto Lacey.

"What's he looking for?" she asked.

Scott shook his head.

Finally, Dukane climbed into the backseat. In each hand, he held a large gold band, the bands Lacey had seen on the arms of the woman who'd whipped her. "I know I hit the bitch," he said. "Saw her go down."

"Who?"

"Laveda. But she's not here now. Just her damn jewelry. Did you see anyone run off?"

"No," Scott said. "I thought we got them all."

"Okay. Let's pick up Hoffman and Nancy, and get the hell out of here."

The car sped forward, bumping over the rough earth, down a gradual slope, and up a rise to the flat area in front of the house. Scott turned off the engine. "You can wait here if you want," he told Lacey.

She didn't want to be left alone. "I'll go in," she said.

Scott pulled the key from the ignition and stepped out. Lacey opened her door. Stifling heat wrapped her like a blanket as she climbed out. She glimpsed the body of the man under the broken window, hammer still clutched in his outflung hand.

She entered the house behind Scott. Dukane followed and shut the door. The house was silent.

"Nancy?" Dukane called.

No answer.

He suddenly broke into a run, vanishing down the hall. Scott and Lacey rushed after him.

The bedroom was empty.

"Nancy?"

From the closet came a muffled sob.

Dukane jerked its door open.

Nancy sat crouched in a corner, half-hidden behind hanging dresses. Her black hair clung to her face with sweat. Though the room was hot and she

wore jeans and a wool shirt, Lacey could see her shivering.

"It's all right," Dukane told her. "It's over. Everything's fine."

"No," she gasped, batting away his hands as he reached for her. Her wide eyes blinked. "Not over. Wanta hide."

From behind them came a scream that washed over Lacey like a vile, chilling flood. It was the scream of a man.

"Get Nancy out of here," Scott snapped, and ran after Dukane.

Lacey dropped to her knees. She tried to grab the girl's flailing hands. "Stop!" she cried. Then she clutched a foot and dragged Nancy from the closet. She pulled the girl to her feet, tugged her into the hall.

From there, she saw Dukane slam the bathroom door, shutting himself and Scott inside.

Screams filled her ears as she led Nancy through the living room. "Wait in the car," she said.

Then she raced to the hall.

The bathroom door flew open. Dukane staggered backward through it, and fell. The wooden hilt of a butcher knife stood upright in his belly.

As she ran toward him, she heard a *whup* like the sound of a wind-flapped canvas. Fire exploded through the doorway.

"Scott!" she shrieked.

The fire lapped her body, forcing her away from the door. She shielded her eyes and gazed into the inferno. Near the floor, she saw a hole in the fire as

if a tunnel had been dug in the flames—a writhing tunnel shaped like a man.

A passage opened in the blaze. It rushed toward her. Smashed her aside. She tripped over Dukane. As she slammed the far wall, she saw a flaming figure race down the hallway, arms waving, hair ablaze.

Scott? She ran after it. As it lurched across the living room, she realized she could see through it: the fire blazed around a hollow shell. It fell against a window. The curtains caught fire. As it lurched out the front door, it turned and Lacey glimpsed its fire-wrapped face, its breasts.

She rushed back to the bathroom.

"Scott!" she cried out. "*Scott!*"

The wall of fire roared.

CHAPTER THIRTY-SIX

Lacey circled the block twice, watching for strangers, then killed the headlights and steered the Firebird up the narrow driveway to her garage. She put it into the garage, and entered her house by the back door.

The lights were off. She left them that way.

Searching the dark house, she remembered how she and Cliff had gone through it that night so long ago—only a few days ago. They'd found no one then. Lacey found no one now. But she couldn't be certain she was alone: she could never be sure of that again.

Though filthy, she was afraid to use her tub.

Though dazed and weary, she was afraid to use her bed.

She arranged blankets inside her walk-in closet, and lay down there. It reminded her of the nest in the hallway that she'd shared with Scott.

Thoughts of Scott swirled through her mind as she tried to sleep. Other thoughts, too. Bad ones that made her shake.

Three times during the night, she heard sounds in the house that made her sweat and hold her breath.

Afraid to investigate, she lay there rigid until exhaustion forced her to fall limp and gasp for air.

Once, as she drifted off, the closet door swung silently open. The dark figure of a man knelt over her. She quaked with terror until he spoke.

"It's just me," he said.

"Scott?"

"I had a hard time finding you. What're you hiding from?"

"Everything."

"Don't be afraid."

"Oh Scott, I thought you were dead."

Then he came down and kissed her, and his charred lips crumbled and filled her mouth with ashes.

She bolted upright, gasping, and found herself alone in the closet. Its door was still shut.

After a moment's hesitation, she pushed open the door. She studied the familiar, night shadows of her bedroom, then crawled over the carpet to the alarm clock. Four thirty.

Time to begin.

Lacey tiptoed through the dark silence of the house. She searched cupboards in the kitchen, found what she wanted, and stepped outside.

She entered her garage through a side door connecting it to the laundry room. A dim light went on inside the Firebird when she opened its door. Kneeling on the passenger seat, reached out and drew its keys from the ignition.

The Firebird was one of the four cars she'd

found after she ran from the burning house and discovered the keys of the Rolls Royce were gone. She and Nancy had dashed up the long entry road, and come upon the cars of the dead people. She'd insisted Nancy take one of them, and leave her.

Now, keys in hand, Lacey crawled out of the Firebird. She left its door open for light, and walked over the warm concrete to the trunk. Taking a deep breath, she unlocked it. The lid swung up.

As dawn lightened the sky, Lacey twisted off the plastic cap. She raised the bottle to her lips. Its strong fumes made her throat clutch, but she filled her mouth anyway to wash out the other taste—the sour taste of the vomit that had flooded out after the blood.

She spat the brandy onto the loose earth at her feet, then upended the bottle. The amber fluid gurgled out, splashing onto the dirt.

When it was empty, she tossed it aside. It fell to the grass beside the cellophane package of beans and the knife.

She put her clothes back on, covering her blood-spattered nakedness.

Then she picked up her shovel. She set it inside the laundry room. Shutting the door, she started for her house.

A man stepped around the corner.

Numb with fear, she staggered back.

The man didn't move.

She gazed at him, at his blackened face and torso, his hairless scalp, his scorched and tattered pants—

and recognized the phantom from her nightmares. She pressed trembling hands to her eyes. At the sound of footsteps, she lowered them.

He was walking toward her, his sooty hands reaching out.

"Thought you'd be glad to see me," he said. "I know I look like a wreck, but . . ."

"Scott," she muttered.

He clutched her shoulders and drew her against his body. His cracked, dry lips pressed her mouth. She felt the wetness of his tongue. His hands stroked her hair, the sides of her face.

"It *is* you?" she whispered. Scott's grimy, grinning face blurred as tears filled Lacey's eyes.

CHAPTER THIRTY-SEVEN

He guzzled half a bottle of Bud, leaned back on the kitchen chair, and sighed.

"That was Hoffman we heard screaming. When Matt and I ran in the bathroom, all we saw was this butcher knife jerking around right above the floor. And the handcuffs shaking. Laveda must've made herself invisible when the shooting started. Must've had a bean left over from the time she'd gone through the process a year ago.

"She went for Matt. That gave me a chance to douse her with gas and touch her off. The whole gas can went up, though. I thought I was cooked, but I dived out the bathroom window. The fall . . . it knocked me out cold. Don't think I was out for long, but by the time I reached the front of the house, I saw you and Nancy running off."

"Why didn't you yell?"

He shook his head and took another gulp of beer. "I figured I could catch up later. The main thing was to get Matt out of the house."

"You went back in?"

"Had to. Couldn't leave him in there. I got to him just before the fire did, dragged him out, patched up

his stomach wound the best I could, and threw him into the car. When I drove up the road, you and Nancy were nowhere in sight. I figured you'd be all right, though, so I drove like hell back to Tucson and got him into an emergency room. I didn't think he'd make it, but he's a tough son of a bitch. They had him in stable condition by the time I left."

"He's *alive*?" Lacey grinned. "Well. What do you know?"

"When I got back to the house and couldn't find you, I suspected you might come back here."

"I didn't know where else to go."

"Not the greatest hide-out in the world."

"I had a plan," she admitted, and lowered her eyes. Until now, the plan had seemed like her only chance for survival. With Scott sitting across the breakfast table, it seemed ridiculous and perverse. She didn't want to tell him about it.

"In your place," Scott said, "I might've tried the same thing."

"You know?"

"I saw the empty brandy bottle out back. And the sack of beans. And where you dug the hole."

"The . . . the rest of the body's still in the garage. I found her . . . near where they'd left their cars. After I sent Nancy away, I . . . a bean was in the dirt by her mouth. That's what gave me the idea. If I were invisible, nobody could get me. I tried the bean, but it didn't make me invisible. So then I put her body in the trunk of a car and . . . God, it was all burned and crumbly and . . ."

"It was Laveda!"

Lacey nodded. "I guess so."

Reaching out, Scott squeezed her hand. "Then it's over."

That night, he dug up the head. They drove far out in the desert, and poured gasoline over the remains of Laveda. The fire burned for a long time. When it finally dwindled, they dug two holes in the sand and buried the smoldering head a great distance from the body.

Turn the page for an advance look at Richard
Laymon's next terrifying novel . . .

DARK MOUNTAIN

Coming in March 2009

CHAPTER ONE

Cheryl heard it again—the soft, dry crunching sound that a foot might make in leaves. This time, it was very close.

She lay rigid in her sleeping bag, barely daring to breathe, gazing straight up at the dark slanting wall of the tent and telling herself to stay calm.

It's probably just an animal. Maybe a deer. A few days ago, camped in a meadow below the pass, they'd been awakened in the night by a deer wandering near their tent. Its hooves had crashed through the foliage, snapping branches and shaking the ground. Bambi the Elephant, Danny had called it.

This was different.

This was stealthy.

She heard it again, flinched, and dug her fingertips into her bare thighs.

Maybe something falling from a tree? Pinecones? They could make sounds like that, she supposed. Plenty of wind out there to shake them loose.

That's it. That has to be it. Otherwise, somebody is standing just outside the tent, and that can't be.

They'd seen nobody for two days. They'd reached Lower Mesquite Lake early in the afternoon. Except

for this small patch of woods, the glacial lake was surrounded by barren rock. They'd hiked completely around it. They'd explored the woods. They'd seen nobody.

Not even when they hiked over a small ridge to Upper Mesquite.

Nobody.

Cheryl took a deep breath, trying to calm herself. *Go to sleep, chicken-shit.*

Cheryl consciously relaxed her legs and rump and back, settling down into the warmth, and turned her head to stretch her taut neck muscles. She felt like rolling over. She wanted to turn facedown and burrow deep, but she was afraid to move that much.

A monster under the bed. Just like when she was a kid and *knew* there was a terrible monster under the bed. If she lay absolutely still, it would leave her alone.

I'm eighteen. I'm too old for this.

Slowly, she started to turn over. Her bare skin made whispery, sliding sounds against the nylon bag, almost loud enough to mask the other sound. She went stiff. She was on her side, facing Danny. The other sound came from behind her—a quiet hissing sigh, a sound such as fingernails might make scraping along the tent's wall.

She flung herself against Danny, shook him by the shoulders. Moaning, he raised his head. "Huh? Wha—"

"Somebody's outside," she gasped.

He pushed himself up on his elbows. "Huh?"

"Outside. I heard him."

"Who?"

"Shh."

Neither of them moved.

"I don't hear anything," he said in a groggy voice.

"I did. God, he's right outside the tent. He *scratched* on it."

"Probably just a branch."

"*Danny*."

"Okay, okay, I'll go out 'n' have a look."

"I'll go with you."

"No point both of us freezing our asses. I'll go." He rose to his hands and knees, still in the double sleeping bag, letting in the cold night air as he searched through the clothes and gear at the head of the tent. He pulled his flashlight out of his boot. "Just be a minute," he said.

Cheryl scooted away. Danny climbed from the bag and crawled to the foot of the tent. Kneeling there, naked, he pulled at the zipper of the mosquito netting.

Cheryl sat up. The cold wrapped around her. Shuddering, she hugged her breasts. "Maybe you'd better not," she whispered. "Come on back."

"Nah, it's all right."

"Please?"

"I've gotta take a leak anyway," he said, and started to crawl through the flaps. He was halfway out when he stopped. He uttered a low groan. One of his feet reached backward.

Cheryl heard a wet thud. Spray rained against the tent flaps.

Danny's legs shot out from under him. He bounced

up and down, knees pounding the tent floor, flopping in mad spasms that seemed to last forever. At last, he lay motionless.

Cheryl stared in horror as Danny began to slide through the flaps. His buttocks vanished. His legs dragged along as if he were being sucked slowly into a dark mouth.

Cheryl was alone in the tent.

But not for long.

CHAPTER TWO

Meg staggered into the living room, a strap of her negligee sagging down her arm. "Good grief, hon, what time is it?"

"Nighttime," Karen said.

"Tell me. Christ, tell me. Call this a vacation?"

"I sure do."

"Yeah, guess you would." She flopped into a chair, hooked one leg over its stuffed arm, and stretched to reach for a pack of cigarettes. "What time's he picking you up?"

"Five thirty."

"Gug. Want me to put on some coffee?"

"I don't want to be peeing."

"Shit. Car full of kids, you'll be stopping every five minutes anyway." She lit a cigarette.

"They're not exactly kids," Karen said. "Julie's sixteen. Benny's thirteen or fourteen."

"Even worse. Christ, kiddo, you're in for it."

"They're okay." Karen propped the backpack against the sofa and shoved in the mummy bag.

"Who's this other family?"

"The Gordons. Never met them before."

"They have kids, too?"

"Three."

"Oh, you're gonna have a *swell* time. Hope you're not planning to screw the guy."

"We'll see." Karen buckled the leather straps of the cover, picked up the backpack, and carried it toward the front door. She leaned it against the wall.

"Sure sounds like loads of fun. Wish I was coming."

"You were invited."

"Give me a break. I need a campout like I need a third boob."

Karen dropped to the sofa and started to put on her hiking boots. They were Pivettas, scratched and scuffed. They had stood in the back of her closet, unworn since the summer she finished her MA four years before, but they felt comfortable and familiar, like good friends from the past—friends with stories of dusty switchbacks, the cool wind of mountain passes, desolate lakes, icy streams, and campfire smoke. She finished lacing them, and slapped her bare knees. "This is gonna be great."

"You're a masochist," Meg said, and stabbed out her cigarette.

"You don't know what you're missing."

"Sure I do. Sack time." She pushed herself off the chair, yawned, and stretched. "Well, have fun if you can."

"Right. See you next Sunday."

"Give my regards to the chipmunks." With a wiggle of her fingers, she turned away and left the room.

Karen glanced at her wristwatch. Five twenty-eight.

Leaning back, she stretched out her legs. Her plaid shirt was gaping open at the belly. She fastened the button, then checked the fly of her cutoff corduroys. All set. She yawned. Maybe she should've taken Meg up on that coffee. She inhaled, a deep breath that seemed to fill her whole body with a light, pleasant weariness. As she let it slowly out, she shut her eyes.

A whole week in the mountains with Scott. Kids or no kids, it would be wonderful. They would find time to be alone, if only at night. It'd be cold, and they'd snuggle together with the wind whapping the tent walls. . . .

The blare of the doorbell shocked her awake. She shoved herself off the sofa and hurried to the door. She pulled it open.

Scott, standing under the porch light, smiled at her through the screen.

"Take your *Watchtower* and shove it," she said, and shut the door. When she opened it again, his face was pressed to the screen.

"I want your body," he whispered.

For an instant, face mashed out of shape, he looked like a stranger. Karen felt a tingle of fright. Then he stepped back and was Scott again, handsome and smiling. "Ready for action?" he asked.

"Yep." As she pushed open the screen door, she leaned out and glimpsed his car in the driveway. The headlights were on. The car's interior was dark. "The kids there?" she asked.

"Just barely. It was murder getting Julie out of bed. Benny was raring to go. I'm not sure he even

slept last night. Then he decided he couldn't live without his binoculars and we couldn't find the damn things."

"Did you?"

"We did. But it screwed up our departure time."

"You're forgiven."

"Thanks," he said. He took Karen into his arms. He smelled of coffee and aftershave. With his mouth pushing gently against hers, she felt so comfortable that she thought she might doze off. Until his hands went under her shirt. She was wide awake as they moved up her back and under her armpits and closed gently over her breasts. They circled. They caressed. Her nipples stiffened under their touch.

"Think I'll send the kids home," he muttered.

"Mmm. I've missed you."

He kissed her again, hugging her tightly. "We'd better get it in motion. You all packed and ready?"

"All set."

She bent to pick up her backpack. "Allow me," Scott said. As he lifted it, Karen hurried to the coffee table. She grabbed her handbag and floppy felt hat, and followed him out the door.

The morning air wrapped around her bare arms and legs, seeped like chilly water through her shirt. Shivering, she waved at the dim face peering out through the backseat window. In the blue-gray light, she couldn't tell whether it belonged to Julie or Benny.

"You can get in," Scott said.

She shrugged, preferring to wait rather than enter

the car without him. They went to the trunk. She stood with her shoulders hunched, arms folded across her chest, legs pressed together, jaw tight to keep her teeth from chattering.

Scott smiled back at her as he unlocked the trunk. "The heater's on."

"The fresh air feels good."

He laughed, and placed her backpack on top of the others. Then he swung the lid shut. "Forget anything?"

"Probably."

He leaned back against the trunk, looking relaxed and warm. Of course, he was wearing long pants and a flannel shirt. "Sunglasses?" he asked.

"Got 'em."

"Jacket?"

"In my pack. Wish I had it on."

"Let's go."

Karen headed for the passenger door, taking her time, waiting until Scott was in the driver's seat before she opened the door. She ducked inside and smiled over the back of her seat. "Morning," she said.

"Hiya, hiya," Benny said, winking one eye in time with the words. He raised a closed hand to his mouth as if holding a microphone. "And a good good morning to you and thanks for tuning in. Have we got a show for you!"

"Can it, Bonzo," Julie said. She gave Karen a quick, tight-lipped smile and turned her face toward the window.

Karen sat down. She pulled her door shut. The

heater blew against her legs. She sighed and settled back, enjoying the warmth as Scott backed out of the driveway.

"All right if I drive?" Nick asked.

His father shoved the station wagon's tailgate into place. "Can you keep it under sixty?"

"If you don't care when we get there."

"Well, our ETA's two thirty. I think we can make it without breaking any speed records. You start getting tired, though, let me know."

"Right."

They climbed into the car. Nick started the engine.

His father twisted around. "Any last-minute pit stops?"

"Gross," Heather said from the backseat.

"Vile," said Rose.

"I think we're all set," Mom told him.

"Sunglasses? Hats? Tampax?"

"*Dad!*" the twins blurted in unison.

"Arnold!"

"High altitudes," he said, keeping a straight face. "Bleeding occurs."

"*Nose*bleeds," Rose said.

Heather giggled.

"Whatever," Dad said. "Can't be too careful. 'Be Prepared,' right, Nick?"

"I've got mine."

His father burst out laughing, and slapped his knee.

"I hope you fellows get it out of your systems before we meet the O'Tooles."

"Scott's no prude." He glanced at Nick. "San Diego Freeway. Runs right into 99 just the other side of the Grapevine."

Nick pulled away from the curb.

"Everybody buckled up?"

Near the corner, Nick flipped on the turn signal though no other cars were in sight. With his father beside him, he planned to drive by the book. He slowed almost to a stop before making the turn.

"What's his girlfriend's name?" Mom asked.

"Sharon? *Karen*. Karen something. He ran into her at a Sav-On."

"A checkout girl?"

"No, no, she was in line with him. I think he said she's a teacher."

"Oh, yuck," Rose said.

"What does she look like?"

"A real bow-wow. Floppy ears, hair on her face, a wet nose. Nice tail, though."

"What *do* you know about her?" Mom asked.

"Not much. You know Scott. Keeps his cards close to the vest."

"I hope she plays bridge. June was so fantastic."

"Don't start on her."

"Well, she was."

"I don't think we want to discuss that person in front of the girls."

"I don't know why you're so angry. She didn't run out on *you*."

"My best friend. Same difference. Now I think it would be wise to drop the subject. You have a green arrow," he told Nick.

Nick made the left-hand turn and headed down the freeway on-ramp, embarrassed that he'd let his mind drift away from the driving. In the past, he'd heard a few references to the O'Tooles' breakup, but never anything so close to an argument. He was intrigued. It was none of his business though. Driving was his business, and he'd better pay attention or his father would take over.

Nick liked to drive. He wished they were taking the Mustang instead of this clunker, but it would've been a tight squeeze with all of them plus five backpacks. Besides, Dad wouldn't want to leave it sitting out in the middle of nowhere for a week. Last year, up at Yosemite, someone had broken a window of the station wagon and had a party inside. They'd come back to find beer cans and a pair of torn, pink panties on the floor.

The break-in had frightened Nick, and he felt uneasy thinking about it now. It was bad enough that some creeps had fooled around in the car, but what if you ran into them on an isolated trail? What if they stumbled onto your camp?

Nothing like that had ever happened to them, but it could. Nick was glad that the O'Tooles were coming along this year. Like Dad, Scott O'Tooles was a big man. If any trouble came up, they'd be able to handle it.

With a feeling of relief, he checked the side mirror, signaled, and slipped into the right-hand lane. He sped up on the overpass. Before it curved over the Santa Monica Freeway, he eased off the accelerator. He picked up speed again on the way down,

signaled a left, and drifted across three deserted lanes of the San Diego Freeway.

His father leaned across the seat to check the speedometer. The needle hovered between 55 and 60 miles per hour. With a nod of approval, he settled back. "You get tired, let me know."

Benny leaned forward. "Hey, Karen?" he said to the back of her head. She turned in her seat and looked around at him. Her face, so near to his, made him feel funny—excited and warm and a little embarrassed. He stared at her, forgetting what he'd planned to say.

He'd never seen her from so close. Her eyes were clear blue like the water of the swimming pool. He noticed, for the first time, the light golden hair barely visible above her upper lip. His cousin, Tanya, with dark hair, had more of a mustache there. Hers looked a little gross, but this on Karen looked so soft and fuzzy that he wished he could touch it. Maybe there wasn't even enough to feel, not over her mouth anyway, but it looked a little heavier on her smooth, tanned cheeks.

"Do you know how to get down off an elephant?" he asked.

"No, how?"

"You don't. You get down off a duck."

Karen smiled and shook her head slightly.

Then she turned away. He could no longer see her face. Sitting back, he stared at her. The rim of an ear showed through her hair. He wished she

would look around again, but first he would have to think of another joke.

He'd only seen Karen once before today. Usually, his father drove off to meet her. But last Saturday, she came over for barbecued ribs. She'd worn white shorts and a loose shirt of shiny red with green and white flowers, and she'd looked beautiful. When Dad introduced him, she shook his hand and said, "Very nice to meet you, Benny."

She had a pale scar curved like a horseshoe on her forearm. He'd wanted to ask her about it, but didn't have the guts.

That day was overcast, so nobody went into the pool and he didn't get to see her in a swimsuit. She sat across the table from him at dinner. It wasn't dark yet, but his father had lit candles. The light from the flames made her hair shine like gold. He thought she was very nice. Julie acted creepy, though. After dinner, Tanya took him and Julie to a movie. By the time they got home, Karen was gone. Dad said she would be coming along on the camping trip, and Julie went crazy. "What do we need her along for? I don't even like her! I don't want to go if she's going." Dad, looking unhappy, asked why she didn't like Karen. "Oh, never mind!" she snapped.

"I think she's nice," Benny had said.

"So do I," Dad told him.

Sometimes, Julie could be a real jerk.

"Anyone hungry?" Dad asked.

"Me!" Benny said.

Julie shrugged and kept on reading her book.

"Julie?"

"I don't care."

"I could use a bite," Karen said, looking toward Dad. Benny saw the side of her face for a moment before she turned forward again. He sighed. Gosh, she was beautiful.

"Well," Dad said. "We'll be at Gorman in a few minutes. We'll stop there and have some breakfast."

"Look out there," Flash said, keeping his voice calm but pressing a hand to the dashboard as a semi swung into their lane. It was moving up the steep grade toward Tejon Pass at half their speed. They were closing in fast.

Nick slipped over one lane to the left, and sped past the truck.

"Stupid fucking bastard," Flash muttered. He lowered his hand from the dash. Nick was looking nervous. "You all right?"

The boy nodded, and licked his lips.

"That . . . He had no business coming over." Flash took a few deep breaths, and slipped a White Owl from his shirt pocket. His fingers trembled as he tore open the cellophane wrapper. He plugged the cigar into his mouth and lit it, then cranked open his window to let the smoke stream out.

"I tell you, Nick, Vietnam was safer than these freeways. Goddamn truckers. Run you down as soon as look at you. Best thing to do is stay out of their way."

Nick glanced at him. The boy still looked shaky. "Too bad this isn't an F-8," Nick said. "We could blow them off the road."

"Thataboy. I tell you, we did our share of that, Scott and me. Nailed whole convoys along the Ho Chi Minh Trail. Blasted the shit out of 'em."

"Arnold," Alice complained from the backseat. She'd heard that one. He glanced around. The twins were asleep, Rose slumped against the door with Heather leaning against her.

"I'll keep it down," he said in a quiet voice.

"Keep it clean."

He tapped off a length of ash, and took a long draw on his cigar. Smoke swirled around his face. *Smoke filled the cockpit. "Blue Leader, this is Flash. Caught a hot one."*

He shook his head sharply, trying to dislodge the memory as his heart began to thunder and his stomach twisted into an icy coil. Oh, Christ!

The station wagon nosed downward, picking up speed.

"Take it slow," he warned.

Nick looked at him and frowned. "Are you okay, Dad?"

"Sure. Fine." He wiped the sweat from his face. He started remembering again. "Well well well," he said quickly to block off the thoughts. "We're over the hump now. The old buggy made it over the Grapevine once again. Gonna be hot as blue blazes in the valley. Good thing we've got our air-conditioning."

CHAPTER THREE

"I offered 'em down, Ettie."

She gazed at the naked bodies of the young man and woman stretched out side by side in front of the tent. The man was facedown, a terrible wound across the back of his neck. The woman, on her back, was bruised and torn. Ettie saw bite marks on her mouth and chin, on her shoulders and breasts. The left nipple was missing entirely.

"I offered *him* with a hatchet," Merle said, rubbing his hands on the legs of his jeans and trying to smile. "The gal, I plain choked her."

"Looks like you did more than that," Ettie muttered.

"She was pretty."

"Merle, you haven't got the sense of a toadstool."

Her son tugged the bill of his faded Dodgers cap down to hide his eyes. "I'm sorry," he said.

"What're we gonna do with you?"

He shrugged. He toed a pinecone with his tennis shoe. "*You* do it," he argued.

"Only when He speaks to me."

"He spoke to me, Ettie. Honest He did. I never would've done it, but He asked me to."

"You sure you weren't just feeling horny?"

"No, ma'am. He spoke to me."

"I saw you yesterday spying on these two. I was afraid you might pull a stunt like this, but I trusted you, fool that I am. I should've known better." She glared at Merle. The bill of his cap rose for a moment as he looked at her. Then it dipped down again. "What did you promise me?"

"I know," he mumbled. "I *said* I'm sorry."

"What did you promise me?" she repeated.

"Not to do it again without asking."

"But you went ahead and did it anyway."

"Yes, ma'am."

"This is gonna make it hot for us, Merle."

In the shadow of the ball cap, she saw a thin smile. "You just can't take me anywhere."

"Wipe that smile off your face."

"It isn't *that* bad, Ettie. I already looked through their stuff. They didn't have any fire permit."

"So?"

He tipped back the bill, no longer afraid of meeting Ettie's gaze. "If they'd checked in with a ranger, they would've got one and said where they were going. But they didn't. So the rangers don't even know they're here."

"Well, that's something."

"Even if someone knows they're gone, nobody's gonna have the first notion where to look. We'll just bury 'em and take their stuff to the cave, and we'll be okay."

Ettie sighed, folded her arms across her bosom, and stared down at the bodies. "I'll put out a spell to ward off searchers, just in case."

Merle looked doubtful. "Maybe I better."

"I can still conjure circles around you, boy, and don't you forget it. I got us safe out of Fresno, no thanks to you. If you'd had the sense to fetch me what I needed—"

"I was seen."

"Wouldn't have taken you half a minute," she said. Merle stood silent, watching as she knelt beside the man's body. She untied a leather pouch from her belt and opened it. "Never should've taught you the Ways."

"Don't say that, Ettie."

"Made us no end of trouble." She wrapped her fingers around a lock of hair, and yanked it from the man's scalp. She pressed the hair into the raw gorge at the back of his neck. Thick blood coated the strands. She twisted them into a string, knotted them once in the center, and poked them into her pouch. Then she lifted his hand. The fingernails were chewed to the quick. She unsheathed her knife, pressed the blade to the cuticle of his index finger, and removed the entire nail. She dropped it into her pouch and stepped over to the woman.

Squatting beside the body, she ripped out a ringlet of hair. She squeezed the breast to force more blood to the surface, and dabbed the hair in it. She tied the sticky cord into a knot. She flicked it into her pouch, then picked up a hand. The plum fingernail polish was chipped. One nail was broken, but the rest were long and neatly rounded. She pared off the tips of four, catching them in her palm, and brushed them into her bag.

"Now, that's all there is to it," she said, looking up at Merle. "Wouldn't have taken you half a minute, and I could've laid down a dandy spell and we'd still be in Fresno today. You didn't even have to take blood. If you'd just had the good sense to bring me hair and nails, I'd have had the essence to throw a cover on us."

"I like it here fine," he mumbled.

"Well, I don't." Her knees crackled as she straightened up. "I like my creature comforts, Merle. I like a good meal and a cold beer and nice clothes and a soft bed."

"And men," he added, showing a sliver of a smile.

"That's the truth." She pushed her knife into its sheath at the side of her dress, and started tying the pouch to her belt. "You deprived me of all that 'cause you were horny and careless."

"I told you, Ettie. He spoke to me."

She didn't believe him. "Don't go laying off your blame, Merle. Now, you take care of the burying and bring up their things to the cave. I'll come along and check before sundown, and I want to see this place looking like nobody was ever here. Do you understand?"

"Yes, ma'am."

"And if you ever offer down again without my say-so, you'll be the sorriest young man that ever walked on two legs."

He looked down at his feet. "Yes, ma'am."

Leaving him there, Ettie made her way along the rockbound shore. At the narrow, southern tip of the lake where its feeder stream splashed down from

Upper Mesquite, she crouched and cupped water to her mouth. Even after spending a month up here, she still couldn't get over the cold, fresh taste of it. Hard to believe that water could be so fine. She knew she would miss it in September, when they had to leave. Wouldn't miss anything else, though: not the heat steaming off the rocks, or the mosquitoes, or the wind that tore around at night so loud it often kept her awake, or the cold when the sun went down, or the hard ground she slept on. She'd be glad to leave all that behind. Not the water, though.

She unsnapped the canvas bag of her canteen, and pulled out the aluminum bottle. After twisting off its cap, she upended it. The old water burbled out. She held the empty canteen under a lip of mossy rock, gripping it tightly as fresh water washed over her hand. When the bottle overflowed, she capped it, then slipped it back into the case. It felt heavy and good against her hip as she stood up.

Staying close to the stream, she climbed up pale, broken slabs of granite to the ridge between the two lakes. She turned slowly, scanning the slopes that rose high above her. Then she peered toward the trail slanting down from Carver Pass beyond the northern end of Lower Mesquite. Once every few days, backpackers hiked by. Until yesterday, when those two stayed and camped, Merle had been just fine.

Blast Merle. Damn and shit!

The trail was deserted now. More than likely, if anyone should show up today, it wouldn't be till the afternoon. The pass was a hard, three-hour climb

from the nearest lake to the east, so Merle should have plenty of time to take care of the mess. Besides, there was the spell. . . .

Stepping onto a flat surface of rock, Ettie unbuckled her belt with all its gear. She set it at her feet and opened the buttons of her faded, shapeless dress. She pulled the dress up over her head. Except for her heavy socks and boots, she was naked. She felt the sun on her skin, the caress of soft breezes. The air smelled hot. It smelled of scorched pine needles, of baking rock.

Bending over, she spread her dress across the granite. Then she sat on it. Through the thin layers of fabric, the rock felt hard and rough. The heat seeped through, stinging her buttocks as she removed her boots and damp socks.

When they were off, she untied the leather pouch from her belt. She crossed her legs and sat upright, with her back arched, her head straight forward. With both hands, she clasped the pouch to her breastbone.

"Into darkness," she whispered, "I commit the essence of my foes. As their essence is obscured, so let all traces of their presence be banished from this canyon, that those who seek them might find no cause to trespass here."

Lowering her head, she opened the drawstrings of the pouch. She pulled out a bloody lock of hair and placed it into her mouth. She chewed slowly, working it into a sodden clump, and swallowed it. She did the same with the second coil of hair. She washed them down with water from her canteen. Then she dumped

the fingernails onto her palm, raised them to her lips, and ate them. She drank some more water.

The rock was rough and hot through her dress. The hair felt thick and heavy in her stomach.

But she was done.

She smiled. She raised the canteen and poured its cold water over her head. It streamed down her face, her shoulders. It rolled down her back. It spilled over her breasts, dripped from her nipples, ran down her belly and sides. Moving the canteen, she let the water fall onto her crossed legs, her groin. She sighed at its icy touch.

Too soon the canteen was empty.

She stared at the glinting blue of Upper Mesquite. Why not? She deserved a treat. Leaving everything, she skipped over the searing rocks to the shore. She waded in, shivering and gasping, and hesitated only a moment before plunging headlong.

RICHARD LAYMON

The Beast House has become a museum of the most macabre kind. On display inside are wax figures of its victims, their bod-ies mangled and chewed, mutilated beyond recognition. The tourists who come to Beast House can only wonder what sort of terrifying creature could be responsible for such atrocities.

But some people are convinced Beast House is a hoax. Nora and her friends are determined to learn the truth for themselves. They will dare to enter the house at night. When the tourists have gone. When the beast is rumored to come out. They will learn, all right.

THE **BEAST HOUSE**

ISBN 13: 978-0-8439-5749-5

THE
PINES

Deep within the desolate Pine Barrens, a series of macabre murders draws ever nearer to an isolated farmhouse where a woman struggles to raise her disturbed son. The boy has a psychic connection to something in the dark forest, something unseen... and evil.

The old-timers in the region know the truth of the legendary creature that stalks these woods. And they know the savagery it's capable of.

ROBERT
DUNBAR

ISBN 13: 978-0-8439-6165-2

Bram Stoker Award finalist

MARY SANGIOVANNI

FOUND YOU

Those two simple words were like a death sentence to Sally. She recognized the voice, straight from her nightmares. The grotesque thing without a face, the creature that thrived on fear and guilt, had nearly killed her, like it had so many others. But it was dead…wasn't it? Sally is about to find out that your deepest secrets can prey on you, and that there's nowhere to hide…for long.

In the small town of Lakehaven something has arrived that can't see you, hear you or touch you, but it can find you just the same. And when it does, your fears will have a name.

ISBN 13: 978-0-8439-6110-2

WATER WITCH

Dunny knew from an early age what it meant to be an outsider. Her special abilities earned her many names, like freak and water witch. So she vowed to keep her powers a secret. But now her talents may be the only hope of two missing children. A young boy and girl have vanished, feared lost in the mysterious bayous of Louisiana. But they didn't just disappear; they were taken. And amid the ghosts and spirits of the swamp, there is a danger worse than any other, one with very special plans for the children—and for anyone who dares to interfere.

DEBORAH LEBLANC

ISBN 13: 978-0-8439-6039-6

EDWARD LEE

What bloodthirsty evil lies buried in the basement of a New York City brownstone, waiting for its chance to be reborn?

When Cristina and her husband moved in, they thought they had found their dream house. But Cristina can feel something calling her, luring her, filling her dreams with unbridled lust and promises of ecstasies she'd never thought possible. The time has come for the unholy ritual performed by the...

BRIDES OF THE IMPALER

ISBN 13: 978-0-8439-5807-2

To order a book or to request a catalog call:
1-800-481-9191
This book is also available at your local bookstore, or you can check out our Web site **www.dorchesterpub.com** where you can look up your favorite authors, read excerpts, or glance at our discussion forum to see what people have to say about your favorite books.

COVENANT

WINNER OF THE BRAM STOKER AWARD!

The cliffs of Terrel's Peak are a deadly place, an evil place where terrible things happen. Like a series of mysterious teen suicides over the years, all on the same date. Or other deaths, usually reported as accidents. Could it be a coincidence? Or is there more to it?

Reporter Joe Kieran is determined to find the truth.

Kieran will uncover rumors and whispered legends—including the legend of the evil entity that lives and waits in the caves below Terrel's Peak....

JOHN EVERSON

ISBN 13: 978-0-8439-6018-1

☐ **YES!**

Sign me up for the Leisure Horror Book Club and send my FREE BOOKS! If I choose to stay in the club, I will pay only $8.50* each month, a savings of $7.48!

NAME: _____

ADDRESS: _____

TELEPHONE: _____

EMAIL: _____

☐ I want to pay by credit card.

☐ **VISA**   ☐ **MasterCard**   ☐ **DISCOVER**

ACCOUNT #: _____

EXPIRATION DATE: _____

SIGNATURE: _____

Mail this page along with $2.00 shipping and handling to:
Leisure Horror Book Club
PO Box 6640
Wayne, PA 19087
Or fax (must include credit card information) to:
610-995-9274

You can also sign up online at **www.dorchesterpub.com**.
*Plus $2.00 for shipping. Offer open to residents of the U.S. and Canada only. Canadian residents please call 1-800-481-9191 for pricing information.
If under 18, a parent or guardian must sign. Terms, prices and conditions subject to change. Subscription subject to acceptance. Dorchester Publishing reserves the right to reject any order or cancel any subscription.